P
UNLOVED

"Earnest, raw, and sexy, *Unloved* brims with tenderness and heart. In her sophomore novel, Corinne delivers the college romance of my dreams. This is more than a love story; it's a journey of self-discovery, a beautiful coming-of-age, and a song about healing and being seen for all those pieces you hide. To be loved really is to be seen, and I guarantee you'll find pieces of yourself in Ro, Freddy, and the rest of the gang at Waterfell."

—Elena Armas, *New York Times* bestselling author of
The Fiancé Dilemma

"Peyton Corinne's storytelling is unmatched! *Unloved* is an angsty, sexy, emotional journey that left me breathless."

—Farrah Rochon, *New York Times* bestselling author of
The Dating Playbook

"*Unloved* absolutely overflows with rich emotion and utter sexiness. I was so engrossed in witnessing Ro and Freddy make their way toward a love they both deserved that I devoured it in one sitting, and then mourned the fact that it was over. Peyton Corinne navigates delicate themes with grace and empathy, and has created a cast of series characters that are so easy to root for. Don't let the title fool you—I loved *everything* about this book."

—Jessica Joyce, *USA Today* bestselling author of
You, with a View and *The Ex Vows*

"Peyton Corinne delivers another slap shot with this college hockey romance. A love story brimming with well-rounded, nuanced characters that keep you hooked and wanting more—with the signature Peyton Corinne heartache wrapped in a happy ending."

—Bal Khabra, *USA Today* bestselling author of *Collide*

UNLOVED

Also by Peyton Corinne

THE UNDONE SERIES

Unsteady

UNLOVED

A Novel

PEYTON CORINNE

ATRIA PAPERBACK

NEW YORK   AMSTERDAM/ANTWERP   LONDON   TORONTO ·SYDNEY   NEW DELHI

ATRIA
PAPERBACK

An Imprint of Simon & Schuster, LLC
1230 Avenue of the Americas
New York, NY 10020

First Atria Paperback edition February 2025

ATRIA PAPERBACK and colophon are trademarks of Simon & Schuster, LLC

For information about special discounts for bulk purchases, please contact Simon & Schuster Special Sales at 1-866-506-1949 or business@simonandschuster.com.

The Simon & Schuster Speakers Bureau can bring authors to your live event. For more information or to book an event, contact the Simon & Schuster Speakers Bureau at 1-866-248-3049 or visit our website at www.simonspeakers.com.

Interior design by Erika R. Genova

Manufactured in the United States of America

1 3 5 7 9 10 8 6 4 2

Library of Congress Cataloging-in-Publication Data

Names: Corinne, Peyton, author.
Title: Unloved : a novel / Peyton Corinne.
Description: First Atria Paperback edition. | New York : Atria Paperback, 2025. | Series: The undone series
Identifiers: LCCN 2024035592 | ISBN 9781668068489 (paperback) | ISBN 9781668068502 (ebook)
Subjects: LCGFT: Romance fiction. | Novels.
Classification: LCC PS3603.O753 U55 2025 | DDC 813/.6—dc23/eng/20240909
LC record available at https://lccn.loc.gov/2024035592

ISBN 978-1-6680-6848-9
ISBN 978-1-6680-6850-2 (ebook)

For AK.
Just in case you don't know the impact your gentle,
steadfast friendship has made on me over the last decade,
this one is for you.
Our friendship wasn't founded in grief, but it was grown in it.
I think that makes it immeasurably stronger.

PLAYLIST

Jump Rope Gazers • *The Beths*

Lollipop • *Lil Wayne feat. Static Major*

Casual • *Chappell Roan*

mirrorball • *Taylor Swift*

Wet Dream • *Wet Leg*

My Honest Face • *Inhaler*

LOVE • *Kendrick Lamar feat. Zacari*

tolerate it • *Taylor Swift*

Pool House • *The Backseat Lovers*

don't worry, you will • *lovelytheband*

striptease • *carwash*

Motion Sickness • *Phoebe Bridgers*

Reflections • *MisterWives*

Linger • *The Cranberries*

This Side of Paradise • *Coyote Theory*

broken • *lovelytheband*

There She Goes • *The La's*

Take Care • *Beach House*

The Smallest Man Who Ever Lived • *Taylor Swift*

complex (demo) • *Katie Gregson-MacLeod*

Cool About It • *boygenius*

Young Folks • *Peter Bjorn and John*

Dreamer (Stripped Down) • *Mokita, Kaptan*

House Song • *Searows*

Chiquitita • *ABBA*

Good Looking • *Suki Waterhouse*

ceilings • *Lizzy McAlpine*

I Can't Handle Change • *Roar*

You Could Start a Cult • *Niall Horan*

Dizzy on the Comedown • *Turnover*

Scary Love • *The Neighbourhood*

Gasoline • *The Weeknd*

Hot • *Cigarettes After Sex*

The Sunshine • *Manchester Orchestra*

As I'm Fading Into You • *Blevins*

Daddy Issues • *The Neighbourhood*

Falling • *Harry Styles*

Smoke Signals • *Phoebe Bridgers*

Big Jet Plane • *Angus & Julia Stone*

Driver's Seat • *Madds Buckley*

Glue • *Nat & Alex Wolff*

We Don't Have to Take Our Clothes Off • *Ella Eyre*

You're Somebody Else • *flora cash*

Liability • *Lorde*

Quiet, The Winter Harbor • *Mazzy Star*

I'm in Love • *Jelani Aryeh*

Fearless (Taylor's Version) • *Taylor Swift*

I Don't Wanna Wait Til Christmas • *Summer Camp*

Kissing in Swimming Pools • *Holly Humberstone*

The Very First Night (Taylor's Version) • *Taylor Swift*

Touch • *Sleeping at Last*

Keep Driving • *Harry Styles*

You're Gonna Go Far • *Noah Kahan*

Sure Of • *Caamp*

So High School • *Taylor Swift*

Jump Rope Gazers • *The Beths*

Forever • *Noah Kahan*

PROLOGUE

Freshman Year—"The Night He Doesn't Remember"

I can be whoever I want to be.

I repeat the mantra in my head three more times before opening my eyes and giving myself another slow once-over in our stuffy dorm bathroom mirror.

I can be whoever I want to be.

Again, I say it as I run my hands over the tight black tank with wispy straps and the black denim skirt, pulling both down again, as if there is any material left to cover my exposed belly button and above-average-length legs. The urge to change again is overwhelming, but . . .

I can be whoever I want to be.

But I feel hot. I feel powerful and beautiful.

There's a knock at the door, and then, "You okay?" muttered in a bored tone through the thin wood.

I swing it open with a confident smile, flicking a few harshly straightened pieces of hair over my shoulder.

"What do you think?" I ask, eyes bouncing across the effortless sex appeal of my new roommate.

Self-consciously, I look down at myself just as she does, because next to Sadie Brown, I'm starting to think I might as well tattoo VIRGIN across my forehead.

1

The girl is tiny and muscular, strong legs and an ass I'd kill for currently wrapped in leather, a baby blue corset brightening her pale skin. Even her makeup—eyes darkened with perfect winged eyeliner and ruby-red lips—makes me feel a bit like a kid who smeared some of her mom's glitter on her eyelids before getting caught.

"You look gorgeous," she says, then without a second glance she's already focused on her phone, absorbed in whomever she's rapidly texting. It stings a little, as it has a million times in the last month since we met on move-in day. But I'm determined I can get her to like me. She'll be my friend.

I can be whoever I want to be.

"Ready?"

I smile again, bright and hopeful, even though she doesn't return it.

"Yeah," I breathe. "I'm ready."

· · ·

I'm overwhelmed in minutes, but in the best way, vibrating with excitement. I feel my spine loosening like a snake charmed by the intoxicating energy around me. Music thumps so loudly I can feel it in my heels, shaking me with the movement as I stumble blindly behind Sadie through the crowd—desperate to keep up with her, even though she won't hold my hand.

I don't need her to hold my hand. I'm not a child.

A body shoves into me, knocking my shoulder hard enough that I stumble off my overly high heels and into a wall. The guy apologizes and tries to smile at me, but I push past him, desperate to keep up with my roommate.

We stop short, standing by the entrance into the main room where everyone is either sitting on couches or dancing in a way that's making my face hot watching it.

My stomach twists with a mixture of want and anxiety.

"You doing okay?" Sadie asks as a massive body brushes behind her and she elbows him off her with a grunted curse.

"Yeah," I say, feeling a bit like I'm shouting. "This is cool."

She nods and scans me again, and my neck feels hot, self-consciousness kicking up at her observation.

I can be whoever I want to be.

Flicking my hair over my shoulder, I smile brighter.

"Do you want a drink?" I ask.

"I'll be right back," she says at the same time, her words and voice drowning mine out easily.

"Where are you going?" I try to ask casually, but I'm gripping her wrist tightly, a life vest in the sea of bodies around me.

She pointedly looks down at where I'm holding her, and I let go.

"I'm gonna follow that one." She points to the captain of the football team, whom I've seen on posters around school. He's a senior, big and handsome and way too popular for freshmen like us.

But he's also looking at Sadie like she's his next meal.

"To the bathroom, but it won't take long. Just wait here, okay?"

I want to say no, it's not okay. That even though she didn't promise it, I thought it was girl code not to leave your friend behind. I don't know anyone here or what I'm doing, and I've never had a sip of alcohol before.

I wanted this night to be different. *I* wanted to be different.

But again, I'm left standing on the sidelines.

"Okay." I smile brightly, tucking my hair that's already started to frizz into curls from the humidity behind my ears. "It's fine. I'll wait here."

Sadie's gone before I even finish the sentence, working the guy like she isn't a foot shorter than him. She barely has to say a word; he just follows her eagerly as they disappear into the darkened hall.

I'm alone, and all the bliss, that floaty feeling I chased earlier, sours in my stomach as I sink against the wall.

My eyes flit across the room, seeing directly into the stuffed kitchen where a makeshift bar has been set up. I want to ask for something to drink, but I have no idea what to say.

I want to let loose, but I'm not sure how.

Frustrated, I blow out a breath and do what I know best: people watching.

There's a group of girls who look friendly enough, but it took me nearly a month to work up the courage to ask my own roommate to hang out. Standing together, they're all pretty girls with cool outfits and makeup that looks professionally done.

I want to compliment them, but my tongue is stuck to the roof of my mouth.

The lights are off, and some weak blue and white strobes hung haphazardly from the corners of the room flicker across the crowd in a continuous, sweeping motion. It makes everything almost surreal.

One couple in the messy, twirling sea of bodies draws my attention like a spotlight. They're moving to the beat sensually, like a scene out of a movie, his hands playing along her waist as she presses side to side, back and forth into him. His hand picks up her silky hair as his chin dips into her neck and he presses a few kisses up to her ear.

It's nearly pornographic, and my neck and face feel a little like they're burning.

A good burn, one I don't want to stop. One I want to feel, explore for myself.

I can be whoever I want to be.

The boy tilts his head at me and smiles, as if he's caught me with my hand in the cookie jar. A lopsided grin that screams trouble of the best kind.

He whispers something to her before letting go, and the girl finds herself spinning into a new set of arms, continuing to dance with them. Just as sensual and jaw-droppingly beautiful. But I'm distracted by the boy now prowling toward me.

Except he takes a hard right toward a different side of the room.

The group he joins is a little rowdier, standing around a table lined with shots, tall cans of different colors clasped in their hands.

It's a group of six or seven guys, a few girls sporadically hanging on to them. All tall and muscular, handsome in a way that's almost daunting. They're playing a game, some of them half dancing to the thumping bass of Lil Wayne's "Lollipop," while their eyes stay keen on the setup before them. Somehow lackadaisical yet harshly competitive.

They're larger than life, and I accidentally stare a bit too long because I cannot physically remove my attention from that same damn guy. And he's looking at me, too.

This time he's in the light more, and I can really see him.

Even better, as he makes his way toward me.

Golden hair shorn short on the sides and slightly tousled on top, as if he knows exactly how to style it. He's got those smile lines that cut his cheeks like carvings in marble, glittering emerald eyes as he grins wider and invades my space. I'm almost certain he can feel my heart beating in time with the music.

"Want a drink?" he yells, but I barely hear him over the pounding noise around us.

My face must be the color of my roommate's seemingly permanent lipstick, but I nod.

"Great. I have an extra," he says, lifting the small plastic cup.

Instead of handing it to me, he loops his arm over my shoulder and stalks behind me.

I grab his arm out of pure fear instinct, eyes wide as I look at the shot.

"I don't know if I can do that." I gesture with my head toward the gleaming drink that flashes blue and amber under the strobing lights. I look up at him, for reassurance or to stare at his gorgeous face, I'm not sure.

He smirks, lifting his hand to lick a drop of alcohol that's sloshed out and down his hand. His tongue is slow, eyes bright, and I realize this is a bad idea.

"Don't worry," he says into my ear this time so I can hear. "You can take it."

My eyes roll back a little, feet shuffling as I regain my balance.

He's way too advanced for me. I need to try a freshman meet and greet, or one of those Super Smash video game parties—the guys there are hopefully more my speed.

I need training wheels. This guy is full throttle on the Circuit de Monaco, no way for me to slow him down.

But before I can back out, his other hand wraps around my neck, tilting my chin up, his palm warm against my throat as he lowers my head back into the cradle of his arm.

His fingers scald my chin, his palm gentle on my throat. It would be easy to step away, to say no and slip beneath the loose hold he has around my shoulders. But I don't want to. I want this.

I can be whoever I want to be.

"Open," he whispers, the command more like a taunt, but his eyes are still twinkling.

He's the most beautiful boy I've ever seen.

Will he kiss me like this? God, I want to feel his lips—they look like pillows.

Pulling myself together, heading off the blush my indecent thoughts are causing, I open my mouth and he pours the fiery liquid down my throat. At first I'm worried I'll gag or spit it out because it burns—but my eyes stay locked on his, on the strange pride gleaming there as he bites his lip and continues to slowly pour until the plastic cup is empty.

I close my eyes for a second, pressing my lips together tightly before I realize some of it's leaking from the corners of my mouth.

He doesn't let me go but tilts my head toward him as he slowly licks the drops of amber liquid from the corner of my lips. I can smell the heady mix of his cologne with the scent of alcohol for a moment,

before—

He kisses me.

Oh God. I let out an embarrassingly loud moan, thankfully drowned out by the music. His tongue is in my mouth.

His arms loop around my waist, and he tugs me tight against his body.

I barely have time to think, not that I could if I tried, because my first kiss being on the tail end of my first shot of alcohol is making me dizzy, my head swimming and fingers numb.

I stumble a little, and he keeps his hands on my lower back as he lets me fall gently against the wall. I don't even remember how or when he switched our positions.

"Whoa," I whisper. He smiles broadly and nods a little, like he agrees. "I— um—"

"Freddy!" a deep voice shouts.

His brow furrows, like he's been jerked away from a dreamy daze, and he turns to look over his right shoulder toward the full table, all watching us now.

"I told you, it's gonna be Matty."

A burly, auburn-haired man shucks his arm around my first kiss's shoulders and shakes him—which jostles me slightly as well, since his hands are still burning twin brands into the bare skin of my waist.

"You don't pick the nicknames, Freddy," he says. "We do. Now, let's go out back—we're gonna play one last beer pong game before heading out. We've still got practice in the morning."

The intruder slips from our bubble, and I'm still staring, open-mouthed, up at Freddy-maybe-Matty.

"I like Freddy." The words spill from my mouth, breathy and quiet. But he hears me and smiles wide, tucking his head into my neck with a kiss and a lick that nearly makes me shout. He sucks lightly before pulling back, only after squeezing me around the middle and lifting me just off the floor.

"I like you," he says with a smirk, reddened eyes glittering like green stars as he sets me down and starts to back away. "What's your name?"

"Okay," I say without thinking. "And it's Ro."

"Okay, Ro." He smiles again, backing away until the only part of him touching me is his hand in mine, drawing me back toward the crowded table with him.

We play beer pong, which mostly consists of Freddy patiently teaching me how to play, despite his friends' protests. Then, as most of the group disperses, Freddy stays by my side. Our heads are pressed together as we whisper random comments about the party-goers milling about, people watching.

His phone rings, the noise loud and intrusive. He peeks down at the screen.

"Oh, um—" His entire expression sobers, and he pushes off the brick wall we've been leaning against. He looks flustered, almost frightened. "I need to take this. I'll come back and get you, okay? Just, don't move."

He stumbles into the table and knocks over a few drinks but doesn't bat an eye before he's headed toward a quiet spot to take the call.

I don't move, even as giddiness and joy threaten to force my limbs to swing and dance.

I don't move, even when Sadie comes back—looking exactly as perfect as she did before, not a hair out of place. Meanwhile, the senior quarterback following her looks thoroughly mussed, breathing hard like he completed a full triathlon with no training.

I don't move while Sadie gets three more shots of Fireball, which I find I love the taste of, but hate the instant swimming feeling in my chest.

I don't move as we wait and wait until the party slowly dwindles.

I don't move when my heart starts to hurt. Not until Sadie convinces me to go with the most sympathetic look she's given me since we became roommates.

"I'm a little embarrassed," I finally tell her as we walk back to our dorm. "I just thought . . . I don't know what I thought."

Sadie smiles at me as I walk past her. "You thought he wanted you. Don't be embarrassed. It happens to me all the time."

I stop short and Sadie follows, both of us turning to face each other.

"Really?"

Sadie furrows her brow, the same displeased expression she usually has. "All the time. I mean, finding a boy at a drunken frat party or a bar is a gamble, Ro. Like, I wouldn't recommend it."

"But you do it all the time." The alcohol makes my lips a little looser and I admit, "I just want to be normal."

Sadie grabs my hand—it's the first time she's reached for me, and she gets me to walk close enough that she can wrap an arm around my waist.

"Wrong roommate for you if you want normal. My life is kind of a shit show— But, honestly, no one is normal. Normal is stupid, okay? Just be whoever you are."

"I don't know who I am."

"No one does. Just—" She huffs like she's annoyed with me, but I'm starting to realize that's how Sadie Brown is. "Just, do what you want and fuck anyone who says you can't, okay? If you want to party, do it. But if you don't want to, don't."

We've reached the dorms by the time she stops talking. There are a few loiterers outside, kissing or laughing or eating fast food, the smell making my mouth water, and I have to resist the sudden urge to beg Sadie to go to Taco Bell.

Turns out I don't have to, as I watch Sadie waltz up to a boisterous group of boys by the fountain in the center of the quad. Of course she struts straight up to the most handsome one—not a moment of insecurity or hesitation.

The tall blond one smiles when he spots her, and pulls her in for a quick hug, which she shoves out of quickly, taking the bag of food from The Chick—which definitely closed hours ago—from his hand.

"Hang out soon?" I hear him say as she starts back toward me.

"Maybe," she calls over her shoulder before giving me a look that screams absolutely not.

I wait until we're back safe in our little dorm, sitting on twin beds opposite each other, before I ask exactly how she does it—so brazenly goes after whatever she wants, especially with boys.

Sadie's expression shifts, her perpetual frown sinking deeper before she puts her half-eaten food back into the bag and sets it aside.

"I mean . . ." I hurry to explain. "You seem so confident. You sleep with whoever you want."

"It's not a crime," she snaps. "I enjoy sex, just like everyone else."

My stomach sinks. "Right." Somewhere in my head an alarm sounds *virgin* over and over. Can't she hear it?

"Are you asking me for advice?" she says, but her tone has lost none of its heat. "Because if so, I've only got one thing I can give you. Don't be like me. Don't even *want* to be like me. Okay? You're pretty and I'm sure you're smart, and trust me, you can be whoever you want to be."

"But I think you're great." The words come out unbidden and I blush, a little embarrassed. It's like I'm wearing a sign that says I Want to be Your Friend So Badly.

"Well, don't."

Her voice cracks slightly and my brow furrows, wondering if she might cry. My arms tingle, ready to hold her, to hug her if she needs one. Like real friends do.

But instead, she straightens and slips off her bed, stepping over to the mini fridge to save her probably already stale food.

Our fragile camaraderie from the night disappears like smoke in the wind. She turns off the lamp and goes to sleep. There is so much anger in her small body; she carries herself like she's always ready for a fight. It makes my chest hurt.

Trying to sleep, I close my eyes and picture Freddy-maybe-Matty, the happy smile across his face, the sound of his voice, the warmth of his skin. I touch my lips again, swearing they still feel swollen from his kiss.

CHAPTER 1

Senior Year—End of July, Present Day

Ro

"Give it to Ro."

I stop short, pausing to survey the open office space filled with the other teaching assistants and tutors for our department. The toe of my sneaker kicks against the moderately heavy door again, managing to hold it open long enough that I can slip through without dropping the giant stack of papers currently blanketing my arms.

Not one of the boys I work with offers to help. No one even bats an eye at my struggle as I plop the over-full folders onto my clean desk space.

It's quiet, but it always is during summer semester—especially finals week—which is why I always opt to come back early. That and the desperate itching need to get back that seems to plague me beginning early July.

"Give me what?"

Rodger, one of the other tutors in our department, tosses me the folder in his hands while Tyler, my boyfriend of two years now, slinks behind me and rests his head on my shoulder, playing with the ends of my hair.

"Rodger doesn't want his student." Tyler laughs, pressing a kiss into my hair. I bristle and freeze, because the last time we spoke over the phone he told me we definitely *weren't* together.

Tyler and I met my sophomore year, my first year as a tutor in my declared major. I'd come to Waterfell knowing I wanted to study biomedical sciences, but not sure of what track to follow. A year above me, Tyler was my mentor and guide for my first year of tutoring.

I looked up to him because he was successful and smart and well respected in our classes. And he relentlessly pursued me—extravagantly, publicly. Flowers before classes, surprising me with lunch at work, offering me rides to and from Brew Haven—and this was all before we ever started dating.

The romantic in me swooned, thrilled that I would finally have the affection I'd always dreamed of. But somewhere along the way, things changed.

"I think we should keep it casual. Keep our options open."

His words from our phone call last weekend ring in my ears like a distant alarm I'm content to ignore.

"Good morning, babe. Welcome to the lair of complaining and being pussies."

His hands stretch out, like he's introducing our office to the HGTV at-home viewers.

"Shove it, Donaldson," Rodger snaps, seemingly more agitated than usual.

Surprisingly, I like him most out of the group. Possibly because I live with someone who has a perpetual anger problem, and she's my best friend.

"Morning," I say, a little distracted as I flip open the file and look at the sample papers before me. My eyes scan the words quickly, brow furrowing. "These look copied. Like . . . word for word. Are they all plagiarized?"

"Every word," Rodger sighs, rubbing his eyes and sinking into a chair at the group table in the center of our circle of desks.

"He used to pull that shit with me all the time. That's why I dumped him off on you last year," Tyler says, shoving Rodger lightly as he moves toward his own workspace.

"I can't work with that guy anymore," Rodger says, mumbling into his hands as he rubs his face and combs back through his messy dark hair. "I had him all last semester, and this summer has killed me. Please, Ro, take him off my hands."

I bite my lip for a moment, sliding my hip against the counter and resting the papers atop it. "Summer is about to close—and besides, I think I have a full stack for fall already."

Tyler hands out coffees from a tray, and I eye him the entire time. When he spots me looking, he rubs the back of his neck. "Sorry, I didn't know what you'd want."

I order the same exact thing every time, no matter the weather—an iced dirty chai—and we've been dating for years, but I give a light smile.

"It's fine. I'll grab one at work."

"I figured." He smiles, walking over and pressing me into the counter. Another kiss before he straightens up. "No way she'll take it."

"Ro'll take it. She's the best tutor we have—better than all of us, right?" Mark—another tutor, and Tyler's closest friend here—says, stretching and spinning in his swivel chair at his desk.

It's not a compliment. In fact, it's the opposite.

If I'm asking questions, then I'm trying to get help or sympathy. I'm weak. But if I'm confident in my skills, then I think I'm better than everyone else.

"I have more students this semester than I know what to do with. And I don't specialize in dyslexia or dyscalculia."

"He's got ADHD, too," Rodger says unhelpfully.

"Can't be that hard." Tyler smirks, leaning to look at the papers I've now started to spread across the counter. "Jesus Christ. He knows how to read, right? Some of these copy-paste paragraphs aren't even, like, in the same universe of relatability."

I grab a cinnamon bagel off the table, a gift from our head professor, I'm sure, and start smothering it with cream cheese as I look back at a few of the more recent papers. It's almost like whoever it is isn't trying.

"A hundred bucks says he doesn't know how to read," Mark says before his eyes scan me and he laughs. "A thousand if Ro takes him and he passes the semester above a 2.75."

"I didn't say—"

"I'll take that," Tyler shouts over me, reaching to grab Mark's hand. "I'll raise another thousand that he tries to fuck her first."

"Tyler," I choke out, eyebrows at my hairline. "Don't be gross."

He shrugs, but there's something terrifying in the smile still spread across his face.

"Wait till you see who it is," he says to me before turning to the boys around him. "No way she even takes it when she sees the name—"

Whatever he says next is drowned out underneath the pounding of my heartbeat in my ears. I almost spit out the bite of bagel already in my mouth, which is suddenly impossible to chew.

Matthew Fredderic.

He might as well be a mythical creature to all of us. They might talk about him like he's the dirt beneath the soles of their newly purchased loafers, but for four years they've envied him as much as I've inexcusably pined over him.

Me and over half the campus.

I push back from the table, silently begging whatever higher power exists that my inadvertent reaction to him—perpetual blushing—doesn't happen right now. I'll never hear the end of it.

I spin back toward Tyler and the entire staff room.

"I'm not—"

"Come on, Ro. He's not going to bite."

"Yeah," Tyler says, barely restraining the laughter in his eyes. "He's gonna try to put his dick in her."

"Make sure he uses protection, Donaldson," Mark laughs. "Don't wanna raise Fredderic's baby who's just as retar—"

"Stop," I snap, spine straightening. "Use that word again and I'm reporting you." *Again*, I want to say. Because I have reported him already, for his use of language and slurs. But no one has done a thing about it.

The cacophony of their *ooo*'s grates on my ears like gunshots.

"I'm so scared," Mark sneers.

I wait, again—and seemingly endlessly—for Tyler to notice the way Mark speaks to me. Instead of disgust or anger, he only shows mild annoyance—but not for Mark, for *me*.

"Just . . . I don't know, take my closing meeting with him and see if you can handle it," Rodger sighs, handing me the other file in his hands. "This is his work from the summer. Maybe you can make sense of what the hell he should do, since he has to pass to maintain his eligibility."

Eligibility to play hockey, he means, because Matt Fredderic is a star campus wide.

The Waterfell University hockey team is one of the top in the nation, for ten-plus years running now. After making it to the Frozen Four last year, Waterfell poured even more money into the sports budget—hockey, specifically.

Posters and cutouts line our campus, displaying the gleaming faces of the players: the handsome golden boy hockey captain Rhys Koteskiy; the stoic pillar of a goalie, Bennett Reiner; and the hypnotizing, crooked playboy grin of Matthew Fredderic—affectionately nicknamed Freddy. Top goal-scorer two years in a row, instigator extraordinaire, and currently signed to play with Dallas.

All bits of information I don't *need* to know—probably *shouldn't* know.

But once upon a time I'd severely crushed on the left winger and read every article or post about him. Embarrassingly followed his social media and saved ridiculous edits of him fans made on social media.

And yet shockingly, I had no idea he'd needed tutoring help, let alone in *my* department.

"Did he pass Sumnter, at least?" I ask, flipping through the stack of biology tests quickly, barely holding in a wince at the harsh red markings.

"Nope." Rodger sits back at the table, sipping on his iced black coffee that I'm tempted to steal from his grip. "But he's gonna have Tinley this time around."

Dr. Carmen Tinley, our College of Science and Mathematics tutoring department supervisor, as well as the woman we are all desperate to impress for a spot on her graduate cohort for advanced biomedical sciences. She takes on the three highest performing students for the spring semester of her intensive program, and there are seven of us competing for the spot.

Beyond that, there's a part of me that idolizes her. She's one of only two women who teach within my major, and she's friendly with her students—different from Dr. Khabra, who is reserved and often brutal in her grading and teaching practices. Where students are scared—albeit impressed—by Khabra's brilliance, Tinley is approachable and warm.

"C'mon, RoRo," my maybe-boyfriend whispers into my ear, dropping his voice. "Do this for us, and I'll let us try something off the list tonight, yeah?"

My cheeks heat.

It's stupid now, how easily he dangles the carrot—how much he knows that I want to cross another item off my Sexy College Bucket List that has sat abandoned for years now.

I almost threw it away a few times, but the sentimentality of it—remembering how Sadie and I became friends over cheap boxed wine, writing everything I'd ever wanted to do but never said aloud onto the foam board, using her dark lipstick collection to leave kiss prints all over the white. Remembering how Tyler and I giggled under cool floral sheets as we held each other's sweaty palms and checked off "lose my virginity" together a year ago, before he covered my body with his in my twin bed and made me feel like something precious.

Remembering how his promises to help me check off each item slowly turned to taunts and jokes.

Remembering how that list has sat, collecting dust for the last year, half empty.

Just like me.

"Off my list?" I can't keep the wonder out of my voice.

He huffs into my neck. "Yeah, babe. Anything you want." It's all teasing, a little mocking, but I grin and bear it because the truth is I really, really want to try it.

"O-okay."

· · ·

"So you're back together then?"

I shrug, feeling Sadie's words drop like a weight into my stomach. "I mean, technically we never broke up, I guess."

It's just after 3 p.m. on a Thursday inside Brew Haven, the coffee shop off campus we both work at part-time, as I help Sadie close, her brothers playing games on my iPad while we clean up. She seems a little more tense than she usually does, but I know things are harder for her now that she's meeting with the lawyer she hired to gain custody of her brothers.

"That's bullshit," she spits, causing Liam to burst into a fit of giggles.

"You said a curse, Sissy," he says happily. She rolls her eyes at him but tosses a crumpled dollar onto the table with a smirk and musses his hair as we walk past them toward the back.

"He blocked you on everything and yelled at you where we work." Sadie keeps her voice low, but her words bite.

I swallow down the lump in my throat at the memory of it, the embarrassment of his screaming and the way our cook, Luis, and his older brother, Alex, who managed the restaurant next door, had to stop him and throw him out.

"I know." I nod. "And he apologized—but we didn't . . ." I close my eyes and rub my temples. "Tyler doesn't want us to jump right back into being together. For now, we're going to be friends and see if we can sort out our issues. We're going to keep it casual."

"Right. Casual." Sadie rolls her eyes, but there's a look there that's more sympathy than annoyance. "Tyler wants you on the back burner while he goes to that stupid conference this weekend and does whatever he wants to do. But once school's back in, he's going to be trying to get back together with you."

I don't say anything. I start to lightly rub the building pressure in my chest.

Because she's right. He does this every year, so he can go play single at the stupid pre-med conference and fool around with the same girl from Princeton who is clearly smarter and prettier and "higher class" than me—whatever that means.

Trying desperately to slow the train of thought, I spin and start to scrub the near-permanent stains beneath the lip of the espresso machine.

"Ro," she whispers. "I'm sorry."

This I hate even more. Because my best friend—one of my *only* friends—is worried about hurting my feelings in her defense of me. She's the one friend I've made in the last three years who has stayed with me, through the ups and downs, through Tyler's behavior and my mini breakdowns.

And I know Sadie enough now to know she won't leave.

Loyal to a fault, like me.

CHAPTER 2

Freddy

I'm going to kill him.

I let out a groan of pure pain from my killer headache, only made worse by the classical music blaring through the house, currently only occupied by me and my awake-and-active-at-the-crack-of-dawn goalie, Bennett Reiner.

"Reiny, *please*," I cry into my pillow, flopping onto my back and covering my entire face and ears.

As if the heavens have heard my plea, the music cuts off and I sigh, until my door abruptly opens, letting in a tall, leggy blonde in one of my shirts and nothing else. Her face is flushed, her back pressed to the now-closed door as if she's hiding.

"Morning, Candice," I drawl. "You wouldn't happen to be the thing that woke the bear downstairs, huh?"

"He was *not* happy that I went down there," she sighs, depositing two yellow sports drinks and two bottles of water onto the bed. "But worth it."

"I'll say." I grab one of the bottles and drain it almost instantly, smirking at the way she seems to need the rehydration as much as I do.

Knowing she's pleased, that she had a good time, is enough to cancel the bad mood and headache Bennett's annoying morning routine started.

She sips lightly on the remnants of her water bottle for a moment before gathering her stuff into a little pile, slipping her own clothes back on and tossing my shirt into the obvious dirty pile in the corner of my "organized mess" of a room.

"Headed out?" I ask, not bothering to put anything on as I stand fully naked and stretch my arms out with a yawn. Her gaze tracks over my body again, hovering longer on the morning wood I'm sporting as I strut toward the small en suite bathroom.

"Unfortunately, I've got Panhellenic meetings all afternoon. But this was fun."

"Fun?" I say, reaching for her waist and spinning her until I'm pressed to her again, my nose running along her jaw. The burst of her giggle feels like praise, and I want to bask in it. But it's still not enough. "Just fun? I think I can do better than that if you stay for a little."

Her gaze fuzzes over but she smirks, shoving away from the heat of my body and gathering her purse.

"It was *more* than fun the first time, Freddy," she says, blowing me a kiss. "You're incredible. I'll see you around?"

Biting down on the desperate response waiting to roll off my tongue, which I know will come across as pathetic, I try not to bristle too much at her departure.

Maybe if you'd done better, she'd stick around. You're off your game.

I salute her with two fingers before heading into the bathroom to wash off the night's activities before my preseason check-in with the full coaching staff.

· · ·

"Rhys comes back this week," is the first sentence Bennett has granted me all morning. I talked nonstop as we ate one of his quick breakfasts over the countertop, and again as we rode to the arena in his truck, but the surly giant didn't grant me even one active-listening sentiment the entire way. I might as well have been talking to a brick wall.

I want to razz him over this stoic silence, but I know that Bennett doesn't joke about our captain, his best friend, Rhys Koteskiy.

I'd like to say I'm part of a trio, but I'm the third wheel if anything. Reiner and Koteskiy have been skating side by side since they were in diapers. Private hockey academies, retired NHL player dads—who also happen to be iconic best friends—Bennett and Rhys are as tightly bound without being blood-related as two people can possibly be.

"Have you guys talked?"

"No. He texted me a heads-up." He clenches the steering wheel a little harder. "Fucking stupid," he grumbles beneath his breath.

Our captain took a brutal hit on the ice during the Frozen Four last spring, delivered by defenseman Toren Kane, known throughout the NCAA as a complete psychopath. The guy should've been barred from team eligibility after his performance at Junior Worlds. Still, he managed to stay on a team while continuing to wreak havoc, throwing illegal hits and fighting, going as far as getting removed from two teams in the last three years.

The hit had nearly killed Rhys; he left the game in an ambulance, and besides the occasional "He's fine" from our coach or Rhys's parents, we hadn't heard from him since.

I knew he probably needed the space—that, or he was hurt badly enough he might not come back. But Bennett took Rhys's icing us out harder, because Rhys wasn't just his captain.

His best friend had completely shut him out. For four *months*.

"Well, that's good. We need him."

Going through our usual preseason activities felt a little wrong without our fearless leader. And after having to opt out of summer intensive camp with the guys for academic recovery classes, I'm antsy to get back on the fucking ice.

Being back in the Waterfell Arena makes my entire mood lighter.

Until Coach Harris decides to burst all my bubbles with his withering look as I take a seat across from him in his office.

The two assistant coaches left before I entered, which nearly made me want to spew up my breakfast as the sinking feeling that I'd done something wrong settled in my gut.

"Coach." I nod, bouncing my knee and rubbing my hands together. "Good summer?"

"Got to spend some time with my wife uninterrupted by a bunch of hormonal adolescents, so yeah, pretty good," Coach Harris says dryly.

"Right." I laugh, but the nerves make it choppy and short.

It doesn't help when Coach sighs, long and loud.

"Listen, Fredderic—"

"Last name only." I cut him off, grinning widely. "Guess that means I *really* did something wrong."

He shakes his head. "I talked to Gavins. Heard you *didn't* reach out to him, or the agent I sent you the contact for."

Fuck.

Jeff Gavins, the GM for the Dallas Stars, the NHL team I'm signed with. Coach Harris has been on my ass about getting in touch with him and the agent he set me up with, trying to give me an early out. I know it's because he sees how much of a struggle the academic side of college is for me, but it's hard not to feel like he's trying to get rid of me.

But he doesn't understand.

There's a reason I'm here, and it's too important to let it go now. This is the one time I won't take the easy way out.

"Gavins signed me for postgraduation. I'm thrilled to play for him, *after* Frozen Four."

"Freddy," Coach Harris mutters softly, rubbing a hand over eyes that don't look like they've gotten any rest in the last two months off.

"Seriously, college isn't for everyone. You could've been playing in the NHL as an eighteen-year-old."

Could have. Key words.

The back of my neck itches suddenly, my knees bouncing higher and faster as I nod.

"Yeah, but I need to do it my way."

It's the same response I've given him every time we've had this conversation in the last three years. I've made it to senior year by the skin of my fucking teeth—at this point, I need to prove to everyone that I can do this.

"All right," he sighs. "I've got two freshman wingers for you to keep an eye on. And as long as you and Dougherty do your usual bullshit, I think we're in for a good year."

The slight praise is enough to have a real smile etching its way across my face.

"Happy to be as disruptive as possible."

Coach Harris shakes his head at me as I stand, but I see the beginnings of a smile playing at the corners of his mouth.

CHAPTER 3

Ro

I've changed my outfit an embarrassing number of times, and yet I still feel ridiculous and *wrong* as I step out of the elevator onto the third floor of the library.

White pleated tennis skirt and a lavender short sleeve, a matching bow in my hair—it's exactly *me*, but for some reason *that's* harder to be confident in these days.

I find a study table easily. Summer B semester is usually empty anyway, but it's the middle of finals week for them, so there's a few people settled around the floor in groups.

The air-conditioning is loud, echoing in the large space to combat the rampant heat pouring through the wall-to-wall windows and poorly insulated walls, so I toss my headphones on and turn to Sadie's Spotify page, spotting one playlist labeled Amped Up.

A loud song by a band I've never heard of kicks on, and I wince.

Skipping to the next track, I bounce my knee to the quick beat as Wet Leg starts up in my headphones.

And, like a scene out of a movie, or one of my dreams from freshman year, Matt Fredderic exits from the sliding elevator doors.

He's as tall and well built as I remember, resembling some type of clean-cut supermodel with that slight mischief burning like green embers in his eyes. It's his personality, the raw sex appeal that seems to drip off him, on and off the ice. He's always dressed heart-stoppingly perfectly, somehow annoyingly never in just joggers and a T-shirt like most of the other sporty boys.

In the summer, though, he's dressed indecently. A baby-blue linen button-down hangs off his broad shoulders, the buttons undone one below what most guys would wear so his shining tanned chest glows even in the fluorescent light of the library. His shorts are short, arguably shorter than the hem of my skirt, with muscular legs on display, one sporting a tattoo that I haven't seen before—a butterfly of all things—on his upper thigh.

There's so much tanned skin showing that my mouth goes dry and I grab my water bottle. Looking like he does shouldn't be legal, all sharp lines softened by boyish charms.

He grasps one girl's swivel chair, spinning her as he walks by with a wink. She giggles and halfheartedly chides him, which he takes like a well-loved class clown. For a moment, his eyes move across the room like he's looking for where he's supposed to be.

But they catch on someone else, a girl arching on her tiptoes for a book off the shelf, the frayed hem of her shorts cutting into her dark thighs. He leans over her and grabs the book she was reaching for. She sinks against the bookcase behind her, while his hand stays planted over her.

And . . . I'm a little worried I'm drooling.

"Hey," Rodger says, and I nearly jump out of my seat, realizing I was so focused on Freddy that I didn't see or hear my coworkers' approach.

"Oh, wonderful," Tyler mutters, sliding into the seat next to me. "He's here."

I feel a little sick, the guilt of mooning over Freddy when I have a semi-maybe-boyfriend mixing with the thrilling lust of being in his presence. Nothing he's doing is inherently sexual, but I've been plagued with dreams about Freddy for years.

"I told you that I didn't need you here," I mumble, still a little frustrated with Tyler's inability to do what I ask. But I'm borderline used to it now.

Rodger has to be here, to officially hand over files and go through the plan change with Freddy present. Tyler most definitely does *not* need to be here. In fact, he shouldn't be. It's a violation of student academic privacy.

Instead, he laughs. "What? Don't want me here so you can pant over Matt Fredderic?"

I roll my eyes and shove him with my shoulder a little.

"C'mon, Ro. Don't tell me you still think he's hot. The guy couldn't pass an STD test, let alone freshman-level bio."

"Stop it."

Tyler's not wrong; Freddy does have a reputation. But it's more complicated than that. I've overheard enough stories about him to last me a lifetime—and not one of them is negative. Girls fawn over him, but I've never heard a single crazy story about him breaking anyone's heart. They have a good time, then they move on. Everyone seems to leave happy.

Freddy is still chatting up the girl at the bookshelf, his hand tracing patterns beneath the hem of her shirt, and she looks mesmerized, like his beauty and aura are a swinging pocket watch and she's the hypnotist's willing subject.

Meanwhile, I'm plastered to the seat, crossing and uncrossing my legs and wishing I hadn't worn a skirt.

As if the shifting in my seat has drawn his attention, Tyler eyes me up and down, his gaze flickering from my ruffled short socks to the lavender bow pulling half my frizzy curls off my face, disapproval evident in his eyes.

"Thought you'd grow out of that look by now," he mutters under his breath.

My face flushes and everything feels too tight. I feel ridiculous, hating how easily his words get to me. I've loved Tyler for years, and

I *know* he hates when I dress like this. But *he's* the one who decided that we aren't together.

Why can't I just ignore him?

I stand without preamble and shove back from the table, nearly tripping as I grab my backpack.

"Whoa, where are you going?" Rodger asks, scooting away in his rolling chair to give me space.

"I—um, the bathroom. It's my period," I say, lying. "Just go over the plan with him and tell him to meet me next week. Same time, same place, okay?"

I'm gone before either of them can respond, nearly running toward the hallway with the bathrooms, my phone in my hand to text Sadie—

—before slamming into a brick wall.

That wall being Matt Fredderic.

"Sorry," I sputter, backing up and nearly tripping over my own feet.

"You're good, princess." He smirks, winking a little as he picks my phone up off the ground and checks it. "Not a scratch. You're in luck."

"Clearly," I blurt, only serving to make myself blush further. My hands fumble for the phone, nearly dropping it again. "I'm—I have to go. Thanks."

I don't think I've ever run that fast in my life.

CHAPTER 4

Freddy

My hands flex a little, eyebrows furrowed in light confusion as I watch the leggy brunette sprint like an Olympic track star for the exit. Someone rolls a desk chair into her path and she dodges it—though she's got the legs, height, and speed to hurdle it—but clips a wall hard with her shoulder.

I watch, with arguably too much focus, the swish of her white tennis skirt, loving how tan her long limbs look in contrast—she's tall, with curls bouncing down her back, loosely tied with a pretty bow.

A pulse of something warm has my feet shifting, body turning like I might follow her.

Focus.

Right. I'm here for a reason, and I'm already—I check my phone—ten minutes late.

I'm unintentionally late *a lot*. Which might be the reason I received a late-night email from my current assigned tutor, Rodger, that I needed to see him prior to the semester start to meet my new tutor.

People might know me as the school slut, a man-whore, but I cycle through tutors far faster than girls. Which I wouldn't mind so much if it didn't mess up my routines so much. It's hard enough for me to keep track of my school and hockey schedules—add a new date and time, new location, every time I switch tutors? It makes it harder to remember and to go to the right place at the right time.

Walking to the back table where I usually meet Rodger, where I've met with him all summer, I come to a dead stop.

My stomach sinks, nauseous at the sight that greets me.

Tyler Donaldson stretched out in the chair next to Rodger.

I've had the distinct displeasure of knowing Tyler Donaldson for two years now. He started as my tutor at the end of sophomore year and continued through most of my junior year. Before handing me off to Rodger last spring—screwing me over before my finals with the sudden switch. He also has never once helped me with accommodations or tutoring. I started to assume he didn't know, that maybe my file was still as incomplete as it had been since freshman year.

But then Rodger started attempting some of my accommodations for this summer, to help me pass my second try with biology, and I realized I'd been royally fucked over by the asshole Donaldson.

Even now, he watches me with that same sneer—like he hates that I exist. To piss him off, I smile a little wider, obnoxiously sauntering their way.

"Rodger." I nod. "Who's the preppy kid?"

"Tyler," Rodger says, distracted by his phone as he usually is. So distracted that he's reintroducing me to someone he *knows* I know—who tutored me for a year.

Tyler fumes, face red in a way that relaxes my false smile into a real grin.

"Funny, Fredderic," he snaps. "Nice of you to show."

I ignore him completely, planting my hands on the table and leaning over them. "I'm not switching back, Rodger. I'll do the semester without a tutor if my only other option is—"

"I'm not your tutor," Tyler says, cutting in. "Sit down and focus for two seconds and maybe we can get through this meeting normally."

He's smart, unfortunately, but uses his brainiac powers for evil, trying to hit me where it hurts. But I'll never let him see that it works.

Sitting across from them, I cross my arms defensively, knee bouncing rapidly beneath the table. *Maybe following that girl would've been better after all.*

"You failed biology. Again," Rodger says, spinning my file toward me.

A blush heats my cheeks before I can stop it, embarrassment and fury mixing at Tyler's sardonic chuckle as he shakes his head at me. I'm sure he doesn't *need* to be here—in fact, I'm betting there are school policies preventing him from being involved in my academics— but I don't want to stir up anything. I want to get the hell out of here.

"You'll retake it in the fall," my most recent tutor says. "And you're going to be with a different tutor now. She's great. She'll make sure you pass."

"She?" I mutter.

"Yeah," Tyler laughs. "Your new tutor is a girl. Think you can refrain from sticking your dick in her for long enough to stay eligible?"

"Think you can refrain from *being* a dick for more than five seconds?" I grin brightly. "Didn't think so."

"All right, Fredderic—"

"Stop it," Rodger grumbles. "You're both giving me a headache." He flips open his worn satchel and grabs another sheet of paper, this one with a new study timetable. "This is the tentative first-week schedule for your tutoring sessions. You'll meet her here for the first one next week, and then you two can decide where to meet."

"Preferably somewhere public," Tyler says, eyeing me.

"Cute," I snap, grabbing the paper and folding it. "Anything else?"

"Yeah." Rodger nods and slips the stapled packet over. "Your fall class schedule—I looked over it already. Your math professor sucks, so get ready for that, but you're with Tinley for bio at least . . ."

He continues talking, but I don't hear a word, heartbeat thundering in my ears at the mention of her name. I pretend to study the schedule, but my anxiety is too high to focus, the words blurring on the page beneath my fingers.

"Is there another biology course open?" I ask, not bothering to apologize for cutting him off. Rodger looks to Tyler, but he shakes his head.

"No," Rodger says. "Not one that doesn't interfere with your hockey schedule."

"Can I take it in the spring?"

"Tinley is great," Tyler says. "She's our boss—she's the best biology professor we have."

"I don't really give a shit, Donaldson." I hate the sound of my own voice, the anxiety leaking into my tone. I sound like I'm pleading, so I force a bit of frustration into it. It's better to sound angry about it than fearful—God forbid one of these geniuses has already traveled down the road I did years ago.

"Whatever." He rolls his eyes, shoving back and grabbing his belongings. "I'm out. You deal with him."

"Nope," Rodger says, talking over me while I sit here, feeling more and more like a child whose parents are deciding what to do with him. "He's Shariff's responsibility now."

I barely hear what he says, still trying to problem solve in my own head.

Turning back to me as Tyler slips away and exits the library, Rodger scratches his head and huffs an annoyed breath.

"You can't take it next semester, Freddy," Rodger says, his voice a little softer than it was now that his friend is gone. "What if you fail? Then you're not even eligible to graduate—then what?"

I close my eyes, trying to breathe a little slower, trying to stop the shaking caused by my bouncing knees. *He's right*, even if he doesn't understand my hesitation. It's this, or possibly not graduating, and then I've suffered through four years with nothing to show for it.

Way to make her proud.

"Okay." I nod, folding the schedule and tucking it around my tutoring papers. "Yeah, I got you."

"You'll be fine," Rodger sighs. "Your new tutor is great. You'll like her."

CHAPTER 5

Ro

"You have to actually tell me if I pull too hard, Ro."

A wince breaks my smile for a millisecond, but I catch myself in the mirror and erase the pain before she sees. I love that she's doing this for me too much to mention how often she yanks on the pieces.

"I'm good," I say happily.

Sadie Brown has been my best friend since freshman year. My only friend, really, but there is a strange comfort in not being alone in that, in knowing I am also her only real friend. We have isolated ourselves in a lot of ways, but I wouldn't trade a second of it—the messiness, the chaos, her brothers, my loneliness. I'd endure it all again for a friend as loyal and strong as her.

But nights like this are few and far between. We both work at Brew Haven, but Sadie works two more jobs on top of figure skating competitively for our school. Add to that her most important job—taking care of her little brothers—and she's almost always gone.

I miss her. But I understand wholeheartedly. I've been the caretaker before. I'll never make this friendship something that weighs on her. There's only room for me to help when I can.

Sadie bites one butterfly clip while using both hands to carefully place another in a twist of my curls. "Almost done."

"It looks amazing."

It does. She's used nearly all my multicolored tiny plastic clips, but mostly the ones that match my striped lilac knitted set—something I made myself sophomore year but haven't had the courage to wear yet.

I check my phone again, seeing the same glaring message announcing it was read ten minutes ago. Which means Tyler will decidedly not be responding.

> **RO**
> *Going to a small party with Sadie tonight.*
> *Hope that's okay! Girls' night :)*

> **TYLER**
> *Doesn't sound like you're giving me a choice.*

> **RO**
> *Are you going to be mad if I go?*

> **TYLER**
> *Are you really just with Sadie?*
> *Send me a picture of you.*

I had: a quick mirror selfie with a shaky smile and my roommate wearing her signature frown and gray silk dress.

> **TYLER**
> *Whatever. Do what you want.*

> **RO**
> *Tyler, please, I'm just hanging out with my roommate.*

TYLER
Ok.

                                                    RO
                        I didn't mean to upset you. I'm sorry.

And since then, nothing.

"Maybe I shouldn't—"

Sadie covers my mouth with her hand, glaring down at me in an unusual reverse of our heights. I'm five foot nine and my best friend is a solid five two, which means we usually look rather comical side by side, even if Sadie Brown carries herself like she's the tallest person in the room.

"We're not doing this tonight, okay?" Her voice is solid, strength pouring off her. I'm desperate to soak up as much of it as I can. "You and I are going to listen to ABBA while playing flip cup for shots in the kitchen, and once you're ready, we are going to a party. We're going to have *fun*. And if Tyler has some shit to say about it, he can say it to me."

My eyes burn a little at her solemn vow.

"Yeah?" she asks.

"Yes."

                            • • •

The party is overwhelming, but Sadie doesn't leave my side.

The frat house is massive and I've never been before, but I know Sadie is a frequent partygoer here—namely for a guy named Sean, whom I am finding I really dislike.

We're currently seated downstairs, amid the flashing lights and loud music that somehow feels like the same fifteen songs on a constant shuffle. Sadie is perched on the arm of a sofa, while Sean ignores her to chat with his friends. Except for his hand, which keeps running up and down her calf.

Maybe Sadie doesn't mind, but the guy wears his bravado like an expensive watch, wrist constantly outstretched. He reminds me of Tyler and Mark—their entire prep school crew.

I don't like it.

My best friend looks ridiculously bored. I make a funny face at her, feeling a little giddy from the cinnamon-flavored whiskey coursing through my body. Sadie smirks—a hard feat to accomplish— before kicking off Sean's hand and heading toward me.

"Wanna play a game?" she shouts over the music. "They said there's beer pong in the kitchen."

I nod, pulling myself off the opposite couch and stumbling a little in my heeled boots. Sadie snorts and grabs me around the waist.

"You sure you're good, Ro?"

Nodding again, a blissful smile on my face, I shuffle into the overcrowded kitchen and take one of the shots being offered as we enter.

I feel free for a moment, from everything that hurts. The alcohol loosens my muscles and hits me like joy pumped through an IV; it feels good, even if it's artificial and fleeting.

"Actually," I say with a giggle, holding Sadie in a loose hug. "Can you help me find the bathroom?"

CHAPTER 6

Freddy

"Don't get him drunk, Freddy," Bennett warned me before we left for the back-to-school house party nearby. "I'm fucking serious."

"Wasn't planning on it," was my minorly snarky response.

And I wasn't. Really, I want Rhys to let loose for at least a second before diving back into hockey captain mode full force.

That, and I'd have to be *blind* to miss the way Rhys stared at my phone over dinner—the photo of Sadie, a figure skater I vaguely remember—like it was the Stanley Cup.

Everyone knows I'm a good-time guy, the life of the party, even if I let our defenseman Holden Dougherty take the lead sometimes. And while I'm not necessarily the best at comforting, especially the captain of my team who I look up to—who seems to be holding on by a thread—I know that I can do this, at least.

Even if "this" means leaving him alone with the twirl girl, who I've never seen smile but *did* see taking body shots off some of my swim team friends at a party last spring—even if it was Paloma Blake going upstairs with both guys afterward.

But the way Rhys and Sadie are looking at each other now as I come up the stairs, I'm thinking I might not interrupt them after all. Even more so because lovestruck Rhysie hasn't even noticed me standing a few feet away from him.

I'm not a mountain like Reiner, but I'm not small, and I'm definitely not quiet.

Especially when a pretty girl stumbles right into me.

I catch her easily, barely resisting the urge to pick her up by her waist and set her back on her feet—just because I can. Like a little advertisement for my skills in the bedroom.

Look, sweetheart, see how strong I am? I can toss you around so easily. I'm gentle, though, but I'll be aggressive, if you want.

I'll be whatever you want me to be.

"Sorry," she says, quiet and shy, her tan skin flushing slightly as she tilts her head back a little to look up at me. Her hair is long, dripping down her back like a waterfall of curls, with little colored butterfly clips swirling through the strands. Then I realize it's the same girl who ran into me—or was it away from me?—at the library last week.

I put on my signature grin, watching it work its magic as her pupils dilate and her cheeks somehow flush further.

"You're good, princess," I murmur, all charm, ready to see if she'll pull me back into the bathroom she came out of or take off down the stairs like Cinderella—considering it's almost midnight. I rub my fingers through the bottom loops of her springy curls. "Need some help?"

"Nope!" Sadie snaps at me.

She goes to pull the girl away from me, but my mysterious stranger's slender hand grabs hold of my wrist behind her back.

I smile down at her grip on me, my other hand tracing along her fingers and taking note of the delicate pearlescent manicure shimmering against my skin. I like noticing details like this, the work people—especially women—put into their appearance.

I don't hear the conversation between my captain and the figure skater, but the girl lets me go too fast and makes a stumbling turn for the stairs. My eyes trail her, feeling a little giddy about the prospect of following her down. She seems fun, full of light.

My body starts to relax just *looking* at her.

But only for a second, before both Sadie and Rhys are barking out a warning to steer clear of her.

I raise my hands up in surrender, fully intent on listening to them—at least for now.

When I turn back to the stairs, she's already stumbling her way down, a little drunker than I first assumed.

Okay. I can't "steer clear" of her when she's got no one watching her.

"Whoa. Easy," I laugh, pulling her to me quickly before she can tumble down the stairs.

"Sorry." She flushes, looking up at me with glassy eyes. "I'm dizzy. And"—her brow furrows—"stairs are hard."

Once she's got her balance back, I follow her down into the living room and then to the kitchen, where she knocks into someone else.

"Damn, babe, buy me a drink first," an equally drunk asshole says, settling his hands low on her waist to help her balance after she's ricocheted off him. "C'mon, over here."

"Nope," I call, diving between them a little roughly. The guy lets go of her instantly, and she bumps into someone else as he looks me up and down, eyes glazed and flickering. "Back off," I growl, feeling testy now.

"She grabbed me," he argues, words slurring. I turn around, shaking my head because I'm definitely not in the mood to fight anyone, especially not idiots with drunken misplaced courage.

"Hey, Ro," one of his friends says, voice softer. Definitely someone I've met before, but I don't remember his name. "Leave her alone, guys," he tells his friends.

"You know her?" I ask.

"Freddy, hey," he says. I shake his hand but don't say anything because I can't remember what his—

"Mitch!" she shouts, grabbing his biceps with a big, dazzling smile. "I didn't know you were here."

Mitch blushes a little underneath his backward hat but looks up at me apprehensively. "We had organic chem together last year. She was on a project with me—is she okay?"

I raise my hands. "I'm just watching out for her. Her friend's upstairs talking to Rhys."

Mitch nods and turns her back around toward me, essentially dumping the responsibility for the beautiful—albeit very drunk—princess with butterflies in her hair back to me.

"Hey," she says, looking up at me curiously, pausing slightly as though she's actually getting a good look at me for the first time in the brighter light of the kitchen. "Freddy."

"You know my name?"

Her eyes go wide as she blanches and then slowly shakes her head. It pulls a laugh from me as I settle an arm around her in the crowded, overly loud room.

"Wanna get some air, princess?"

"Okay," she acquiesces, melting into me slightly as I steer us out to the back patio and pool area.

"You didn't tell me your name," I say, lips to her ear so she can hear me over the thumping speaker as we pass by it. "It's only fair, since you clearly know mine."

She steps out the door first, with me trailing behind as I pull the sliding door shut.

"Rosalie," she offers a little loudly before blushing and smiling shyly. "But everyone calls me Ro."

It's quieter out here, and she instantly heads toward the pool, kneeling to dip her hand in.

"It's warm, kinda," Rosalie calls back to me before sitting down and unzipping her boots, pulling her socks off quickly so she can stick her feet in the water.

I shake my head but follow her and do the same, carefully setting my pristine shoes away from the water, pulling her boots to lie next to them. I stick my feet in beside her, thigh pressed lightly to hers. She sways gently to the music playing out here—it's a calmer vibe, with Kendrick Lamar and Zacari's "LOVE" playing through the hanging-by-a-wire porch speakers.

I take her in for a minute, while drawing in a breath. Usually I thrive in the bustling, never-lonely environment of a party, but this feels better somehow. She's beautiful, warm tawny skin and curling brown hair trailing nearly to her waist. Glassy hazel eyes—a little more green than brown—and a rosy tint to her cheeks from the alcohol. This close, she smells a bit like Fireball cinnamon whiskey and something softer, a clean floral perfume.

Her outfit is a stunner, too, shorts and a sleeveless knit top that make me want to ask if she *made* them.

"These are cute," I say, reaching out to pull lightly on one of the pink butterfly clips weaving down through her curls. "Pretty. I like your outfit."

Rosalie blushes more deeply and pulls away, tucking her chin. "Oh, thank you. I—um, I don't dress like this usually."

"Oh?"

She shakes her head.

"Why not? It's cool."

"Tyler says I look like a dumb little kid," she blurts out, then grimaces like she wasn't planning on saying all that. Something shutters in her eyes, and she starts pulling at the clips, trying to tear them out of her hair almost harshly. "They're stupid anyway."

I stop her before she can yank a whole chunk of her curls out and smooth them down, reclipping one of the discarded butterflies where she'd pulled it loose. Only three of them are left in her hair, a colorful graveyard of discarded butterflies littering the concrete around us. "They're not stupid. Tyler is stupid," I grumble. I don't know who the guy is, but he sounds like a prick I'd love to meet fist to face.

Which might be the reason I can't stop myself from asking, "Is Tyler your . . . ?"

"Boyfriend? Yeah— Or, I mean, no," she murmurs before her cheeks heat. "I forgot. He's my ex-boyfriend now, I guess? I don't know. He's confusing and says we're not together, but we're 'casual.'" She throws sarcastic air quotes around the word, and I chuckle a little. "But he'd kill me if he knew I was talking to you."

"Jealous type?"

She snorts like I've told some funny joke, kicking the water with her feet a little. "Not at all. But you're *you*."

I'm used to it, but for some reason the words land like a solid punch. For a moment, I don't want to be known for what I am.

"Ahh, am I truly that big of a slut that everyone's heard about me?" My voice isn't carefree or relaxed anymore; even the chuckle in my words is darker, and I think it frightens her a little.

"No," she finally says, her eyes wide and brow furrowed. "No— it's . . . Because . . . I mean . . . I have a crush on you."

I pause for the punch line, but Rosalie starts to talk nervously.

"We've met once before, at another party, but you probably don't remember, and I sound insane, but you've always been my, like, celebrity crush."

A smile spreads across my face before I can even control it, happiness bubbling in my stomach like champagne. I almost want to giggle like a kid.

"Aren't celebrity crushes supposed to be celebrities?" I nudge her shoulder with mine a little, and my foot accidentally bumps hers in the water.

She laughs and nods, cheeks flushed and eyes intoxicatingly bright. "Yeah, sure—but you will be one someday." She says it with such surety I find myself blushing for the first time in years.

"Oh yeah?"

"You're incredible."

I've heard those same words so many times, but the way she says them, they sound more genuine somehow. Like this isn't about my body at all. Sex is easy to me; I've been a quick study since I was far too young. Hockey is even *easier*, and I'm better than most because I work hard beyond how much comes naturally to me. But outside of that? I'm . . . nothing. I'm a fucking failure at using my brain—anything beyond the physical is pointless for me to even attempt because I'm nothing when I'm not using my body.

But . . . this feels different.

"Thanks. Big hockey fan?"

"Sure." She nods profusely. "Never been to a game, but I'm sure it's amazing. I've seen videos. Very cool."

I laugh because she looks confused and sympathetic all at once. Like she's appeasing a kid who wants to talk about his obsession with dinosaurs. Something that makes my chest feel warm.

"Videos? Of who?"

"Just like top NHL plays and stuff. Or like if it's on TV. They're pretty amazing. I think Sidney Crosby is very handsome."

I reach out boldly to tuck a curl behind her ear and spin my hand through her mass of ringlets. "You haven't seen amazing yet, princess. Not till you see me play."

It's a fucking line, and probably one of my worst. And I watch her sink back a little as it has the opposite effect than I wanted it to.

"I'm gonna get in now."

Rosalie is up and gone too quickly for her words to register before my eyes shoot wide and I jump up to follow her. She climbs the side ladder onto the top of the tall storage shed at the edge of the cement pathway around the pool's edge. The frat calls it a "high dive" where the more adventurous partygoers like to flip and dive off—but more than one person has broken a limb misjudging their jump.

My stomach lurches as I realize exactly what she's about to do.

I race over to stand in front of her, heart in my throat for reasons I don't want to think about.

"Hey, princess—whatcha doing?" I ask, voice shaking slightly.

"I wanna do something fun."

"Talking was fun. You want to play a game?"

"I want to be someone else," she blurts, and her eyes start to well. I want the stars back, the bright honeyed hazel eyes that look at everything with wonder. "I want to be like you."

"No, you don't," I laugh sharply.

"I'm not brave or cool or anything fun, I'm just . . . I'm careful. I'm good, and it's still not enough. I want to be more."

"You can be whatever you want to be."

Like my words have caused her physical pain, she shuts her eyes tightly. "I wish—" Her feet slip a little and my stomach somersaults.

"Rosalie," I bark. "Wait for me." I flick my eyes around, noticing that we have an audience now, before walking to grab one of my shoes and yanking out the lace.

Fuck it. The shed is a bit taller than my reach, but if I can jump and latch on to it with my hand, I can pull myself up without taking my eyes off her to get to the ladder.

So I do, gritting my teeth at the sharp metal of the shed roof cutting my palms as I pull myself up to stand in front of her. I grab her by the waist like I'm a little worried she might try to jump anyway.

"What are you doing?" She sounds breathless, and I have to close my eyes not to let my imagination run away from me.

"If you're jumping, I'm jumping." I shrug.

"You are?"

"Why not?" I smile. "Unless you want to do it alone."

Rosalie shakes her head rapidly. "I hate being alone."

Me, too.

"Great. Then I'm not leaving you alone, Ro," I whisper, my breath fanning her hair as I reach over and pull the last few clips from her hair, tucking them into my pocket, before gathering her curls up into my hands, piling them high on her head, and carefully tying the shoelace around them to keep them out of her eyes.

"Thank you," she says, blushing.

We're too close but I don't move. "You don't have to thank me. I just wanna make sure you're okay."

"I'm okay." She shivers beneath my hands, which are settled on her shoulders now.

I take her hand in mine and step to the edge. Thankfully I've seen some daredevil frat boys jump from this stupid thing before. I know it's doable.

"Ready?"

"Ready."

I count down, my hand locked on to hers as we jump. The water feels cold on my overheated skin—crippling anxiety over a girl will do that to you. I surface and flip my hair out of my eyes, hearing wheezing giggles from Ro as I swim right over to her and paddle in so close we share breath.

"You're very nice." She smiles.

I preen under her compliment. "Yeah?"

She nods, but the smile slides off her face quickly and my stomach sinks, a desperate need to bring it back plaguing my mind.

"What's wrong?"

"I wish it was always this easy."

"What do you mean?" I ask. I've been called easy plenty of times, but never like this.

"I think it's hard for people to like me. And I try *really* hard." Tears well up in her eyes for a moment and my throat closes a little at the sight. At the sentiment, too, because I understand it deeply.

So I offer her a piece of my own vulnerability to match hers.

"I hate that. Sometimes I feel that way, too." Goose bumps break out across my arms at the earnest confession, but I can't take it back now.

And . . . I don't want to.

My eyes trace droplets of water as they cascade down her honeyed skin, dripping off her curls kept high off her long neck by my shoelace.

There's pure joy in her eyes and she's finally relaxed—like the tension in her shoulders has melted off into the water. Everything feels gentler, like time itself is moving slower as we wade across from each other. I'm sure I'm giving her the same moony expression she's giving me. I'm confident, by the rapid beating of my heart in my ears, that I am.

It's different, this tentative thing with her, whatever it is. My chest is warm and tight all at once, because it feels like she might kiss me. And I want that, desperately. It doesn't matter how many people I've indulged in before; it feels like the nervous excitement before a *first kiss*. I want to freeze this moment, to slow it down somehow so I can feel this way over and over—

"Freddy?" Rosalie asks, voice whisper-soft and breathy.

"Yeah?" I say, my voice matching hers. I drift closer to her, until our hands brush beneath the water.

"Thank you."

I tuck one of her stray curls back behind her ear. "Anytime, princess."

"I think you'd be really easy to love," she says. It's a lax, whispered compliment, one she doesn't know sounds like a gunshot in my head, hitting me straight in the chest.

My words disappear, until I'm left standing and staring at her, only shaken by the appearance of my captain and the figure skater bursting our contented little bubble.

I think you'd be really easy to love.

It echoes in my head on a loop, tethering my ever-spinning mind.

CHAPTER 7

Ro

"You look like shit."

I barely raise my head, instead turning my neck so I can peek up from the blissfully dark paradise my crossed arms on the table have created.

Sadie smirks, setting down two cups of coffee from our second-hand Nespresso—a gift from my mother the first and only time she visited—in front of me.

"You try waking up with a pounding headache and 'tolerate it' playing on repeat like a sad, terrifying alarm."

Sadie bursts into a laugh, wiping her mouth with her sleeve where some of the coffee sputtered. "Please don't tell me that was your speaker playing all night on a loop."

I groan. "I think I started with 'Getaway Car,' and then at some point during the night I got sad and weird."

"That's less surprising considering your absolute knockout kara-oke performance in the back of the car last night."

I slam my hands down on my face, head shaking. "No, please say you're kidding."

Sadie raises one perfect eyebrow, her lips still stained from her usual dark red lipstick, hair slicked back into a bun. Even undone, she's perfect, elegant. And I'm . . .

A lumpy mass of frizzy, tangled curls and swollen eyes.

"You really don't remember?"

"I blacked out after those last shots, Sadie," I whine, rubbing my eyes and dramatically slumping back in the wooden chair at our little breakfast table. "I don't remember anything."

Sadie's face looks almost stricken and something sinks in my gut.

"Oh God," I moan. "Your face—just tell me. What is it?"

"Your little sing-along might have been in the back of Matt Fredderic's car." She chews on her lip for a moment while I feel my face slowly drain of color with each word she says. "And you might've somehow ended up in the pool with him."

"In the pool? What? How—"

"You jumped off the top of the shed like a lunatic." Sadie snorts. "Kinda scary, but also kinda amazing."

Oh God.

I hate that my first thought is of Tyler, wondering if he saw, if someone at that party filmed me acting insane and told him all about it. I *wish* I didn't care about his opinion of me, but I still do, because I love him, I think. And I want him to think highly of me, as an equal and a partner.

Not a drunk party girl jumping off roofs with playboy hockey players.

Instinctively, I reach for my phone and open our text thread.

Nothing.

Just two unanswered, unread *I'm sorry* texts, from me to him.

My entire body jolts as I do a double take at the time staring up at me from my phone.

1:39 p.m.

"I slept past one!" I shriek, nearly knocking the chair back in my haste to stand up.

Sadie, who has put her trusty corded headphones into her ears, looks over at me with a piece of butter-and-jam-covered toast half hanging out of her mouth. She reaches up to pull one earbud out, then reaches for the toast.

"Yeah," she says, dragging it out, arching an eyebrow. "I think we were up until nearly four, Ro. I barely survived getting the boys to their practice this morning, and immediately went back to sleep when I got back. Why—what's wrong?"

I'm groaning already as she finishes and I unceremoniously shove a piece of toast into my mouth and grab a water bottle.

"I'm supposed to be at the library in twenty minutes."

"Damn, Ro!" Sadie smiles. "I think I'm proud of you for this, actually. First ever day you're late to anything."

I'm already desperately searching the cabinets for a protein bar—anything to tide me over so I don't pass out on Matt Fredderic mid-session.

Matt Fredderic.

I pause in my rapid retreat to my room, spinning back toward Sadie to beg, "Please, please, *please* tell me Freddy and Rhys were so hammered last night they also blacked out?"

Sadie pauses, her face slowly morphing from confusion to a beaming, evil smirk.

"I didn't see either of them holding a drink once. Sorry, Ro." She shakes her head at my stricken expression. "Don't worry, Freddy is probably obsessed with you now. Might be good payback for you spending the entirety of freshman and sophomore years pining over him."

I shake my head hard enough to stir up my headache again full force.

"I have to go tutor him now." I rub my hands over my face again and nod, turning for my room before her mocking rendition of "Getaway Car" can fully reach my ears and irritate my already pounding head.

• • •

He's late.

It's a blessing and a curse, considering the absolute sprinting gymnastics I performed to get myself ready and here *on time*. It's not my best look—an oversized bright pink tee dotted with hearts and butterflies in different shades of pink, a pair of comfy, thin cream cargo pants, and a thick, black fabric headband pushing my absurdly more-unruly-than-normal curls back.

At the least, I'm clean and have successfully washed out any lingering cinnamon liquor smell.

My head is almost too heavy to hold up, so I rest my chin in my hands and close my eyes, sucking down more water from the ridiculously large bottle I've lugged with me.

"Hey."

God, how can he make one word sound like that?

I straighten, smiling lightly even as I feel the heat start to rise in my cheeks. It only grows hotter as Sadie's retelling of the night forces its way back into my brain.

He's infuriatingly handsome, as he always is, dressed a bit more casually today than his usually well-planned outfits. Still, the material of his soft navy Waterfell University Hockey shirt stretches perfectly over his defined chest and shoulders, looser over his trim waist.

Golden hair sits in soft, short waves, perfectly styled, and those same smile lines carve out space, sharpening his smile into an unsuspecting weapon.

"H-hi," I breathe, clearing my throat as I realize I'm still *staring* at him.

His eyes crinkle at the corners as he settles his body into the chair, which suddenly looks small beneath his weight. There's a lightness to his face, like we're sharing some inside joke even though neither of us has said more than a greeting to each other.

"Good to see you again, princess," he says, the words soft. My cheeks heat. "I missed you."

"I—good to see you, too." I fumble for the words. "I should apologize for last night."

"For which part?" He smirks, leaning forward, hands on the table suddenly so close to mine they nearly touch. "Getting me wet?"

Freddy bites down on his lip, tamping down his smile as he looks at me. I watch him right back, like studying intensely for a test in a subject I don't know.

He almost looks like he wants to kiss me—which is ridiculous. But his face is so similar to the version of him I remember from that summer party freshman year. The flush of his warm skin, the taste of cinnamon on his tongue—the flavor of *him* on *my* tongue.

Does he remember that kiss? Does he wake up from dreams about his arms around my waist like I do about him?

Icy shock has my eyes jolting back to lock on his half-lidded green gaze.

Did we . . . Did we kiss? I can't ask him that. I don't want to admit that I remember *nothing* from last night. It's humiliating that it happened at all.

"No. I mean—yes, but—I don't—" *What did he say?* My brain has gone blank.

I clear my throat and refocus on my usual script. "We're here today to do a quick assessment of—"

"Rosalie," he coos, trying to calm me as he sets a hand on top of mine. It has the opposite effect, jolting me a foot off my seat as I yank my hands back to sit on them.

Rosalie? Oh my god. My cheeks stain darker somehow; I can feel the heat. I told him my full name? No one knows my full name—I never use it. Not even Tyler knows what Ro is short for, but he also never asked.

"It's Ro," I say, my voice small and squeaky. "I mean, that's what I go by."

There is a sliver of hurt marring his expression before he laughs it away and sinks into the chair across from me, still leaning over the table with his large forearms and big hands. It's distracting. *He's* distracting.

"Not what you told me," he says in a singsong. "Besides, I *like* Rosalie."

I can feel my control of the situation slipping, so I straighten up a little in my seat and slide my notebooks and folders into a straighter line, busying my hands and watching my movements so I don't have to look at him.

"I might've had too much to drink," I say, biting down on my lip and swallowing the shame-induced lump that forms in my throat. "I'm so sorry."

"Don't apologize, Rosalie," he says, smirking at me as I blush again over the use of my full name. It rolls off his tongue like a song. "I really, *really* enjoyed last night."

"I know I may have, uh, *behaved* in a certain way at the party last night, but I want to assure you that I am usually very professional—"

"But we didn't know each other yet," he says, frowning.

A dull ache throbs in my chest, but my smile still shines as I finally meet his confused gaze.

"Right," I say before sliding over the packet I usually use for assessing learning differences. I clear my throat unnecessarily again, straightening my spine. Freddy mirrors me slightly, but his bright green eyes are still dancing. "Rodger and Tyler left me a few notes about you to go through. But I figured that we could—"

"Hold on." Freddy holds his hand up like he can physically shove the words I've said back into my mouth. "Tyler—your asshole-maybe-ex-boyfriend—is Tyler *Donaldson*?"

My mouth gapes, opening and closing a few times before I settle on a response that doesn't include *I talked to you about Tyler last night?* in a screeching scream. Instead, I try to grab hold of my fragile professionalism.

"That's inappropriate," I snap. Freddy slumps back in his chair, brows furrowed in thought and eyes pointedly aimed away from me for the first time since he arrived at the table. "But, yes. Tyler Donaldson and I . . . date."

Date. Present tense, because I'm not quite sure what to call this weird, uncomfortable dance we're currently doing with each other.

A jovial smile works its way across Freddy's face as he crosses his arms and meets my eyes again, "Of course. Makes sense why he warned me about *you* the same way they've warned you about *me.* Seems both of us have a bit of a reputation."

The words sound like a joke, a purposeful jest. But I feel a little sick—more from the anxiety than from the aftereffects of the alcohol.

Tyler warned him about me?

The list of things he might've said feels so long and overwhelming I don't know where to start—which only ratchets up the anxiety and fear to an insurmountable level. *Ro's had a crush on you since freshman year. She swears you were her first kiss, even if most of us don't believe it happened.* I can almost *hear* his mocking laugh grating over my ears.

Or worse—my bedroom habits.

Tyler says I behave too brazenly, to put it kindly. I'm overeager, too loud or dramatically vocal. I ask for too much, or to do things that Tyler sees as *"beneath someone smart like you, Ro. It's degrading."* Would he mention something so personal to Freddy? Could that be the *warning* he's talking about?

Could that be why Freddy found me at the party last night? Looked for me then and is flirting with me now? My heart drops again, like I'm on a never-ending thrill ride that's easily shaving years off my life.

Maybe Tyler has been right all along. My behavior should reflect the respect I expect. If I want to be seen as brilliant and smart, I should be more reserved with sex, like Tyler is. Like I'm sure his prep school New York friends he spends his summers with are as well. If I do that, maybe I'll finally be good enough.

I wipe my clammy palms across my pants and pull on a loose curl, wrapping it around and around my finger soothingly.

"Listen . . . If Tyler said something or I was weird to you last night, or something . . . just know, that's not me."

His brow dips, furrowing at my words as his fingers draw circles on the wood of the tabletop. His lips are twisted down, and I feel like somehow my words are upsetting him.

"What about what you said—?"

"I don't remember anything from last night," I finally say, my voice a little harsher than I intend, skin hot with humiliation. Nodding my head a little roughly, I press on. "It's probably best that way. Let's start over. Forget last night ever happened," I cut him off, reaching my hand out like a formal greeting.

Freddy looks at my outstretched hand, hurt rolling across his features as his shoulders slump. Does he know how openly he's wearing his emotions in this moment, without his perpetual flirty smile?

He shakes his head, muttering, "Right," beneath his breath. He doesn't meet my eyes, his gaze drifting to the ground like he's working something out in his head, before finally grasping my hand in a quick, halfhearted shake.

As I flip open the folder, he stands so abruptly his chair gets knocked back. My eyes go wide.

"Where are you going?"

He has his backpack already tipped onto one shoulder, giving me an awkward salute before heading out the door and into the empty silent floor of the library.

"Wait! We haven't even started!" I shout, somewhat too loud, flustered as I chase him down.

I grab his backpack strap and stumble back a little with the accidental force of my pull. I'm surprised he manages to stay upright, but I'm *not* surprised that I can't. A squeak bursts from my mouth as I crash backward onto the floor.

He flicks his eyes over my now-prone form, sprawled embarrassingly across the terrible nineties-patterned carpet. I wait for him to leave, tempted to shut my eyes not to see the mocking smile I'm sure he's sporting.

But instead, he bends over me, his palms gripping my waist over the billowing fabric of my too-large shirt, and lifts me up, setting me steadily on my feet. As if I weigh nothing—like I'm some tiny girl, and not the five-nine lanky girl that I *know* I am.

There's a moment where his hands linger a little, and I swear I feel them *squeeze*—

Freddy takes off again, and I startle.

"Wait, Freddy. Where are you going—"

He snaps his fingers and spins to answer. "I forgot— I have, like, hockey stuff," he says, a fake smile spreading over his lips. "You get it!"

I shake my head a bit to keep his charm from settling over me. "No— I—"

"I'll see you next Tuesday!" he shouts, getting another stern *shh!* with a wagging finger from the summer librarian.

"It's on Thursday," I shout back, rolling my eyes as the librarian gives me a shocked expression. There aren't any other students here currently, no need to be silent.

He leans against the door and shrugs with a cheeky smile. "I'm dyslexic."

He pushes out the door before I can even *begin* to come up with a response to his self-deprecating humor.

Day one of tutoring Matt Fredderic and I've already lost all control over our dynamic.

CHAPTER 8

Freddy

My entire plan hadn't helped.

Texts unanswered, or with quick, apologetic responses—but I'm still alone in this house.

Mostly everyone I'd usually invite over for company was busy doing other things, being with their friends—enjoying the ease of the beginning of the semester.

I'm glad they're busy, but it doesn't make the slight feeling of abandonment hurt any less.

Even now, as I heat up microwavable bacon and scramble several eggs in the one pan Bennett allows me to use, I hope that I'll return to excited responses on my phone. At least one *"I miss you Freddy"* or *"On my way!"* to mend the hollow ache starting to grow in my chest.

I slam my bedroom door shut behind me and the echo of it sounds in my head.

I'm alone. The house is empty. Rhys comes back tomorrow, and Bennett isn't here—he never came home last night. Still, I feign ignorance to dampen the sting as I sit in my empty room. *You're fine. Everything is great.*

Forcing a quick smile like it might liven my spirits, I eat everything on my plate before curling up under the covers and trying to sleep. Even as *her* voice plagues me again.

I think you'd be really easy to love.

• • •

I'm on time today, a rarity for me, but I've barely been able to think of anything except this upcoming tutoring session—be it in the form of anxiety or anticipation, or both.

She asked me to meet her in the coffee shop on the third floor in a shortened email only minutes after my desperate run from our last meeting. It's the first day of fall semester, so the library is relatively empty—most everyone has no reason to be here this early at the start, apart from perpetual strugglers like me.

Still, I barely slept, deciding to spend my morning at the sports complex gym, which means I'm wearing shorts that show a bit too much thigh and the last of my clean T-shirts—I desperately need to do laundry—from my current collection in the backseat of my car.

I spot Ro before she sees me, seated in a corner booth. She's still as pretty as the first time I saw her, if a little more buttoned up today. A sweater vest top like a tank that looks more professional than her comfortable style from last time. But she's still got a funky clip—chunky with embellished cherries on it—in her hair, which makes me feel a little lighter. There's a pencil pressed to her lips, and she rolls it mindlessly across them before *tap tap tapping* it on her mouth. It's distracting enough that I stop for a moment and watch her.

Like I've announced my presence, her eyes leave the papers spread in front of her and lock on mine—but not before gazing a little too long at the butterfly tattoo on my upper thigh. I flex the muscle a little on my next step, a brazen smile taking over, the need to perform for her in some way almost overwhelming in intensity.

People watch me all the time, run their eyes over my body like it's on show just for them. But the way Ro watches me feels different. Not covetous, but inquisitive, like she's trying to see something deeper.

Or she's trying to remember the night she wants to erase from existence.

The grin on my face falters slightly at the unbidden thought, but I manage to shake it away physically with a quick jerk of my head as I step up to her alcove.

"Hey," I say, dropping my voice. The effect is immediate, her skin flushing rose gold. My smile only widens; I *love* that I have an effect on her.

"Hi."

Ro's hazel eyes, wide and wonder filled, drop to my thigh again before darting quickly back to my gaze.

"Have a seat," she says, voice sterner than her expression shows. I follow her instructions happily, leaning on my forearms as she starts to speak again. "So, I double-checked your schedule and cross-checked it with—"

"Cross-checking? That's illegal." The joke is pathetic at best, and anyone else might groan in annoyance or ignore me completely. But as usual, *Rosalie* is different.

Ro grins like she can't really help it. It's like pouring gasoline on a fire for me, and I'm desperate to pull another smile or laugh or any positive reaction she'll give me more than I care to pay attention to whatever she's trying to show me.

"Funny," she says.

"I'm *very* funny—as I'm sure you remember." I'm testing her, trying again to see how much she might recall from Friday night. Maybe a few days have given her some of those memories back.

Her brow furrows slightly, "No. I—" She clears her throat and looks up at me hesitantly. "I'm sorry. I just . . . I really don't know what happened last Friday. I don't remember."

Her words pull the warmth from my skin and replace it with a cold, clammy flush.

Ro looks like she's waiting for me to fill in the gaps and I freeze, smiling despite the little ache at the reminder that she doesn't remember anything.

What's a nice way of saying, "*You were so upset that you wanted to jump off the roof into a pool just to feel something different*"? Or maybe, "*You told me your boyfriend sucks and then tilted my entire world by saying that it would be easy to love me? When it's a fucking hardship for everyone else*"?

Instead, I smile and shake my head. "Don't worry about it. Please, continue. I promise not to interrupt." I make a show of zipping my lips closed, locking them and tossing the key over my shoulder, before straightening my back stiffly, hands clasped. The picture of a perfectly attentive student.

"Anyway . . ." She's still smiling as she points to the papers she's laid out in front of me. "It looks like these dates in pink are the best ones for us to meet. I put the times on them as well. Once I get a better hold on what your hardest subjects are, I'll break it down further to focus on what we need to tackle first. Make sense?"

I swallow hard. "Sure."

"Okay," she continues. If she notices I've barely glanced at the papers, she doesn't say. Ro hands me another printout, this one thicker and stapled together. "These are the topics for today's pretest. I put a mini break under each one as a refresher, mostly because I don't want you to be overwhelmed. What you score on the pretest doesn't matter, obviously, but it will help me know what our starting point is."

Looking at the paper, I bounce my leg beneath the table. The amount of text is staggering, enough to have me giving up before I've even started.

"Yeah." I nod, skimming my eyes over the document. "All looks good. Should be fine."

Shoving the paper back toward her, I plaster a smile on my lips before looking up. She's less relaxed now, brow furrowed as she looks back and forth between me and the paper.

She knows. I skimmed too quickly; I'm usually pretty good at fake-reading, covering my own ass for years when it comes to these moments. But I'm too nervous around her. She read the list in my file: dyslexia, dyscalculia, ADHD—but no one ever knows how severe the dyslexia is for me, how I struggle to read my hockey schedule, let alone a textbook on biology.

We both stare at each other, my gaze jumping more than her clearly focused one, and the moment feels like it passes for an eternity before her hand spins the paper back to face me.

"Okay, well," Ro says, voice serene. "It's a requirement to go through these together, for my team. So if you don't mind, I'm gonna just read them aloud to you."

There's no way in *hell* this is a requirement from her team—now that I know her team consists of Tyler and Rodger and anyone else who's tried and failed to help me. I bite my tongue to avoid offering some snarky version of exactly that in rebuttal.

But she's lying because she wants to help me. Without embarrassing me or calling me out.

"Okay." I nod, swallowing tightly. "I'm listening."

CHAPTER 9

Ro

"And everything is going well with your friends? What about that bowling class you said you were taking?"

I take in a deep breath, shoving a hand through my hair as I spin around in my desk chair slowly.

It's my weekly phone call with my mom, though I've called her twice this week. Tyler thinks I call her too much, that I'm "too attached to her" for my age.

"I ended up dropping it before summer, actually. I needed more time to focus on my research paper for Tinley."

I hear my mom starting up her usual argument about balance and enjoying my time at school, but I cut her off quickly because this entire conversation will inevitably lead to a confession that I don't want to make. Especially not at ten o'clock at night before the first day of school.

"I'm really tired," I whisper, ignoring the ache in my chest that even the idea of ending the call with her brings.

She sighs into the phone, and I clench my eyes.

"All right, *yavrum*," she says softly. She's called me *yavrum*—which is Turkish for "my little one" or "my darling"—since I was young. My dad always chides her lovingly for babying me—meanwhile, he called me jellybean until I started high school. Hearing the endearment over the phone when I'm so far away always feels like she's wrapping me in a warm blanket. "Call me soon, please. I love hearing your voice."

"I love you," I say, hoping even a fraction of how I feel manages to come through. The words don't feel like enough. "And tell dad I love him, too."

"I will. We love you. And remember," she says, her voice filled with deep love, "your father and I are so, so proud of you."

"Good night, Mom," I choke out before ending the call and tossing myself onto my twin bed, burying my teary eyes in the sleeves of my dad's Waterfell hoodie.

It feels almost cathartic to let myself cry. I spent half the summer with my parents, but it's never enough time to be with them. And knowing I won't go home until Christmas is almost too overwhelming to think about now, so I don't.

Instead, I wait for the tears to stop, wash my face, and braid my hair before setting my alarms and laying out my clothes for the first day of fall semester. I double- and triple-check my schedule, pack up my backpack—anything to distract from the pressure on my chest.

Eventually I manage to exhaust myself. I reach for my phone on the desk, where it's currently playing "striptease" by carwash from one of Sadie's playlists. As the singer croons softly from the speaker, I notice a text notification.

UNKNOWN
Still on for tomorrow? This is Freddy btw.

There's an entire line of random emojis beneath it, with multiple fiery hearts and winky faces, as well as several stacks of books.

I type FREDDY into the New Contact name line—before biting my lip and erasing it. Texting my students isn't something I do, choosing email to keep professionalism in an environment where I'm often the same age or younger than who I'm tutoring. If Sadie, or god forbid, Tyler, saw his name on my phone, they'd have more questions than I would ever have answers for.

> **RO**
> Yes, before class. I'll go over everything
> for the pretest again.

STUDENT
That sounds like cheating . . . I love it.

> **RO**
> It's not. Just test prep like I would
> with any student. See you tomorrow.

STUDENT
Aren't you going to ask how I got your number?

Butterflies roar to life in my stomach, harder and more insistent. Texting with him doesn't feel like part of my job, it feels like flirting. Like excitement and inside jokes. *You're his tutor,* I remind myself. *Not his friend.*

> **RO**
> Good night. Get some sleep before your classes
> tomorrow. Rest is important.

STUDENT
Sweet dreams, princess.

There's a winky face and a kissy face tacked onto the end of that last message, but I dismiss it as quickly as I dismiss my overheated cheeks. I plug my phone into the charger and roll over to try to sleep, only to see Freddy winking and blowing me kisses in my dreams.

· · ·

The room is tense as soon as I enter, all conversations halting.

It's a weird feeling I'm mostly used to. Being the only girl in the department makes me wary, and I'm usually excluded by the prep boys who run the place, but Tyler is their ringleader and my sometimes-boyfriend, so I've always expected that maybe that would earn me some sort of place with them.

And yet . . .

"Good morning," I say, stepping over to slide my backpack onto my desk chair and scoop my curls up into a bun off my neck, the walk across campus and the anxiety of how Tyler might behave, especially in front of his favorite audience, now churning in my gut making me sweat.

"Ro." Tyler smiles, but it's tight and strained. He ambles toward me, the entire group behind him walking carefully as if they want to eavesdrop but think they're being subtle. "Can we talk, baby?"

My stomach drops. I want to say no, because I already feel a little nauseous and the way he's looking at me ensures that feeling will probably only get worse.

Instead, I say, "Sure," and smile, albeit uneasily.

We step into one of the small study rooms—there are only three of them in the offices, which we mostly use for teacher-student meetings or extra testing time, but right now they're all empty.

The room has floor-to-ceiling windows, which makes me feel like I'm in a fish tank and our peers are all watching, ready to tap at the glass.

"The guys and I were talking about the cohort applications and

I just . . ." He trails off, pushing a hand through his mussed auburn hair. "Maybe you should consider trying for one of the other tracks."

My brow furrows, heart beating faster as I try to stay utterly calm.

"I haven't even tried for this one yet. The application isn't even due for two more months. I don't— Why are you—"

"Hey," he says. "Don't get worked up about it. It's just a suggestion."

I think my reaction is perfectly normal, considering *he* is on the selection committee with Tinley.

"I don't understand. You said my thesis idea was perfect—"

"Forget I brought it up. Your idea is *great*, Ro. You're a genius," he says, tucking me into his arms for a gentle hug. "I feel like it's going to come down to you and Mark for the spot, and Mark plays dirty. I don't want you to get your feelings hurt with that whole mess. I'm looking out for you."

Mark *does* play dirty. He deleted one of my papers sophomore year when we were both going for the same grant. As Tyler explained it, Mark was desperate to stay at Waterfell after his parents cut him off for "something ridiculous" he'd done over the summer.

I didn't ask what at the time, because I didn't feel the need to. Because Tyler *had* looked out for me, defended me and threatened Mark to keep his distance. Since last summer, however, Mark and Tyler had grown closer.

"I think I can handle him. And you're on my side, right?"

I hate how small my voice is as I ask, but I need that reassurance from him. Even if things are "casual" now, I do miss him. I miss how it was before, when we ate homemade lunches on my break at Brew Haven and debated uses for AI in the medical field, what we'd do as postgrads, where we'd go together.

"Right," he sighs. His lips press a soft kiss to my forehead and I melt a little. "If you're set on this program, then I'm on your side, RoRo."

CHAPTER 10

Freddy

My stomach is churning as I step down to the bottom level of the lecture hall.

My eyes flick from the gossiping semicircle of TAs, who are actually my age, to the line of freshman students waiting to talk to their new professor. Among the first group, I easily spot my curly haired tutor.

Ro looks over at me and I offer her as much of my usual smile as I can manage. She waves back at me before gathering the rest of her items in her green backpack that's got a ribbon tied to the zipper pull—a ribbon that I played with to occupy my hands while I focused on her words a few hours before.

She steps toward me, away from the other TAs, and a real smile takes over her face. A little of the anxiety in me fades. Mostly because when Ro looks at me, I don't feel like she's judging me.

She might be the *least* judgmental person I've ever met.

"Hey," she says, her hands wrapping around her spiral-bound planner. "How did it go?"

"You tell me," I say.

She adjusts her backpack a little, turning to the side. "Got it in here, so I'll let you know soon. But I'm sure you killed it."

Pretty sure I bombed the thing, but I'll take whatever misplaced praise I can get.

"Ro," a voice calls from the top of the lecture hall where, at the main entrance, Tyler Donaldson and his gang of assholes in boat shoes are now standing. "If you want a ride, you need to come. Now."

The rough command makes me tighten fists at my sides, especially when Ro's tawny skin heats in embarrassment, turning rosy gold where I can see along her profile.

"Right," she calls to him. "Just . . . wait for me by the car. I'll catch up, promise."

Tyler rolls his eyes and stalks out into the hallway. I have to ball my hands to keep from flipping him off and yelling something back at him like, "*Do your khakis come like that or do you have to shove the stick up your ass yourself?*" But I manage to hold it in when Ro breaks the tension with a little laugh and tucks back a curl.

"Sorry about that," she says a little awkwardly.

My brow furrows. *She's* the one apologizing?

I hate the guy. He's never had a nice thing to say to me, and I can't imagine how his need to put others down doesn't leak into his friendships and relationships. In fact, after the party and my chat with Ro before diving into the pool, I *know* it does, and I hate him a little more for it.

Tyler says I look like a dumb little kid.

Fucking asshole.

I tighten my grip on my backpack, cracking my knuckles a little with the movement.

"I . . . I should go. But I'll see you—"

"I have to ask." I stop her, my hand grabbing her wrist as she's started to leave. "Why the hell are you dating that asshole?"

Her cheeks turn darker.

"That's an inappropriate question to ask me. I'm your tutor. And your TA," she stammers.

There's a dangerous thrill zinging up my spine, distracting me from the dwindling crowd around our professor and my actual reason for staying after class. Making Ro blush and stammer might be a new favorite pastime of mine—great for me and my desperate need for distraction; terrible for her and my grades.

I grin a little and shrug, carefully raising my hand to scratch the back of my neck and stretch, watching with glee the nervous dart of her eyes to the exposed sliver of my lower stomach.

"Not that inappropriate for a friend to ask, though." I lean in to where I'm nearly whispering in her ear. "And aren't we friends?"

"We aren't— I mean, Freddy—" Ro huffs and grabs my arm, yanking me toward the wall, as far from the students lingering by the lectern as possible.

"C'mon, Ro. Let's just agree to be friends."

"It's inappropriate."

"Yeah, yeah." I shrug, smirking sardonically. "Just think about it. Might make the whole study partner thing a little more bearable for you."

"Bearable?" she asks, her brow and nose scrunching as she looks up at me.

God, I hate talking about this. I can almost feel my hackles rising, along with my frustration at the way she's playing this. I push those feelings down and smile as I pull at the end of one of her braids. "Yeah. Somehow you got stuck with me, the dumbest kid in our entire school. Three-year reigning champion. I'm going for the sweep."

"Freddy."

The softness in her voice, the sympathetic gentleness of the chide, makes me sick.

"You should go. Get out of here." I say it all with a smile, lifting my hands to readjust her backpack. "I'll see you at tutoring— promise. Now go catch your ride."

"I'm surprised you're still here," she stalls, stumbling over the first two steps of the staircase.

I give her a firm look, arms crossed. "Easy, princess. Watch where you're walking."

"Yeah, yeah," she mimics me lightheartedly, but I see the moment she turns from playful to worrying. "Sorry— I'll—"

"Last two standing," a smooth, dark voice announces. It makes the hairs on the back of my neck stand up, anxiety reignited in my gut. "Need something?"

Carmen Tinley stands between us now, closer to me—close enough that I can smell the triggering scent of her usual perfume. She flicks her gaze between Ro and me a few times before Ro finally steps back down toward her.

"Sorry, Dr. Tinley," she says with a glittering smile that sends a fresh wave of nausea plowing through me. "We were just chatting. I'm Freddy's new tutor, actually."

Carmen's striking crystal blue eyes grow wider. I feel the heat of her stare across my face, waiting for a reaction I won't give her.

My muscles tighten, bracing for impact as she sidesteps me and stops one step closer to Ro.

"You're applying for my cohort in the spring, right? I think Tyler told me you were planning on it."

"I am," Ro says before a brighter, closed-mouth grin spreads across her face.

"I know this is Freddy's second time in my class, so if you can help him pass this time around, it would really impress me. I would love to see him succeed."

They both turn to look at me, but I focus only on Ro's features.

"Me, too," Ro says, and it brings a little warmth to my cold, uneasy body.

"Just stay focused." This time, Carmen's words are directed at me. "I don't want you seducing my best girl."

She laughs, like she isn't making jokes about my reputation to my tutor—as my professor. Ro wrinkles her brow and I want to hug her for even realizing how inappropriate this entire thing is.

Ask me, Rosalie. Please. I think I could tell you.

"I should go," my calm, confused tutor says, ending the awkward silence. "Freddy, do you want to walk with me?"

Something squeezes in my chest. I step toward her, feeling a weight lift from my shoulders—before it slams right back down as Carmen wraps a hand around my bicep.

"I need to speak with him for a moment. Do you want her to wait?"

I shake my head, my shoulders melting in defeat. "No, go ahead, Ro. I'll see you Wednesday."

"If you're sure . . ." She trails off. Ro waits until I've assured her before she trips her way up the stairs, enough times that she pauses halfway and turns to make sure I'm not watching—which I am—before she finally makes it to the top, leaving me behind.

"Freddy," Carmen says. "It's nice to have you back in my class. Do you want to go over the syllabus? Make sure everything is clear?"

So, we're playing it like this.

I shake my head a little aggressively. "I want out of the class."

Her eyes narrow a hair, but she nods and steps back, beckoning me lazily to follow her into the connected hallway and through to her office.

Dr. Tinley's black high heels click on the linoleum and grate on the already loud space inside my own head. I'm trying to focus on the speech I've been mentally preparing the entire lecture, but I find my attention lingering on the length of her legs in that dress and wondering why she wore it. Has she worn it before? Did she do it on purpose?

Stop.

Dr. Tinley unlocks her office door and flicks the light switch, a warm lamp illuminating the darkened room.

It looks the same as it did before.

I wait what feels like a lifetime for her to settle into her desk chair, playing almost tauntingly with her short vibrant hair, painted lips pursed as she furrows her brow and looks at me.

God, I hate the way she looks at me. Like I'm a child, some pathetic little kid she's been charged with watching over.

"You want out of my class?" she asks.

I nod. My throat feels thick. It's too hot in here.

"I'm divorced now, Freddy."

"Good for you."

She pauses, a flash of pain and sympathy stretching across her pale face before she leans forward and speaks more softly, her voice a caressing whisper.

"I'm sorry. I should've been more careful with your feelings—"

"Stop it," I snap, jerking back in the chair when I realize I'd been subconsciously leaning toward her. "I'm not a child. Just let me drop the course."

Carmen huffs and taps her manicured nails across the desk, the clicking sound grating on my ears enough that my shoulders hike up. My knee continues to bounce restlessly, even as I press a hand down on it to try and stop it.

"Unfortunately, Freddy, I'm teaching the only sections this semester," she says, her voice back to the polished certainty it usually has. "But my TAs will be mostly in charge of the class, considering how low the classification is, so it'll be fine. And you'll have Ro here, and tutoring you. You won't have to see me much—unless you want to . . ."

"Great." I jolt to stand, pulling my backpack strap up on my shoulder. If I stay in here a minute longer, I think I'll spontaneously combust. Or say something impulsive that I'll desperately regret later.

I need a fucking drink. And a girl, someone else to bury my head in until I feel normal again.

My mouth opens like I'm going to say something—probably some awful, taunting, cruel thing—but I only let out a shaky, shame-filled breath and turn on my heel toward the door.

I have to unlock it to get out, a fact that makes it hard for me to sleep that night.

CHAPTER 11

Ro

The first half-week of school had been perfectly uneventful. I went as far as celebrating with Sadie by scream-singing MisterWives' "Reflections" while dancing around the apartment and cleaning up.

After Ms. B, Sadie's elderly neighbor who has been a huge help with Oliver and Liam, agreed to watch them over the weekend, we spent Saturday night playing drinking games with each other on the floor of our apartment and watching all our favorite romantic movies.

I'd woken up at four in the morning passed out on the ground, holding hands with my snarky roommate. Then snuck a pillow under her head, fixed the blanket over her, and returned to my room to sleep in, only waking when I hear the front door slam and a trail of little voices announcing that Sadie had brought her brothers over.

Pulling myself from bed, brushing my teeth and trying to look at least *slightly* like I didn't get hit by a train last night, I'm greeted by a happy sight in our little kitchenette—Sadie and Liam making pancakes and Oliver setting the table.

"You're starting to impress me with your"—she makes a drinking motion with her hands behind Liam's back—"abilities."

"God, my head hurts." I laugh and start to shake my head, but the pain makes me freeze and I lay it in the cradle of my arms on the tabletop instead. "I think the sugar content is doing me dirty."

Sadie smiles and squeezes my shoulder as she steps by. "Well, I don't know where this new side is coming from, but I for one am loving it."

Because I usually don't drink or party with her. I'm as straitlaced and well-behaved as I can be. Sadie knows I don't drink around Tyler, and she doesn't ask. Besides the party, the one I don't remember and don't *wish* to remember, considering how much I must've embarrassed myself in front of Matt Fredderic and Rhys Koteskiy, I haven't really gone out with her much since sophomore year.

Not since meeting Tyler.

We eat our pancakes mostly in peace, Liam talking nearly constantly with his mouth full. Oliver stays quiet, eating slowly and watching over Sadie and Liam carefully. He might not be the oldest, but he acts like he's the man of the house already, and it makes my heart squeeze painfully in my chest.

The boys eventually excuse themselves to the couch and our TV.

There's a loud knock at the door and both Sadie and I groan, hands clapping over our ears.

"You get it," I say. "I never want to see the light of day again."

Sadie snickers at my exaggeration, hitting my shoulder with her hip lightly as she crosses to the door. The pancakes are gone, but my stomach is still growling, so I head to the fridge to scavenge for some string cheese and the giant tub of watermelon, managing to balance a water bottle under my arm as I take my loot and head for my room.

Then Sadie calls my name, in that voice tinged with attitude, and my stomach drops.

"Tyler is here," she says, coming back over to me, taking the snacks from my hands and allowing me to steal back one of the sealed string cheese packs.

"Hey." Sadie stops me, quirking up an eyebrow. "Say the word, Ro, and you know I'll make him go."

"I know, but it's okay." It's not a lie, but it's something I would never ask of her. "I should probably talk to him anyway."

She takes everything to the counter and heads for the couch with her brothers, pulling her hoodie back on as she goes.

Tyler isn't in the doorway when I open it, and for a moment I feel a little calm, until I poke my head out and see him leaned against the wall. He straightens and smiles at me, that same soft smile that makes me feel like he *truly* cares for me, like I'm the only woman he's ever seen. Then his gaze drops, making its usual assessing perusal of my body as I close our door and lean against it.

"You look like you had a rough night."

It's an accusation, and suddenly, my walls start to move back up. "I don't . . . what?"

"Ro." He sighs heavily, like the weight of the world is on his shoulders. He runs his hands through his hair, making it fly around at odd angles where leftover gel seems to stick to the strands. "I know you probably saw the pictures and—"

I can't hear him over the sudden buzzing in my head. *The pictures?*

My mind races, heart thumping. *Pictures of what?* An image of Freddy and me in the pool, flirting or giggling, flits through my mind. Then another: me, drunk and making a fool of myself, dressed like "a child," as Tyler would see it.

"What happened?" I ask, crossing my arms but leaving my tone open and sympathetic even as a knot settles in my stomach. He shoves his hand into his pocket and reaches across to hand me his phone.

Tyler's eyebrows dip and his eyes shutter, and his face looks so hurt that I find myself wanting to reach for him, because I do love him. I don't want him to feel hurt or upset.

I want it to work with him . . . *right?*

But apparently he's more concerned with getting his hands on Lucy Hamilton while spending the weekend at home in New York.

Because the photo I'm looking at is Tyler, dressed in a beautiful suit I would kill to see him in, with a leggy blonde on his lap, silken hair in a chignon and a deep red dress pouring over her like a model on the cover of a magazine. His face is tipped down to hear whatever she's whispering in his ear, his hands on the skin exposed by the high slit of her dress, eyes locked on to her cleavage.

They were both on the Academic Bowl team—her at Princeton and him at Waterfell—before graduating last year. Tyler stayed here for grad school, garnering a leadership role over Tinley's cohort, while studying directly under her. But his *childhood friend* Lucy Hamilton ended up at NYC for business school.

I'd wanted to be on the Academic Bowl team, once upon a time. But Tyler begged me not to try out for it, claiming we needed space from each other and deciding that Academic Bowl was *his* thing. I wasn't allowed to be part of it.

"*You need your own thing, Ro. The Academic Bowl is . . . I don't think you'd like it. Too stuffy and academic for you. That's just not you.*"

Not me, because I was "so girly," as he often said. Something he liked about me once. And then he graduated and suddenly I needed to be more sophisticated but failed in every way.

But Lucy was sophistication personified—the preppy, gorgeous Ivy League soccer player and apparent academic genius, who fit right in with his wealthy, elegant family. The girl who he'd continued to claim was "just a friend" until last year when a few photos were sent to me anonymously of him with his tongue down her throat in a snooty Prohibition-style bar while on a weekend at home in New York.

We broke up, but only for a week, before the endless attention—flowers, delivered lunches, excessive gifts appearing at our dorm door—and his romantic, heartfelt apology texts convinced me to talk to him again.

It was forgotten as quickly as it happened, and anytime I'd bring up "the misunderstanding," as he referred to it, he said I was trying to sabotage our relationship. "*Why do you want to rake me over the coals again, Ro?*"

As if he wanted me to forget, to swallow the hurt until it was buried deep enough. I didn't think that was possible.

He'd never taken me to meet his family, but spent every vacation "running into her," and then calling me crazy when I asked exactly what was going on between them.

And we *just* talked last week about trying again. About dating slowly, *casually*, because he told me after one of the COSAM introductory dinners that he was proud to have me by his side and that we could be perfect together.

Anger flushes my cheeks, and I hate the way my body wars between crying and screaming.

I settle for biting my lip and wiping slyly at my eyes, because if Tyler sees me cry, I'll never live it down. It won't be about his mess anymore; it'll turn into a lecture about my overdramatic emotional reactions.

He'll use it against me.

I'd sobbed in front of him once before, completely broken down about missing my family, and he'd told me to stop behaving like such a baby. To "grow up." It hurt, but I swallowed my pride because maybe he was right. I'd never seen Sadie or any of my friends from work or classes cry openly over homesickness.

Grow up.

"I honestly didn't think she'd be there, Ro. I would've told you," he says. Considering he hadn't told me once in the times this happened before, I doubted that. "But you know our families are close, and she's so incredibly smart, so it was good working with her. We won the entire thing."

"Good for you," I snap, shocking myself and him equally.

"Don't snap at me like that. This wouldn't even be a problem if you'd just—" *Do better. Be better. Act right. He wants to say it; he has a million times before.* Tyler cuts himself off and runs a hand through his hair, making himself look a little more like a mock version of 2008 Edward Cullen, the strands standing nearly straight up and out to the sides. It's funny enough to keep back a few more tears. "Look, never mind. I didn't come here to fight with you."

"Seems like you did," I mutter, but his proximity and the anxiety rushing through me is enough to have me wanting to make things good again between us.

Calm, at least. I hate fighting, so much that I concede every time. It's easier that way.

"I'm not mad." The lie burns my throat enough that I reach to hold it. Like that will stop the lump from forming. "I need some space, okay?"

"I promise, it was an inconveniently timed photo." He puts his hands up defensively. "Truly, Ro, I need you to believe me. Don't make this a bigger deal than it is, okay?"

How many times did he practice saying those words like an acceptance speech? The version of me that wants to shout at him, yell and scream, maybe slam the door in his face, is buried so far beneath the need to keep the peace that I'm not sure if she exists anymore. Instead, I'm piling hurt on top of hurt.

And I have a sinking feeling in my stomach that I will probably forgive him, and end up right back where we started. Right here.

He kisses my forehead, seeming pleased when I don't push him back or shrug off his embrace.

"I'll call you tomorrow, okay? We can talk more. Whatever you need."

I wait in the hallway until I'm sure that I can swallow the tears back so Sadie—and more important, her brothers—don't see.

CHAPTER 12

Ro

I spend the next two days avoiding a constant stream of calls and texts from Tyler.

I'm not ready to talk to him about it, even knowing I'll have to face him nearly every day of the week. I manage to skip out on Monday's lecture with Tinley to catch up on some grading work, but it's my one pass.

Tuesday comes quicker than I'm ready for—and I find I'm more anxious about seeing Tyler than I am about my tutoring session with Freddy, which is usually my main source of the nauseating butterflies in my abdomen. In fact, I'm excited about the session, because I've spent the entire last week researching new ideas and instructional tools for dyslexia and dyscalculia, specifically in cases with co-occurring ADHD.

It's quiet in the little alcove coffee shop this morning. Most of the students at Waterfell prefer the environment of Brew Haven, which makes this spot easy to snag, and it's far enough from most distractions that it's perfect for our morning sessions before my classes.

Coyote Theory's "This Side of Paradise" plays over a crackling speaker at a low volume—after my research on music for concentration, which so far seems to be working—as I tap my pen to the beat and watch Freddy slyly between nonsensical doodles.

"Done," Freddy cheers, slapping his paper down with a moony smile. "I deserve something for speed on that one."

"Speed means nothing if you got every answer wrong."

He makes a *pfft* noise with his mouth and runs a hand through his purposefully disheveled morning hair.

"Hey, Freddy," a cheery voice says, and my student spins in his seat to wink at the pretty blonde at his side. "Good to see you. Are you coming to Zeta later?"

"I might—are *you* going to be there?"

She blushes, and regrettably, so do I. "Yes," she giggles, seeming a little flustered by his mere presence. "My roommate and I heard a rumor about you and wanna know if it's true."

If I wasn't watching his profile like a hawk, focused on the strong column of his throat and the line of his jaw, I probably would've missed the minuscule flinch.

"Oh yeah? Is it how magnificent I am with my hands? Or maybe my mouth?"

Her giggle ratchets up higher, but my entire body tenses.

Why is he joking about this?

She dips down toward him, her messy braid swinging down to brush against his skin. She whispers the question, but I hear every word.

"Is the profile yours?"

This time, his eyes close entirely, like he's taking a punch and not flirting with an eager female. My brow furrows further.

"Ah." He nods, shrugging with that same too-big smirk. "A man never kisses and tells." He presses a finger to his lips before nodding toward where she seems to have forgotten my presence at the table.

"I'm in the middle of a tutoring session and don't want to be rude, but I'll catch you at the party later."

It seems to be enough to appease the girl, her entire body seeming to float away with the lightness that Freddy injects into everyone around him. But he looks . . . exhausted. Worn down completely.

I want to ask him what is going on, maybe find out why he looks like he'd rather pull his own fingernails out than go to that party. But I also want him to stop looking like *that* because my chest is starting to ache.

"You got almost half right," I say, feeling cruel giving him a bad grade when he still has the expression of a beaten dog. "But I think we can stop for today, because I left my other material at home."

"Or we could go for another hour," he says with a shrug.

"I don't think your fan club would love me for that."

The snarky taunt slips out of my mouth before I can stop it, my eyes widening when I realize what I've just said. *So much for professionalism.*

And yet it seems to light him up.

"Jealous?" An open grin crawls across his face. "Don't be. Underneath *all* this is a one-woman man," he says, running his hands down his body to emphasize his point. The gesture makes my face tingle, heating at even the *hint* that Matt Fredderic might be flirting with *me.*

"I have a boyfriend," I say, ducking my head to focus on the papers in front of me.

Do you? I think. *Because it's looking like he spent all summer feeling up some blond Yale genius when you were supposedly dating.*

"And I score on defended nets all the time." Freddy shrugs, then leans across the now-too-short table to peer up at me with playful eyes and a pretty smile. "The goalie makes scoring more difficult, not impossible."

Three years ago, this would've been a dream. Now it only serves to make me squirmy and hot. I can't remember the last time anyone flirted with me. Tyler was my first boyfriend, and with him it was never playful; it was almost overwhelmingly serious.

"Besides." His hand tugs lightly at one of my springy curls that's fallen in his way. "I love a challenge."

I jolt back, pulling away from his sudden closeness.

"You have to stop."

"Stop what?" he asks, expression suddenly innocent despite the flicker of excitement still clear in his emerald eyes.

"Y-you—" I huff, shoving my curls back off my neck. "You know what! The . . . *that* thing!" I point at him, my voice still nothing but a harsh whisper. "The *flirting*. I need to focus."

"Am I distracting you?"

Distracting is one thing, but it's more . . . unsettling. It doesn't feel *real*. It feels off, somehow, like this is some continuous play that I didn't agree to watch.

"I'm trying to be professional," I say, keeping my tone soft, but serious. "Please, Freddy."

My phone buzzes again—probably the tenth call in the last few minutes.

The playful look that is usually permanently fused to Freddy's face melts away to a light concern. "Seems like someone *really* wants to get ahold of you, Ro."

"Yeah." I frown, stomach rolling, because I know exactly who it is, but am unwilling to admit how regular an occurrence this is. I click the phone over to Do Not Disturb before shoving it into my bag. "Okay, let's focus. I promise to get you out of here on time. Now, did you get the audiobook?"

"Yeah." Pink colors his cheeks and he scratches the back of his neck. "You were right, Dr. Fincher is a lot better about handling stuff."

"She is. Her son is dyslexic." I had Dr. Fincher freshman year and loved her. So much so that I ended up joining the literary magazine staff first semester.

Freshman year I'd signed up for just about everything. Then I met Tyler. He suggested dropping most of my extracurriculars so I could focus on my studies. And on our relationship. I trusted him, because he was older than me and smarter, and compared to his worldly life, I was a bit sheltered.

More accidentally than intentionally. Because I loved being at home. I loved my parents. And then when my dad . . .

Well, I didn't spend much time out.

So I didn't party, stuck to studying and spending every waking moment with my mom and dad. I'd gone to my dad's alma mater. They'd offered a full scholarship and it was far enough away that my parents wouldn't worry about me, wouldn't stress themselves with trying to take constant trips to see me.

I was careful, too. I only told them about the good things, the successes. Because that is what they deserve—everything good.

The only problem is that I miss them. Every day.

"You okay?"

I blink, realizing I've zoned out completely.

"Um, yeah—".

As if zoning out in the middle of a tutoring session wasn't enough for one day, tears start forming in my eyes, my chest tight.

"Oh fuck," Freddy curses, stepping out of his side of the booth and sliding into mine, pressing me toward the corner. "What's wrong? Did I say something that hurt you?"

Why he's blaming himself, I can't begin to figure out, but there's a strange comfort to his presence that's easing the loneliness of missing my family, a feeling that is always pressing down on me like a fathomless weight.

"T-this is s-so embarrassing," I cry, rubbing at my eyes and shaking my head. "I'm sorry."

"Hey, hey, hey." He gentles his voice, a quiet *shhh* sound pouring from his lips into my space. I'm nearly pressed to the wall, his large body expanded to form a wall around me, like he's protecting me from the rest of the library so I can have my mental breakdown in peace. "Don't apologize. I'm the one who should be sorry."

"No." I shake my head adamantly. "You didn't do anything wrong." I manage to calm myself down with slow, soothing breaths that eventually stanch the tears—enough that I can wait until I'm in the safety of my apartment shower to fully lose it.

"Sorry, I . . . I miss my family. I'm a little homesick," I admit honestly. I'm embarrassed, but the last thing I want is for Freddy to think he's done something to make me this upset, when he hasn't done a thing wrong.

He leans back, his face relaxing as he nods and scans my face with his eyes again. There's something genuine there now, an openness I haven't seen from him before.

"I get it," he says, voice calm and quiet. It's deep, but soft in a way that has me almost leaning into him. "I . . . I miss my mom. A lot."

I don't say anything, and that seems only to relax him even more. Instead, we stay silent like this for a few moments longer. His arm is stretched across the table, shoulders broad and protective, cocooning me here. We aren't touching, but I swear I can feel his warmth emanating off his skin. It feels somehow more intimate and comforting than any moment I've had before.

It's shocking in a way, because I've never felt this in my intimate moments with Tyler, who rarely hugs me or holds my hand—which he considers to be displays of "pathetically desperate PDA." Still, this is different from anything I've felt before, even *with* Freddy.

If I close my eyes, I can feel him wrapping his arms around me in the darkened living room the night he doesn't remember. Part of me always thought this moment would never come again. The other part of me figured I'd have some kind of mind-melting breakdown if it did.

But I don't feel overheated or unsure of how to respond. Instead, I feel . . . comforted. Truly at peace, with his arms holding space for me.

"You okay?" he finally asks, relaxing back.

"Yeah." I nod. "We should probably call it a night."

It isn't even 6 p.m., but I'm pretty sure I'm on borrowed time before my actual breakdown. Stress is tightening my shoulders painfully; my neck aches and my entire body feels ready to give out on me.

"If you're sure," he says hesitantly. "We can stay here as long as you need?" It comes out as a question, like he's unsure about the entire thing.

I shake my head. "I think I just want to go home."

I sound more vulnerable than I planned, but it works to relieve the tension. He backs off, sliding out of the booth. We silently gather up our things. He walks me out into the parking lot, the sun still brilliant and gold, a beautiful warm evening.

And I still feel wrong, twisted up.

"I'll see you tomorrow morning, for class."

He nods, his eyes still on my face, scanning me repeatedly. There's something about how openly worried he is about me, the vulnerability he's displaying, that finally makes me say, "I'm okay," as I grab his bicep and squeeze.

Freddy smiles, all gentle and genuine this time. Real.

"Okay," he says, the quiet calm of his voice covering me like a blanket.

CHAPTER 13

Freddy

The dressing room is dead silent for only a minute before it explodes.

With Holden and me leading the charge.

"This is utter bullshit," Holden shouts. I stand beside him, crossing my arms as we stare off with the entire line of coaches in the middle of our locker room.

"You can't possibly expect us to play with him."

"I do," Coach says, calm, not even a flinch at our raised voices and the endless support rallying behind us. "I expect you to play with him *on your line*."

I toss my head over my shoulder to look at Bennett, but he's gone pale. His jaw clenches as he wipes the cleansing pad up and back down his leg pad again. Clearly he doesn't agree, but he won't be the one to rock the boat—not publicly at least. It wouldn't surprise me to learn he'd already spoken with Coach about it.

"No." I shake my head. "No way in hell. Kane's a fucking psychopath. Why the hell would he even *want* to come here? Think about it."

Coach Harris blows a breath and readjusts his cap.

I hate this. Mostly because I admire Coach; he's one of the only male figures in hockey I've known this well and managed to trust. I respect him enough to do nearly anything he says, follow any order—but not this. This doesn't make sense.

Toren Kane is a menace. And an incredible defenseman when he isn't in the penalty box or blasted across sports news outlets for one scandal or another. He *should* be in the NHL already, but he screwed up enough that this seems to be the only route for him into professional hockey.

Last year, during the Frozen Four tournament, Toren Kane made a nasty hit against our captain, Rhys. Knocked him unconscious, left him sprawled on the ice, and left all of us with a sick feeling in our stomachs. We lost the game after he was taken off, none of us able to focus without Rhys—especially Bennett in goal. But it didn't matter anymore; the win would've meant nothing without him.

I *know* Coach Harris admires Rhys, has trusted him as our captain since sophomore year, because he's always been the most mature, serious, and put-together player on our team. Rhys was our captain *before* he was our captain, a leader down to his bones. So why would Coach bring the guy responsible for sidelining Rhys—nearly *killing* him—onto the team?

"Kane's on the team. Koteskiy knows, and he's accepted it. Either get on board or get out of my fucking rink."

Not a single word is said with malice, his tone never rising. He's calm and collected, and it somehow settles everyone into a peaceable quiet.

"You're a team. No matter what happens, remember that. Now, let's go," he says, exiting the room as our assistant coaches start barking out orders and demanding we get our asses on the ice. The tension never dissipates, but everyone falls in line.

• • •

I'm barely inside the house when I decide to text her.

FREDDY
Hey, are you okay?

PRINCESS
Didn't peg you for a worrywart, Dad.

She sends an eye roll emoji and a quick follow-up text to assure me she's kidding. Still, the taunt makes my stomach swoop with the anticipation of bantering with her—mostly because I think it means she's actually comfortable enough to joke with me.

FREDDY
I prefer Daddy, if we're speaking on titles.

It's a risky text; the taunt without my voice might come across horrid. Bubbles show she's typing—then stopping, then typing again before finally a text comes through with a string of puking emojis. My smile only grows as I spin in a circle, like a preteen girl getting a text from her crush.

FREDDY
How was your day today? Better?

PRINCESS
Yes.

And then, separately:

PRINCESS
Thank you for checking on me, Freddy,
but you don't need to worry about me.

FREDDY
I do need to. How else am I going to pass my test?

There's another long moment where I watch the bubbles appear and disappear repeatedly. I'm nearly ready to send some funny GIF to make her smile from this far away, hating the memory of her reddened eyes and distraught face in the corner booth last time I saw her.

Leaning back against the door, I tap my fingers along the side of my phone, desperate to cling to this conversation and keep it from ending.

FREDDY
Let's play twenty questions. Favorite movie?

PRINCESS
I should probably get some sleep, but Ever After.

I don't know it, but I immediately search for it on my phone, trying to figure out where I can stream it, debating asking her to come watch it with me, my constant want for relief of loneliness beckoning yet again.

FREDDY
I don't have a favorite, there's too many.

This time, the wait is too long between messages and I impulsively call her, a little shocked when she answers on the second ring.

"Hello?"

"I figured this is easier for me to ask all my questions and get all my answers in real time. I hate texting."

"Hi, Freddy," Ro says. Swearing I can feel her smile through the phone, I flick through the apps on my hand-me-down Xbox and select the one that I know has her favorite movie on it.

"If this movie sucks, I'm going to be very disappointed, Rosalie."

"Wait—which movie?"

"*Ever After*, your favorite one," I say with inflection, like her question is ridiculous.

"You're watching it? Right now?"

"Just queuing it up—but I want to talk to you first." I try to keep my timbre calm and quiet, matching her sleepy tone. "Unless I woke you up."

She waits a long moment and my heart starts to sink before her hesitant voice whispers, "No, I'm good. We can continue your twenty questions."

"I've got way more than twenty, princess, but we can start there." She laughs and makes my stomach swoop like a free fall. "Favorite color?"

"I don't have a favorite. There's too many," she says, repeating my words from earlier back to me. "You?"

"Green—like, any shade, I like them all." I clear my throat and relax against my headboard, feeling any earlier tension leak out of me as we talk. We toss questions back and forth, Ro choosing some after warming up to me a bit more.

She asks me for someone I look up to. I tell her Archer, one of my dad's coaches, and Rhys. I ask her for her favorite thing to do, and she tells me about her fashion projects and affinity for sewing.

"Will you make me something?"

"Maybe, if you pass biology."

The mention of the class sours the good feeling for a second before I smother any threatening memories.

"Most embarrassing moment?" she asks, a light crinkle of bedsheets in the background. The thought that she's lying in bed, letting my voice lull her, makes everything feel softer, more intimate, even through the phone's speaker.

Lighthearted contentment fills me as I tell her about my first junior hockey game. My mom was sitting at the ice with Archer, holding up a giant sign and ridiculous foam fingers in our team's colors. I went a little too quick onto the ice, falling flat on my face and causing a massive dog pile after tripping my teammates coming in behind me. I tell Ro my hurriedness was from nerves or embarrassment, but it wasn't—I remember seeing my mom and Archer, having this bursting feeling inside me, a desperate need to get closer to them.

She chuckles as I recount the story, especially when I admit I was never allowed to be first out of the tunnel again. I'm so desperate to keep her happy, to pull more laughs from her, I can't stop myself from continuing.

"And then there's the time I got caught having sex," I say, pausing as I hear her choke on something at my confession—maybe water. "Well, actually, I've gotten caught *a lot*, but this time was worse."

Recounting the story of Archer and my mom catching me with the literal girl next door isn't as painful to tell, especially when I leave out the fact that we were both fifteen. I do tell her it was my first time, because that alone is embarrassing.

"What was really painful," I tell her, "was the splinters of wood from the treehouse in my ass and the humiliation of having Archer remove them with tweezers."

We both cackle at my expense, my smile so big my cheeks ache.

"What about you?" I ask once her giggles have subsided. "Most embarrassing moment?"

"Too many to count." Ro pauses, and I let her think, humming the *Jeopardy* theme under my breath as she gathers her thoughts.

"Okay, um, I had to go to this retreat with my team last year in New York for the weekend. It was my first time going on a trip with my boyfriend and I decided to, um . . . buy these kinda *sexy* things to wear."

My grin is uncontainable. "You can say lingerie, Rosalie."

She clears her throat, and I know if I could see her face, it would be that same beautiful rose gold hue. "Right. But, um, Tyler and I had the same bag—because he let me borrow his—and they got mixed up in the Uber. So when he opened it, there was all this frilly girly *lingerie* . . . " She struggles to say the word, almost whispering it. "And it was so humiliating. I'm the only girl on our cohort, and the guys would not let me live it down."

"C'mon," I say. "It would've been *much* better to razz Tyler than you. I can think of at least five perfect jokes right now."

The words seem to cheer her up as she nervously giggles into the phone. "Yeah, maybe. It was kind of all for nothing, too."

My eyebrows dip. "What do you mean?"

"Tyler didn't like it." She yawns. I try not to say anything, biting my tongue with the insults I want to sling Donaldson's way. Instead, I'm quiet, letting her fill the space. "He was so embarrassed he told everyone we were on a break—that it wasn't for him. He wanted me to throw it all away, said it made me look like a slut. Which is terrible, and I'm not. I swear."

Again, the words are said on a laugh, and I'm ready to punch this kid because he's somehow warped her into thinking this *awful* story about her being treated horribly by her *then boyfriend* is somehow embarrassing for her.

So I'm honest. "The only person who should be embarrassed is Tyler."

We're both silent for a little too long before she concedes. "Maybe you're right. That wasn't a good story. I'll think of a better one."

I don't want to let her go, but she's yawning between every other word.

"All right, why don't you tell me next tutoring session?"

"Mm-hmm," she whispers.

Ro's asleep, I realize, and I don't want to hang up. So I leave my phone on the pillow, muting it as I head downstairs for a water. Rhys's bedroom door is shut tight, and there's an almost overwhelming pull to knock and check on him on my way back, but I grit my teeth and turn to my own room.

He doesn't need my brand of help. Reiner is better for him anyway.

After a quick shower, I tuck into bed with my phone next to me, the quiet sound of Ro's breathing lulling me to sleep.

• • •

When I come downstairs the next morning, Rhys is dancing in the kitchen.

It's weird enough that I stop, watching him from the doorway for a moment. He's got headphones in, blaring loud enough that he doesn't hear me in the room, and he bobs around as he makes his coffee.

"The music thing is new," Bennett says, making me jump four feet into the air.

"You know," I say with a sneer, "for such a big guy, you're silent. It would be nice to let people know you're walking around. Get a heavier footstep."

The goalie only chuckles once, then moves past me into the kitchen to start his usual morning breakfast rituals. Rhys sees him, clocking me in the corner, and blushes, pulling out his headphones.

"Hey," he says sheepishly. "Sorry."

"For dancing in your own kitchen?" I press a hand to my chest. "Apology accepted."

Rhys hovers awkwardly as the machine finishes his coffee—my mouth is watering. It's a nice, fancy machine that either Bennett or Rhys contributed to the house, nothing I could afford myself. Too anxious to ask them how to use it, I usually wait until someone's making coffee and request a cup.

Surprisingly, that system has worked for years now.

"Well," Rhys sighs. "I need to . . ."

He points upstairs and trots off, not bothering with anything else. Which isn't like him—Rhys thrives in our group, happy around everyone and always the brightest star of us all. Holden and I might bring the laughs and good times, but Rhys is the *good* friend. Kind, smiling, always happy. Golden.

Now his face looks a little pale, light dimmed as he heads upstairs to close himself back up in his room—the new normal, it seems.

I wait until I hear his door click shut before asking Bennett, "Have you talked to him?"

"Yes."

I roll my eyes. "I mean, about how he's doing? Something seems . . . off."

Bennett clenches his fist, almost breaking the egg in his hand prematurely. He pulls his shoulders back and shifts his neck toward his shoulder, like a quick twitch of muscle. A sign he's uncomfortable or upset. Clearing his throat, the hulking goalie continues to make breakfast.

"He won't talk to me," he huffs.

"But you're his best friend."

I don't mean it as a reprimand, nor a call out. It's my own helplessness, of feeling disconnected from Rhys, that's bleeding into my tone.

Our entire group feels like it's half fractured. Bennett seems more distant than usual. Rhys is floundering, something clearly wrong that he won't admit to or ask for help with.

Giving up on talking to either of them, I run back upstairs to shower and change before my dreaded class schedule for Fridays.

Mostly, the one taught by the woman who hurt me most.

Being there every other day, listening to her lecture, is a certain kind of hell for me. Seeing Carmen alone is enough of a trigger, but I'm also torn between wanting to tune her out completely and needing to listen to what she says so I can pass the course this time.

Still, as much as I hate biology, I can't help the slight excitement I feel going to the class because it means I get to see Ro outside of tutoring.

I already like her, want to be a friend to her. I've never really felt comfortable around a girl enough to want to be her friend, but this feels warm and safe. I want to see her around, more than tutoring. And . . . I think it could be good for her, too.

CHAPTER 14

Ro

"I tried."

Sadie huffs into the phone. "Ro, please, please, *please*, don't let him do this to you."

"He's not." I shake my head, doodling a bit as I try to distract myself. "It's my fault. I just . . . I don't know what he wants."

"It's not your fault," Sadie says. There's a slam in the background. Then I can hear the little giggles and squeals in the back that let me know she's picked up the boys from school, and I feel guilty using her any more than this. She's already stretched too thin.

"I know." I clear my throat a little before calling brightly, "Hey, Oliver. Hey, Liam."

Liam's screech drowns out Oliver's quiet but steady greeting. I tell Sadie I'll see her later, tomorrow if things go well, and she tells me she's staying with the boys tonight.

The coffee shop within the library is closing, so it's quiet and darker in our hidden corner. I moved our usual spot to here this week—to avoid both the girls desperate to distract Freddy and Tyler, who is also tutoring somewhere in this building.

Tyler is supposed to come over tonight, and I've been tearing myself apart trying to figure out how to fix things—or if I even want to.

My stomach flips, because it's a reach toward the unknown. I know Tyler—I know what to expect from him in anger, in love, in the bedroom . . . everything. I *know* it isn't the best relationship, but the loss of it feels like jumping from a plane with no parachute. There's safety in knowing; there's comfort here.

But if I stay, things have to be better than they are. I have to fix it.

I need to know how to make things good between us again. Namely, sexually.

Because we haven't had sex since last semester.

My relationship with sex is complicated, especially with Tyler. I'm not a virgin, but I can count on one hand the number of times we've had sex in our nearly two-year relationship. My curiosity and innocence were endearing to Tyler at first, like most of me, until it—I—became an annoying nuisance.

"Ro."

He likes the Ivy league girl, though.

The thought comes unbidden, and I nearly flinch, because it haunts me silently all the time. *What is it about her that's better than me?* More deserving? Maybe she's more refined when it comes to the bedroom.

"Ro?"

I wanted to be spontaneous, to try new things—hence my forgotten Sexy College Bucket List—but I've had enough embarrassment in trying to last me a lifetime.

I've tried to work around Tyler's rules and wants. Sex with him is careful, controlled, and only in one position. Tyler is always silent, which does near constant damage to my self-confidence. And sometimes I'm so loud he tells me to tone it down. He doesn't like to go down on me; says he doesn't enjoy it. But he won't let me do it either.

It's degrading. I can hear his voice in my head, my gut churning because his reprimand is somehow more degrading than being on my knees, having his dick in my mouth. *You shouldn't even* want *that, Ro.*

"Rosalie."

The sound of my full name sliding off Freddy's tongue like a song makes me startle, cheeks heating as I realize how long he's been trying to get my attention. Two palms playfully smack down on the table across from me as Freddy slides into the booth with a beaming smile.

"Sorry." I tuck my falling curls behind my ear, tempted to toss them all up off my neck because my flustered thinking and Freddy's intense gaze are making me sweat. "I've been distracted, I'm so sorry."

"You're fine, Ro, take a breath." He relaxes in his seat, which looks ridiculous because he's so large, muscular. "Besides, I'm kinda enjoying not being the one who is lost in their own head."

I smile, mostly because he *does* tend to get lost in his own head, and nod. He slides the papers I'd been grading to the other side of the wood table between us.

"What's got your head all spinny?"

There's part of me that's tempted to talk to him about it, to *ask* . . . but I can't get the words out.

"Stupid stuff," I huff.

Freddy presses his forearms to the table, tapping his fingers swiftly as he looks up at me, turning his head nearly into the table to catch my downturned eyes.

"C'mon, *Rosalie*," he says. "I like stupid stuff."

I roll my eyes, but my expression quickly changes to a pleased smile, because as usual when I'm around him, I feel more at ease.

"Okay." I tuck my hair back again, nervous energy crawling up my spine, making me jittery in my seat as I lean forward. "Let's say, hypothetically, that you were dating a girl for a few years."

He crosses his arms. "All right. Hypothetically, am I in love with this girl?"

"Um, I think so?"

"You think so? Sounds like something you should be certain about."

I shake my head. "Okay, so, hypothetically, you're dating this girl for a few years. And maybe things are a little, um, off between you."

"Off?" His eyebrows raise and lips purse. "How?"

"Like . . ." I lean forward again, arguably too close to him before admitting quietly. "Sexually."

His eyes blow wide before he turns back to that same neutral expression. Still, there's a light color to his cheeks before he huffs lightly. "What's the question?"

"So, hypothetically—"

He raises his hands. "Of course, hypothetically."

"What is a way she could, like, seduce you?"

"Seduce me?" The usual, ridiculously pretty smile reappears on his lips as he sinks low in his seat and gives me wide, sparkling green eyes.

"Yeah, I mean . . . You're good at sex, right?"

The grin on his face only grows. "Is my tutor asking me for sex tips?"

Jesus. I throw my head into my hands and groan. *Way to be a total cliché. Teasing Sadie about her hockey player while* you *play tutor to an athlete who needs help and instead talk about sex.*

"God, I'm sorry, Freddy. I shouldn't have said a word—this is so inappropriate. Please, *please*, forgive me." *And please, never mention it again.*

"It's fine—"

"No. No, it's not fine! It's objectifying you! I'm so sorry."

He laughs, the sound bright and soothing.

"You're fine, Ro, honestly. Relax." He leans forward, resting on his forearms again as he talks softly to me. "I'm good at sex," he says, and I can feel how hot my skin gets almost immediately. "Great, actually."

Even without the reputation he wears like a nice piece of clothing, he *looks* like he would be.

Matt Fredderic might as well be dripping sex. It's almost too easy to imagine him on top of some girl, his tight, thick muscles bending and stretching as he thrusts slow and hard, his hands rough in the best way. Would he use his callused palm to grip her throat? I imagine he's not selfish, but obsessed with pulling pleasure from his partner's body with precision and skill.

With that same panty-melting smirk that makes my stomach swoop every time I see it, even if it isn't directed toward me.

"So, if a girl wanted to—" My throat closes, and I drop my voice even lower. "Go down on you, what would make you want that?" The words start pouring from me too fast, tumbling from my mouth as I lose control. "Like, a striptease? Or dirty talk? Maybe some nice lingerie or—"

Freddy's face goes bright red as I continue until he finally lays his big palm across my mouth, effectively covering my face up to my eyes.

"Jesus, Ro."

He drops his hand.

"What?" I ask, fanning my neck because it's so hot I'm sure I'm sweating. The lump in my throat is back, and I'm a little worried if I don't get it together I'll cry tears of pure embarrassment. "I-I just want to know if I'm doing it right. I want it to be perfect."

His expression softens at the aching vulnerability in my voice, his fingers lightly tracing the skin of my arm laid flat on the table between us.

"Hey, it's all right. You didn't do anything wrong." He takes a deep settling breath, and I close my eyes for a moment, focusing on the swirling pattern of his fingertips on me.

"If you were my girlfriend, Rosalie," he says, his voice deep and rough. My full name is like warm honey dripping from his lips. "You wouldn't have to do anything to convince me. Just a fucking smile and I'd be a goner, okay?"

Suddenly his voice loses its huskiness, and the smiling happy face is back.

"But I'm the school slut, right?" he says with a shrug, relinquishing his touch and slumping back lazily against the booth. "So maybe ask someone smart, like Bennett or Rhys."

"Okay," I say. "Do you have their numbers?"

His eyes go wide, body shooting upright. "Do *not* ask them anything."

"But you just said—"

He looks mildly frantic. "Forget what I said," he growls, and rubs his hands over his face. "My brain hurts. I don't know what I'm saying. Just . . . just tell him you want him. Kiss him and tell him exactly what you want him to do to you, okay?"

"Okay." I nod, but I'm already resigned because I've *tried* that.

"I think we should be done for tonight. I've got somewhere to be," Freddy says, standing quickly.

My stomach drops. I try to say thank you or apologize, but he's gone too fast, nearly sprinting out of the library like he can't escape fast enough.

CHAPTER 15

Freddy

My phone is ringing, and after a week of only talking about reading strategy and working on biology homework, I'm hoping it might be Ro calling to talk about nothing again.

Unfortunately, it's not.

"I've been calling you for a week straight."

The gruff voice has my back up immediately. "I'm busy."

"Not too busy to meet with Gavins."

"How did you—" I close my eyes and massage the pulsing between my eyebrows. "You know what? Never mind. I don't care. What do you want?"

"Did Archer get you the in with Dallas?"

"No," I growl, rising to the bait he dangles so easily. "My fucking skills did that, asshole."

My father laughs. "More like me every day, huh?"

I'm nothing like him. I'm nothing like him. I'm nothing like him.

"Dallas gave me the deal. Me, alone. And it's better than you could've ever done."

"Sure," he mocks. "Before or after Archer played father at the conference table?"

"Fuck off," I shout, pacing my room in earnest now. "I'm not talking about Archer."

"So defensive—"

I hang up, throwing the phone back toward my bed before crank-
ing up the volume of the TV—on the screen is some internet show
I've watched for years that comforts me even now—before heading
into the bathroom for a long shower, hoping the steam and heat will
wash away the hatred and gnawing guilt and fury swirling in my head.

• • •

Practice is shit.

I'm frustrated, for multiple reasons that I don't *want* to think
about, but also because of this. Hockey is my one thing, my escape.
But we're playing like shit and it's all Toren fucking Kane's fault.

We've been running the same drill for nearly half an hour and
our line—*first line*—can't get the puck down the ice because Holden
and Kane can't get themselves together.

Part of me wants to scream at them to handle themselves, while
the other part of me is ready to come to blows with Coach Harris
to point out exactly how fucking stupid bringing Kane on the team
is. Expecting a loyal junior like Holden, who thrives under Rhys's
attention and guidance, who views him like a near god, to play
defensive partner to the player who nearly killed him? It doesn't
make sense.

And then there's Rhys, who still looks a little worse for wear. I
won't admit it to the others, but I see him struggling a bit. Every now
and then he starts breathing harder, like he's out of shape when I
know he isn't . . . It's something else.

But if he wants to keep his pain and secrets to himself, so be it. I
know my place. I'm not *really* part of the Koteskiy-Reiner duo. I'm
the pretty third wheel.

"Again."

I wait for a moment, licking the sweat starting to drip off my
lips and trying to calm the heavy breaths sawing out of me. My eyes
flick to Rhys again, waiting for him to say something, to speak to

what we're all feeling. But he stays silent, seething as he looks toward Kane.

It'll have to be me, I guess.

"Respectfully, sir," I sigh, still breathless. "We clearly have a defensive problem, and you're running us all ragged for it."

Holden flinches, and I want to apologize to him—I will, but right now, I stand firm.

"You might as well be playing keep-away, superstar," Toren says, seeming unbothered despite his hard breaths from the overexertion.

"At least *when* I pass, I'm passing to my line—not the other fucking team."

"All right," Coach yells, his voice holding its usual heavy authority but stronger. Because Coach Harris doesn't yell. He's not that kind of coach. Instead, he thrives on respect to lead us, something I admired from the first time we met.

Everyone sinks back, watching as the middle-aged man rubs his face repeatedly before looking us over once more with a dismissive wave.

"Do whatever you want with them, Coach," he calls to the assistant coach on his right. "I don't care. I don't want to see any of them until they get their shit together."

He starts heading off the ice but pauses again and looks toward Rhys.

"It's your team, Koteskiy. Remember that."

Rhys's face tightens, but he nods. Ever the golden-boy captain, even under the annoying strain that is Toren Kane.

So instead we spend the last third of practice skating suicides until I'm pretty sure we're all about to puke. Everyone is huffing and barely standing by the time Coach Johnson lets us go for the day.

Back in the locker room, things are quiet, tension thick in the air around us.

Rhys slides his AirPods in the instant he's out of the showers, hair dripping as he tugs on his clothes and heads out, head bowed. A shadow of our golden captain, wearing a smile as a mask he thinks we all don't see through.

I showered quickly, too, mostly because I've got a test tomorrow morning and I'm going to try to get some rest for it.

"Ready to go?"

Holden slaps my arm as he comes to stand by me, waiting because he offered to drive me after Bennett said he had somewhere else to be and rushed out before the rest of us. I shove the last of my things into my bag before nearly slamming my head into the panel of wood above my cubby.

My entire body spins toward the only person who would purposefully smack into me.

Toren fucking Kane.

"Excuse me, *teammates*," he sneers. His tattooed, still-wet body shoves over to his locker cubby as he rips his towel off and tosses it onto my gear bag.

"Fucking disgusting," I grumble, grabbing the towel and snapping it at him hard before tossing it back. He only smirks over his shoulder despite the red, whiplike mark across his back where I've hit him. I want to be able to contain the words, to be the bigger person, but my mouth is already open. "Why don't you pack it up and shower at home next time? No one fucking wants you here."

He nods, pulling sweatpants over his legs before turning and stretching his arms wide.

"Well aware."

"Then why are you fucking here?"

He steps closer, shirtless, black ink on display. The tattoo that takes up the majority of his side and torso looks mildly familiar; I feel like I've seen it before.

"If you think I *want* to be here, you're more of an idiot than I thought."

Don't be a fucking idiot.

My fist is flying before I can stop it, slamming into his cheekbone. He has plenty of time to protect himself, to grab my arm or dodge, but he doesn't. He lets the hit land.

"Your dad teach you those moves?"

"Shut the fuck up," I snap, shoving his bare chest so his back hits the side wall of the corner we're in. I'm petrified that he knows something he definitely shouldn't. I've kept my father's identity under wraps, tight. Not that anyone would know the washed-up third-string player that was John Fredderic. Only Coach Harris and I know. But I'm more furious that this fucker has the audacity to say something about it. I lean in toward him, quietly seething. "You don't know what the fuck you're talking about."

He smiles brighter at my sudden ferocity.

"I think I do, pretty boy—I did my fucking research."

I shove him harder against the wall, furious he isn't retaliating.

"Freddy," Holden calls, grabbing my arm and pulling me back. "He's not worth it. Back off him. Let's go."

Holden looks mildly disappointed—but not in me, it seems. In Kane, his new partner.

I shrug his grip away and grab my stuff, stalking out the door with yet another crushing weight on my shoulders.

· · ·

It hasn't been this bad in a while.

Piling on my dad's phone call with the shitty practice and Toren Kane getting on my last fucking nerve, I feel about ready to scream by the time Dr. Cipher's teaching assistant passes out last week's math quiz.

A fucking 45.

Not just a failure, but *worse* than last time.

And I tried—really, *really* tried.

My face is burning hot with embarrassment at even the thought of telling Ro. I crumple the paper in my fist before shoving it into my bag and darting out the door the second we're dismissed.

For a moment, I debate canceling our tutoring session altogether. But when I open our text thread, I see our last conversation—the little emojis she sent—and I turn my ass back around and head toward the COSAM center, where she asked to meet.

I even stop to grab an iced dirty chai and a black iced coffee for myself—as if bringing her a treat might soften the blow of her disappointment once I show her the test results.

I want the smile her go-to drink order will bring her before the inevitable letdown.

"Look what the cat dragged in."

Every bit of stress that had escaped my body at the thought of seeing Ro comes thundering back tenfold at the grating voice calling to me the second I enter the tutoring offices.

Donning my usual smirk, I nod toward him. "Donaldson."

"Fredderic," he says, leaning against the countertop. "What are you doing here? Lost?"

I feel a desperate need to needle him, and I can't help responding with, "Just here to pick up my girl."

A light snickering from his cluster of cronies listening behind him echoes in the tense silence.

As if summoned by thought alone, Ro emerges from the back office—Carmen's office, I realize, my stomach plummeting.

Dressed in white pants and a sage-green top that shows a sliver of the tan, brown skin of her stomach, Ro looks gorgeous. She's so smart, kind, and funny, too. And again, I find myself wondering why in the hell she's dating Tyler Donaldson.

"RoRo," he calls, moving to stand by her desk.

I know it's hers because her backpack with a ribbon tied to it is resting on top.

She gives a quick, small smile to Tyler before looking my way a little anxiously.

My palms feel sweaty.

"Hey, Freddy," she says kindly. My shoulders relax, any lingering anxiety in my body melting away at her open, sincere smile directed to me. "Let me get my stuff and we can go."

"Take your time."

I see it coming long before it happens. Tyler steps into her space, crowding her enough that I can hear the desk creaking with their weight. My stare darts to the ceiling before my curiosity gets the better of me and I watch them kiss.

Her questions about sex have plagued me since the day she asked. I want to know where they come from—or better yet, why she's asking *me* and not talking about it to the person she's having sex with.

Which is *not* something I want to think about.

Though watching Tyler attempt to devour her face is dangerously close to making me laugh. The surprise on Ro's face tells me even more, that this public display is more for my benefit than for hers—or even his.

Tyler finally releases her. Ro's face is bright red as she walks to me, an embarrassed, shameful set to her shoulders that erases every teasing remark from my brain. Instead, I open the door for her, shooting Tyler a quick glare before following closely behind her.

"You okay?"

"Me? Yeah. Fine," she says, but her voice is shaky. "Why?"

I shrug. "Just checking."

I hand her the sweating plastic cup with a smile. She takes it, confusion wrinkling her brow.

"What's this?"

"Iced dirty chai. That's what you like, right?" She looks so confused and mildly upset that a bolt of panic shoots through me. "Did I get it wrong? I'm sorry. I'll buy you something else at—"

She cuts me off. "No, no, no, it's my favorite. I can't believe you remembered. Thank you, Matt."

My given name feels like a warm blanket falling over me as it rolls off her tongue.

"No big deal."

I take a sip of my iced coffee and walk closer to her as we cross campus to our quiet library spot. We chat the entire way, returning to the favorite-movies topic since we both continue to think up *more* favorite movies to add to the list.

I've almost forgotten about the test altogether until she asks, after we've settled into the booth and unpacked our bags. But . . . things feel good, and I don't want the pleased expression she's been sporting since I handed her the drink to disappear.

My plan to lie disappears in the face of her calm, gentle expression.

"Actually." I scratch the back of my neck and avoid her eyes. "I failed."

Waiting for the crush of her disappointment, I busy my hands with fumbling for the horrid thing, paper slicing into my thumb as I shove it toward her.

"Pretty embarrassingly, actually." I chuckle, cracking the joints in my fingers—anything to *not* look at her in this humiliating moment.

But then her hand settles over mine, stopping my fidget. Ro's voice is quiet as she says, "Not embarrassing. Just tells us what we need to work on. It'll be okay."

When I finally arch my neck up to look at her, she's fiddling in the smaller pocket of her backpack for something. She meets my gaze, hazel eyes glittering with mischief I'm enlivened to match. Her hand opens to spill a pile of butterfly clips across the table.

"Okay—"

She explains the problems, or more so the proper order of equations that I clearly did not comprehend, and I try to focus and listen. My heart races with exhilarated bliss.

I keep waiting for the other shoe to drop. For there to be something to offset the pure luck of having Ro on my team, that she's truly on my side—that she cares so deeply about what I understand that she truly *wants* to help me.

"Does that make sense?"

Her voice drowns everything out for a moment and my cheeks heat with slight embarrassment, but I finally feel comfortable enough to shake my head in honesty. *No, it's still not clicking for me.*

There is no frustration, only a gentle smile and nod before she tries a completely new way of explaining.

In the middle of her statement, Ro pauses, realizing she doesn't have enough clips to finish this particular problem, before reaching into her hair and pulling the two from her curls.

The motion is too similar to the pool, the clips the same as the ones I have stashed on my bedside table from the night she doesn't remember; I like to look at them when I can't sleep.

I rub at the ache in my chest, the edge of sadness that she remembers none of it too heavy to truly bat away. I'd give anything for one of those moments with her again, walls down, complete vulnerability and real affection.

But it's enough for me to have *this* with her, too, to be her friend, if she'll let me.

I make a vow then to protect her, the pretty girl with butterflies in her messy curls, even if she'll never really be *mine*.

CHAPTER 16

Ro

TYLER
Tonight is going to be perfect.

RO
I can't wait for a fresh start. 🖤 🖤

My last text is left on read, unanswered for twenty minutes. My anxiety is loud and raucous in my chest as I apply two more unneeded layers of my favorite pineapple-flavored lip balm, making them overly shiny and slightly sticky.

My text remains unanswered as Liam knocks at my door and asks if he can tie the bow in my hair.

"Like I always do," he says with a shy smile. "I'm the best at it." Even though his words seem confident, there is a perpetual fear of rejection in everything he asks.

I've been sitting on the end of my bed, fully dressed and done up, for thirty minutes. I need to leave soon if I'm going to—but something is holding me back.

This feels wrong.

I can't shake the feeling, even as I call an Uber to the restaurant.

It's not too fancy and part of a strip of restaurants in quaint down-town Waterfell, which means it's a little far from campus. And, for a girl with an unreliable car, that's not ideal.

I've been stranded more times than I can count, so rideshare has become a good friend of mine since freshman year. Sadie and I had bonded once over our car issues, and how illiterate we were when it came to anything about them. And although I knew it would take one text, one *mention* of an issue with my car for my parents to swoop in and save me, I'd kept my mouth shut and made do with what I had.

Stepping into the restaurant, I shiver a bit—wishing I'd opted for a cardigan to pull on over the shimmery white thin-strapped dress—and then send a quick text to Tyler to let him know I'm here. The waitress seats me by the window and offers the bread service, which I happily indulge in while I wait.

And wait.

Thirty minutes, to be exact.

The restaurant continues to fill up, a popular date spot on a Friday night in early September. Each happy couple that enters only fuels my mortification—even the *un*happy ones, because at least they showed up in their misery.

I text Tyler again and again, even chancing his wrath by calling him.

No response.

Unshed tears blur my eyes as I eat my weight in bread and olive oil before asking the waitress if I can pay for my Diet Coke and leave.

She gives me a sympathetic look and a to-go order of cheesy bacon fries on the house, which only makes holding back the impending breakdown harder.

Walking on shaky legs—made worse by the strappy, impractical heels on my feet—I barely make it out of the tinted glass doors before slamming hard into someone.

"S-sorry," I choke out, the word mushed with a sob.

"Shit," a deep, soft voice curses before cool hands brace on the overheated skin of my biceps. "Ro?"

Matt Fredderic.

As if this couldn't get more humiliating.

"Hey, Matt," I murmur, attempting some sad excuse for a smile through my tears. "W-what are you doing here?"

"Ro, are you okay?"

His voice sounds more serious than I think I've ever heard it. He looks mildly frantic, searching around me like we're about to be attacked.

I finally take him in, only now realizing there's a wide-eyed pretty blond girl with dip-dyed tips of blue standing next to him, looking at me worriedly.

"Oh my god."

Now I'm really crying. This is truly the most embarrassing moment of my life.

"You—I'm . . . Freddy, I'm so sorry—"

"Rosalie," he says again, his hands framing my face, tilting my head up until my eyes lock on his. "What happened? Why are you crying?" His face suddenly changes. Anger crawls across his usually jovial features and leaves something harsh and fearsome behind. "Ro, did someone hurt you? Who—"

"No. No, I'm fine."

"Where's Tyler?"

I shake my head silently because I *can't* get the words out. I can't bring myself to admit my boyfriend stood me up and left me here, especially to Matt Fredderic of all people, but to admit it *while* accidentally crashing his date? Absolutely not.

"I'm sorry," I say again. "I didn't mean to intrude. I just—I'm gonna call an Uber—"

"No, Rosalie." Freddy runs a hand down his face. "And don't apologize anymore. I'm giving you a ride home."

The girl with him doesn't look angry, only confused and concerned.

"Can you guys wait in the car for a minute? I . . ." Freddy steps away, muttering about grabbing something he left behind in the restaurant they just came from, before leaving his date and me to stand and stare awkwardly at each other.

Well, awkward for me, at least, considering she immediately sidles up to me.

"Are you okay?" the girl asks softly.

"Yeah. I'm so sorry." Taking a shaky breath, I wipe away the rapidly drying tears, trying to salvage the mess of mascara I'm sure is caked under my eyes. "I'm Ro."

"Nice to meet you, Ro. I'm Sarah." She hesitates before asking, "Would you like a hug?"

I snort out a wet laugh and concede with a quick nod. "Yeah, actually."

Sarah wraps her arms around me, squishing her head into my collarbone. I'm tall for a girl, even more in the kitten heels that I know Tyler would've complained about if he were here, considering they'd make me his height. Not something I've ever cared about, but it bothers him.

The physical contact is comforting. I like to be touched, to be hugged. And it's not often I really get that anymore, except from Sadie and her brothers. But she's been gone more often than not lately.

Sarah releases me and walks us to Freddy's car, which looks a little worse for wear. I grab the handle on the back door and slide in before she can offer me the front, because I can *feel* that she wants to.

"You two are close?" Sarah asks, sitting in the front seat reluctantly. We both wince as the door squeaks loudly when she pulls it closed. I slide to the middle of the backseat.

"I'm his tutor."

"Oh." She smiles conspiratorially. "Fair trade, huh? He's amazing, right?"

I get the feeling we aren't talking about his hockey skills, which I have yet to see in person, nor his pedigree as a student, and it causes an uncomfortable twist in my gut.

"We're just friends."

Her brow wrinkles and she turns in her seat, flinging her long hair back behind her. There's a dark red spot on her neck that looks fresh, like someone has been sucking on it, and I have to look down at my lap to stop myself from imagining Freddy giving it to her—how his lips might tease and play along her throat. The idea of him biting down to mark her pale skin makes my skin feel tight and overheated.

Inappropriate. Stop being so desperate.

"Freddy doesn't have 'just friends' who are girls," Sarah says, but it comes out like a question. Like she doesn't quite know him enough to say whether it's true or not.

My shoulders bunch. "He is with me."

Except . . . that's not really true, is it?

We aren't friends—I don't think. I've made that mistake before, hoping we were friends and realizing with overwhelming embarrassment that it was all one sided.

The driver's-side door opens and Freddy hops in, suddenly handing back two personal-size pizza boxes to me.

"One cheese and one supreme—I wasn't sure what you'd want, so I grabbed both."

I blame my multiple breakdowns for how quickly tears start to gather in my eyes at the kindness of it. He didn't ask if I'd already eaten, didn't ask if I *wanted* anything . . . he just did it. For me.

It's quiet for the most part as we drive back. Sarah asks a few general questions—like "What's your major?" and "Where are you from?"—which I field with ease. But I'm distracted slightly by Freddy, who isn't doing anything really, but he's enigmatic, and it's nearly impossible *not* to be drawn to him.

The way he drives is annoyingly attractive, one hand on the wheel and one free, currently smoothing over his plump bottom lip. When he backed up, he lifted his arm to rest on the passenger headrest, looking over his shoulder and giving me a wink before concentrating on the steady stream of weekend traffic.

His muscular thighs are obscenely on display again in shorts, and spread enough that I can see where the side of his right one presses hard against the center console. And that damn butterfly . . .

He checks the rearview mirror often, eyes meeting mine like quick check-ins. And for every tentative smile I give him, he repays me tenfold. The three of us fill the ride with lighthearted stories, most of them funny. He listens to Sarah talk to me, occasionally adding little quips and jokes. The smiles lines in his face stretch and expand at the laughter he gets from us, like a kid receiving exactly what he wished for on Christmas morning. As if our praise and attention is the gift he's waited for all year.

We pull up to an off-campus apartment complex I've never been to before. For a moment, I manage to pull my focus from studying him.

Sarah gets out and smiles at us, hand on the door.

"Tonight was great, Freddy. And Ro, it was so nice to meet you. Hope your night gets better." The last sentence is said with a smirk and wink that makes my face flush.

"Don't, Sarah. She's my tutor," Freddy says, still grinning, but there's a hardness to it. An underlying sternness. "I'm serious."

She crosses her heart and gives him a little salute before flouncing toward the staircase behind her.

"Sorry I ruined your date," I blurt.

"Not a date."

"Still, I didn't mean to mess up—"

"Rosalie, I promise, you didn't," he says, his tone brokering no argument. "Now, why are you still back there?"

He leans back and grabs my hand, pulling me gently to crawl awkwardly—bumping my head a few times for good measure—over the console and into the passenger seat.

CHAPTER 17

Freddy

Ro's hand feels warm, soft, and delicate in mine. I don't want to let go.

"Take Care" by Beach House plays through my speakers that desperately need some love and care. I've brought us to a park between downtown Waterfell and the dorms, refusing to take her home just yet.

She's eaten half of the first pizza. I'm not hungry, but I watch her nearly soak her pizza crusts in garlic butter and savor them most. Her tears have stopped now, but the pain is still there—buried under marinara, cheese, and a desperate need to make me smile.

This I know because she keeps peeking up at me with the same grin I give when I'm trying to decipher if someone is upset. If I need to please them somehow, to make it better.

I want to ask her what happened. Instead, I offer, "Do you want to watch something?" Because I can't take another gentle glance from her like she's done something wrong. I fumble for my phone, setting it up like I have a thousand times on my dash—a perfect, precarious balance. "Do you want to watch your movie?"

"My movie?" she asks, brows furrowed and mouth full enough that the words mush together, almost incomprehensible. Her blush is immediate as she chews—mouth sealed tight—and swallows.

"Yeah," I laugh, pulling up one of my streaming apps; *Ever After* is already queued. "I downloaded it for my next away game. Figured I could watch it on the bus. I fell asleep the other night, so I didn't finish it."

Hazel eyes alight on mine, more steadily than they have all night, and I feel a wave of deep relief at the beautiful sight. She grins as the opening starts playing, watching it as intently as I am watching her.

After a few minutes, I'm sucked into the story easily—a princess story for the girl I'll always call princess feels almost too perfect.

"Do you have a comfort movie?" she asks quietly, as if we're in a movie theater and she's afraid to speak too loudly and disturb the other patrons.

I consider her question for a moment but shake my head, resting my elbow on the center console so our arms touch. "Not really. I mainly watch YouTube videos—I like *GMM*." I don't say that I watch them all the time, often to fall asleep or when I first wake up; it weirdly makes me feel not so alone.

"But," I say, my mouth moving before I can even *think* about what I'm saying. "My mom loved *Love Story*. It always made her feel better. We used to watch it all the time, especially when she—"

My words fall away and I drop my gaze, pulling my arm back from the comfort of her skin to run a hand through my hair and scratch the back of my neck. Eyes burning slightly, I swallow hard against the press of emotions. *Don't cry. Stop fucking crying—it's been four years. You're not even saying anything sad.*

"Are . . . you okay?"

She's hesitant in asking. My stomach somersaults again before I nod.

"Yeah, sorry. I—" Clearing my throat again feels like a stall tactic, but my voice is stuck to the back of my throat, hoarse and scratchy.

"My mom died," I say, then rush to continue with my usual, "but it was like four years ago. And I'm fine now, so it's okay." Every word is more placating than the last.

The truth is that some days I barely feel anything, if I even think about it. And some days it hurts like she died *yesterday*.

Ro's eyes watch me again with the same intensity she's always had that makes me feel stripped bare, vulnerable. "It's okay to miss her, you know. And to cry about it. I cry about missing my parents all the time, and they're just far away."

Her words feel like a hug and I lean into it, meeting her gaze with my reddened eyes, not trying to hide or joke around this moment.

"Yeah?"

"Yeah." She nods before biting down on her plush bottom lip and fiddling with a curl, one of her nervous tells. "Do you ever get lonely?"

A disbelieving laugh bursts from me before I can help it, but I nod and smile at her. "All the fucking time."

"Yeah?" She asks it this time.

"Yeah."

"It's— I love Sadie, she's my best friend," she says, words flowing as her comfort level grows. "But she's my only friend and . . . and she's busy, a lot. She has a lot going on." Her voice fades slightly, and a bolt of irritation with the figure skater rouses me yet again—for Rhys and for Ro. "I don't see her as much when she's busy, and last semester I barely saw her at all. It's not her fault."

It is, I want to argue, but I bite down on my tongue.

"So." She shrugs. "Sometimes I can't help feeling really, really alone." A huff of laughter finishes the statement, but there's not a drop of humor in it.

"I'll be your friend, Ro," I say. "I want you to see me as your friend."

"I'd like that, Matt."

She smiles, small and gentle, and I feel another layer of care and protectiveness reach out from me to her. *A friend*—not because of being on the same hockey team or some kind of trade-off.

Just my friend, because she *wants* to be.

· · ·

Arguably, I enjoy my friends' birthdays more than my own. And today is Rhys's birthday.

We decided last week on a more low-key party at our beloved Hockey House, inviting the team and some close friends. I even splurged on the fancy local IPA bottles so Bennett would be enticed to drink, which has paid off considering he's on his third and smiling across from me in spite of the mess in his beloved kitchen.

The problem, it turns out, isn't our beloved goalie's usually surly nature. It's the deeply felt absence of the pain-in-my-ass figure skater.

Rhys informed us both last week that he invited Sadie. His smile was obnoxiously big, dimples gleaming as he confessed that he "didn't care" who we invited or what we wanted to do—just that Sadie was coming. It was all that seemed to matter to him, which only raised my apprehension tenfold.

We try playing a few drinking games, but Rhys is distracted the entire time, eyes lighting up every time the door opens, and going dark as soon as it *isn't* Sadie.

Even Paloma makes an appearance, wishing Rhys a quick "happy birthday" before joining Holden and a few of the second line playing King's Cup in the living room, which Bennett surprisingly joins as well.

Meanwhile I try—and mostly fail—to entertain Rhys. Several girls flirt with our handsome captain, but he won't even look at one of them, eyes trained on the door. It's hard not to drop a snarky comment or two about the missing figure skater, but I can see it hurts Rhys's feelings more, so I try to tamp them down.

"Actually," he finally says, with a smile so fake it's half cracked. "I think I'm gonna go up. I just . . . I'm tired and my head is killing me."

He's done this a few times now. It's frustrating because he uses the injury that he won't actually talk about so we don't press him on whatever the issue is—and he *won't* talk about whatever's going on with Sadie.

Meanwhile, my anger toward the girl only grows with every hesitant step my captain takes up the stairs, eyes over his shoulder.

It's late now; most of the party has headed downtown or dispersed. Holden and Bennett are back at my side—the latter looking more relaxed than I've seen him in a while, a light smile on his lips as he cracks open a beer. I can't seem to muster the same peace or joy—I feel like an utter disappointment. Rhys is upstairs, miserable and hurting over a girl I could've warned him about at that very first party. He's in too deep now.

I'm about to bother Bennett about the entire situation when someone steps into our kitchen with clicking heels.

Sadie Brown—in a very short dress, a big leather jacket, and tall black heeled boots, with her signature dark red lips—is two hours late.

"Freddy." She nods. "Hey—have you guys seen Rhys?"

"Look who finally decided to show," I say, finishing the shot Holden's poured into my cup. "A little late for him, actually."

She looks upset, and my stomach lurches a little, like I've done something wrong. But I shake that thought from my head quickly—*she's playing with Rhys's feelings. She's a bad friend to Ro. They deserve better.*

I give Bennett a quick once-over. He's uncomfortable, his smile gone completely as he hunches massive shoulders over the table, avoiding both Sadie's and my glances.

"I know I'm late," she says, her voice shaking a bit. "But I need to talk with him."

"Not happening," I snap, more harshly than I mean to. "Get out."

"Freddy." Bennett finally breaks, sounding frustrated, hardened. He looks at Sadie—something like sympathy or deep understanding flickering in his blue eyes. It only ignites my frustration further, as if *I'm* the one who doesn't understand. The outsider. The broken, left-out other to the Bennett-Rhys-and-now-Sadie triad.

"No." I crush the cup in my hand, fury flushing through my blood. I toss it into the trash can, narrowed eyes never leaving Sadie. The words I want to say to her are all jumbled in my head. I want to yell and rage over her friendship with Ro as much as I want to erupt on her about Rhys.

I may not know Sadie, but I know of her—especially last year. Every single party I attended, she was there. And never alone; she even showed up with Paloma a few times, but she always found what she wanted—alcohol, an athlete, and a quick romp in the bathroom. It's not judgment of her that makes me disapprove of her with Rhys. It's the fact that I *know* Rhys couldn't do a one-night stand if he tried. Friends with benefits don't exist for Rhys. He's an all-or-nothing kind of guy, and I admire him for it.

The same way I admire Ro, her devotion to her friendships that becomes more apparent with every interaction we have. And I can't help but want to tuck them both away from Sadie where she can't hurt them.

And yourself, right? Because if anything, you're just like her.

I stomp out the threatening voice inside before turning to Bennett instead of the small figure skater in our kitchen entryway.

"You saw him, Reiner. He stared at the fucking door all night waiting for her." I barely give him time to speak before I'm back to Sadie—the slight leash on my anger disappearing. "You've already hurt him once tonight. Considering your track record, I think it'd be better if I stop you now."

Each word seems to hit her like a slap, but I can't stop myself. It's like acid, burning my throat as I push it all out.

"You don't give a shit about him."

The room feels too quiet—even with the music trilling through our speaker system. Still, there's a cold flush to my skin now. I feel hollow.

"If I didn't give a shit about him, Freddy, I think you'd know. But this isn't like last semester. And Rhys is . . . different."

I roll my eyes and mumble sarcastically beneath my breath, which seems only to set off the mini volcano that is Sadie Brown.

"I love sex as much as you do, *Freddy*, and that's not a fucking crime just because I'm a girl. But I guarantee I care more about Rhys than you've ever cared about a girl you put your dick in."

Each word hits like an arrow, finding her intended target until I'm bleeding out.

You're not better than her. You're just like her. If she doesn't de- serve Rhys, then you don't deserve to even be friends *with Ro, let alone whatever fantasy you're already spinning in your head.*

"He's in his room," Bennett finally says, but his words sound garbled and distant in my ears. She takes off, a desperation to her movements that makes me feel like I may have crossed a line.

"Little harsh, Freddy," Holden mutters, wincing. "Let them do what they want."

I shutter my eyes to all their reactions before reaching for the dark bottle of Jim Beam. Bennett knocks my hand away with a hard shake of his head.

"You're done."

"I'm fine," I snap back.

He grows in size, pulling his spine straight and staring down at me darkly. "You're done. Hang out with us and get over it or go to bed."

"Fuck off, Reiner."

He means well, I know he does, but it feels too much like a re-minder that I'm like a kid brother trailing behind him and Rhys. I feel ridiculous, embarrassed and annoyed, so I swipe my phone off the table and start to march off.

"Make sure everyone goes home safely," I hear Bennett mumble, probably talking to Holden. "You can stay here in the spare room if you want. I'm gonna make sure he's okay."

He's silent as he trails me up the stairs, but I can feel him all the same. I stop in front of the space between our doors.

"You're upset," Bennett says, voice flat. It's an observation, noth-ing more, but from him it feels like a hug. "I'm sorry. I didn't mean to make you upset."

Bennett and I don't have conversations like this—heart-to-hearts aren't our vibe. I annoy him out of love and he grumbles like an irri-tated bear, also out of love, I assume. But Bennett is harder to get to know than most.

Rhys explained it to me once. "*Bennett needs you to be clearer. He can't always pick up when you're serious and when you're joking. Try not to be so sarcastic.*"

At first it felt like I'd done something wrong. But what Bennett really wanted was to be my friend. He didn't understand me the same way I didn't always understand him.

We still tend to irk each other, but it feels more like it's purpose-ful. Like a family.

"You don't make me upset, Ben. I'm frustrated with Rhys and Sadie and . . . myself. I don't know." I shake my head. "I didn't mean to act like an asshole."

"You usually act like an asshole." He shrugs his big shoulders and the hint of a smile echoes even as he stares down at his feet. "Makes things feel normal. And, with Rhys . . . maybe Sadie will help."

I doubt it. I bite my tongue not to word-vomit yet again.

"Yeah, maybe."

"She's not so bad. And she makes Rhys happy, so, maybe she can help more than we've been able to." He opens the door wide as he speaks and his black lab, Seven, lifts his head from the bed before stepping gently over someone in Bennett's bed.

My eyebrows shoot up—because Bennett doesn't date or even sleep around, from what I know. And I've known Bennett Reiner for going on four years now.

His service dog pads toward him with a whine and nudges his hand with a wet nose. Bennett whispers, "Go back to her," so quietly I can barely hear him.

Still, I can see Seven settling back against the lump beneath the covers, partially covered by the door and Bennett's body as he protectively pulls it farther to block my now searching gaze.

"Get some sleep," he says distractedly, and I nod. "Everything'll be fine."

He's more positive about this than he has been, so I trust in Bennett's solid presence and say a quick good night before heading to my room, ignoring the jagged edges of loneliness that beg me to find someone to occupy my mind.

Instead I turn on *Love Story* and fall asleep to a lull of memories— my mom's hand in my hair, the flavor of slightly burned popcorn, the sound of Archer asking, "*Is he asleep?*" before carrying me in his arms to my room.

"*You're my favorite kid in the world,*" he'd say, voice quiet as my mom lightly giggled.

"*No,*" she would say, soft and happy. "*You can't have him. Matty is all mine.*"

"*Fine,*" Archer would say. "*Just let me hold him for a little longer.*"

The mix of their tones in my memory is more soothing than any lullaby.

CHAPTER 18

Ro

"I know you aren't gonna believe me, but." Freddy smirks. "I think I got it."

He spins the paper back toward me across the table in Brew Haven, but instead of his usual deflection tactics, he sits quietly waiting for me to check his work.

It's not our usual tutoring time, because Freddy has an away game series this weekend, both exhibition games to settle into their team dynamic for the season.

I've barely looked over the sheet before he's interrupting.

"As you can see." He clears his throat and waggles his eyebrows as he slumps self-satisfied against the back of the booth. "I'm *amazing*."

The wide smile that mirrors his is immediate, impossible to contain even if I wanted to—and I don't want to. He's joyous about *math*, and I want to do a little dance in my seat that my hockey statistics-related questions are what caused this change in his demeanor, but I manage to hold in the urge.

"You are," I say, laughing at how his smile somehow grows, the lines around his face digging deeper. "And you did that one right. I have more."

As he starts in on the next one, reading and rereading the paragraph as I look over his file and fill in a few notes on his usual accommodations, a slight plan forms in my head. Today is a good day for math with Freddy, but that is very abnormal. Biology might be a big strain for him, but it's math that is destroying his GPA. And his self-confidence.

"Hey, Freddy?"

His eyes dart up to mine before dropping to the pencil in my mouth and hooding slightly. Enough that I flush and pull it away from my lips.

"Yes, *Rosalie*?"

It's embarrassing how much of an effect my full name from his mouth has over my body. I shiver slightly, but continue. "It's okay if you don't want to talk about it, but are you—do you not take any medication?"

His brow wrinkles.

"For ADHD, I mean."

A grin pulls at the corner of his mouth. "I figured," he answers a little sarcastically. "But I don't—I tried it when I was younger, and it didn't work for me. I could focus, but it made me crash and messed with hockey for me. I could barely eat and I hardly even wanted to play I was so tired. Worn out." His cheeks heat and he avoids my gaze. "It's stupid, I know. Picking hockey over being smart."

"Medicine doesn't make someone smart. And ADHD doesn't make you not smart." My voice is a little harsher than I intend, but I roll with it. I need him to *hear* me. "Neither does dyslexia or dyscalculia. Medication is a step stool, not a cure."

He grins and shakes his head, gazing at me with what looks like awe in his eyes.

"What?"

"My mom used to say that."

I press a hand to my heart to soften the deep bittersweet ache those words incite. "She must've been a genius, then."

Laughter spills from his mouth. "Yeah. She definitely—"

"Freddy," a delighted voice beckons. A tall brown-haired boy sidles up to the table wearing a Waterfell Basketball shirt with his number emblazoned underneath. He smiles brightly and flips his hat around backward. "What the hell, man? I figured you'd be at the hockey dorms tonight."

"Brandon." Freddy smiles tightly, tapping his pencil on the table more rapidly with a new tenseness in his shoulders. "Not tonight. I've got too much to work on."

"Damn, that sucks," Brandon says in a way that does not sound sympathetic at all.

As if he's only noticed my presence now, Brandon runs his gaze over me—in a way that's too similar to how most people look at Freddy, like he's half naked. I cross my arms over my chest self-consciously. "Sorry, I'm Brandon."

"Ro," I say, reaching to shake the hand he's offered. He holds it longer than necessary, turning my wrist over and petting the skin below my bracelets. "These are cute."

"Thanks. I made them." My cheeks burn hotly with his intense stare.

"Really?" he says, seeming genuinely interested, still holding my hand. "That's so fucking cool—"

"We should get back to studying," Freddy snaps, sounding more irritated than I think I've ever heard him.

I yank my hand back from Brandon's grip, holding back the apology I want to give Freddy.

"C'mon." Brandon laughs, planting his hands on our table and leaning over. "What the hell do you need to study for anyway? Last I heard you're sitting pretty with an NHL contract."

Freddy nods. "Yeah, postgraduation."

As if he didn't even hear him, Brandon continues, "And besides, aren't you still making bank with the OnlyFans shit?"

My eyebrows might as well be plastered to the ceiling, unable to hide my reaction.

I wait for Freddy to deny it, but he doesn't even look surprised by the statement.

"Yeah, yeah," he mutters in the same sarcastic way he always says those two words. "Still, I've got a test to pass, so . . ." He lets the words hang, spreading his arms over the stacks of papers and textbooks around our workspace.

So go away, I imagine he wants to say.

"Just come over when you finish." Brandon waves him off. "I bet Ro wants to come, too. Right, babe?"

Something in his words has Freddy stiffening and rising to sit a little taller. His face is menacing, frustrated and angry.

"Knock it off."

"Please, Freddy, you have plenty of girls waiting for you. I can keep Ro company. In fact, I need some tutoring help myself." His gaze switches back to me, and he drops to his elbows so his face is suddenly too close to mine.

I suck in a shocked breath, trembling in discomfort. My body wants to move away, but I'm frozen, eyes drilling holes in the wood between my spread palms.

"I'll even stay after class and show you how—"

"Fuck *off*," Freddy snaps, shoving up from his seat aggressively. Brandon matches his stance, expression wary.

"Chill, Freddy. I was joking." He looks over at me. "I didn't mean—"

"I have a boyfriend," I blurt, closing my eyes. "And we're over our time already, and Freddy isn't coming to the party right now. So if you wouldn't mind leaving."

I shuffle the papers in front of me as a distraction and an excuse not to make eye contact with Brandon as he apologizes again and leaves us in a bloated silence.

Freddy looks sick, face pale as he sits back across from me. Anxiety crawls up my spine; I'm unsure if I overstepped, if I did something wrong.

"Freddy?"

"Sorry—I'm sorry," he says, shaking his head with a bitter laugh. "God, I hate that guy."

"He was kinda rude," I say, playing with my manicured green nails. "I'm—why did he say that?"

The question spills out before I can stop myself, but I can't look at Freddy when he says, "Because he's an entitled asshole and you're beautiful. I'm sorry if he made you uncomfortable. I didn't know you and Ty—"

"No," I say, cutting him off, raising my head to meet his eyes. "I mean . . . about the OnlyFans?"

Freddy grimaces at the reminder and I'm seconds away from taking it back, saying *never mind* and moving right along with our next math problem, when he speaks.

"It's not mine. I've seen it, and whoever it is has the same tattoo on his thigh, but it's not me." He tips his head back to stare at the ceiling and shakes it slightly, another weird, half-broken noise that sounds more like a cry than a laugh blurts from him. "People talk. It's just a rumor."

He chuckles, a forced laugh, and wipes a hand over his face. "It's okay if you don't believe me. But it's not mine."

"Why don't you *tell* people it's not yours?"

He shrugs, like none of this matters. "It's a rumor about me. One of thousands—it doesn't affect me."

Only, clearly, it does. I shake my head, a million previous inter-actions shooting through my brain. His hesitance to ask for help, his constant insistence of his stupidity, and now this?

"You're . . . you're more concerned about people knowing you struggle to read than you are about an OnlyFans account that's not even yours?"

His mouth opens and closes a few times, before settling on, "Yeah. Can we stop talking about this?"

It's the harshest he's ever been with me directly. I shut my mouth, despite wanting to push him on this.

He only just became your friend. Give him time.

"Okay."

"Sorry." He shakes his head. "I'm just frustrated."

"We can talk about something else," I say. I feel like I would do anything to erase the defeated, angry look on his face.

"Okay. How about: When did you and Donaldson start dating again?"

Anything but that, please. Desperate to please him, I answer, "We aren't. We just . . . He asked me to hang out this weekend. On . . . a date."

He nods, crossing his arms tightly. "Like the date where he stood you up?"

"Freddy—"

"Sorry, I shouldn't have said that."

"He wants to make it up to me." *I think.*

Tyler asked me to spend Saturday with him, to take a little day trip. He said it was going to be a surprise, but that it would be good for us to get closer and enjoy time together uninterrupted.

I still feel the same, confused and frightened of every possible outcome, but I agreed.

Though I regret it slightly now, a twinge of wrongness striking my stomach as I admit my agreement to Freddy.

"As long as you're happy, Rosalie." He smiles, but it's the mask one he always uses with everyone else. My stomach sinks further.

But I match his mask with one of my own and lie. "Yeah. I'm happy."

CHAPTER 19

Ro

"You said we were spending the day together, just us."

I *despise* the whining timbre of my voice echoing in the car.

"Change of plans," Tyler says coolly, watching the GPS carefully. "The guys from the Academic Bowl team here got us tickets, so we're meeting up with them. I told Rodger, Mark, and Davis to Uber here and I'd drive us all home."

His cutting gaze slides to my stiff form in the passenger seat as his hand settles on my upper thigh with a barely there squeeze.

"I'm sorry, Ro," he whispers before smiling. "About missing our date last time. But this is better, right?"

It isn't, really, but I nod anyway.

"Thanks, babe." Tyler leans in and kisses my cheek before saying, "Mind hopping in the back? You're skinny, so we can squeeze everyone in."

And because I'm pathetic and have lost every inch of my backbone, I do. Which means, when we pick up the guys, I'm stuck between Mark and Davis in the backseat, Rodger sitting in the front. It's my personal hell, especially with Mark's continued sharp comments (and equally sharp elbow "accidentally" hitting my abdomen) all snidely directed toward me.

"Excited to see your favorite student?"

I want to snap back at him, but hold my tongue. I'll give him nothing.

The truth is, I *am* happy about the change of plans for that reason alone: that I get to watch Freddy play hockey. There's a giddy rush to my steps from the car all the way until we grab our decent seats in the arena.

I'm the only girl, and not a single one of the guys—from Waterfell or the Vermont school—attempts to chat with me. Which feels like a strange sort of blessing.

Especially once I see Freddy emerge onto the ice, following Bennett and Rhys.

The arena is fairly empty—an early exhibition game not drawing as many students as I'm sure an in-season, high-stakes game might. Which means that it takes barely a minute for someone to spot me— the hulking goalie, who grabs Freddy by the scruff and turns him toward me.

I can't help the beaming smile and wave I shoot his way from my spot three rows up. His brows dip before his eyes meet mine and a bright, breathtaking grin spreads across his face, deepening the lines in his cheeks. He skates a little closer to the glass and taps it with his stick with a wink.

"I'm just gonna say hi," I mumble, tripping over the seats with my long legs, hopping over the two rows separating me from the glass. Tyler murmurs something rude that gets a laugh, but I ignore it, drawn to the smiling boy with his helmet off.

For a moment we stare at each other. I'm usually closer to his eye level, being a tall girl myself, but now he's in skates, adding a few inches to his height.

"Rosalie." He smirks. "Fancy seeing you here."

"Surprise!" I say, a giggle bursting. "It was a last-minute thing. But I'm excited to see you."

"I'm excited for you to watch me." Our smiles feed off each other, growing wider to the point they're almost ridiculous. "Thanks, princess."

Freddy takes off backward, eyes still on me as he circles and starts warming up. I climb back over the seats to sit next to Tyler.

Rhys circles behind Freddy and waves to me as well, eyeing the guys—searching, I think, for a certain best friend of mine at first before his gaze turns wary at my company.

My thumbs-up does little to dampen the intense expressions of the now-three overprotective hockey players—two forwards and a hulking goalie—watching, especially when Tyler grabs my chin and turns my face toward his a little roughly.

"I thought you were here for me," he whispers in my ear.

"I am," I say, but my words come out almost aggressive. I'm angry—he's the one who changed our "casual date plans" into a prep academy reunion of smart rich kids getting drunk at a college hockey game.

My attention stays rooted on the ice, on number twenty-seven mostly. I know the basics—I've taught myself a good bit while coming up with real-world examples for Freddy's math tutoring sessions—but seeing them in real life is completely different.

He's fast—shockingly so—and larger than life on the ice. My heart thunders to the beat of the music they play between periods and never lets up, too excited. He's so in his element, like he was truly born to play. It's clearly a natural talent, one that he's honed and trained to perfection. He's so beautifully happy.

I think I could watch him play forever.

As we enter the third period, however, the mood shifts—on the ice and off. Freddy seems agitated, frustrated. The team has barely scored, and it seems like there's almost constant arguing on the bench, even between the coaches and a few players.

Meanwhile, Tyler and his entire friend group are drunk, getting rowdier by the minute, and *still* going back for more.

"Damn, he's fast," someone comments as Freddy speeds by on a breakaway that doesn't score.

"Oh yeah." Mark laughs. "Fredderic is fast on the ice, fast running through girls, but . . . he's pretty *slow*."

Anger heats my face and I ball my fists in my lap not to snap.

"We've all tutored him," Tyler says, taking a hefty swig of his cheap beer. "The guy's a fucking idiot. Right, Ro?"

I ignore him, jerking away to slump forward and focus on the game, shame curdling my stomach for not speaking up.

By the time the game ends—a Waterfell loss, two to one—they're stumbling and shouting as we exit the arena.

I see a few campus security guards watching the group closely, my cheeks going hot as Tyler slams an arm around my shoulders and demands a kiss on his cheek, which I give a little hesitantly.

"What's wrong?" He sneers. "Too busy making goo-goo eyes at your student, RoRo?"

He says it loud enough that laughter bursts into the crisp night air from his audience of drunken guys. I scoot out from his arm as we start for the car.

"I'll drive," I say, reaching for his keys, but he whips them back, furrowing his brow. "Seriously, Tyler, knock it off. You're all drunk."

"You weren't drinking?" one of the Vermont guys that I don't know blurts, smirking as he leans on his friend. "Figures. You look like a fucking prude."

"Try the opposite," Tyler mutters with a grating laugh. My stomach knots, eyes darting around like maybe I need to escape.

"We're all adults here," Mark says, "You're not better than us. Act like it all you want."

I've barely said five words to any of them the entire night, but somehow, *I'm* the one acting a certain way. Foolishly, I look to Tyler, like he might stop whatever this gang-up-on-Ro session is. He's talked horridly about Rodger and Mark behind their backs to me, but when faced with us all at once, he's never chosen me.

This is your last chance. Please let me be wrong about this. Defend me publicly for once.

Instead, Tyler only sneers. "The only reason you aren't drinking is because you can't handle your alcohol."

"Stop, Tyler. It's embarrassing—"

"*You're* embarrassing," he snaps, like the tether on his patience has broken entirely. "I mean, my god, I don't know how I even tolerate you at this point. I must be a goddamned saint."

Tyler moves toward me, almost caging me against the brick siding of the building. He's shouting now; sympathetic looks shoot my way from a few of his friends, but none of them stop him. No one bothers to intervene.

"Fucking pathetic, Ro. Honestly—"

"Do you mind?"

The voice that stops him is gruff, but with a sickeningly smooth quality threaded in the deep tone. And the man it belongs to, now grasping Tyler's shoulder tightly where he was starting to box me into the corner, is more terrifying.

He's massive, tall even to me, with warm russet skin and black hair dripping wet. A player, I assume, based on the black-on-black suit he's wearing, but I've never seen him before tonight—even on the roster I studied a few weeks prior.

"Private conversation, man. This is none of your business."

"You're screaming at a girl in public—I think that makes this everyone's business," he says before flicking his frighteningly bright eyes toward me. "You okay?"

I nod.

"Do you want to keep talking to this loser?"

"Fuck off," Tyler growls, trying to yank himself away from the force field of a man in front of us. "My girlfriend is fine."

The guy's golden eyes swirl with mirth—not with anger, but like a gladiator with the spectators chanting *more*! He grips Tyler a little harder before yanking him away from me and slamming his back into the brick.

"Now you're just pissing me off." He smiles, lifting Tyler off the ground so his feet scrape to find balance. "How is it little pricks like you even—"

"Let him down."

Everyone stops at the presence of another giant entering the scene. Tyler's friends, who haven't scattered, but haven't intervened either, freeze like pups in the presence of an alpha as Bennett Reiner walks toward the stranger still mildly strangling Tyler.

The guy puts him down, and Tyler trips backward for a moment before saying something under his breath that has the golden-eyed stranger shooting a fist toward his face.

"Fuck," Bennett curses, pulling him back from going after Tyler again. "Goddamn it, Kane, don't make me save your ass."

"I've been saving yours all night," Kane grumbles halfheartedly. "Fair's fair."

Shockingly, I see a small grin spread across Bennett's face as he manhandles Kane away with a rough shove. "Go get your stuff on the bus. I'll take care of this."

Bennett turns and I see a visible change in Tyler. He could easily win with words over fists with some guys, but not Bennett Reiner. He's from a family far wealthier and more connected than even Tyler Donaldson's.

Threats to sue mean nothing to the towering heir to the entire Reiner fortune, not to mention the son of a hotshot corporate lawyer.

"Reiner," Tyler sighs. "We were just leaving."

Bennett nods, arms still crossed as he stands over us all with shower-soaked curls and in a crisp blue suit sans tie.

"Then leave."

His voice brokers no arguments from the group as they all start to walk away. I turn to follow them, head ducked low in shame, but after we've left the spot where the Waterfell goalie still stands, Tyler grabs my arm.

"Find another way home," he says. "We're not taking you."

"You can't leave me here." I try to press some authority into my wavering voice, hating the catch of a cry in my throat. "How am I supposed to—"

"You're a big girl, Ro." He sneers, swaying a little from the beers he's been chugging. "Use that big brain to figure it out."

CHAPTER 20

Freddy

My entire mood postgame is always determined by how I played—win or lose—and tonight, a certain curly haired tutor was in the stands, which should make me happier. But instead, I'm wallowing.

I played like *shit*. My turnovers were highest on the damn team, as our lovely assistant coach reminded me for ten minutes postgame. And for *this* to be Ro's first time watching me, I'm upset, disappointed . . . embarrassed. I can barely read, suck at math, and now the one thing I'm supposed to be incredible at, I'm failing in front of her.

And Tyler Donaldson, my brain kindly reminds me. I grunt in frustration as I grip my bag a little too harshly.

"Tell Ro and her friends 'thank you for coming,'" Rhys says, patting my back as he passes by. "Was really nice of her."

I nod. "She's great."

But I'm almost certain he doesn't hear me because he's already putting in his headphones. I swear, he never has them *out* of his ears.

Following behind him, I'm nearly to the bus when a meaty hand grasps my shoulder—almost too hard. I wince.

"Fuck, Reiny—" I cut myself off at the incensed look on his face. "You okay?"

He tilts his head back.

"Whoever she was here with left her here."

I look over, following where he's gesturing to see Ro, sitting on the ground against the brick of the stadium building. A curse bursts from my lips, but I don't say a word to Bennett before I'm jogging across to her.

It isn't very cold, but she's shivering as I approach.

"Ro?" My voice is calm, tentative, but I plaster on a smile to hopefully soothe her.

She looks up at me, a little shell-shocked. Her hazel eyes are red and swollen, hair falling from the pretty high ponytail she was sporting when I first spotted her behind the glass.

I hate how small she looks. I hate the way my body feels like it's looming over her, so I drop down into a low squat, my thighs screaming in protest. I may have played like shit, but I sure as hell pushed myself too hard for a goddamn exhibition game.

"Freddy," she stutters. "Hey." She smiles, too, and it warms my heart as much as it rips it to shreds. "You were amazing."

"I really, really wasn't." I shake my head, ducking my eyes from her. "But thank you for coming."

"It was really cool." She smiles, but her eyes look waterlogged. "Just now leaving?"

I nod behind me.

"Team bus is about to head out." I bite my lip, taking a few breaths so my voice is calm when I ask, "Are you okay, Ro?"

"Y-yeah!" She nods rapidly. "I'm just about to call an Uber."

My brow furrows. "Where are your friends? Tyler?"

"He, um . . . They left. Tyler drove me here, but I—" Her voice breaks off into a rough sob, one it's clear she was trying to swallow before it escaped.

A curse falls from my lips as I kneel completely and crawl to her, pulling her up and folding her slender form into my body.

"Shh," I coo. "You're okay." I stroke her back as we both kneel on the concrete.

I try to give her as much time as she needs in my embrace. How many times have I wished for exactly this? For someone to give me simple affection and ask nothing else of my body? True comfort.

So I can give her this. I want to, desperately.

And not just for how good it feels to be needed, but for how it feels to be needed by someone like *Ro*.

Because I respect Ro; I look up to her, like a role model. She is kind and welcoming, helpful—and there's no ulterior motive.

She's creative and strong and independent. She's nothing like me. She doesn't need other people's praise to feel like she's *worth* something. Doesn't need pretty words to drown out the echoes of the ugly ones always shouted in my dad's voice.

Ro doesn't *need* anyone.

But right now, she's in my arms and I'm the one giving *her* comfort. I bask in it.

There's no way in hell I'm letting her ride an hour back into town alone at 10 p.m. at night in a rideshare. I'll carry her the entire fifty-something miles back to Waterfell before I let that happen.

"Rosalie?"

Saying her full name feels intimate in the quiet dark, pressed against each other like this. Still, she looks up and pulls away, gently wiping beneath her eyes.

"S-sorry."

I shake my head. "Nah, none of that." I try to pull a smile from her with one of my own. "Can you wait here for me to check on something?"

Her eyes scrunch, but she nods and sits back down, moving her long, lean legs to stretch out in front of her.

My skin feels too tight, heart thundering and mind scrambled as I make my way to the bus where Bennett is standing next to Coach Harris. They both stop speaking as I approach.

It isn't until I'm standing next to them both that I realize I left my bag with Ro.

"Your girl okay, Freddy?" Coach asks, brushing a hand through his short, well-kept beard. His stance is serious, face displaying zero hints of how he feels, as usual.

"She's my tutor. And she got left here. Is there any way I can ride back with her? I don't want her to go alone."

Coach purses his lips and shakes his head mildly, straightening his suit jacket. "You know the school would have my ass if I let you break that rule. You have to ride back with us."

My stomach drops while my mind flies in thirty different directions, trying to come up with some sort of plan.

"What's her name?"

"Ro, sir."

"Tell Ro she can ride on the team bus."

My eyes widen. "Really?"

He looks offended. "I would never leave a woman stranded, Fredderic. Have a little more faith in me than that."

"Of course, Coach." I smile and nod, resisting the urge to pick him up and twirl the man around in the air with my gratefulness. Instead, I jog back to Ro and quickly convince her to get on the bus. She is hesitant, but agrees, which helps to finally relax some of the tension in my shoulders.

Only some.

Ro is quiet, holding her arms around her middle in a way that makes my stomach hurt. Small and curled in on herself, she walks up the short stairs of the charter bus. The chattering stutters to silence as the guys spot the leggy brunette decked out in Waterfell gear and I say a silent prayer that none of them makes a joke.

The anxiety of it is enough to make me wish she was here with someone else, someone worthy of her. That no one would raise their eyebrow at me to ask if I was bringing her home or assume silently that I'm sleeping with her.

Ro doesn't deserve that.

Rhys stands and wrinkles his brow, stopping her midstride with a soft touch to her arm.

"You okay?" he asks, voice low.

"I'm fine." She matches the quiet whisper of his voice. "Please, please, don't tell Sadie about this."

Sadie, the figure skater our beloved good-guy captain enjoys breaking his heart over.

It's strange for me to remember that *my* Ro is best friends with a girl nearly infamous for her unapproachable demeanor and bad behavior—a stark contrast to the vibrant, friendly, and almost overwhelmingly welcoming Rosalie.

You're just like her. You and Sadie. If she doesn't deserve Rhys, why do you deserve—

No. I shake my head and stare back up at my captain.

Rhys looks like he wants to protest, but at my hard glare from behind her, he nods.

"I won't."

I point to the empty row two seats behind Rhys, letting Ro go first and slide in.

Before I can follow her, Rhys grabs my bicep and lowers his voice, mouth nearly at my ear to whisper, "I wouldn't classify this as hands-off."

There's a bitterness to the smile I grant him. "I'm not sleeping with her, Rhysie. No need to issue me a citation for getting too close to your bratty figure skater's roommate."

He lets the barb slide, but his grip on my arm tightens.

"Ro is Sadie's best friend. I'm just watching out for her."

"And who exactly is watching out for you?" I ask, a little miffed. *Or me,* I want to add. Instead, I swallow down the words like sand, grating as I smother them. "Someone needs to. You're gonna get hurt by her."

"Watch it," he snaps, fierce in his protectiveness over the girl he "isn't" dating.

"Ro's tutoring me. That's it," I sigh, ducking my head closer to him. "And she got left here—hours outside of town—by her asshole boyfriend, okay?"

Rhys bites his lip and relaxes his grip. "That Donaldson kid was an asshole to her in front of me the one time I met him. Sorry, Freddy. I think I'm just . . ."

I wait for him to finish. *I'm just . . . not okay. I'm trying to make everyone smile but I look like I'd rather be anywhere else when I'm playing. I faked an ankle pain to not play, something I'd never do . . .* I wait for anything to show me that my friend needs me.

That he trusts me enough to need me.

But he smiles and shrugs, patting me on the back and settling into his seat again, slamming his headphones back into his ears aggressively.

CHAPTER 21

Ro

Breathe in. Breathe out.

My entire body feels like an open wound, my arms tightly wrapped around my waist the only thing keeping me from tearing open and bleeding out on the scratchy fabric seat of the Waterfell hockey team charter bus.

Freddy isn't even looking at me. Part of me believes he's giving me privacy, but the frayed edges of my heart are screaming out how annoying, how childish and embarrassing I must be to him.

I turn to speak to him, to say what, I'm not sure. Perhaps beg him to let me call an Uber or offer to study with him on the ride, to make myself useful, needed somehow. But I pause at the tense set of his shoulders.

Freddy grows in size, like a living human shield over me. I look up to see what caused this reaction in him, only to be greeted by the same terrifying gold eyes of the man from earlier.

Maybe not greeted, but startled by, frightened.

Even armed with the knowledge that this man defended me, nearly fought Tyler, I find myself petrified at the sight of him. Freddy's obvious reaction to him only validates my feelings.

He flicks his eyes over me briefly, whether to assess me as a friend or enemy, I'm unsure. But there is no malice, only cool indifference as he lumbers to the back of the bus to sit alone.

The overhead lights flick off, comforting darkness swathing over me as the rumbling of the bus smooths out. Subdued conversations float from somewhere in the back, muffled music playing in different pairs of headphones.

"Are you okay?" Freddy asks.

I force myself to meet his gaze now.

Tyler's voice echoes in my ear like a continuously pounding drum, the backing track to the collapsing of my chest.

I don't know how I even tolerate you at this point. You're embarrassing.

Every time it happens, I wait for it to hurt less. I wait for the moment people talk about, the numbness. He's done it so many times that eventually I'll ignore it and move on. But it never comes. I feel everything like a frayed nerve, open and throbbing with the pain of it all.

Freddy puts his hand on my knee and squeezes, a smile smoothing the worry lines on his cheeks, but his brow stays furrowed.

I try to smile back, to reassure him that I'm fine, but my stomach somersaults again and I hiccup a sob instead, ducking my head.

"Shit," he says under his breath, looping an arm around my neck and burying my face into his chest, giving me a private dark space to quietly break down. "Go ahead, Ro. Let it out."

I shake my head against him, but he presses a surprising kiss to my hair and only holds me harder.

"It's okay. The lights are off—everyone's sleeping or got headphones in. You're fine, cry if you need to. I've got you."

I believe him.

Freddy, as I really know him now, is someone I am learning I can trust. I can rely on him.

Matt Fredderic has been a thousand different things in my head. After meeting him freshman year, I romanticized him endlessly. In my dreams, he was the cool, popular boy who took off my metaphorical glasses and fell in love with me. A knight come to save me in my tall ivory tower. The gentle lover who took my virginity with quiets whispers of "*is this okay?*" or "*you're so perfect*," and then confessed his devotion to me in an epic, movie-worthy "*It's you. It's always been you*" moment.

And then, after I met Tyler, I abandoned those fantasies of Matt Fredderic in favor of what I thought was a real chance at a love story. What I can now see as me *begging* him for even a modicum of something romantic.

Something he deemed unrealistic.

"*Real people don't act like they do in your books, Ro.*"

But it wasn't even the romance I'd wanted. It was my desperation for wanting to feel something real. Something overwhelming, but worth it.

I spent my life safely at home, close to my parents because it was comfortable, and their love was a warm and tangible thing. Then, after my dad's stroke, I spent every waking moment with them out of fear. I didn't want to miss a second—just in case.

But I'd lived entire lives, thousands of them, in books. And part of me always imagined what falling in love would feel like.

I'd longed for it.

Maybe Tyler is right.

Maybe I am ridiculous and naive, but even admitting that in the safety of my own head is embarrassing. How could I possibly ever admit to anyone else that I spent a year of my life begging to have sex with someone who called me desperate when I told him I loved him?

That I spent *two years* continuously seeking validation from a guy who consistently measured me against another girl to show me my flaws.

As if just being better—more serious and sophisticated, smarter, more competitive—as if *that* would earn me his love. Shine brighter, Ro, but not too bright; not brighter than him.

And now?

I feel . . . disgusted with myself.

Why did I do that? What made me so desperate to be enough for him that I continued to bend and shrink myself into the box he wanted to put me in?

The realization is somehow worse than anything Tyler spewed at me tonight.

So many of my pieces, the things that make me *me*, are gone, chipped away so that I don't know who I am anymore.

I feel lost. Floating without a tether.

I rest my head against Freddy's warm, solid chest and he holds me, whispering soothing nonsensical words so calming I find my tears drying up, a numbness slowly seeping into my bones, and I feel safer, so I lean into it.

CHAPTER 22

Freddy

Ro doesn't speak for the entire hour-long ride back.

I give her one of my AirPods to listen to, putting a playlist of Taylor Swift on because I vividly remember her bright, wide smile and beautiful voice singing loudly in the back of my car.

Though I can't remember the song now. Probably because my brain likes to play Ro's voice saying, "*I think you'd be really easy to love,*" on repeat like a torturous soundtrack of the night she doesn't remember.

A night I couldn't forget, even if I wanted to.

Back at campus, we pile out of the bus and into the arena parking lot slowly. I thwart a few of the guys' curious, worried glances at Ro with a quick shake of my head.

But everyone is kind. If anything, they're concerned.

Ro looks around, lost. And although she's stopped crying, her eyes are red-rimmed and watery as she looks toward me. The heartbreaking vulnerability there makes my throat tight.

The guys hang around, Rhys and Bennett closer than the others, all watching her just as worriedly as I am.

Coming to Waterfell might not have been my choice, but I am honored to play with my entire team—with the new exception of Kane. My teammates are good fucking guys who would take care of Ro if I wasn't here. And she isn't even my girl—she's my tutor.

"Ro?" I ask, because there is panic bleeding into her expression.

"I—I'm sorry. I don't know what to do." She raises her arms helplessly, eyes darting around. "I . . . He has everything. He took everything—"

She's working herself into hysteria. I quickly sweep her into a tight hug, one that she instantly returns.

"I don't have my car or my student ID, not even my dorm keys," she mutters into my neck.

"It's okay. Let's take my car. We'll figure it out."

"I'm sorry."

I shake my head, hugging her tighter as I subtly gesture over her head that *we're good* so my lingering teammates can go home.

"No apologies. Now, let's go. I'm starving."

· · ·

I inch a bag of waffle fries toward Ro across the console as we leave The Chick parking lot—only after I scarfed down two grilled chicken sandwiches.

It takes a long moment before she finally takes the fries out of the bag. I even catch a hint of a smile as she spots the couple of pounds' worth of special fry sauce, logging that reaction in my head under "Things That Make Rosalie Shariff Smile."

I try to start a few mindless conversations with her, but Ro is silent. She's somewhere else, deep in her thoughts. And I, better than anyone, know what being lost in your own mind feels like. So I let her sit with it all, as much as I hate how clearly she's hurting.

"Cool About It" by boygenius plays softly while I slowly weave through the backstreets, taking the long way back to campus. Even with the soothing guitar riff and warm voices, tension pulls my muscles tight.

"Do you want to talk—"

"No," she says. It isn't cruel, just a quiet rejection.

It doesn't matter. It hurts just as much.

I clear my throat, and then say, "I was in love with someone, too, who treated me bad. And . . ." I huff a bitter laugh, gripping the steering wheel harder to keep my voice steady and soft.

"But she didn't love me. She never said it back—fine, but she held that shit over my head. And it worked. I wanted her to think about me all the time, like I did her. I would do anything for it. And it took me way too long to really see what she was doing to me."

Ro doesn't say anything, but I can feel her rapt attention like a spotlight heating the side of my face.

"And it wasn't until we weren't together anymore. And I felt so ridiculous and stupid . . . and embarrassed. And she was fine, because she didn't care."

"It was fun, Freddy. But that's not . . . You're not what I need."

I shake my head in a poor attempt to clear her voice from it.

"Why . . ." Ro starts, her voice raw and scratchy before she clears it and sips her Diet Coke. "Why are you telling me this?"

To look like an idiot, clearly.

I can't find an answer, and the silence stretches out between us while I try to put what I feel into words. Her patience and the stillness of her presence soothes me.

"Because I wish someone had stopped me before I got lost and broken. And . . . because I care about you. You're my friend, Ro."

Her face brightens as she blinks wide-eyed at me.

"Yeah?"

"I thought we covered this," I say teasingly. "Unless—"

"No. No, I'm your friend." Her nod is enthusiastic, and it tugs at the knot in my chest. "I love being your friend. I just—I've had trouble with that in the past, thinking people were my friends and . . . anyway, it's embarrassing."

My chest aches enough that I raise a hand to rub at it, because

I understand that feeling. I've made that exact mistake more times that I can count.

The car idles in front of the dorms, and Ro hesitates long enough that I'm about to offer for her to come stay at the Hockey House. Because I'm starting to think that Ro's like me.

That she doesn't want to be alone.

Instead, I stay quiet as she grabs her drink from the cupholder and reaches for the car door before she pauses and looks over her shoulder at me.

"I'm glad I'm your friend." Ro's hand rests on the handle, and she shifts her tall body around to face me. "For what it's worth coming from me, whoever that girl is, she's an idiot. I think . . . I think you're amazing, Matt. You're a good guy."

The praise warms my stomach and I smile. *Coming from you, it's worth everything*, I want to say. But instead, I nod and say, "A lot easier to tell someone else that, than yourself, huh?"

She flushes and nods. "Yeah." There's a charged silence, and then, "I should go. Thank you for saving me—again. And for everything else." She hops out, hand on the door to close it.

"Thank you, Rosalie," I say, my voice soft in a way I can't seem to control around her.

"For what?"

"For helping me. The math and reading stuff can be . . . hard." I shrug, vulnerability making me sweat through the thick Oxford shirt. "You've never made fun of me, once." The words are sensitive, and it hurts to say them to her, but I need her to know.

"I wouldn't. Never—"

"I know."

Our words are all whispers, like we're both too scared to break the other.

Then she shuts the door gently and starts toward the dorms. Her phone lights up in her palm again, and she shoves it into her coat pocket. And I watch as every bit of strength that she had when she left the car seems to melt from her, shoulders sinking, head bowed. Defeated.

My hand hits the steering wheel, head swimming over the image of her through the fogging window. At the entrance, she turns back to me and tries to smile again, barely managing before she knocks, and an RA lets her in.

It takes me an hour to drive away.

I spend most of it convincing myself not to follow her inside. She doesn't need someone like me.

CHAPTER 23

Ro

"You look tired."

I grumble something nonsensical—and probably incoherent—at the twelve-year-old scrounging for food in the pantry before I head to the coffee machine.

My lack of response must be enough to confuse Oliver, because he's staring at me as I turn around, eyebrows raised like I've let a barn animal into the apartment or am wearing a giant inflatable cowboy suit instead of my pajamas.

I look down, just to check.

"Are . . . you okay?"

Jeez, I must look worse than I thought.

"I didn't sleep well."

I wait for a quick retort, like Sadie might make, but remember that this is Oliver I'm dealing with.

He watches me make a cup of coffee, which I don't often drink, with mild concern. Enough that I finally tell him, "I'm fine. Just had a bad night."

After a long gulp, I jump up to sit on the countertop. It's only 6 a.m., so I'm not surprised we're the only ones awake.

There's a chance neither of us even went to sleep.

"How was your night?"

He shrugs. "Fine. Nothing bad."

"But you didn't sleep."

He shrugs again, and I know I've guessed right.

"If you're having trouble again, we can get you in to see someone."

Oliver is already shaking his head before I've finished my sentence.

"No, Sadie can't afford all that. She just got me new skates. I'm . . . I'm fine, Ro."

He's upset enough for me to drop it, for now, but I log the information.

Living in a dorm with my best friend and her two little brothers was *not* part of my Sexy College Bucket List, but I wouldn't trade them for anything else. I love Liam and Oliver like they're my own brothers, but helping them means I'm helping Sadie, and . . . I'd do anything for Sadie.

I don't think I would've made it through being so far away from my family for the last three years without her.

And it hurts my stomach to know that she might not know that—that she's not a burden to me. That she's the opposite.

By the time I reemerge from my room, Sadie is awake and my phone has racked up twenty-six missed calls from Tyler. It isn't until I'm out of the dorm building and walking toward the gym for a quick indoor track run that I finally answer.

"What?"

Stay firm. Be strong.

"Jesus Christ, Ro," he says, his anger nearly making me stop completely and turn back for my room. "I've been worried sick."

"Not that worried, considering you left me stranded an hour outside of town."

"I'm the one who spent all night trying to call you and check on you. *You* ignored *me*."

"I told you I was home safe and needed to be left alone. I needed space—"

"I said I was fucking sorry, Ro. I shouldn't have left. And honestly,

I wouldn't have, but you were kind of being a bitch and I got really upset and needed to go home."

"You left me there alone, Tyler, without any of my stuff. It's not okay."

Good. I want to pat myself on the back. Quick, but firm. *Don't get drawn into this again.*

"It was one time."

I almost scream.

"It wasn't though, was it? It wasn't even the second time. Literally less than a month ago you left me stranded at a restaurant for hours."

"I said I was sorry for that," he bites out. "But go ahead and rake me over the coals for it, again."

This is the first actual conversation we've had about it, but sure.

"Tyler—"

"Stop punishing me, Ro. I said I was fucking sorry."

Less than twenty-four hours of space, and I'm punishing him.

"I need my stuff, Tyler."

"Meet me for coffee and I'll give it to you," he quickly responds.

"Leave it in my office and I won't report you."

I can feel more than hear the fury rise in him. I wish I could be happy we are doing this over the phone, away from each other, but Tyler's best weapon has always been his words.

"Stop. You're acting like a fucking bitch, Ro."

"Don't call me that." I'm proud of the way my voice doesn't shake.

"I didn't," he sighs, like I'm some petulant child. "I said you were acting like one."

"That's the same thing. You're insulting me over and over—sometimes I'm a bitch, the next moment I'm acting like a child. Pick a different tactic; these insults are making you sound dumber than you are."

Maybe I shouldn't goad him, but for some reason I'm walking a little taller after my word vomit, feeling good. Confident.

"Don't put fucking words in my mouth. You were the one who wanted to get back together. You practically *begged* me the other night."

I stop walking, my stomach swooping as I'm struck by that same sick feeling. Like I'm looking in a mirror for the first time in two years and I *hate* what I see.

"Stop calling me, Tyler. I'm done."

There's a disbelieving laugh that grates my ears. I kick the brick of the building I'm standing in front of, because I want to scream and cry and maybe test how far I can run before I pass out from exhaustion to get it all out.

"You're acting like a kid, Ro."

Laughing a bit too loud as he does *exactly what I said he would*, I nearly swallow my tongue, but manage to calmly reply, "I'm not. I'm serious. We're breaking up, Tyler."

"We aren't. Stop being dramatic."

"By your standards, we weren't even dating. We were 'casual.' I'm being nice by even saying this to you—I don't want to do this anymore. I want to be done."

"Sure," he grumbles. "We'll talk later. When you're not as emotional."

He hangs up. And I think about trying the classic male *punch my fist through a wall* coping technique.

. . .

By the time my session with Freddy comes around on Monday morning, I've got a stack of thirty-plus missed-call notifications on my phone and a seemingly endless thread of texts.

Tyler Donaldson is cool, calm, and collected in person—but through a phone call or text, he's brutal.

Still, I've somehow managed to avoid him for two days. My tutoring sessions take place in new locations, all my students willing to meet me wherever I ask. I even take my office hours at other school offices or in private library rooms.

But today is our overlap as GTAs in Tinsley's class, which is unavoidable. I am a live wire of tension.

The sound of the door makes me jump, and one look at Freddy tells me my reaction did not go unnoticed. His brow furrows, the smile previously on his face melting to apprehension.

"Did I . . . do something wrong?"

The question is so opposite of everything currently blasting across my phone screen I almost laugh.

"Not at all," I say. "Sorry, I'm just— It's a bad day for me today."

He's still standing at the door, tall body covering the entryway easily. His entire posture—from the set of his shoulders to the one-handed grip on his backpack strap—screams uncertainty. It's not a look I've seen often on the popular hockey jock, and I quickly decide it's one I truly don't like.

"Did you want to cancel?"

"No. I'm good, I promise."

I manage to release a shaky smile, but it's enough to have his shoulders relaxing as he makes himself comfortable across the table from me.

Going over the math assignment takes me far too long, mostly because I keep getting distracted by my phone ringing.

And ringing.

Now with new, randomized caller ID numbers—a fact that makes my stomach drop.

The very first time we had a fight, Tyler left in a rage and blocked my number, my social media—everything. It was an unsettling shock for me, one I didn't know how to handle because he was my very first boyfriend. I didn't know if it was normal behavior or not, and with Sadie swimming in endless responsibilities with her brothers and dealing with her dad, I didn't have anyone to ask.

He came to Brew Haven to apologize two days later, saying that he needed me to understand how upset he was. Sadie said it was a fancy way to say he was punishing me.

Which now I know to be true.

Then, after another fight, I didn't let him punish me. Instead, I blocked him. That had somehow made things worse. And since we got back together again and again, Tyler continued to see it all as a success.

Hence the random numbers currently blowing up my phone.

Finally, when the ratcheting anxiety is nearly ready to burst from me, I toss my still-vibrating phone into my bag—too harshly, as my student stops his scribbling and looks up at me, eyebrows high before his eyes narrow as he takes me in.

"You sure you're okay?"

"Fine," I squeak out. But for some reason there are tears in my eyes.

I am not *crying in front of him* again.

Freddy, as usual, sees right through my lie. Yet he doesn't call it out.

Instead, he shuts his textbook, a move that has me double-checking my watch and the loud clock on the wall.

"I have an idea," he says, palms flat on the table as he leans slightly over it. "Why don't we skip class?"

A denial, full and resolute, should be spilling from my open mouth. Instead, it's a quiet, blushing confession.

"I've never done that before."

He grins—not the one he usually dons; this one is all innocent boyish charm. Gentle, genuine.

Real.

"Me neither."

"Really?" I laugh. "That's . . ."

"Surprising?"

I shake my head. "No, actually, that makes a lot of sense."

"Yeah?" he says, sounding skeptical, but intrigued. He leans forward.

"Yeah." I nod, smiling softly up at him. "You'd never want to even *chance* letting someone down. You . . . you always show up."

There's a hitch in his breath, and if I didn't know him better—the fact that I'm sure everyone has complimented him enough to last a lifetime—I'd say he's yearning to hear the words.

They wash over him like water on a sunflower.

He reaches for my backpack to sling over his other shoulder. It makes my entire body feel warm—not because the action is inherently romantic, but because it is gentle and kind. Something I want, desperately.

We head out of the library and toward the small covered parking lot. Freddy smiles brightly as several people stop to greet him. I try to stay back a step to give him some space, but every time I falter, he turns back to wait for me.

Almost worriedly. Like I'm going to disappear.

Eventually, we make it to his car, where he tucks me into the worn leather passenger seat, shutting the door before jogging to his side.

"So, what do we do now?" I ask. My knees bob up and down, brain swimmy from the adrenaline coursing through me. I feel almost giddy.

And sure, maybe it's the relief of not having to see Tyler today. But I think it's more the Matt Fredderic Effect.

He makes everything ten times better. I've always known he was intoxicating to be around—since the first time I met him I've been entranced—and it has nothing to do with his beauty.

I look over at him, see his bright green eyes crinkling with a grin. Plush, too-pink lips and smile lines carved into his cheeks.

No. It's not about what he looks like at all. It's *him*, just as he is, like a magnet pulling forever at my focus until all I can see is him.

Tyler makes me feel small and naive, silly.

Sadie makes me happy, but with her there is always the weight of responsibility. The need to care for her is ingrained in our friendship.

But Matt is different.

His presence feels warm and vibrant. Being around him is like the climb before the drop of a roller coaster—bright anticipation filled with the safety to free-fall without getting hurt.

Around him, *I* am the fun, exciting one. Not the tagalong or the audience to him.

"What's something you've never done but always wanted to do?"

My mind fills with images, all inspired by my dusty Sexy College Bucket List somewhere on my desk, under a pile of printed articles on creativity and its effect on the brain.

Freddy holding up a funnel for me, or showing me how to shotgun a beer. Freddy with his hands in my hair, letting me try everything with him . . .

Freddy skinny-dipping with me, bodies wet, water making his golden hair dark against his skin—easy to see with my curls all piled high, tied up off my neck with a . . . with a shoelace?

Why does that feel so familiar?

Shaking my head, I settle for a safe, "I've never been ice skating, actually."

He freezes, mouth opening and closing before a mischievous glint appears in his eyes and he's starting the car.

"Where are we going?" I ask.

"To the arena."

"Are we allowed in there?"

He shrugs. "We're already skipping class, princess. What's another rule broken?"

CHAPTER 24

Freddy

The arena is locked, which only means I get a nice twenty-minute drive with Ro quietly humming to the radio as I take us through historic downtown Waterfell and toward the community rink.

It's moderately warm for an early October day, so I have to dive into the rumpled clean clothes pile in the back of my car for a jacket—smelling each before I find the cleanest one, a Waterfell University Sports half zip with my number on the sleeve and my last name emblazoned on the left pocket.

"Arms up for me, princess," I say, slipping the fabric over her head and settling it over her hips. I lean in and zip her up, fabric grazing her chin as she grins at me sweetly. I grab my skates out of the back before locking my car.

The cold sting of the arena settles my nervous system as we enter. I'm about to have her sit while I grab her a pair of skates, when she squeals.

Ro tackles me, my back hitting the lightly padded flooring as her long limbs tangle with mine. She's tall for a girl, and clumsy, enough that I can imagine her as a gangling teen.

"Shit—sorry."

I smirk up at her through a sea of curls as she scrambles to pull them back over her shoulders, even as they keep escaping. "You know, I think that's the first time I've heard you curse."

She blushes further before shoving on my chest and peering through the window overlooking the rink.

"It's Sadie. She's here."

My eyebrows raise as I slowly push up, letting Ro continue to hold on to me—something I'm not sure she even realizes she is doing—while I do.

She's whispering, so I do, too, brushing back a few of her curls and politely ignoring her full-body shudder as I lean in.

"You know they can't really see us up here, princess."

"Oh," she whispers before clambering away from me and standing, cheeks stained dark red.

I follow her gaze and look through the dark glass at the half-filled rink. Public skate is designated to the outside circle, but in the middle is my captain and the figure skater with a group of about six baby skaters.

Rhys watches Sadie with a singular focus, head following each movement. Like he would another player, as if he's unlocking the secrets to their moves, their plays. The kind of focus only Captain Rhys is capable of. And I might've noticed it slightly at the party, but here, under the hard fluorescents, it's impossible to miss.

Maybe I was wrong.

Because it seems like Sadie looks at him in the exact same way, careful and intense.

Like they both watch over each other, constantly.

"Is he a good guy?" Ro suddenly asks.

The question surprises me slightly. My eyebrows dip as I examine her profile while she watches them. She looks anxious and worried, hand splayed on her chest, fiddling with the collar of her shirt, and chewing on her lip.

"It's just," she continues before I can answer. "I've never seen Sadie really *like* a guy. And she has . . . a lot going on. I want to make sure he's as good of a guy as he seems to be."

"No— Rhys is the best guy I know. I'd trust him with my life. She's in good hands."

Something sours in my stomach, because I suddenly can't get Rhys's birthday party out of my head. It isn't my fault, I know, because going off my party-based interactions with Sadie, why wouldn't I be protective of my friend? ·

But Ro is *good* and kind. And if she is protective of Sadie, if she loves her this much, then perhaps there is more beneath the surface.

Like there is to you?

Or do you want *to believe that because Ro loving Sadie despite her flaws means she* could *love you as her friend? In spite of* your *flaws?*

As it always is, the voice in my head sounds like my dad, and I have to shake my head to clear the spiral before it starts.

Except now I can't remember what she's said because my brain is far away from our last interaction. So I scrub at the back of my neck and nod to her.

"You have to pick something else."

Whether what I said was on topic or not, she grins and I relax.

"Me? What about you?"

"Nope. We clearly aren't going skating today, so . . . you have to pick something else." I turn and head for the door, loving how quickly she follows me with a small *hmm* noise as she thinks.

I stop in front of my car, raising an eyebrow at her and tapping my foot.

"Okay. Well, I've always wanted to get a tattoo."

My eyes flare. Not what I expected, but I can work with that.

"What did you have in mind?"

Her gaze flicks down to my legs. I'm wearing jeans today, but I might as well be naked with the searing intensity of her eyes right over where my thigh tattoo rests.

"A butterfly," she blurts out before shaking her head rapidly and covering her face with her hands. "No, wait. Sorry, I actually don't know."

I stay quiet, knowing my ego might not be able to handle her matching her first tattoo to mine, and I open her door for her.

I drive to the tattoo parlor I've used before, in historic downtown Waterfell, nestled between a popular pizza joint and a vintage candy store that hasn't changed a thing in the past hundred years.

Pulling into one of the hard-to-find slanted spots a few buildings down, I help Ro out and lay a hand on her middle back to guide her quickly across the road.

Inside the old brick building, the parlor is a mix of bright cream and soft greens, framed designs and some full-sized canvases cluttering the walls. It's relatively empty, with a girl getting her back tattooed on one of the tables.

"How about you look through the book and I'll get the paperwork."

Any other guy might fill it out for her while she looked through the shop's portfolio and picked a design, but I can barely read it, let alone write down her answers as she says them out loud to me. We'd be here for hours.

So instead I grab a pen and the papers before turning back—

—only to find that Ro is gone.

My heart drops for a second before I spot a mop of curls as she paces awkwardly fast back and forth outside.

"Jesus, Ro." I smirk as I exit the shop, crossing my arms and standing in front of her to force her to stop. "I thought you'd left me here."

"No!" she says quickly. "I'd never do that—I kinda freaked out for a minute. And maybe . . ."

She trails off, her face sinking.

"Maybe you don't want a tattoo yet," I say.

She nods, looking highly apologetic as she quietly whispers an "I'm sorry."

"Don't apologize, Rosalie." Desperate to bring her mood back to what it was, I look wildly around us. "Actually, I came here mainly because I'm starving, and they have the best pizza in Massachusetts."

Ro looks to where I point next door.

"They do?" she asks, disbelieving.

I shrug. "According to a"—I look closer at the newspaper taped on the inside of the window—"1995 *New York Times* article, yes. And honestly, that place looks like it hasn't changed since, so I think we're in luck."

I pull open the door for her.

It's a small building with three tables total, looking like the early 1990s threw up in it. Complete with two quarter machines in the entryway, one full of gumballs that look like rocks, hardened with age. The other has exactly what I'm looking for.

After paying for our pizza in cash and asking for quarters as change back—ignoring the annoyed look from the pimpled teen behind the counter—we decide to take it to-go.

Mostly because one table has a couple enjoying their early dinner, and the other two are covered in boxes that I'm betting aren't getting moved for us to sit.

Somehow I manage to get two of the colored balls out of the machine without Ro noticing, even if I look like an asshole making her carry the boxes out to anyone passing on the street.

Still, I think the surprise will be worth it.

CHAPTER 25

Freddy

We end up at the dorms after Ro gets a text from Sadie that she won't be home.

She doesn't tell me exactly what the text says, which only bothers me because I can *tell* it's bothering her.

Protectiveness has never been my thing—with friends or girls. Clearly, I've never been good at taking care of them. But with Ro, the budding friendship I have with her feels important. And *that*, I'm protective over.

Every light in their apartment-style dorm is off, but the TV plays music, currently "Young Folks" by Peter Bjorn and John at a medium volume. Ro walks in first, flicking on the mismatched lamps on their tables by the couch.

I follow her lead, sitting after she prompts me with one of the floor pillows on the pallet they've clearly constructed. She's still standing, looking around nervously, before darting back into the kitchen area.

"Want some wine?" she asks, grinning as she reaches and pulls down two multicolored glasses.

"Sure."

She pours from a bottle of white wine out of the fridge, carefully setting both glasses on the low coffee table and opening one of the pizza boxes on the floor.

I raise my cup. "To 1995's best pizza in Massachusetts!"

I'm rewarded with an open, happy laugh that feels like the first rays of summer sun warming my body.

We clink our glasses together as she repeats my toast before we chat quietly and enjoy the food.

. . .

"So," I say, polishing off my fourth slice of pizza, still on my first glass of wine. She steals one of my crusts from the pile I made her after lying about hating the crusts, and dunks it in the garlic sauce. "I may have grabbed us a surprise so we can both complete our 'never have I ever' task."

Her hazel eyes twinkle, bright in the lamplight as we sit on the piles of pillows and blankets pulled down from the couch over the carpeted floor.

"What is it?"

I pull out the two colorful prizes from the machine from where I tucked them earlier, before grinning and juggling them lightly in my hand.

"Temporary tattoos."

Her smile is near blinding.

"What are they of?"

"Didn't look," I say, and shrug. "Figure we could choose at random and put them on each other."

"Really? You'd do it, too?"

I crinkle my brow. "I'm not letting you have all the fun without me, princess. Now, come on. Pick."

Without a moment's hesitation, she grabs for the purple one, leaving the green plastic ball in my hand.

She pops it open to reveal a crown tattoo, silver and sparkly.

"Perfect," I laugh, reaching for it. "A crown for a princess."

She rolls her eyes at the tease but bumps my shoulder with hers. "What did you get?"

It's amazing how free she seems. More than I've seen her before. Granted, she's nearly polished off her second glass of wine, but she's soft and smiley—not drunk. Calm and relaxed.

A version of Ro I don't think I've ever seen.

I pop the lid on mine, sighing and shaking my head at the little tattoo in there.

"I can't," I groan. "I'll never hear the end of it."

"You promised," she laughs, peering over my shoulder to see Hello Kitty staring up at us both.

"I know, I know." I *also* know exactly the look I'll see on Holden's face. I can nearly *hear* the jokes he'll throw in the locker room until it washes off.

Something makes Ro pause.

"You don't have to. Not if you don't want to."

"I know." I fluff her hair affectionately, smiling at her with a shake of my head. "I want to. Promise."

It seems to appease her, the smile I've been aiming for all day pleasantly back on her face. Making her happy, pleasing her, makes me—

Stop. We're not doing this again.

Remember last time.

Shaking my head, I stretch and push the nearly empty pizza box away.

"So, where do you—"

"You first," she blurts before standing and running to the kitchen.

"Okay," I say, pulling off my shirt and settling back on my forearms. "But you gotta promise to get it perfect, Rosalie. It's bad enough showing up with Hello Kitty on my chest. Even worse if she's all mangled on—"

I pause, because Ro has malfunctioned, standing completely frozen in the corner as she was reentering the living room.

Her eyes are wide and round, mouth slightly open and face

blushing rapidly. It's enough of a change that I press up to sit, anxiety rolling down my spine.

"What's wrong?"

"Nothing!" she says, but it's high-pitched and squeaky, which means it's very much not nothing. "I just . . . you're—you took off your shirt. I wasn't prepared."

I relax a bit and have to swallow down the urge to ask if she likes what she sees. I'm well aware of her weird relationship with Tyler Donaldson, one he's made distinctly clear to me is none of my business. But it's second nature for me to preen like a goddamn peacock at the slightest hint of attention.

Fucking pathetic.

"Sorry, Ro. I didn't mean to make you uncomfortable." Because that's what she's feeling, right? Discomfort? "I was gonna have you put it on my chest, but—"

"No, no," she says, stopping me, shaking her head, which seems to work like a reset button for her entire body as she darts forward, back onto our makeshift pallet with a bowl of hot water and a thin roll of paper towels. "Sorry. That was probably so weird. I'm . . . sorry, Matt. You're unfortunately very handsome."

"Unfortunately?" It makes me laugh. I've been told I'm attractive more times than I can count, but none of them quite so backhandedly.

"I'm not—" She shakes her head. "Sorry. I probably made you uncomfortable just now. You don't have to do this to make me happy—"

"Trust me, Rosalie," I say. "Nothing else I'd rather be doing."

I get comfortable again, leaning back on my forearms while she kneels at my side.

She snickers, drawing my eyes back to her.

"What?"

"Nothing. You're splayed out like you got injured in a battle. And

I"—she gestures to herself briefly, to the ceramic bowl and paper towels at her side—"look like I'm here to heal you. It's all feeling very bodice ripper."

My eyebrows shoot up as I repeat, "What?" But a lot louder, as her cheeks turn crimson.

"The books, with the ladies in dresses on the front and the shirt-less men?" She bites down on her lip. "They're called bodice rippers."

"They're sexy books?" I wink, suddenly *very* interested in this hobby.

"Yeah, but they're romantic."

"You like them?"

I hate that she looks mildly shamed as she nods, dipping the paper towel into water and pressing it to my skin. "Yeah. I like all romance, but . . . I like those best. I used to have this massive collection of them."

"You didn't bring any here? I wanna see one."

"I did, but—" She cuts off, eyes darting to the floor. "Um, actually most of them are gone. I think I have one; my favorite one."

She gets up, stumbling a little, and I take over holding the paper towel to my pec.

The book in her hand is torn on the edges, worn and well loved. Maybe it was bright green at one time, but it's faded to a soft sage now. She hands it to me delicately.

Marked in Fire, the title scrolls across the cover, the bottoms of the letters brushing the overly chiseled chest of the half-naked man with long red hair, a kilt his only piece of clothing. He embraces a dark-skinned woman with a mass of curls, one hand on her hip, the other tangled in her hair.

"What's it about?" I ask, biting down on the teasing smile that wants to appear. She looks too unsure, slightly hesitant for me to even hold the book, let alone look at it.

"It's, um, a reformed rake story."

My brows dip. "A what?"

"It means"—she clears her throat and plays with the end of the blanket beneath me as I flip the book over like I might read the back—"that the hero was a rake, a playboy, and he changes his ways to be with the heroine, because he loves her."

Ro pauses and pulls on a strand of hair, a buzzing nervous energy around her.

"Keep going," I say, intrigued.

"Well, um, in this one, everyone thinks Callan, the guy, is this womanizer. And Rosalina has been taken from her father to pay his debts, carted all the way to Scotland."

I smile now, tilting my chin down so I can meet her eyes. "*Rosalina*, huh?"

She blushes. "It was the first time I saw something like my name, but that's not the reason it's my favorite. It's—she's scared at first, and when they auction her off—"

"They *what*?"

Ro is looking at me now, her finger to her mouth. "Let me finish. They auction her off and Callan puts in the most money—no one knows *why* he would want to settle down. He can have any woman he wants, but no one understands that he's lonely."

My stomach hollows out a bit and I look back down at the shirtless man on the cover. *Yeah, Callan, I get it.*

"But Rosalina does. Because she's lonely, too." Her lips press together and she tucks her hair back behind her ears. "To be loved is to be seen—and she's the first person to really see him. That's why they fall in love."

It's quiet, except for the music humming low in the background.

I'm lonely, I want to say, almost desperate to compare myself in some way to the oiled-up man that Ro clearly has a soft spot for. *Can you see me? Can you feel how lonely I am?*

Are you lonely, too?

Ro reaches to touch my hand, but only pulls the paper towel away from my skin, blowing lightly on the tattoo as I speak nearly into her hair.

"I . . . I liked to read. I mean— I like books. I couldn't read well, as a kid." *Nor can I now*, I think, but refrain from saying. Even though I know she's well aware now and would never tease me about it. "But my mom used to read Harry Potter to me. And then *Lord of the Rings, Eragon*— I loved them."

But then I got older and decided skating with my friends and blowing off my curfew was more fun than listening to my mom's voice. And before I could get my brain fucking right, my mom got so sick she couldn't hold her head up, let alone read me a fucking book, so I never finished any of the ones we started.

And now I won't. Ever.

Clenching my jaw, I wait for the wave of grief to recede.

Ro looks up at me, not realizing how close we are. I can see the flecks of pure gold in the swirling moss of her eyes.

"Which one was your favorite?"

I smile. "*Lord of the Rings.* I liked Samwise."

Her eyes soften, like I've revealed some great truth about myself, and it's so achingly tender I pull back before she can see something she doesn't like if she looks too closely.

I don't think I could weather her disapproval.

"Your turn, princess."

We switch positions, and our movements are gentle, but skittish—both afraid of frightening each other if we go too quickly.

Mokita and Kaptan's "Dreamer (Stripped Down)" plays softly as Ro settles beneath me, lying flat on the multicolored blankets like a patchwork background to her tawny skin, exposing the long column of her throat and her flushed skin.

"I want to put it here." She gestures above her hip bone. "If that's okay."

I nod, not trusting myself to speak.

For a moment, I wish I wasn't attracted to her. That everything I felt for her was *purely* friendship, because that would make this far easier.

Then I wouldn't think about the way she shivers as I raise the fabric of her shirt. I wouldn't notice the softness of her skin underneath my fingertips, the gooseflesh that fans out across her entire stomach as I press the damp paper towel to the tattoo. The audible puff of breath she releases as I blow lightly over the crown.

Trying to give myself room to breathe without begging her for a kiss—or even a fucking pat on the head at this point—I stand and discard the wrappers and pizza boxes, cleaning up our scattered mess.

"Thank you," she says quietly. "For rescuing me so many times lately . . . with Tyler. I know that's probably annoying—"

"It's not." I shake my head, stuffing the boxes into her too-full trash bag before tying it and setting it by the door to take it out when I leave. "It's only annoying that he treats you like this. You deserve so much better. You're amazing, Ro."

I peek over at her, and see her arms lying over her eyes, her shirt still raised and showing where the crown shines like a beacon—high enough that I turn away almost immediately.

"Yeah, well, maybe I'm not so amazing, once you get to know me."

Her words are a soft mumble, and when I ask her what she means, she doesn't answer.

It's quiet again as I finish cleaning up. I return to the pallet and sit by her side.

"When I was little," I say, my tone low because her eyes are closed, "I used to ask my mom to read me the books from school. She would read them to me first, and then I would read them after her. She'd go through them over and over again with me, until I got every word perfectly."

I can almost picture my mom as I speak, her comforting embrace around me as she turned the pages and softly corrected the words I missed.

"I know now I was memorizing more than I was learning to read better, but it didn't matter. She *knew* it embarrassed me on our read-aloud days in school, so she made sure I felt confident before each one."

If you want to stay home today, it's okay, Matty.

How the world's softest woman ended up with the worst narcissist alive always feels like some grand cosmic joke.

A deep sigh heaves out of me as I look down at a sleeping Ro.

"You remind me of her sometimes, especially when you teach me. I think you're amazing and . . . and I hope you think you're amazing, too."

I should go, I *need* to leave. But I can't let her sleep on the floor like this.

So I stand, reaching my arms beneath her head and knees to pick her up, trying to be slow and not jostle her awake.

Her head lolls onto my chest, brow wrinkling as she mumbles beneath her breath.

"No, don't. I'm a giant."

I smile slightly. "You're tall. But I'm taller."

"And stronger," she breathes, snuggling closer as I walk into her room. I feel like preening, puffing my chest a little.

"Yeah, princess. And stronger."

I shoulder the door open, entering her room. It's small and neat, but well lived in. The decor here lets me know she has a heavy hand in decorating the rest of her and Sadie's apartment, with its bursts of colors and endless pillows and throw blankets.

I lay her on the bed, using one of the blankets hanging off the end to cover her. My heart feels like it's gonna beat out of my chest, and the smile on my face is manic at best. But I can't bring myself to care, not when she looks like that.

Soft, relaxed, and happy.

Turning to leave, I catch sight of a cardboard sign propped up on her desktop, next to a mini sewing machine, half covered by printed articles. A list, I realize, skimming over a few of the items:

Dance on top of a bar like Coyote Ugly.
Third base in a car.
Skinny-dip! (But don't get caught or go to jail!)
Go on a crazy spring break trip. (But don't get arrested!)

A mix of handwriting, neat and scribbled, with little doodles and drawings.

And checkmarks, notably beside a few of the more sexual items on the list. There's a pang in my chest, pressure that makes me rub at it. I know it was Tyler who did any of that with her, and I can't help but hate him all the more for it.

I look away from the cardboard, back to Ro's sleeping form, and blow a breath out. It's easier to relax, to let it go, when I see her so vulnerable and trusting.

So I file the information away—that the list exists at all—into my Rosalie Shariff folder, and secretly hope that it'll be *me* next time drawing checkmarks in the margins with her.

CHAPTER 26

Freddy

There are two texts from Archer and two missed calls from my dad waiting for me after I finish the morning portion of our two-a-day practice.

I swipe away the texts, hoping enough people will message me to bury them deep in my inbox, away from my curiosity.

I'm here if you ever need someone.

Desperate to get Archer's gruff, sad tone out of my head, I call my father back before he loses his shit on me in my voicemail—again.

"Hey," I say carefully when he picks up.

"What the *fuck* was that?" He is nearly growling. I hear a door slam closed in the background before he really starts in. "You lead as top scorer for your exhibition games, then sit on your fucking ass waiting for the real shit to start?"

I'm ten years old and I'm cold.

I reach for my bedroom door and pull it shut, like the action will shake my mind away from dangerous territory. "I didn't—"

He cuts me off. "I sent goddamn *scouts* to see you, dumbass," he says. "You ungrateful asshole—might as well quit now. It would be the right thing to do, considering all you keep doing is fucking up everything I've built."

I'm ten years old and my dad won't look at me.

"You're a goddamn embarrassment, Matt."

My mind is splintering, every thought making my head pound harder and harder.

I'm ten and I'm cold.

I'm ten and I'm cold, nerves making me shiver more than the briskness of the rink. It's already crowded, kids around my age scattered along the benches, their fathers kneeling to tie skates for the younger ones, some chatting with each other.

I look up at my dad with a gap-toothed smile, but he isn't looking at me—he's looking around the room.

"Should I put my skates on here?" I ask, still smiling, even though it's making my cheeks hurt now.

"If you aren't having fun, tell him you want to go home. He'll bring you right back."

My mom's voice reverberates in my ears. But I don't want to go home. I want Dad to like me.

"Yeah," he says, sliding my bag off his shoulder and dropping it onto the bench next to me. "Just . . . get your skates on and get on the ice. Gotta talk to someone real quick."

He's gone before I can say that it's still hard for me to get the laces just right. That sometimes my mind starts to wander, and I forget where I am or what I'm doing, so I need someone to watch me do it—to help.

There's a weird pressure on my chest for a moment as I stand by my bag, pulling on my sweatshirt strings as my dad jogs to the other side of the space, slaps another man on the back, and shakes his hand.

His smile is wider than it's been all day.

"You good, champ?"

The new voice rocks me, and I tilt back to look up at the very tall man in front of me. There's a boy standing next to him around my age, maybe older, because he's kinda big for a kid. Bigger than most of the kids on my team, with his arms leaning on his stick.

"I, um . . ." I scratch at my neck. "I need help with my laces."

The man nods and smiles. "That's all right. They're complicated sometimes. Why don't you sit on the bench there and I can help."

I nod again, sliding over and dragging my bag next to me. Pulling my skates out, I sit on the bench and try not to kick my feet.

"Hold your breath for five seconds and blow it out for five. Don't think about it." *My mom's voice echoes through my head as I follow her usual instructions.*

My eyes start to wander as he laces my skates, flitting across the Winnipeg Jets logo on the gray fabric stretched across his chest.

"The Jets," I say, nodding a little. "Henney is a beauty this year."

The man laughs, nodding as he smiles. I feel foolish, but I know he probably agrees with me. I may not be the best in school, but I watch hockey constantly. I think about it all the time.

And Coach Archer says I think like an all-star already.

"He is," the man says, pulling my other foot into his lap while I stretch my ankle and check his work. "Do you like the Jets?"

"Yeah, but I'm a Dallas fan." I smile. "My dad plays for them."

"Oh yeah? What's your name, champ?"

"Matt Fredderic," I say, peeking over at the kid my age who hasn't said a word, still just staring at me. "But my team calls me Matty."

"Nice to meet you, Matt." He smiles. "Your dad is John Fredderic, huh?"

There's an edge to his voice and I hesitate because I've heard that before. The adults always act like that with my dad. But I nod anyway.

"Yeah, he brought me today to skate with me. I don't get to spend a lot of time with him."

"Reiner," my dad says, rejoining us with a plastered-on smile that looks almost painfully fake as he reaches a hand out—even though the man is still working on my laces.

He pointedly ignores my dad and loops the last double knot.

"How do those feel, champ?" Mr. Reiner asks, smiling at me. I still

*feel like I might be in trouble, stomach sinking, so I nod quickly before
even checking the left one.*

*Finally, he tilts his head up and stands, taller than my dad—he
looks like Coach Archer, super tall, dark hair and a short beard, but he
isn't as tan.* "John. Good to see you."

"Sorry about this," *my dad says as he gestures vaguely down at me.*
"Didn't know the kid can't tie his own damn skates."

*He laughs, and I decide as soon as they're done talking I'll ask him
to take me home.*

I just want my mom.

*They talk, but I can't hear the words, I only feel a couple of gentle
touches from Mr. Reiner across my back or on top of my head—like he's
giving me a bit of kindness or strength before he goes.*

*And then my dad is dragging me out of the rink, still in my skates,
into the bathroom where the blades scrape over the tiles as he speaks,
low and cruel into my ear.*

"Don't ever pull that kind of shit again. A goddamn embarrassment. When we go back out there, you better show them all up. You're
not on a team—you show them *you're fucking worth something* on
your own. *Be a superstar.*"

"I have class," I mumble, head pounding, cutting him off entirely.
Not that I've heard the last few minutes of his tirade.

But I do hear his final words.

"I'm coming to the Harvard game. Mess this up and I'll blow up
your contract with Dallas."

Fury pulses through me. "You're not my agent. You can't do
that."

"Watch me. Besides, who the fuck else is going to do this? Elise is
gone and it seems Archer left this burden to me—as if I didn't have
enough on my plate, having to deal with *you.*"

Right. Because having me as a child was such a liability.

"I don't need you."

He laughs. "I'm your father. Your name is *famous* because *I* made it so."

"Leave me the fuck alone." I hang up, feeling a little sick, and a lot worse for wear.

• • •

I feel as out of place as possible sitting on the too-small stool in the biology lab with thirty-plus students from my lecture. But Ro told me it was a good idea to show up to the optional evening review, so I did. I'd rather not spend more time with Carmen Tinley than I must.

"And that's active transport?" I blurt the question, knee bobbing and pen rocking in my fingers as I shove my other hand through my hair. Tyler's sudden smirk makes me shrink back a bit, regretfully. "Or . . . passive, I guess?"

I bite down on my tongue not to mutter "never mind" like I usually would, to force them to move on and leave me behind. It's one concept you don't get. Except, it's not. Every foundation in biology seems to build on the ones before, and the second I fall behind on one, I'll never catch up.

"You've got to be kidding," Tyler mutters, slumping on the table.

Ro stands from her chair, confident and relaxed.

"Think about it this way," she says, clasping her hands. "Passive transport is like rolling a giant stone down a hill—it uses no energy, right? And active transport is like taking the same stone and actively rolling it up the hill, which would use a lot of energy. So, a sodium-potassium pump is . . . ?" Ro pauses, tapping her nail against the whiteboard where the large diagram is drawn. I have a suspicion she drew it, knowing now how artistic she is.

"Active," I answer, smiling. It might be the first time I've answered a question in a class setting aloud—*hell*, it might be the first time I've *asked* a question in class since I was fourteen.

"What a stupidly simplistic explanation," Tyler sneers, looking at Ro. "Sounds like you're talking to a child."

A few of the student who are listening laugh, enough that I see Tinley look up from her one-on-one discussion with a table near the back. She doesn't move, thankfully, but Tyler doesn't seem even slightly concerned by her attention.

"Tyler—"

"If you want to listen to the future kindergarten teacher with bows in her hair, I'm sure she'll give you a little gold star and smiley face on your paper. Might even hold your hand while you take the exam." Again, a few students laugh, but I shoot a quick glare over my shoulder that shuts half of the underclassmen up. "But if you want to pass, then you need more than whatever the hell she just said."

Ro blushes furiously, but maintains her heightened posture and doesn't back down from Tyler's irritating smirk. *That's my girl.*

"We haven't even gotten to the breakdown yet. They need to understand this concept to understand the—"

"Ro," Carmen cuts her off.

My eyes shutter at her voice.

"If I needed your help to teach, Ro, I would ask."

"Freddy had a question—" Ro says, trying to defend herself.

My mouth opens to help before it seals shut as Carmen's hand lands on my shoulder. "Now, what can I help with?"

"Nothing," I grit, wanting desperately to rip my skin out from underneath her grip. "I'm fine. Ro helped me."

Ro's face goes slightly pale at my sharp admission. Carmen squeezes slightly, brushing her hand through the ends of my hair as she walks behind me around the table, to the front of the class. She says something to Ro beneath her breath, chastising her as Ro nods, cheeks red in humiliation.

Ro's beautiful, haunted hazel eyes keep darting to mine, but she doesn't move. Everyone in the room is silent, watching as my tutor lets Carmen finish before finding a seat near the side of the room.

There's a beaten-down set to her shoulders that mimics mine, both hunched and afraid, but frozen in this stupid classroom.

I wait for Carmen to say something to Tyler, to chide him for his much larger disruption, but she doesn't. Only steps up beside him and takes over where she paused.

The session ends minutes later, and the only thing I remember is Ro's explanation. I want to run, to bolt from this room and let the energy of a sprint take the edge off my hyperactivity—even if I know it won't. Instead, I stay while Ro helps hand out extra study sheets and packs her bag.

Tyler watches her. Carmen watches me. But I never take my eyes off Ro.

Finally, I stand and toss my bag onto one shoulder, heading toward her to be the last student to leave the room.

"Hey," I whisper, huddling in close and blocking her slender form with as much of my body as I can. She fiddles nervously with one of the bows in her hair until I grab her hand and pull it away. "You okay?"

"Yeah. I'm fine—"

"Fredderic," Tyler snaps, sidling up beside us. I try to block him subtly with my shoulder and height, but he manages to catch Ro's eye easily even as he speaks only to me. "Good to know Ro's been so helpful to you. You know, we used to have a bet that you couldn't read." He laughs at this and shakes his head, like we're old buddies sharing in his hateful humor. "But my bet was better—I bet you'd fuck her first."

He doesn't drop his voice even a notch, so I know Carmen hears his words.

"Ro loves being hands-on with instruction, right, RoRo?" He

sneers, a flare of regret mixing with hatred in his eyes as he looks her over again. "But sleeping with a student? That's low, even for you."

"We aren't—" Her voice is shaky, eyes welling with tears that she does her best to hold back. If we weren't in the classroom of the one authority figure I know won't take my side, I'd knock him on his ass.

"Jealousy isn't a good look on you, Donaldson," I say before hardening my face to stone. "Leave her alone."

He pats me on the back and drops his voice to a quiet whisper. "You two might be perfect together. She's even more of a slut than you, Fredderic."

Ro shoves off the wall and darts past me to sprint from the room. It's deathly quiet for a moment before I peek over my shoulder at Carmen, who is carefully watching, even as she pretends to be busy with whatever papers lie in front of her.

"Don't talk to her again, asshole." My words are sharp edged and swift, loud enough that our beloved professor can intervene, but as long as I don't raise my fists, I know she won't. "I'm serious."

"Nice threat, but I'm not scared of you." Tyler shrugs, as though my words have no effect. "She and I are far from over."

"Wanna fucking bet?" I snap before storming out and breaking into a run, hoping to catch her.

I don't have to go far. Ro is standing by the restroom entrances, a hidden corner spot, with her head cradled in her hands.

"Rosalie," I breathe. Her head darts up, curls tumbling as she sucks in a hard breath and forces out a smile despite her reddened, watery eyes.

"Freddy, hey," she says, wiping her cheeks. "Did you have another question?"

It hurts, her deflection, but the boundary she's drawing is clear. We're not friends right now, or anything more—she's my tutor, my TA, and I'm the student. I can't comfort her, take her in my arms and hold her like I so desperately want to.

"No, I'm fine. But . . . I'm worried about you."

"I'm okay," she says. "Honestly, don't worry about me."

I nod, like it will make her feel better, shuffling my feet before adding, "If there's something bothering you, you can talk to me about it."

"I'm good." Her words are shaky at best, eyes darting around me. "I should go."

I nod, swallowing the sting of her unusually quick rejection.

"Okay. That's fine. I just want you to know I'm here, and I'm a good listener." I sound so much like Archer that my teeth ache and I quickly add a flirty, "At least when it comes to you."

Her eyes close tightly, squeezing back tears, and she clings desperately to the smile on her face.

"Good night, Freddy."

She's gone before I can say another word.

CHAPTER 27

Ro

"What next?"

I blush and toss my phone down before haphazardly grabbing it to click the screen off. Sadie eyes me strangely from where she's pouring herself a decaf coffee from our old Nespresso. It's ten o'clock at night, but I'm not tired, and I know Sadie wants to stay up with me. Even with how deeply tired I can tell that she is.

When she offered to have a girls' night with me at the cafe earlier, after I confessed to the official severance with Tyler, I was more thrilled than I let on. I've missed her—I've missed *this*. Movie nights and laughs and loud, ridiculous karaoke sessions. I've missed Sadie, but I would've been happy if her brothers were here, too. They're just as much a part of my Waterfell family as she is.

But this, just us, girl time, is filling my heart with pure joy.

"Hmm?" I ask, distracted by the image still assaulting my brain. I can turn the phone screen off and away as much as I want, but the image is stuck behind my eyes.

Matt Fredderic sent me a photo. Of himself. Shirtless. With a Hello Kitty tattoo on his pectoral. I've seen him shirtless now, but not slick-wet with sweat, the camera angled down toward a very suggestive V, only cut off by the thick hockey pants he's wearing. Somehow, *that* addition only made it hotter.

And now, I'm sweating.

"I asked whether you want me to tattoo your face now or later," Sadie deadpans. All I hear is *tattoo* and my face goes red as I picture Freddy again, the whisper of his fingers on my hip bone, his breath over my skin. The fading crown that's still there.

"Earth to Ro-row-row-your-boat?" Sadie laughs, sipping on her coffee noisily as she sits back on our makeshift pallet and turns the movie credits off. "Distracted much?"

"No," I say too hastily.

She flips through her Spotify playlists on the TV, finally selecting one appropriately called "BOYS SUCK," and letting ABBA's "Chiquitita" play over the speakers. I laugh and Sadie grins.

"Are you 'Chiquitita'-ing me?"

"That's not a word," Sadie argues. "But yes. I'll keep playing it louder until you tell me what happened with you and Tyler."

I shake my head, but my smile is too big to contain as she turns the volume up. "Liam is gonna be sad he missed this."

Instead of agreeing, Sadie takes her phone and films a clip of us sing-shouting the words and dancing, texting it to Oliver with a quick message to show it to Liam. And that she loves and misses them both. My heart clenches tight, a sliver of guilt forming because I know she's not with them only to keep me company.

"I'm really okay," I say, trying to convince her, and maybe myself. "He sucks and this should've happened a long time ago, honestly."

"I couldn't agree more."

I smile at her haughty attitude, now that she's finally allowed to show her distain for Tyler more openly. "You didn't have to stay with me tonight."

She turns the volume down and collapses beside me, our heads side by side.

"I need you sometimes, too, you know," she says quietly. "I know I'm not the best at it, but you're my best friend."

My eyes and nose burn sharply, but I shake my head.

"You're a great friend." Memories of her flash across my eyes, days when I've broken down over missing my parents, over Tyler's hot-and-cold behavior, over feeling like I'll never be enough. And no matter *what* was happening in her messy, chaotic life, she's always been there to hug me. To lift me up and tell me to be a badass. "You're my best friend, too."

Our hands find each other in the air over our heads, fingers winding together as her upbeat playlist continues to thump in the background.

"So . . . are we gonna talk about Rhys?" I watch her from the corner of my eye, seeing the emotions she's trying to stifle dance over her features. An almost giddy happiness at the mention of the hockey star, before a shuttering regret and pain. I don't want her to be sad. "Have you guys hooked up?"

"What? No."

"You swear you haven't had sex with him yet?"

I'm mostly teasing, because she's told me already that she hasn't actually done the deed with her hockey boy yet—which is surprising with the amount of time I hear suspicious noises coming from her side of the apartment, no matter the time of day.

"*He's really good with his mouth*," she'd said when I pestered her, and my full-body blush took a full day to fade. But even knowing how satisfied Rhys Koteskiy seems to be keeping Sadie, this isn't the norm for her.

Trying to pester her for more only ends with her sniping back at me with, "I thought *you* said no talking about boys." She waggles her eyebrows. "If that's back on the table, you need to tell me about the Student."

She asks about *the Student*—Freddy's name on my phone—because though she doesn't know who it is, she has seen me texting the mystery person with a too-wide smile several times at Brew Haven.

My back stiffens, but she laughs, mumbling sarcastically under her breath, before asking me about tutoring Freddy.

"It's fine. Easy."

"I'm surprised he needs a tutor. Isn't he sleeping with all his professors for good grades?" *Ouch.* "Or does he not have any female teachers to seduce this year?"

I want to chide her for the comments, but I feel unsure of *how* to do it. Instead, I settle on a quickly muttered, "Very funny," as my mind races over the words. It isn't the first time I've heard those kinds of rumors, but this is the first time it rips such a deep hurt through my heart. I feel protective of Freddy, as I always do, but there is a possessiveness there that I'm not ready to acknowledge.

But then Sadie's phone rings, and our night of peace takes a hard left turn.

• • •

Sadie's anxiety is palpable, even if she puts up a good front. We push through the throng of bodies, searching for Bennett Reiner, who is six foot six and broad framed, so it shouldn't be that hard.

The second Rhys's best friend called Sadie's phone, I could *see* how desperately she cares about the hockey boy she claims is only a "friend with benefits." She's on a rescue mission now, shoving through people much more aggressively than I am, despite her much shorter frame.

Music makes the walls thump and gooseflesh spreads across my very exposed skin. It's not like I haven't worn something so revealing before; more that there's a difference between my well-put-together "going out" outfits, and the blue and white silk shorts and tank pajama set I'm currently dressed in. Complete with a white ribbon tied through my thick, curly ponytail and the ridiculous white sneakers I slipped on without socks in our rush, I feel a little foolish.

And a lot out of place.

I see Tyler before Sadie does, tripping back a few steps subconsciously as his reddened brown eyes lock on mine. He shoves Sadie with his shoulder, and the back of my neck prickles as my fingers curl into fists.

If anyone can take care of themselves, it's Sadie. But I don't want her to have to—and especially not with this.

His attention never leaves me, almost like he doesn't know he bumped Sadie.

"Nice outfit, Ro," he snaps, his voice haughty and taunting.

I nearly flinch but manage to hold it back.

Stepping in front of Sadie, I send her off toward where I can see Bennett and Freddy hovering, though I avoid any eye contact with either of them, thankfully. I know she doesn't want to leave me here—with a drunk Tyler especially—but from her demeanor after the phone call, something is wrong.

And she can deny it all she wants, but she likes the hockey captain—*a lot*—so after my second reassurance, Sadie reluctantly goes.

"What are you doing here, Tyler?" I ask, not really caring but knowing if I don't talk to him now, he'll follow me around and possibly make a scene.

Sober Tyler would be mortified to make a scene, but *drunk* Tyler is always trying to start something. I stopped going out with our group from lab because he nearly got in a fight almost every night after one too many, and the pattern was exhausting. It was never fun, so that part of my college experience just stopped.

"Still throwing a tantrum, I see." Tyler smirks, eyes grazing my skin as his fingers reach out to tug and snap at the thin strap of my tank top. The silk has too much give, and I see his eyes dart down to see my bare chest beneath before I pull back and cross my arms.

"If you wanted my attention—"

My skin heats, eyes burning a little at the implication of his gaze and smirk.

"Stop it. I'm not doing this—"

"I said I was sorry," he slurs halfheartedly, tripping over his feet and crowding me into the wall, hard enough that his hip jostles the table to our left. I'm not short, and Tyler is only an inch taller than me, but he's suffocating this close. My skin is hot, the back of my neck sticky with anxiety and frustration that I have no release for.

"Actually, you didn't," I huff, tucking a few stray curls behind my reddened ears. "A-and it wouldn't even matter if you did. Now get away from me."

"Don't be ridiculous, Ro."

He reaches up and grips my face. The gesture isn't rough, but it's humiliating.

It's almost painful how he's the one making a scene, and yet I'm the one left feeling like a chastised child, embarrassed and trying not to cry.

"Stop it," I snarl. "Get off me."

I'm sure my voice is too quiet for anyone in the booming, darkened party atmosphere, but someone hears me because the heat of Tyler's body is gone the moment I close my eyes.

"What's going on here?"

Even though I want to sink into the ground out of pure embarrassment, I can't help the wave of calm that loosens my muscles at the sound of his voice alone.

I blink and Freddy is next to me, standing like a buffer so even if he's facing both Tyler and me, his shoulder is slightly angled to shield me.

Tyler doesn't turn his bloodshot gaze from me, but now he looks more unhinged, and my stomach sinks.

"Go away," Tyler spits.

Freddy clicks his tongue, still smiling, golden hair perfect, pale skin still somehow peachy like he just left the beach, his shirt open slightly so a sliver of his bare chest shows. He looks perfect yet again, and I feel more ridiculous.

"Nah," Freddy says. "I don't think I will."

And then his hand snaps out and grabs Tyler's chin, tugging hard so he has no choice but to look at the taller, stronger man holding him. His eyes try to dart back to mine, but Freddy jostles him again. Freddy's hand looks so big against Tyler's face that I worry he might break his jaw by accident.

"I'm not gonna ask again. We gonna have another problem, bud?"

Tyler looks on the verge of a furious outburst, but instead he tries to jerk his chin out of Freddy's grip again. This time he manages, but only because Freddy has let him go.

"Wasn't aware we had a first problem, Fredderic." Tyler clips the last name almost condescendingly. He seems to have sobered up, like the fear of possibly getting into a fight with a six-three hockey star might have chased away his buzz.

"Oh, we do." Freddy smirks, crossing his arms casually as his eyes flicker from me to Tyler and back. "About yea high," he says, tossing his hand up to gently pat the top of my head, careful to avoid my ponytail. "Curly hair." His hand dusts down to tug lightly at one of the curls loose around my face. "Usually wearing a bow." This one he says with a giggle—not mocking, but with pure joy as his hand skims over the silk ribbon in my hair. "And loves her sexy books."

Freddy whispers the last part, so low I don't think Tyler hears it, but I don't look at him to check. I'm too distracted by the heat of Matt Fredderic's gaze on my lips, my cheeks flushing deeply under his attention.

And for now it doesn't matter if this is part of some macho stand-off. Freddy's attention feels good.

The moment seems to lengthen and grow between us, until I'm sure we've been staring at each other for far too long. Someone clears their throat. Tyler, I realize, who I'd almost forgotten was still here while I got lost in the deep green of Freddy's eyes.

Freddy scowls as he looks back over at Tyler, stepping fully in front of me.

"And it all revolves around *you* treating her like fucking shit."

For a moment, Tyler looks furious. But I watch with my stomach churning as his face slowly morphs from rage into absolute delight.

"Holy shit," Tyler says, still smiling like he's won the lottery. He flicks a finger between Freddy and me. "I mean, I knew you were dirty, Ro, but really? *This* is what you want? I guess I was right to make that bet after all. I wonder what Dr. Tinley would think—"

As Tyler speaks, I see every muscle in Freddy freeze, pure fury bleeding over his usually happy and mischievous expression. It's almost frightening how quickly his mood shifts, and something in my head screams out *wrong, wrong, wrong.*

Freddy shoots forward to grab Tyler by the collar.

"Shut the fuck up," Freddy snaps, jerking my ex-boyfriend to slam him against the wall.

"Freddy." My voice is sharper than I mean it to be, but my heart is racing and everyone in the foyer and living room now has their attention on us. "Leave it."

Freddy shuts his eyes for a second, releasing his hold on Tyler.

"Taking a ride on the school slut to make me jealous, Ro?" Tyler snaps at me again. I can't help it, but I flinch and move back, hitting the table and knocking myself into Freddy's side.

It's like Tyler knows his best shot at hurting Freddy is through me.

And it seems to be working.

"Aww, Donaldson." Freddy smiles, his entire persona blending into a mix of the previous fury and his usual mischief. "Worried the school slut can actually make your girl come?"

"Freddy!" I try to shout, but my throat is suddenly tight, like I can't breathe, so it comes out hoarse and pathetic.

Freddy turns his body toward me, eyes scanning my face as if the impact of what he's said starts to wash over him. Regret fills his eyes, and he shuts them tight. "Rosalie, wait. I'm sor—"

It happens too fast for me to shout the warning, Tyler's hand snapping out to sucker punch Freddy in the mouth.

Tyler stumbles back, almost knocking into me because I'm still so close to them. Fury darkens Freddy's gaze as he looks toward someone in the crowd.

"Get her the fuck out of here," Freddy snaps, pointing at me. Arms wrap around my waist, an apology whispered in my ear before someone pulls me back into the crowd.

But as soon as I'm a safe distance away, Freddy's eyes shine with excitement as he spins on Tyler, his mouth still dripping with blood as he wipes it away with a smile.

"Been waiting to do this for years."

Years? Why would Freddy—

Freddy grabs the collar of Tyler's shirt again, a move I've seen in every hockey fighting video I've ever secretly watched, dazed at the startling brutality. His fist hits hard against Tyler's jaw, head smacking back against the wall before Tyler tries to swing back at Freddy—missing.

Tyler isn't a fighter. I know from the number of times I've dragged him out of a bar for starting something he never can finish, so I know that if I don't stop them, it's going to be a bloodbath.

I look up and see Holden behind me. I don't know him, but I know he's on the team, so I ask him, "Where's Bennett?"

"Haven't seen him in a while. You okay?"

"Yeah." I barely have the word out of my mouth before I'm slipping around him and pushing through bodies for the one person I know can stop this.

CHAPTER 28

Freddy

God, it feels fucking good to finally hit Tyler Donaldson.

Partially because he's tormented me for years with his asshole comments during our previous tutoring sessions. But mostly because of the look on Ro's face I've seen one too many times.

If I get even slightly tired or distracted, my brain tosses up the image of her, crying, red eyes and butterfly clips halfway pulled out of her hair, with another image of her waiting in the cold because he fucking *abandoned* her in a random town an hour from home.

And it hadn't been the first time.

It's almost too easy to conjure the mental images of other times he'd left her stranded, alone, and without me to guide her back.

I throw my entire body into the next one, unashamedly proud of the blood that starts to trickle across my fist.

Glancing over to where Ro should be, I realize she's gone. Holden is still there, but he just shrugs at me.

"Sad you can't show off your muscles for her now?" Tyler snaps.

He's a talkative fighter, but I love to chirp, so I smile.

"I'm sure you're happy she's *not* watching me kick your ass right now." I land another hit to his side, hearing the air gush out of him as he stumbles back. "Besides, I think I'll be the one she's going to be taking care of after this."

Two thick arms wrap around my chest, yanking back my arms with enough force it makes me wince. At the same time, I see Holden jerk Tyler back by his collar, which is now stretched ridiculously from the beating he's taken tonight. He doesn't fight Holden. Clearly, he's lost, and he doesn't *want* to keep fighting me.

But he won't. Shut. Up.

"You good?"

It's Bennett, I realize, holding me back, and I nod, trying to relax so he'll release me. Especially when I see Ro heading toward me, her expression a mix of concern and restrained anger. Like she wants to hit me, but then nurse me back to health.

I'd happily let her do either.

"Are you okay?" she asks.

"I'm fine, princess," I answer immediately, and Bennett drops my arms, grumbling something under his breath as he steps back.

Holden starts to walk Tyler out the door, but not quickly enough as the little idiot turns around to us and spits out, "Better add 'Get an STD' to that stupid sex bucket list of yours."

Ro's face drains of color. I want to tell her that I saw the list, that it's nothing to be ashamed of—but she's embarrassed, clearly upset. And that's more than enough for me.

But I also want to hit him again, so I snap forward. Bennett is surprisingly quicker for all his size, jerking me back.

"Stop," he commands, quiet and steady. "Holden, get him the hell out of here."

Holden does as he's told, but Ro still looks borderline ill.

Wrapping my arm around her shoulder doesn't seem to shake her. Even as she patiently cleans up my blood from the one or two hits Tyler managed to get in, she barely breathes, eyes distant.

By the time we emerge from the bathroom together, Bennett looks distressed.

"Go home. Make sure Rhys drinks some water before you

leave him in his room. I'll be there soon to deal with it," Bennett snaps. As if handling the sad, drunken Rhys situation and breaking up a fight in the living room wasn't enough, I can see something else has clearly happened to fray the edges of his careful control.

But I'm too worried about Ro to ask, so I nod and take her hand as we go down the back staircase and outside, rounding the house toward Sadie's car parked down the street.

We're barely past the yard before I try to stop Ro.

"Princess," I say, but she doesn't even pause her stride. "Hey, Ro, wait."

Coming to a sudden stop with my hand wrapped around her wrist, she looks up at me, eyes glassy.

"You don't need to be embarrassed about whatever he was talking about." *Real subtle, Fredderic.* "You can talk to me about it. I'm not—I want to know."

It's not the right thing to say, but I can't stop thinking about it. I can't stop wishing I knew his address to add a few more injuries to the count for making Ro feel like this.

"Just drop it, Freddy," she sighs, tugging her hand away.

It makes me feel alone, that trickle of abandonment playing at the edges of my mind. I try to shove the voices back, already trying to tell me what a *pathetic idiot* I am. *A whore. A brute.*

"Rosalie—"

"I said I don't want to talk about it, Matt," she snaps, and I almost flinch. "Especially not with you."

Her words might as well be fucking knives for how they land. Swift kicks to the stomach would be preferable.

But instead of letting any of it show, I nod and slip a tiny smile onto my face as we walk to the car.

The ride is silent.

Even Sadie doesn't play any music.

• • •

I wasn't expecting a text back from Ro—I even thought she might dump me off on another tutor after my display last night. So her last-minute agreement to meet up with me at Brew Haven has me jumping out of bed and throwing on a hoodie and sweatpants lightning fast.

Thankfully, I woke as early as Bennett, surprisingly—early enough to hear the whispered conversation in the hallway and wait until the front door closed to make my entrance.

"You're up early."

It's more of an inquiry than it is a true statement, because Bennett is *always* up early. He looks upset, but nods while continuing to stare at the front door like he's trying to make some sort of decision.

"Didn't know you even came home last night, let alone with a houseguest," I say, sliding on my shoes by the door, carefully tying the white laces. Even now, nearly two months later, it's hard to erase the memory of that string weaving around Ro's hair, looping the lace and the feel of the frizzy curls against my palms.

The overly loud clearing of my throat seems to shake Bennett as he finally turns to face me. He's in long sleep pants, shirtless, and his chest is heaving slightly . . . like he's holding back panicked breaths.

"You okay?"

"Fine," he mutters before stomping up the stairs and heading to Rhys's room to knock loudly. There's a muffled groan through the door—sounds like a hungover Rhys—before Bennett shouts, "We need to fucking talk."

And I think that's my cue.

It's getting cold faster now. You'd think after nearly four years in the northeast I'd be used to the temperature drop, but I'm shivering by the time I duck into Brew Haven after parking down the block—

with it being a dreary Saturday morning, the coffeehouse is busy enough that the small back parking lot is full.

Suki Waterhouse plays softly over the old overhead speakers, "Good Looking" making the scene almost dreamy with the cloudy mist outside. The line for the counter is long enough that I would leave were it any normal day.

But Ro is there, shining and bright against the mahogany booths on the left side. The tawny skin not covered in her oversized cobalt-blue hoodie is warm and beautiful. Her hair is a mass of curls piled into a scrunchie on her head, some falling loosely around her face.

When I picture Ro in my head, which is becoming a more common occurrence lately, she's always like this, soft and comfortable—except her hair is tied with my shoelace. And even more, she's holding me—

Stop.

I nearly trip in my stride to her before shaking the precarious thoughts from my head like she can hear them. She's so brilliant it wouldn't really surprise me if she *could* read minds, especially mine.

But, no, she's still smiling shyly up at me as I stand awkwardly by the booth for a beat too long.

"Morning," she says quietly, tucking her hair back behind her ear, even as it immediately falls back into her face. "Thanks for meeting me."

"Thanks for inviting me," I reply, voice matching hers in softness as I settle my body back against the wood. My knee is already bouncing too rapidly, so I keep my hands off the table so I don't shake the entire thing.

"I made you a coffee—I think I got your order right."

I think I'd drink rotten milk if she made it for me.

"Thanks, Rosalie," I breathe, basking slightly in the flush hearing me say her full name brings to her cheeks.

There's only a beat of silence, before—

"I'm so sorry—"

"I'm sorry—"

Both of us speak at the same time before stopping in unison to let the other speak. And then, nothing but laughter, giggles from her and soft chuckles from me. The sounds settle some raucous thing in my gut.

"You first," she says.

I'm happy to oblige.

"I'm sorry about last night. I just . . . I got a bit carried away with Donaldson. Not just because of you, Ro. He's been a jerk to me for years—you . . ." I trail off, trying to figure out the best way to say it without scaring her off. "I care about you. And he was being an ass-hole. He's *been* an asshole to you all semester."

"Yeah, he has." She shrugs with a little self-deprecating smile that makes my chest hurt and hands tighten into near fists atop my thighs. "But it's okay. Thank you, actually, for defending me. I'm sorry I didn't—"

She cuts herself off suddenly with a shake of her head.

"What?"

Ro leans forward on her elbows, and I match her posture. Even tucked into the booth, a private corner, she wants this to be quieter.

"Tyler was using something private against me, and he was being mean to you, too. And I just . . . I realize how naive I was being. I was upset and I took it out on you last night, so I'm sorry, too. Are we friends again?"

I smile, heart too full of the goodness of this moment. "Were we ever *not* friends, Ro? C'mon—I don't scare that easily."

She laughs, and it feels like she's stitching together pieces of me I didn't know were torn—the parts shredded by my insecurities with friendship and mistakes and *not being fucking good enough for any of it.*

We talk quietly for what feels like minutes, but it's actually hours before she heads back into the kitchen and returns with a full breakfast spread of her favorites for me to try.

We're only halfway through our shared meal when I realize my cheeks hurt from smiling so much, and not one of them has been for show.

Just like everything else when it comes to Ro, it's so *real*.

After we finish eating and the cafe is mostly cleared out, she orders us another drink from the girls behind the counter—Sadie isn't here today, otherwise I'm betting she wouldn't have met me here since our connection, our *friendship*, is still somewhat secret.

But I don't mind it. It feels like for now, it's just ours. Nothing our friends can taint as long as it's just ours. They're all so busy, too wrapped up in their own dramas to pay any real attention to us anyway.

She's still laughing at the story I've just told her—involving costumes from the sophomore year Halloween party and an accidentally naked drunk Bennett, who had to sprint to the bathroom covering himself with a torn toga, ass on display—when I finally work up the nerve to ask her about Tyler.

"So . . . can I ask about Donaldson? You guys still together or—"

"No." She cuts me off, emphatically.

"He broke up with you and he's being mean to you about it? Why?" As soon as I ask, I shake my head and put my hands up like a surrender. "You don't need to answer that. Just . . . let me know if I can help, like, get him off your back or something. If he's bothering you and you want my help, I could keep him away from you. Like, maybe play up the flirting with you? Or threaten him? Sic one of the guys on the team on him. Or multiple—"

I'm rambling but I can't seem to stop, so instead I take one of the forks and swirl it in the leftover sauce, drawing an infinity symbol and tracing it over and over.

"Actually . . . yeah. Tyler is bothering me. He's—" She stops, biting her lip and shaking her head a little so the springy curls surrounding her heart-shaped face sway. "He already thinks we are sleeping to-gether." She barely manages to say the words with a deep blush. "So, maybe you could . . . I, um . . ."

She looks at me pleadingly, as if begging me to fill in the gaps here.

"Sooo." I drag out the word, leaning on my forearms on the table. "You want me to . . . ?"

Even though I think I know what she's hinting at, I won't say it for her. *She has to be the one to ask.*

"Not, like, go out of your way. But maybe, at least before or after class, you could just flirt with me. Like you usually do, but—"

"Like, kiss you?" I say a little too excitedly.

Her nose wrinkles like what I've said disgusts her, and for some reason the reaction makes me laugh.

"No, Tyler knows I don't move that fast."

"That fast?" I ask, smirking. "Are you a virgin?"

"No!" she nearly shouts before glancing around as if anyone could hear us in our secluded spot. She wraps her arms around her-self protectively even as she lengthens her spine and neck haughtily. A contradiction of anxiety and bravery that I can't quite figure out. The silence hangs heavily between us before she slumps and bites down on her lip.

"Why?" she asks, her voice softer, quieter than it was before. "Do I seem like a virgin?"

I have to hold my breath to keep from laughing because her ex-pression is devastatingly serious.

"I'm not a baby."

My eyes widen, hips hitting the table hard as I scramble unco-ordinatedly to stand, my hands gently grasping her upper arms. Gentle, yes, but enough to get her attention. Because her expression and the tone of her voice are hurt.

"Ro, no. I didn't mean it to sound that way."

She shakes her head. "No, it's fine. I mean—I'm not. I've had sex. With Tyler."

I am unfortunately aware of that, as per my snooping. But I'd rather not hear another word about it. My hand shoots up between us as I settle back into my seat. "Please, spare me the details."

At least when it comes to Tyler Donaldson. Inadvertently, I have thought about what she might be like beneath the right touches. How quickly she'd break apart under my hands, tawny skin flushing red, hazel eyes sparkling.

Stop. Stop. Stop.

She's your friend.

"So, what exactly do you want me to do?"

CHAPTER 29

Ro

Tyler doesn't show up to class on Monday or Wednesday, finally coming back on Friday after claiming to be sick with a stomach bug.

Mostly to hide the bruising from getting his ass kicked by Freddy.

My nerves bubble to a boiling point as he enters the classroom and greets our other TAs—his friends, not mine, I am quickly reminded—before he turns toward where I'm stacking quiz sheets.

"Ro," Tyler says, crowding into my space a little. This close I can see the yellow fading on his face, a small cut line on his lip. It nearly makes me smile.

I could greet him, make nice, and then politely ignore him. But even acknowledging him feels dangerous considering how many times that's led me right back into his hold.

"Little too close, Donaldson."

Turns out, I don't need to make a decision, as Freddy reaches from behind me to press a hand to Tyler's shoulder and push him back.

His false bravado takes over quickly, but I don't miss the slight flinch from my ex-boyfriend.

"Just talking, Fredderic."

I take a step backward, not realizing how close Freddy is standing behind me until my shoulder is pressing into the warmth of his chest.

"I'd rather you not be so close when you talk to my girl." His arm comes up to circle my shoulders, fingers gently tracing my exposed collarbone in maddeningly light strokes.

I'd said no kissing because I truly didn't think I could handle it—handle *him*. But this is somehow even worse. My skin feels hot, my oversized, off-the-shoulder sweater somehow suddenly too warm.

Tyler laughs a little, but his brow furrows in a way that has me pressing myself farther into Matt's arms, and his other hand finds my hip to stabilize my too-rapid movement.

"Like I said," Tyler says with a sneer. "Excellent choice, Ro. He will *absolutely* be able to check off everything you wanted—let me know when you're done playing around."

It's not the dig at myself that has me ready to snap—it's a foreign sensation of protectiveness toward Matt. A defensiveness I've never felt once in the face of Sadie's scathing comments about Tyler.

"Hey," Freddy whispers, turning me toward him and settling his heavy palms on both my shoulders. "You okay, princess?"

"Yeah." I nod, resisting the urge to peek over my shoulder and see how Tyler might be reacting.

Students are filing in, and it feels a bit like every eye in the room is trained on the touch of Matt's hands to my bare skin.

Specifically, Dr. Tinley's eye. She clears her throat to catch our attention and the classroom's. "I have a no-PDA rule, Ro. Your behavior is inappropriate."

My stomach sinks, but Freddy curtails it all with a curt nod over my shoulder to her.

"It's my fault," he says. "I'll try to control myself." He looks at Dr. Tinley again, brow furrowed, before pressing a quick kiss to my forehead with a dazzling smile that nearly makes me melt into a puddle, then quickly sliding up the slipping fabric of my sweater to cover my shoulder a little more before turning to find his seat.

But the Matt Fredderic Effect doesn't wear off after class ends. Tyler doesn't bother me all day.

· · ·

The slam of the apartment door startles me enough that the spoon in my mouth drops and clatters to the floor, the sound muffled by the pitter-patter of feet signaling Sadie's brothers are here.

I walk out of my room, smiling and quickly greeting Liam with a hug and Oliver with a wave as they head to her bedroom, toting their shared hockey bag.

"Showers and bed," Sadie says before shouting a quick "And brush your teeth" after them as they run along.

She looks . . . haggard. Beautiful, in the way Sadie is always beautiful, fierce and unflinching, but she's rubbing her hands over her eyes like she hasn't slept in a week.

"Hey." I greet her gently, placing the spoon in the sink and replacing it with two from the drawer to offer her some of the ice cream I'm holding.

"Hey," she replies, kicking her shoes off and pulling her slicked-back bun down, combing it harshly with her fingers. I want to offer to brush it out for her, to sit her in one of the chairs and take my time smoothing out the tangles so the stress lines marring her face disappear.

"Everything okay, Sadie?"

She heaves in a deep breath, stopping at the corner of our cozy kitchen breakfast nook and shaking her head.

"Honestly, I don't wanna talk about it."

"Oh, yeah. Totally understand."

Actually, *I don't*. I hate it. Anxiety swirls as I try to think over every conversation we've had in the past week—maybe even the past month. Is it possible I've done something to upset her? Something that would make her *not* want to talk to me about whatever is bothering her?

The urge to apologize is nearly too strong to bite back, but I manage to strangle it in my throat and only nod with a too-bright, too-fake smile.

She turns for her bedroom without another word, while I call after her with a "Good night."

The apartment feels empty, despite it being overly full, as I pad back into my room.

My phone vibrates and the shock of it is enough that I nearly drop it.

MOMMA
How is my girl? Resting well?

The sight of her text has me closing my eyes and imagining her arms wrapped around me, my head tucked into her shoulder while she scratches her nails lightly up and down my arm to soothe me.

For a moment, I consider calling her and telling her everything I'm feeling—how worried I am over Sadie, the fear I feel every time my phone rings, the complicated feelings I have for Matt—but the second tears start to well in my eyes as I consider what I might say, I toss my phone into a drawer and slam it shut.

My mom and dad are everything good in my life. They don't deserve my complaints—they deserve my success for how hard they've worked to get us through the last seven years.

So I swallow it all down—a healthy dose of *is she mad at me* followed by a scoop of homesickness and heartbreak, the fear that nothing will ever be *good* again—and turn on my sewing machine.

It's past midnight by the time I stop, a pile of reworked clothes scattered across my floor like a fashion major's project threw up in here, but the tie is on top. Navy blue with the Waterfell Wolves logo patched into the end, and white letters embroidered on the back.

When I check my phone again, there are twenty-five missed calls from two unknown numbers and my stomach sinks. I delete the notifications and slam my phone back into my drawer for the night, because even *thinking* about what to do with that problem makes my temples pulse with an oncoming headache.

I force myself to study my actual major classes for an hour before falling asleep atop my comforter with a hardback textbook as a pillow.

CHAPTER 30

Freddy

My knee is bouncing so rapidly I'm worried I'm gonna pull something before our away game this weekend, but the flurry of emotions is too high.

A fucking mandatory adviser meeting, with my math professor, like they've been invited to sit front row at my shame fest. All because I failed another test.

My mom stands in front of me like a warrior, barking words I don't understand at my principal and the mean teacher who doesn't like me.

I wait quietly, kicking my feet back and forth to keep from getting "spinny." That's what my mom calls it when my brain starts to go too fast and I can't stay present or listen well.

Coach Ace's car idles in front of the school, and he gives me a quick smile and buckles me in the back before getting in to drive us.

"He's only in third grade," he says to my mom, his hand grabbing hers. "It'll be okay."

"Archer, you should've heard the way they spoke about him, with him right there."

They keep talking—hushed whispers that I can barely make out, but that one word they keep saying is confusing, so I finally ask, "What's discount-ca-lala?"

Mom turns in her seat to face me. Her nails—green with white smiley faces and cool patterns—dig into the leather as she gives me a soft smile.

"Dyscalculia," she says before giggling a little. "It's a hard word, huh?"

"Very hard," Coach Ace says. "I don't think I can say it, either, Matty."

I laugh a little with them and smile. "What's it mean?"

"You just have trouble with numbers sometimes, bud. Not a big deal, but it's good to know so we can make things easier now."

My mom nods in agreement with him. "Right, Matty."

I can't help bouncing my knee a little again. "But . . . I'm not good with words. I thought the numbers would be easier."

We're stopping, I realize, in front of my mom's house. She unbuckles her seat belt and opens the door before the car has completely stopped—which I'm pretty sure is a big no-no, especially considering the bad word Coach Ace nearly shouts when he throws the car into park so hard I jerk against my seat belt.

My door opens, my mom's beautiful face filling my vision.

"You are so smart, Matty, okay? Just because words and numbers might be hard doesn't mean you can't do it. You can do anything, *understand? I need you to tell me you understand."*

She looks like she might cry—and I hate when mom cries, so I nod. "I understand, Mom. Promise."

I unbuckle myself just in time for her to grab me in a tight hug and kiss the top of my head. Coach Ace joins our hug for a moment before backing up so my mom can put me down and hold my hand to walk inside.

"Don't do that again, Els," I hear him whisper to my mom. "You nearly gave me a heart attack."

But my mom's not paying attention, only looking at me with a bright, wonder-filled smile. "No matter what, I'm so, so proud of you, Matty."

"Matthew?"

I shake my head, focusing on the man in front of me—my adviser, though I can't remember his name.

My feet shuffle back and forth, the toe of my sneaker lightly kicking at the table leg over and over as I try not to bounce my knee.

Focus. They asked you a question.

"Is it just math, then?" he asks, but his tone tells me he's already asked it. My cheeks heat.

"Failing? Yeah—I think—"

Someone knocks at the door before opening it and letting themselves in.

My professors, specifically Dr. Cipher, followed by a living nightmare.

"Dr. Tinley," my adviser says, surprise evident in his voice. "I didn't realize you'd be joining us today."

Carmen smiles, tucking her short, wine-red hair back behind her ears and shaking his outstretched hand.

"I just got Freddy's weighted grades finished to estimate his semester average, so when I saw the email, I figured I'd pop by."

Pop by. Sure.

Fists clenched at my sides, I eye both teachers as they settle across from me at the conference room table.

"I thought this was math-specific," I manage to spit out, but my tone is gruff enough that it seems to land like a hit to Carmen. "I'm passing biology. She doesn't need to be here."

There's a tension in the room now, and I immediately regret my words and the attention they might bring. But my desire for her *not* to be here is remarkably greater than something unsavory being discovered about her student relationships.

"Freddy," she says, clearing her throat and sitting up a little straighter in her sharp blazer. "I'm not here for negative reasons. If anything, I'm here as an advocate."

Yeah. And I'm a Nobel Prize–winning physicist. Biting back the disbelieving laugh is a physical feat.

"Whatever." I shrug, leaning forward but bouncing my knee a little harder underneath the table to push the energy swirling in my body *somewhere*, because there's nothing on this table I can fiddle with. "Let's get this over with."

Dr. Cipher clears his throat and carefully passes out the papers in his folder, photocopies of my last two failed tests. Carmen busies herself with picking at her nails, but out of the corner of my eye I clock her concerned gaze running over my test and then over my face.

It feels like nails scratching my skin there, and I close my eyes to heave a breath.

"As of now, Mr. Fredderic is going to fail again," Dr. Cipher says plainly. He's been an asshole all semester, and I'm pretty sure he's never once bothered to glance at my file—considering I haven't gotten a minute of extra time on anything.

Not that the extra time would help. Even with my mom and Archer's help, I'd barely scraped by to graduate from high school. Now . . . I look around the room again.

Now that I'm alone, there's no way I'm going to manage even that.

Someone knocks on the door, loud and impatient, interrupting whatever Dr. Cipher was in the middle of saying.

My adviser looks around and finally heads to open the door, seeming miffed at the interruption. Even more so when he opens it to reveal the odd couple in the doorway.

Coach Harris, stern-faced, arms crossed. And in front of him, dressed in an agglomeration of light green like it's the first week of spring and not the middle of October, is Ro.

Ro with hair braided half up, her signature ribbon high on the top of her head, springy curls like a halo around her face—also stern, matching my coach like an intimidation tactic.

"We're in the middle of a meeting—"

"I think we are supposed to be part of it, Mr. Hibberd." *Right*—now I remember his name. She pushes lightly on the door, letting herself inside the room without his permission, missing the glare Coach Harris sends the man on her behalf.

"Ms. Shariff, I believe I told you in my email that your presence was unnecessary for today."

Ms. Shariff. The name makes me smile, but pride bleeds in. Her sweatshirt has a little kitten playing with a ball of green yarn that matches the color of her linen pants that look a little like pajama bottoms. She's dressed exactly like herself, and *still* holding her own against a bunch of stuffy collegiate assholes.

A little absurdly, I want to take a picture. Maybe send it to Tyler with the words *fuck you.*

Ro surveys the room briefly, her composure only cracking for a quick wink my way as she settles at my side before placing a thick binder on the table.

Coach Harris pats and squeezes my shoulder as he comes to stand on my other side.

"You did. However, as per school policy, considering Mr. Frederic is a student athlete here on an athletics scholarship, his coach is *encouraged* to attend, if not often required. I am also his school-assigned tutor for the semester, and therefore should also be in attendance."

Mr. Hibberd seems frustrated, which nearly makes me smile.

Ro hands out the packets she's got in her folder. They're highlighted and tabbed, I realize as she hands me a copy as well.

Carmen gives her a smile, but it looks a little forced. Ro doesn't seem to notice—or if she does, she doesn't care. And somehow, that makes me feel even better.

I'm not spinning anymore. There's a peace in knowing Coach has my back, in knowing Ro's here in *defense* of me.

"Matt Fredderic has documentation for his ADHD, dyslexia, and dyscalculia. I have been tutoring for four years now here at Waterfell, specifically with ADHD and dyslexia students, but this is my first student with dyscalculia."

She flips the page and everyone in the room follows her direction.

"I have logs of his tutoring assistance dating back to freshman year. He has managed to stay within eligibility for three years now, failing only two classes, one of which he is in the midst of retaking—and succeeding in." Ro gestures to Carmen Tinley quickly, who nods slightly and relaxes back in her chair, I'm sure admiring Ro in the way I am, too.

Mr. Hibberd gruffly cuts in. "We are aware of his success in biology, Ms. Shariff, but that isn't the concern. Mr. Fredderic is failing his singular math credit."

"He's a communications major."

Mr. Hibberd's brow wrinkles. "So?"

"So? What are we torturing him for?" She flips through to another page, tabbed with purple sticky notes on everyone's packets. "These are ten cases of comparable students who substituted a critical thinking course for mathematics in cases of dyscalculia. I think this is not only a viable option for Matt, but I believe it is the *only* option this school can offer without bringing an internal investigation in the handling of learning differences and accommodations that have not been reported, nor offered, in this case."

The entire room stretches in the silence, while my joy feels almost tangible.

No one, since my mother, has defended me so fiercely.

I think I'm in love with her—not even romantically, but on some soul level. I feel devoted to her.

When no one speaks, Ro clears her throat and stands up again, only to hand out another, single sheet, this one on online critical thinking courses offered and their costs for the school.

"Matt is a brilliant, talented student. When offered the correct accommodations, he thrives. It would be quite disappointing to see this school fail him in this."

She smiles at me again, squeezing my shoulder with her delicate, slender fingers. I have to resist the urge to grab her in a hug and spin her around the room.

·   ·   ·

I'm walking on clouds as we leave the conference room, registration number for my new replacement course clenched in my hand as I follow a stomping Ro like a lost puppy.

"Ridiculous," she mutters. "The way they treat you is absurd. Have they been like that to you the entire time?"

She doesn't wait for my answer before continuing to stomp across the green, wind pulling some of her curls free until she looks a little more haphazard, softer, and I can't stop staring at her.

"Accusing you of not applying yourself? God—I'm insulted *for* you. To fight me on that? They don't know *anything* about you."

Ro swings back toward me, finger wagging toward my face. "Don't listen to a single thing they said. You're so smart and kind and I'm proud of you, so . . . So screw them! You're better than all of them anyway, Matty. Smarter, too."

I should laugh, but I can't breathe.

Matty. It pours over my skin like warmth and comfort. Home.

My entire soul feels like it's fracturing, and she has no clue, still stomping across the parking lot toward what I now realize is her car. And I'm still following her.

"Sorry, I'm just." She growls a little and shakes her head. "I'm done. I swear."

"You can keep going," I stammer. "I like you angry for me."

She grins and laughs a little, breathing in deeply and out slowly as if to calm herself down.

"I am. Very angry for you. But I know you've got a practice to get to and I made you something."

She opens her car door and reaches in for a little gift bag, handing it to me shyly.

"It's silly, but I wanted to make you something for your first away game this weekend and the official start of your last season. So . . ." She shrugs again, all the fire from earlier seeming to bleed away into self-consciousness.

That has me ripping into the bag faster, pulling out a length of silky blue fabric. It's a tie, embroidered with the Wolves' logo and my number in pretty cursive with a star.

"A star?"

"You're gonna play for Dallas, right? I felt like it would be good luck. It's—"

"It's the best gift I've ever gotten. Ever, Rosalie." I crush her into my chest without hesitation, kissing the top of her head and laying my cheek there as I rock us back and forth. "Thank you."

CHAPTER 31

Freddy

It's actually been awhile since I've done something this impulsive. But after yesterday's meeting—and the gift I'd carried like a precious jewel into my room later that evening, tracing and retracing the embroidery—I want to do something for her.

So I've found the perfect place to take her today. Granted, asking her for her schedule or if she's even free ahead of time might have been a better option, but after finding out how close the store was, I could barely sleep from the bubbling excitement.

I park outside her dorm and try calling her, but it goes straight to voicemail.

My brow furrows as I opt for a text.

FREDDY
Can you come outside for a minute?

I add a few emojis, until it looks minorly ridiculous. Her phone is on Do Not Disturb, but once she reads the text, the notification disappears and she's typing.

PRINCESS
Are you at Millay right now?!?!?!

It's her voice in my head as I read the text slowly. Her typing continues for a long moment, arguably too long for me, before a voice note comes through.

We often send each other voice notes instead of texts—she started it, but I adore them just as much. Not only is it easier for me, faster when I'm in a rush, but I've become quite addicted to the sound of her voice.

A few times—when I've had to go away for the whole weekend or miss a tutoring session for a two-a-day practice, and especially when studying for an upcoming exam—she sends me audio files to go over the missed topics. I'm sure the guys on the team bus think music is thumping through my ears. But it's the voice of my favorite girl in the world.

"Heyyy," she says, dragging out the word, sounding like her mouth is full as she steps away from the phone and back. "I figure this is easier—but what are you doing outside the dorms? You finished practice, like"—she pauses—"less than ten minutes ago. That's crazy."

A little giggle and then, "Anyway, I'm coming down. Let me just find my pants. Okay, be right there!"

There's some rustling before the recording ends and I'm beaming, blushing a little from the unbidden image of Ro without pants—which I shake my head to clear.

Just in time, it seems, to spot a girl in a pretty lavender sweatshirt and pleated white tennis skirt skipping and scurrying down the steps of Millay to my idling car with the hazards on at the curb.

The same curb I dropped her off on the night she doesn't remember.

I think you'd be really easy to love.

She stops at my rolled-down passenger-side window, leaning into it as she pops up on her toes and smiles at me.

"I couldn't find pants," she blurts before biting her lip and shaking her head like that wasn't what she planned to say.

"I can see that," I say, shifting in my seat. "Ready to go?"

Her hazel eyes widen. "Do I need to bring anything?"

"Just yourself. Hop in, Ro. We've got places to be."

She acquiesces easily, pulling open the creaking door and sliding into the seat.

She doesn't ask where we are going, just hooks up her phone to the aux cable like she's comfortable here with me. Like she's done this a million times, and settles back against the headrest while "Dizzy on the Comedown" by Turnover plays as I keep the windows rolled down and pull away from the curb.

· · ·

Ro can't get a word out, frozen in shock, while I watch her with a grin so big it hurts.

"We can go in whenever you're ready."

"How did you even find this?" Her voice is whisper soft, even though it's just us and the car radio still playing music off her phone as it has for the hour-long drive. She didn't question me once, no *Where are we going?* She didn't even ask for a hint. Her trust is exhilarating.

I shrug. "I did some digging." *I spent all night searching for something to even slightly show my appreciation for what you've done for me.* "I thought you'd like it."

Eyes wide, she's still staring at the faded yellow building smooshed between plain redbrick storefronts. The awning is green and white striped, with an old pink sign that reads In a Clinch. Painted across the window are the words Sweet, Spicy & Vintage Bodice Ripper Romance.

Ro stumbles a little into the front door, and I grab the loose brass handle to open it for her. The smell of old books mixes lightly with faint hints of tea, coffee, and butter from the little cafe nestled in the back.

I know it's there because I called the owner.

Shockingly, the In a Clinch bookstore has little online presence. Opal is the store's owner, whose number I found on a nearly empty business page after hunting it down. She was kind and sweet answering all my questions, offering more than enough information to know that making the drive with Ro would be worth it.

Just Ro's reaction on seeing the little bookstore is enough to feed me for a lifetime.

Her fingers drift across the plastic-wrapped special editions displayed by the door, violin music playing overhead. She eyes a few signed editions up front before wandering toward the used books on the far wall.

"Hey, Ro," I say, snagging her attention. "There's a cafe in the back. I'm going to get us a coffee and chai if they have it, okay? Take your time looking around."

Ro nods distractedly as her eyes continue to flicker around the room.

I find Opal in the back, a white-haired woman dressed in floral pastels with a gentle demeanor. We talk quietly, desperate to preserve the dreamy quality of Ro's time.

Once Ro finishes—a large stack of books balanced in her hands—she joins us. Opal gushes over her choices, book by book, before offering a few suggestions of her own. They're entranced by each other.

"Did you make this place?" Ro asks, complimenting her on every little detail. Opal smiles and shakes her head, grabbing a picture frame off the checkout counter and setting it between us.

"Sue," she says, and points to the tall redheaded woman in the picture wearing bright burgundy lipstick. "She built this place for me. Her parents left it for her as a little cafe, a soda shop. We both loved to read, both loved romances. So when I moved away to New York to try and become a writer, she turned it into a bookstore. When my book finally came out, it flopped. But it was nearly a best-seller here, because of her.

"I moved back home and we got a cottage together. I kept writing and she kept expanding the store. It didn't really flourish, but . . . I want to keep this place open for as long as I can. For her memory."

"It makes you feel closer to her." The words slip from my mouth unbidden, but Opal nods and smiles, patting my hand across the little wooden table.

"Exactly."

Opal rings us up. I worked out payment in advance so Ro doesn't even have the opportunity to *try* to pay for it.

I pile her copies, some new and some old, into the tote bag we've also purchased, setting the pastel pink bag on my shoulder and heading for the door with Ro behind me. She reassures me she's ready to go every time I ask if she wants to stay a little longer when I catch her lingering.

"This is . . . the best thing anyone's ever done for me," Ro says, practically floating as she follows me out. "Seriously . . . I can't be-lieve this place even *exists*."

Laughing, I open the car door for her and then the back door so I can pile her books carefully on the seat. Climbing in and starting the car, I smirk toward her again.

"I'm glad you liked it."

"That was probably so boring for you," she says, sidetracked as she pulls her phone out and takes a picture of one of the books she's kept close to her. A pristine edition I recognize as the one she showed me before. Her phone goes off with a loud ringtone before she cuts it off with a double click and tries to take the picture again.

I shake my head. "Not at all. Seeing you look dreamily at shirtless men on book covers might be my new favorite pastime. Besides." I shrug and look away from her. "I might've grabbed some audiobook CDs while we were there, so I could read your favorites."

Marked in Fire is old enough that my options were a cassette tape that I didn't have the system for or a CD that Opal managed to pull from her donation pile.

It felt like kismet.

I reach into the glove compartment, my arm grazing her exposed thigh, to pull the sage-green CD jewel case out and hand it to her.

She tosses her phone into a cupholder—a picture of Sadie, Liam, Oliver, and Ro all making funny faces lighting up the screen—as she grabs for the CD and examines it with a disbelieving laugh.

"No way—"

Persistent cell phone vibrations pull my attention to the cupholder as I turn onto the two-lane back roads to avoid the highway traffic. An unknown number with another area code I don't recognize pops up on Ro's screen. It rings a few times and then disappears, but Ro's too distracted.

I ignore it, but it starts again. And again, from a new number every time.

"Someone's calling you again," I say, albeit unhelpfully, as I scratch at the back of my neck and pull to a stop at a red light.

She blushes and turns her phone away.

"It's nothing; just leave it."

Annoyed with her dismissive tone while there is clear fear in her eyes, feeling a little childish, I grab the phone and turn it back toward me. It stops ringing then, and I see Ro's shoulders tense like she's waiting for it to start up again.

It does, now resting in the palm of my hand. A different number calls right after, twice.

The phone is locked but the notifications scroll, endless calls— about five or six from each number, all with different area codes.

I feel a little sick, scrolling down the seemingly endless list. All from the last two days.

"Are these, like . . . I don't know—scam calls?" I ask, knowing full well they aren't, but having trouble piecing it together. "Ro, who is calling you from all these numbers?"

"Matt," she says, bottom lip trembling. "The light's green."

Least of my problems, I think, but pull into the empty parking lot of a closed laundromat right next to us, throwing the car in park.

"What's going on, Ro?"

She raises her hands like she wants to reach for me, but also wants to protect herself. She settles for hugging herself around the middle and my stomach drops. "He does it to bother me—"

He?

"Tyler?" I ask, a little disbelief peppering my tone. "All of these are him?"

"Usually." She nods reluctantly, like *she's* the one doing something wrong.

"Rosalie, this is fucking harassment. It's illegal—you have to report him."

"He didn't hurt me—he does this sometimes when he's trying to get my attention. Keeps making more profiles online or using other numbers. I don't know what I'm supposed to do." Her voice breaks and I feel like I can't breathe.

"Princess," I rasp, voice barely escaping the tightness of my throat. I open the car door and circle the idling car, ripping her door open a little too hard. "Come here."

She steps out of the car and melts into my arms. I tuck her too tightly against me, pressing kisses into her curls as I rub circles into her back and swallow back the fury and anger that's coursing through my body.

The phone rings again and I can't stop myself from grabbing

for it, stepping back from her huddled form so that my fury doesn't infect her.

"What the fuck do you want, asshole?"

The pause is long, drawn out, before "Is this not Ro's number?" comes from a voice I'd know blind.

"Rhys?"

"Freddy?" He chokes.

I'm far enough from Ro that she can't really hear me, but she can see the confused worry on my face. "What? It's—what's wrong?" she asks, approaching me.

I bite my lip, desperate to soothe her anxiety. "We're, um, studying right now." Hand to the mic like I can block it, I whisper to Ro, "It's just Rhys, princess, I can handle it." Then, back to Rhys, I fire off my main concern—why the fuck is he calling Rosalie?

"Why am I—" He matches my irritation. "Sadie wants me to bring her brothers to Ro at the dorms."

This time she hears him and I can't stop the clear guilt that washes over her. So I yield to her, handing off the phone.

"Hey. Sorry, I've been having a problem with spam calls." My fists tighten, jaw clenching tighter. "Um. I can—" She looks around, as if she's suddenly remembered how far away we are. "I won't be back for a few hours. Shoot."

Rhys says something in his usual comforting way. It soothes her, and I hate the irritation at my friend that subconsciously rises. *Rhys and Bennett are both the calm to your chaos. How would you ever be soothing to her?*

The phone call ends and she gazes up at me slowly.

"I think we should go home."

My eyes shutter as I agree, despite the ache in my heart that wants to turn the car around, drive her back to that little pastel bookshop, and keep her away from everything that hurts.

CHAPTER 32

Ro

It's a quiet Thursday night, my favorite kind, because I'm watching Oliver and Liam.

I never mind watching Sadie's brothers, but tonight I'm downright excited about it, because Sadie is spending the night with Rhys Koteskiy. I'm giddy for her, as if I'm the one with a hot date.

The boys are stretched out between the sofa and the pillow pallet on the floor watching whatever animated movie Liam chose tonight; Oliver gets to pick next. There are coloring and craft supplies tossed around, a messy and welcoming sight. It feels like a home.

A knock at the door has all of us looking at each other before I finally head to check the peephole—eyes lighting up at the sight of Matt Fredderic on the other side of my dorm room door.

"I come bearing gifts," he says, lifting up the pizza box in his hand as he smiles at me the moment I open the door.

"Freddy." I slump against the doorframe, biting my lip. "Now's not a great time."

His cheeks pink while his entire demeanor deflates like a kicked puppy. "Oh, right. Sorry, I didn't know you had someone—"

"You ordered pizza?" Liam asks, coming around into the frame and staring up at a wide-eyed Freddy. Liam cocks an eyebrow at me after finishing his quick examination. "Did you scare the pizza man? Sadie *always* scares the pizza man."

I laugh and shake my head. "No, this is my friend Freddy. Freddy"—I grab Liam around the shoulders and pull him toward me—"this is Liam, Sadie's brother."

"Hi." He grins sheepishly.

"Do you want to come in?"

"Yeah." He blows out a breath, stepping across the threshold.

Following Liam toward the living room area, I quietly eavesdrop as Freddy answers all the six-year-old's bubbling questions—*Are you on the hockey team? Is Rhys your bestest friend? Do you score all the goals?*—the last one followed quickly with, "No *way* you're better than my brother. His name is Oliver." He points to his sibling unnecessarily.

Freddy smirks at the stoic twelve-year-old. "Yeah? What position do you play?"

"I used to play wing, but I'm on the D-line now." He shrugs. "I'm the biggest on my team."

He isn't arrogant, just stating a fact.

Liam bursts in with, "Yeah, and Coach Max says he's got—um, what did you call it again?"

"Protective instincts." Oliver blushes a little with a frown still emblazoned across his face. He looks like Sadie, dark brown hair and gray eyes, but even more with his lightly freckled skin flushed in embarrassment and the wrinkle in his brow.

I grab a stack of paper plates off the high shelf in the kitchenette and join them in the living room, where Freddy is leaning over Liam, who is now sitting on the pillows we laid on the floor, to open the pizza box.

Every flavor of pizza, different-sized slices shoved together to make a mismatched whole pie.

"What's with the hodgepodge pizza?" Oliver asks, lip curling a little at the entirely random assortment of slices in the box.

"Nice word, Ollie," I quietly praise as I pass by.

"It's the leftovers from the hockey team dinner at Koteskiy's," Freddy says, clearing his throat. "I thought it was sweet, but now that I'm looking at it, it's just weird and kinda gross."

His hand curves around the back of his neck, scratching and fussing with golden waves. He sits with his wide back toward the kitchen, Liam to his right, Oliver grabbing another water bottle for his brother.

I can't resist touching Freddy, reaching as I set the stack of plates on the coffee table to mess with his hair and shoo his hand away.

"Very weird and kinda gross," I repeat teasingly. "I love it."

He relaxes, almost preening up at me.

"Yeah?"

"Yeah." I nod. As I start to step away, his hand trails up my exposed calf, squeezing gently before letting me go.

The goose bumps trailing after his touch linger long after I've settled onto the floor pillows on my side of the coffee table, grabbing the remote to start the movie back up.

• • •

Liam falls asleep less than an hour later, slumped slightly onto Freddy's bicep. The usually fidgeting hockey star doesn't move a muscle until I stand and offer to take Liam.

"He can sleep in Sadie's bed for now. I haven't rolled out the mattresses."

Freddy wrinkles his brow slightly before whispering, "Is it okay if I carry him?"

But he isn't asking me, he's asking Oliver to his right. The elder of Sadie's brothers nods, and my throat catches a little as Matt Fredderic tucks his palm against the back of Liam's head and angles him to his front so he can stand with the six-year-old already cradled in his arms. He pads lightly to Sadie's room, shifting his little cargo to open the door with ease.

I turn to say something to Oliver, but a loud, incessant knock on the door interrupts me.

"Probably the RA?" I say to Oliver, who has hiked his shoulders up in response to the abrupt sound. It shouldn't be the RA, though, because I tutored her all last year for free in exchange for "no questions asked" about Sadie's brothers' frequent stays.

"Ro." A low moan echoes through the door as I approach. A voice I know well enough for my stomach to bottom out.

Oliver is at my shoulder, hand on my upper arm to stop me. "Maybe we shouldn't open it."

The banging starts up again, and I try to plaster on a convincing smile for Oliver's sake.

"It's fine, Oliver. Promise. Why don't you go check on your brother?"

He shakes his head firmly. "I'll just be right here."

God. I nearly swallow my tongue. *Maybe I don't open it and just let him knock all night.* That feels even more disruptive to the two kids here that need security and safety, and this little dorm is one of the only places they have that all the time.

So I pull open the door slightly.

Tyler nearly falls into me, pushing over the threshold. He's drunk, eyes glassy and face red, reeking of alcohol.

"Ro," he sneers, grabbing my arms to keep himself up. I struggle a little but freeze when I remember we have an audience.

"Hey, back off," Oliver shouts, shoving forward to defend me.

But before he can, Freddy grabs Oliver's shoulder and pulls him back gently. Freddy steps forward, shielding Oliver and wrenching Tyler away from me and up against the now-closed door easily. Like he weighs nothing in the face of Freddy's ire.

"Want another fight with me, huh, Donaldson?" He sighs a little, pulling at Tyler's polo collar.

"Fuck off," Tyler snarls, words slurring. "I'm here to talk to Ro."

"For a smart guy, you're really fucking stupid," Freddy laughs before his voice turns razor sharp. "Stay away from Ro. Stop calling her, stop using fake numbers. Leave. Her. Alone. Am I clear?"

"Or what?"

Freddy pulls him forward and slams him back against the wall again, a little harder.

"Or I'm going to get a transcript of Ro's call and text log to send to Adam Reiner for a favor."

The mention of Bennett's dad makes Tyler pale. "I didn't do anything—"

"It's called harassment, asshole. You are *harassing* her. I think a restraining order in this situation means you'd have to leave Waterfell altogether."

Freddy takes Tyler's silence as him acquiescing, guiding him by the collar like an animal to shove him out the door.

"Don't drive, but go the fuck home. Don't make me call campus security." He grips his collar one more time and Tyler nearly yelps, flinching away. "I'm serious, Donaldson. Get behind the wheel of a car this drunk and I'll kill you myself."

He lets him go and slams the door closed within a breath. My entire body feels like it's paralyzed—or shaking, I'm not sure. Steeling my spine, I turn to Oliver, who looks a little red-faced and can't tear his eyes away from the door.

"You okay?" Freddy asks us both, eyes flickering between Oliver and myself. I nod quickly, letting his eyes settle on the fearsome twelve-year-old with his shoulder angled in front of me, protective as always.

"Oliver?" he asks again, stepping a little closer. "Are you okay?"

"Fine," the kid mutters.

"Do you want to talk about it?"

His brow only furrows further, looking so much like the angry roommate I adore so much that my heart aches. "None of your business."

"Okay." Freddy nods before ducking down to get closer to Oliver's level. "But if you need to talk about something, Rhys is a really, *really* good listener. And a great protector. He'll always watch out for you guys."

There's a pause, Oliver silent for a long moment, before he asks, "And Sadie?"

"Yes," Freddy and I both say together.

Freddy ruffles his hair, seeming not to mind when Oliver rapidly shrugs away from him.

"My captain is *crazy* about your sister. He's very serious, and I would trust him with my life. I promise, you can trust him with Sadie."

I watch the words hit Oliver, knowing he takes them to heart. Oliver is harder to get to know than even Sadie, both in sharp contrast to heart-on-his-sleeve Liam. Oliver is protective, has been since the first time I met him freshman year as an angry, frightened nine-year-old who scowled at me until a pillow fort that I helped build for him and a three-year-old Liam seemed to win him over.

"I'm gonna go to bed now," he announces a little awkwardly before turning without preamble and heading to Sadie's room.

Freddy looks at me, an unsure smile spreading for a moment before I shake my head.

"That's just Oliver," I say. "He's fine."

His face slowly melts into soft concern as his hands come up to cup my face gently. It's half inspection, half veneration, eyes trailing over every inch of my skin.

"You're okay." I think he meant to ask it, but it sounds more like he's reassuring himself.

"Yeah, I'm fine." I turn around and walk into the main room to start cleaning up. "More embarrassed than anything."

He frowns, stopping me with a hand to my arm. "No reason for you to be embarrassed, Ro. You haven't done anything wrong."

I nod, deciding not to argue with him. "Thank you for coming tonight. Sorry it probably wasn't what you were expecting."

His hand drifts down my arm slowly. Fingers dancing together, wrapping and unwrapping until they're intertwined. My heartbeat speeds up.

I lean toward him and he follows, like a magnet. It's the same way I felt at eighteen in that dirty fraternity house.

Kiss me, I think, entranced by him. *Kiss me. Remember the first one.*

I lean back, the realization that he *doesn't* remember hitting a little harder this close to him.

"Don't apologize. It was perfect. I just wanted to hang out with you, without tutoring."

We are standing at my bedroom door now, and it would be so easy to lean back into him. To pull him over me with floral sheets cool against the heated skin of my back.

"Yeah." I nod, swallowing hard. "As friends."

The word makes his brow dip, like it hurts him. But he manages my least favorite Matt Fredderic smile and hits my shoulder with his.

"Yeah, yeah," he says, his favorite catchphrase. "Friends."

CHAPTER 33

Freddy

Winning a hockey game is the equivalent of a high, which is one reason I've never bothered with anything harder than booze—that and the continuous threat of random drug screenings.

But winning a game with Ro sitting right near the glass, shimmering prettily underneath the arena lights, is somehow *more*. Now, I'm antsy to see her, leg shaking and body jittery as I check the sliding door over and over for Sadie and Ro.

Which doesn't take long. They step onto the back patio as Rhys and I jump up a little too excitedly.

"I like the jacket, Sadie," I say as they scoot through the mingling crowd into our half circle of friends—mostly our entire first and second line, sans Toren Kane.

"Thanks," she says a bit offhandedly as she keeps her piercing gray eyes trained on my captain. "Ro made it."

Sadie passes me by, and Ro stops at my side with a shy little smile. "Yeah?"

"Yeah." She blushes. "And this one." She does a little twirl, showing off the unique, vintage patchwork-style denim. "And I have a surprise for you."

"Because I won?" I ask, slinging an arm over her shoulders and squishing her into my side.

"Sure." She smirks before turning her wrist over in my hand, showing me the sleeve where she's embroidered a 27.

My heart is thundering. I want to kiss her, but I know I can't. Instead, I hold her hand to my chest over my heart like she'll feel it beating and *know* how I feel for her. The immeasurable level of admiration for her gentle, glimmering heart that she wears on her sleeve so that *everyone* always knows how much they're seen and loved and cared for.

"Freddy," Holden calls, heading toward the beer pong table. "Ready?"

I nod before tucking a straightened piece of her hair back.

"You look beautiful." It slips out before I quickly cover it with a nod to the table. "Wanna play with us?"

. . .

The first round of beer pong is fine. Perfect, even.

Ro and I easily win against Holden and a *very* drunk Paloma Blake, and I hug her around the waist in celebration, lifting her slightly off the ground.

"Fuck off," Holden huffs, but his eyes dance as he shakes his head at me and slumps back into the empty chair behind him, where some of our friends have been watching the not-so-fierce competition.

"Ro?"

The deep male voice saying Ro's name like *that* has my attention before it has hers.

She spins, her soft mouth curving into a wide, genuine smile as her gaze locks on the tall, familiar guy behind her. With dark brown skin and tight curls atop his head with a sharp fade, he's a handsome guy, unfortunately.

"Walker," she says. "Hey, how are you?"

He smiles and steps between us. "I'm great. Actually, we won our game yesterday. Did you go?"

She shakes her head, while my mind races trying to remember exactly where I know this douche bag from. *Game yesterday . . . mildly familiar . . .*

Walker Taylor—wide receiver for the Waterfell football team. Super senior.

"Damn," he says, hand lifting to his chest like his heart is hurting. I find my own hand reaching in the same motion, my chest feeling a little tight. "You promised last semester—"

"I know." Ro groans a little and nods. "I'm sorry about that. Things got busy, but I've been more adventurous this semester."

His eyebrows skyrocket and I close my eyes, cursing beneath my breath at her unintended innuendo. Ro rarely ever *means* to be flirty like that, but *my god* if this guy isn't taking every little word as a trail of crumbs to follow.

"Yeah? Enough to play a round of beer pong with your old student?"

Old student.

She was his fucking *tutor*?

Suddenly, I am rubbing the center of my chest, an ache permeating my body.

Paloma knocks into the table again, giggling even as beer sloshes all over both her and me, and my gaze flicks away from the flirty vignette across from us.

Holden stands quickly, putting his hands on Paloma's waist and coaxing her into the seat he's vacated, which she easily goes to. She's beyond drunk, and something about it feels . . . wrong. If I had any ability to focus on something other than Rosalie Shariff, I'd try to figure her out or find one of her friends.

Actually, I've never seen Paloma with friends. Not any real ones, at least, and no one I could name. She's always alone.

Thankfully when I look back at her, Bennett is already there, kneeling by her side and whispering something quickly to her, at which she shakes her head and closes her eyes. His jaw clenches tight, but he doesn't move. I relax a little knowing I don't have to watch her so closely anymore—I trust any of my team to take care of her, but Bennett above most everyone else.

"Freddy?"

I spin, realizing only then that Ro has called my name a few times, but she's stepping away from our side of the table, Walker at her back, one of his hands hovering over her waist. I want to know if she can feel it, if she knows it's there or he's waiting for the right opportunity.

"Yeah, princess?" I smirk, pushing the smoke and drawl into my voice that I know will turn her cheeks a pretty shade of rose gold.

Walker shifts his stance at my words, finally making the final push to put his hand on the curve of her waist. My jaw aches from the strength of my back teeth bearing down.

"Do you want to play again?"

I smile at her, a real one this time, and nod. "Sure."

• • •

When I agreed to a second round of beer pong, I definitely didn't intend to link myself with an overly competitive Holden, who tried to insist we chug an entire beer for every point.

And I definitely, *definitely* didn't want Walker *fucking* Taylor—the football hotshot with a last name for a first name, and a first name for a last name—all over my goddamn tutor.

"Get it together," Holden snaps, slapping my back so hard I almost lose the Ping-Pong ball in my hand. It's annoying, but it manages to break my hazardous focus, and less than appropriate thoughts about slicing off Walker Taylor's hands every time he uses them to "adjust" Ro's stance. His fingers keep grazing circles on the bare skin of her arm, now exposed since she's discarded her jacket.

I sink the ball easily, gaining my tutor girl's attention with a bright-eyed smile as she takes a long, deliberate sip of her drink and moves the cup away.

When Holden sinks his, he calls for the balls back, and Walker rolls them to us across the sticky table covered in Sharpie signatures and faded phone numbers. I take the green ball and dunk it into one of the cups of water, looking up to take my shot when Walker decides to rest his chin on Ro's semibare shoulder and whisper something into her ear that makes her flush.

The ball leaves my fingers, missing every cup and the table entirely, bouncing onto the floor by Walker's feet.

I wish I'd hit him in the fucking mouth.

"Damn it," Holden mutters, stepping up and hitting the rim of a cup before it falls out. "I think I'm done for the night." His hand pats my back a little harder as he turns away from us. "Anyone seen Paloma?"

I don't answer, don't look around to help—because I feel a little bit like I'm burning up from the inside. Watching Ro flirt and smile *should* make me happy . . . If I still thought of her as a friend, it would. But something feels wrong.

And I can't shake the desperation to be the one on the receiving end of her smiles. Just like I'll never be able to pluck the memory of her telling me how easy it would be to love someone like me from my brain.

I think it would be simpler to live the rest of my life without those words ringing in my ear, without knowing how easily she defends me, uplifts me . . .

Living without her at all now seems like some difficult thing. But so does living *with* her, because my admiration and respect for her are becoming a deep well with an end I'll never find.

"Ro?" I ask before the football boy can find his way to her lips. "Can you help me with something really quick?"

If I was anticipating a snappy reply, I'd be let down by her immediate concern and quick apology to Walker before she steps away from him to follow me into the house through the back door.

"Everything okay, Matty?"

Matty. A possessive feeling rolls through me, but not over her— of *her* over *me*.

I down the rest of the room-temperature beer in my hand and set it on a table, grabbing her hand as I take us toward the stairs. A few small groups are clustered by the entrance, front door open to let slightly cooler air flow into the overheated, darkened house.

When I spot the couple on the middle of the staircase, I start to snap at them that they're in "off-limits" territory before I realize it's my roommate.

Bennett is with a girl sitting two steps down from him, her arms wrapped around his massive thigh and calf, blond hair pouring over his jean-clad knee where his hand gently combs through the strands, careful and slow. He isn't looking at her, surveying the party as he usually might. But—

Steps faltering, I do a quick double-take as we pass them and realize it's Paloma, face serene and eyes closed as she lies in Reiner's lap while the stoic goalie carefully guards over her.

He barely flicks his eyes up to meet mine, but his face is a stone mask before he nods to Ro on my heels and gives me a stern, disapproving frown.

You're the one with Paloma fucking Blake sleeping like a puppy on your thigh while you pet her hair, but sure. Let's question my *decisions.*

I shake my head and continue up past them, my pulse thrumming in my ears. Ro never falters in following me into the shadowed, unlit hallway between our rooms. Rhys's door is closed, music spilling out from where I'm sure he and his new girlfriend are having a fantastic time celebrating the win.

I almost laugh at the realization that everyone who *lives* in this house isn't currently attending the party, but Ro grabs my arm.

"Freddy, are you—"

I turn and corner her, hand over her head pressed into the wall as I settle my body nearly against hers.

Her eyes go wide and dark, pupils dilating in the shadowy light. "Is Tyler here?"

The question makes my stomach sink, flaring with a little leftover jealousy and heat from downstairs that hasn't let go of me fully.

"Why in the hell would I invite your dumbass abusive ex-boyfriend to this party?" I grit out. "No. Tyler's not here."

"But . . . you're." She vaguely gestures to where I'm partially leaned against her, pushing her into the little hallway alcove leading to my bedroom. "You—"

I should focus on the fact that Ro believes every ounce of my affection for her has been *because* of Tyler. But I can't.

"Were you gonna go home with Taylor Walker?" I blurt out, running my hand through my hair before licking my upper lip. I feel it tingle when I catch her watching the movement. My reflexive response is to watch her mouth right back.

"I think it's the other way around."

"Ro." I shake my head, waiting for her eyes to meet mine. "Were you going to sleep with him?"

"No," she replies, quickly but assuredly.

I nod. "Kiss him?"

"Maybe . . . yeah." Her cheeks are flushed, making her tawny skin glow. The heat from the packed house mixed with the alcohol we've been drinking is making her straightened hair start to frizz, little waves forming around her face.

I nod again. "Okay, I can work with that."

"What do you mean?"

My heart is in my throat, butterflies hammering my stomach—which has never happened before. I'm usually bleeding confidence at this point with a partner; *this* is my comfort zone.

"Did you want to kiss him because you like him?"

I'll back off, I swear to myself. *If she says she likes him, I'll let go of her.*

She shakes her head.

"You just want to kiss someone?"

She nods.

The music seems louder, The Neighbourhood's "Scary Love" is thrumming against the walls in a way that leaves me questioning if it's from Rhys's room or downstairs.

"If you wanna kiss someone, I'm right here." It comes out breathy, but I'm smiling as my hand works its way up her side to rest against the right side of her neck. I lean in, skimming my nose along her cheek. "And I'm way fucking better at it than him. I promise, princess."

Her tongue, cherry red from whatever fruity hunch punch drink she was sipping during our games, flicks out to lick at her plush lips. She bites down over the same spot—and I lose my slipping grip on my self-control.

I kiss her.

Despite the hard grip of my hands on her, despite the fierceness of my feelings for her and my racing heart, I'm as gentle with her as I can manage as I press my lips to hers.

I pull away, just barely, so our lips still bump and brush with the breath we're sharing, my forehead pressed to hers.

"We're friends," she says, a little dazed. Her voice is shaky and breathy, gentle in the shared space. "Friends don't—"

"Friends can do this sometimes."

"T-they can?" Her hands timidly reach for me, until one grasps my forearm, the other sneaking up my bicep to the ball of my shoulder. I refrain from asking her to squeeze it—to press her pretty patterned manicure into my skin enough to leave a mark beneath the fabric of my shirt.

"Absolutely," I say, pressing another kiss to her heated neck. "I'm so good at this, Ro. Please, let me show you." Another press of my mouth. "Just a kiss."

I wait only a beat, but it's enough for her to nod before pushing up on her tiptoes to reach my mouth enthusiastically. It's all the permission I need to wrap her up and haul her nearly into me, desperate for her warmth and the swirling coconut floral scent of her hair.

She's beautiful like this, her hair soft and smooth, but part of me aches for the tangles of her curls to thread my fingers through like I've dreamed about for weeks.

Ro's breath stutters as she pulls away this time before slamming a little too hard into me, teeth clinking as I stumble before catching her. I could carry her, but she's so perfectly tall her legs tangle with mine as we stumble back against my bedroom door. My hand fumbles to open it before we both stumble in with laughs forcing our lips apart.

Her gaze drops a little self-consciously, hands smoothing the fabric of her silk top. I'm distracted by her teeth chewing relentlessly on her swollen bottom lip.

We both stand quietly, a beat too long, until matching flushes work their way up our necks, climbing through the skin of our cheeks. I want to touch her again, but—for the first time since I was fourteen—I don't know how.

"Can I kiss you again?" she asks, and a smile bursts across my face. I want to close my eyes and bask in the feeling that her question gives me, but I nod instead, opening my arms for her to come to me.

She does, suddenly unshy as her lips press to mine again, hands grasping at my shoulders as I fall back into the door to steady us both.

My thigh presses higher, hitching her to her toes as she gasps into my mouth, tearing away like that pressure is distracting enough that she can't focus on the kiss anymore. Her hips move a little experimentally at first, before her head falls back and my arms wind around her waist to keep her steady as she rocks.

I tug at her, just slightly. She easily tumbles forward, little puffs of air from her parted lips making the skin of my neck tingle.

"There you go, princess," I mumble before my tongue traces the sharp hinge of her jaw, up to her ear. I press a kiss to her cheek and smile, whispering, "C'mon, Rosalie. Tell me if it feels good."

She whimpers and pants, scrambling higher on my thigh as she rides it faster now, her fingers digging harder into my shoulders like she's—

Fuck. She's already there.

"Matt," she begs before convulsing rapidly against me, bucking with abandon.

"That's it, baby. Take what you need."

Her moans are so loud I swallow them with my mouth as she rides out the orgasm, slowly coming to a stop.

Her head drops into the crook of my shoulder. I feel a little high, hands smoothing up and down her spine—so I *feel* the way she tenses.

Ro's whole body turns to stone, and suddenly she's pulling herself off my thigh, with her chin tucked down. Eyes to the floor like she's . . . like she's ashamed.

Silence roars in my ears, stomach plummeting as I try to slap on a gentle smile and angle her chin upward.

"Hey, are you okay?"

My voice sounds a bit like I've been gargling sand.

"Ro?"

She nods and tilts her head up, eyes watching me like prey caught in a predator's stare. Which only makes my anxiety spin out a little, because minutes before she was soft against me, overwhelmingly willing in my arms. Now she's all stiffness and hesitation.

"Sorry." She gathers her hair into a ponytail, twisting it up before letting it spill down her back as she shrugs. "I don't know what came over me. I—I'm not . . . " Her eyes shutter before she blinks up at me.

"I think I'm just drunk," she whispers, like it isn't a knife against my throat.

"I'm not drunk," I sputter. "Are you drunk?"

I'm certain she isn't, having not stepped away from her side all night. And yet something like relief flutters through my stomach when she shakes her head.

"This is so embarrassing." Her hands lift to cover her reddened face again. "Can we please just pretend that didn't happen?"

If it *was* clear embarrassment for this happening with *me*, for being with *me* like this, I would let it go at her request. But something about this seems wrong.

Use your head, Matt. You know this girl.

Even as I try not to jump to conclusions, I know her enough to nearly feel the presence of Tyler Donaldson in the room with us— and it makes me a little sick with rage.

"Rosalie," I say, tone calm but louder than my whispered words before. "Nothing about what just happened is embarrassing to me. It was incredible—*you* are incredible. Why are you embarrassed?"

CHAPTER 34

Ro

Don't cry. Don't cry. Do not *cry.*

It's impossible not to let some tears escape.

They'd already started to form out of pure mortification, but Matt Fredderic's words tip me over the edge . . . *You were incredible*, he said. And the contrast between those words and the echoing remnants of Tyler in my head swirl through me. The gentle admiration and wonder in his gaze for the moments after it happened, the soft caress of his hands on my skin.

"Why are you embarrassed?" he asks again, calm.

"*You sound ridiculous, Ro.*"

"*No. We're not doing that—why the fuck would you want that? It's degrading.*"

"*I just don't see you that way, and I don't want to. Don't you want me to respect you?*"

I want him to hold me again, let some of his strength seep under my skin so my voice doesn't tremble when I quickly admit, "I don't want you to think I'm a . . . a slut. I know something's wrong with me and I can't control myself. I get carried away."

Clearly it isn't what he's expecting me to say.

Some combination of disgust and shock hardens his entire expression, his eyes going wide like a nightmare come true. I choke on another sob, because I know Freddy has been with other women before, lots of them, and I feel ridiculous. Ridiculous for coming that fast. For ruining the moment after. For humping his thigh in the first place like some animal in heat.

"Rosalie," he says calmly. "Why do you think that?"

"You look like a slut, acting like that."

Something crosses over his face—an emotion I can't name but wish I could banish from his handsome features. And then, almost reluctantly, he settles his back against the door, huffing out a heavy sigh.

Vulnerability hangs off him like a well-worn, damaged cloak.

"Remember the girl I told you about?"

I nod, because not for a second have I forgotten a conversation with Matt Fredderic—let alone one as sensitive and important as *that* one. The one that told me Matt isn't all simpering smiles and class clown romanticisms, that he's a boy with a heart I'm starting to think is softer than my own easily broken one.

"She made me work for her affection all the time. And I was so . . . *desperate*. I wanted it so badly I would've done anything she asked. And I did, for a while. But she . . ."

He shakes his head and closes his eyes as he continues.

"It was never about love for her; it was all about control. And I know it's not the same, but I think you might know how that feels. Trying everything for affection?"

I nod again, heart practically blocking my airway as I try to swallow. "Yeah."

"Yeah," he repeats. "Okay."

"I—" My voice shakes as I desperately try to clear the catch in my throat. "It was like no matter what I did I always managed to do something wrong—to mess up. And I was never perfect enough. Never smart enough or sophisticated enough. And with sex . . ." My words drop to a whisper. "I was a virgin, but I wanted— I wanted it. I like it, and sometimes I get too into it, and act like a whore."

"Hey," he chides gently. "Let's not use those words to describe ourselves."

I've heard Matt Fredderic describe himself as a "whore" or the "school slut" more times than I can count. But Freddy is more protective of every other person in the world than he will ever be of himself.

"He has all this power over me from so far away and I hate it."

"It sounds cliché, but believe me, I understand. I gave her a lot of power, even after everything." He grimaces. "Without her even there, I was still doing things with her in mind, but it was like I was moving in a fog, going through motions with no direction except a mean voice in my head.

"I trusted her—it was harder because of that." There's a catch to his words, like maybe he still struggles with it. "So I know how hard it is to clear that voice." He presses a soft, chaste kiss to my forehead, reaching for my hand again. "But I think it helps to talk about it."

"I'm scared."

"Ro," he croaks, a sad smile marring his perfect features. "You're breaking my heart, princess." Another kiss to my temple. "It's okay. You don't have to tell me—"

"No," I say, cutting him off with a quick shake of my head. "I want to, I'm just— I don't want you to see me differently."

The confession is raw as it falls from my lips that still tingle from his kiss.

"Never."

He smiles, and it's so blinding it feels like standing in the sun on a warm California beach day. Like home.

CHAPTER 35

Ro

"I look ridiculous," I say quietly, biting down on my lip as I turn slowly side to side in the mirror.

"Let me see." Sadie's voice chirps from the video call she's currently on, though I've pointed the camera to the ceiling while I change.

Even at the height of Sadie's party-girl phase, before Rhys Koteskiy's appearance in her life, Sadie had always spent Halloween alone with her brothers. All holidays, really, despite my continual offers to accompany her, plan a party, or even to take her back home to California with me.

"Ta-dah," I mutter, propping the phone up against the mirror and stepping back awkwardly for her to see the whole thing. On my phone screen, Liam flips Sadie's Wookiee onesie hoodie up—the same costume she wears every year and will continue to don as long as Liam is *Star Wars* obsessed.

"Hot," she says. Her intense gray eyes are hard not to shrink from for most people, but Sadie is my best friend. I only find comfort in the icy cold of her gaze.

"The game was good," I prompt her, checking the red ribbons tied into my long pigtail braids. "Rhys played amazingly."

She rolls her eyes, but I see the slight tinge of worry in her gaze. "He seemed okay?"

Sadie asks this particular question a lot, and though she won't tell me everything, she's confided that he took a really nasty hit on the ice last spring, and sometimes she gets anxious about him skating—specifically if she can't be there to watch him.

I told her that it was cute how she fretted over him. She faked a grimace and pretended to throw up, but her smile was bright underneath it all.

"He was incredible. Bennett had a shutout."

"Look at you," Sadie coos. "Learning all the lingo."

I giggle a little, relaxing as I balance on one leg to roll up the white stockings to my midthigh. Accompanied by the blue-checkered puff-sleeve dress I've owned for years and never figured out how to style, I look like the perfect blend of sweet and sexy.

For the first time in a long time, I feel hot, *and* I feel like me.

"You sure you're good to go by yourself?" she asks. Sadie may be the queen of attitude and seeming not to care, but she cares *a lot*. I know if I told her that I wasn't okay by myself, she'd call someone to get me or spend her *birthday* with me instead of her brothers. I'd never take that from her.

"Yeah, I'm gonna Uber. It's only, like, a five-minute ride. By the way, happy birth—"

"Don't say it," she growls. "Or I'm hanging up on you." Her eyes dart over both shoulders, before she hunkers down farther on her couch and pulls the phone closer. "So, you gonna tell me what's going on with you and Freddy?"

"Nothing," I say quickly, but stumble over the word slightly as an image of him flashes in my mind's eye: heaving breath and whispering praise into my ear as I—

Heat shoots up the back of neck.

"We're friends." I clear my throat. "And I'm still his school-assigned tutor until the end of this semester. He's just . . . he's flirty."

And touchy, I want to add—but I know the conclusions she'll draw, the connotation behind the words. And it isn't how I mean them.

Freddy is warmth and sunlight, shining and shimmering across ocean-blue water. The kind you want to bask in. His gaze is like heat on my skin. And he's always reaching out to touch some part of me—physically affectionate in a way that has *nothing* to do with attraction.

He's the same way with his friends and teammates—a pat on the back or squeeze of a shoulder, tight hugs and body slams after goals, helmet to helmet as he cheers with them. His need for touch even platonically is easy to see, but it's even easier to imagine him casually intimate with someone he did find attractive, maybe a girlfriend.

A hand on the thigh while driving, kneading circles into skin. Holding hands, always, fidgeting with her fingers on the tabletop as they chat. Or under the table, before slipping up my skirt and pressing into me, until I can't hold back my—

"Ro?"

I shake my head, trying for the thousandth time to somehow remove the mental image of Matt Fredderic against his bedroom door, freshly bitten lips and shirt rucked up *by me*, before it destroys every brain cell I have left.

"Yeah?"

"Have fun tonight." Sadie's gaze is piercing, like her words are more threat than suggestion. "Or else."

"Anything else, my ice queen?" I mockingly bow.

"Yeah." She smiles. "You should use my lipstick. It's on the bathroom counter."

• • •

RO

I'm here!

I text Freddy as I walk up through the open door. The party is in full swing by the time I get there, stepping into the overcrowded thumping living room space, dancers plastered to each other and the walls on all sides.

It's overwhelming for a second, and when I don't see Freddy or get a text back, I start for the bathrooms, needing a quick breather.

The door is locked, marked with a sheet of paper that says "Chicks." I lean against the wall where it's a little quieter, looking out to the patio and bonfire going in the distance, a group of guys and girls laughing and chatting.

The sliding door opens a little roughly before two bodies stumble through. The girl is dressed as Poison Ivy with green tights and a green corset, vibrant red hair, and—

Paloma Blake.

Paloma Blake with red hair and reddened eyes storming into the house with someone massive on her heels. She enters the vacant bathroom with a crude sign that says "Dicks" and slams the door shut.

The other newcomer in my quiet hallway space doesn't say anything, only leans against the opposite wall. I can't tell if he's looking at me because he's wearing a Ghostface mask, a lazy choice, as shown by the simple jeans and half-buttoned nearly translucent button-down that's soaking wet and sticking to his skin.

He undoes the remaining buttons and pulls it from his tan skin, and I almost swallow my tongue. Muscles on muscles, amber in the light from the single standing lamp that *screams* "boy dorm decor."

The mask comes off next, and I realize it's the guy who hit Tyler— Toren Kane.

After our run-in and hearing him announced at the home game, I looked him up. He's as terrifying as I thought, somehow worse in person. And the Ghostface costume doesn't help that image.

He's covered in tattoos, and I can't stop my eyes from scanning them slowly, realizing that I recognize quite a few.

Starry Night wrapped half around his torso. *Bedroom in Arles* on one bicep. A unique design that seems to mix Van Gogh's famous self-portrait with the sunflower vase on one arm. *Almond Blossom* twining down the other, nearly reaching his fingertips. He's covered in Van Gogh's work.

And not just famous pieces, but more unknown ones—

Skull of a Skeleton with Burning Cigarette, but surrounded by blends of landscapes and pastorals I can only assume are based on the famed artist's work. All done in grays and blacks, but still recognizable without the color.

He's caught me staring now, and embarrassment stings my cheeks as I stutter, "Big fan of Van Gogh?"

My question has his entire body tensing before he eyes me a little strangely.

"Excuse me?"

My mouth goes dry, neck damp with sweat at the intensity of his eyes. Molten gold. Furious, a match waiting to be set alight.

"You—your tattoos. There's, like, an entire collection of Van Gogh."

His eyebrows shoot up.

Maybe no one has asked before. Maybe they've only recognized *Starry Night* and the sunflowers but didn't bother to realize he's made a shrine to the artwork on his skin.

"Yeah. I . . . like his work."

His right hand raises to his bicep, fingertips dancing along the inked skin there absentmindedly. I narrow my gaze to where, between the perfect sleeve of Van Gogh paintings and sketches, there is a cluster of lilies. In fact, there are several bunches, scattered between different images all over his body.

"I didn't know Van Gogh painted lilies."

Whatever I've said shuts his entire body down, like pressing an off switch. Muted fury flutters across his face before he shudders, letting out a heavy breath and nods to me.

"If you click your heels three times, do you think you'll end up in your dorm or Fredderic's bed?" he says with a snarky smirk before grabbing his mask and sliding it back on, gripping his shirt in the other hand and storming out.

CHAPTER 36

Ro

There's a Ninja Turtle dancing his way to me—so perfectly timed to the eerie beat of The Weeknd's "Gasoline" that it feels like a fever dream version of my first time seeing him freshman year.

I've never asked Matt if he remembers that we met once before. That I waited for him for hours and then days and then weeks three years ago. I don't think I could handle it if he says he does remember, or that he doesn't—there's no good answer.

I shake my head with a simpering smile at the painted-green shirtless body of Matt Fredderic as he shimmies playfully around me.

"Hey, Rosalie," he breathes in my ear when he's close enough.

"Hey, Matty."

He grabs me in a tight hug that makes me squeal and jerk back to check that his green body paint hasn't transferred to me.

"C'mon, princess," he says, playing with the end of my pigtail. "You know I'd never mess up your cute outfit. You worked so hard on it."

A smile pulls at my mouth as I examine him.

The green and yellow paint across his face, neck, torso, and arms looks messy, like whoever did it had to battle a constantly fidgeting and distracted Freddy. I imagine even-keeled Bennett giving up midway through, which explains why most of his arms are patchy, barely painted. A purple mask with roughly cut eyeholes is tied tightly around his head, fluffing his golden locks around it in a hand-somely disheveled way—as is usual for Freddy.

"Which Ninja Turtle are you supposed to be?"

He smacks a hand to his chest. "I'm insulted that you don't know this."

"Only child who didn't watch the show or movies," I say with a shrug.

"Yeah? Too busy with Beethoven for Babies? Or movies to improve your child's IQ, my little brainiac?"

My face is on fire. I giggle and nod, feeling warm from the two drinks I've had. Not even tipsy, but completely drunk on his presence. It's almost too easy to bask in the warmth that *is* Matt.

It would be so easy to love him, I think.

I barely manage to bite back the comment, grabbing his hand and jerking him closer to me.

"Dance with me?" I ask.

He smiles and touches his nose to mine. "Always."

He pulls back and gulps down his full beer in a way that has my eyes tracking his Adam's apple, mouthwatering as he swallows.

Matt takes my hand and spins me. I drag him a little closer, very aware that I'm playing with fire. But I don't care.

"You're so beautiful," he whispers into my ear before darting back to give me a light, dopey smile that's all softness and zero flirt.

My chest aches as I circle my arms around his neck and pull him closer. He smells like whiskey and body paint, and he feels danger-ously like mine.

• • •

Matt Fredderic is a dopey drunk.

Eyes glazed from the shots we took—especially the ones he took in my stead when I wanted to stop drinking for the night, while the group wanted to keep playing whatever game we were on.

He laughed and joked with his teammates, but always made sure I felt included in it all. Freddy never makes anyone feel like an outsider, I'm realizing. He's kind with everyone. He's attractive, physically, yes, but he's truly attractive because of how he treats those around him.

Bennett drove us to the Hockey House, offering me a ride to the dorms from there, which sparked a very quick argument from sleepy Matt in the back, who tucked his arms around me over the seat. The goalie shook his head but offered to help us inside. He looked antsy, so I assured him I'd be fine getting Freddy in on my own.

Which is proving harder than I thought.

Slowly climbing the steps with the added weight of a six-three muscled hockey boy is difficult, but I manage guiding us into his bedroom—even with the distraction of his puffs of breath on my neck, where he's leaned his head.

He rests heavily on me, his body glowing under the soft lamplight in his messy room. It's organized chaos; I can recognize it now. As soon as I turn to close the door behind us, he slides onto his back on the bed.

"Good night." He smiles. It's so boyish and sleepy I can't help the starry-eyed look that comes over my face.

"Not so fast, Matty," I chide, shaking his arms as I pull at his hand until he props back up.

"I want to sleep. Don't you wanna sleep with me, Dorothy?" The huff beneath my breath must come out a little louder, because his mouth quirks and he squeezes my hand in his lightly. "Or do you like princess more?"

"C'mon." I pull at him again. "You're not sleeping in this green body paint. We need to get you into the shower."

"And you'll wash me?"

"If it gets you in there? Sure."

His smile is breathtaking, and suddenly every ounce of energy that had seemingly left him is back in full force. He's up and nearly sprinting to his en suite bathroom.

The shower is small, a tight square that we both definitely won't fit into. So I get him to sit on the lid of the toilet as I turn on the water to a soothing warm spray.

Hunting through his drawers and cabinets, I find a container of baby wipes, hidden behind a messy jumble of unused products and a tower of multicolored towels.

I grab the thickest one, setting the plush material atop the limited counter space. Taking two of the wipes and quietly instructing Matt to close his eyes, I remove his mask and wipe away the paint on his handsome face. His skin reddens slightly with the motions, but he relaxes, breaths growing heavy and deep.

Reaching for a washcloth to soak under the warm spray, I hum a Cigarettes After Sex song lightly under my breath.

Continuing to his neck, I rub off the fading green body paint, careful to move his chain and make sure it's clean, even the intricate pendant—a small, delicate carving of two winged figures embracing. I inspect it further now, able to see it more closely than I ever have. It's a carving of something I recognize, a famous depiction of Psyche and Cupid. I want to ask him about it, but his eyes are nearly closed. Is he already sleeping?

Despite the warmth of the cloth, gooseflesh ripples across his exposed skin. I raise the towel to gently wipe his face.

"Do you like him 'cause he's smarter than me?"

His voice is so small that for a moment I'm convinced he didn't speak. That it was some whisper of my imagination.

My hand pauses, hovering over his cheek as I flick my eyes to meet his gaze—but his eyes are downcast, fingers playing with the hem of my too-short skirt.

"Who?" I ask after clearing my throat.

"Donaldson. You dated him so long. Is it because he's smart?"

Both of his hands are distracting me, one palm warm against the back of my thigh like he's trying to keep me here between his spread legs. The fingers of his other hand twirl patterns from the high cut of my stockings, playing with the fabric and my bare skin between the lace and my skirt.

But his voice isn't the flirty or humorous Matt Fredderic. He isn't hiding the insecurity in a joke.

"Matt," I say, but my voice sticks. "We are broken up. For good. And he's not that smart, I promise. In fact, I think you're smarter in a lot of ways."

He peeks up at me, a few speckles of green looking like freckles under his eyes, and a beautiful smile spreads across his full lips.

"Yeah, yeah." He rolls his eyes playfully. "I wish I was smart like you. You're amazing."

My heart squeezes tightly before thumping hard like it's aching to reach for him as much as my arms are.

"*You're* amazing, Matt," I whisper, wiping away the lingering green at his hairline. His face is clean now, but I keep sweeping in gentle, soothing motions over his skin. "You're so smart and creative and funny. You're amazing."

He sighs, and as his breath flutters against my fingers, I realize I might as well be tracing his lips.

"I want to kiss you again so bad," he huffs, but shakes his head. "But I promised 'just friends.'"

I want to kiss you, too.

Desperately so.

But my friendship with Matt is too important to me, so I swallow back the dry mouth that accompanies my desperate want for him.

"I love being your friend, Matt," I say, because it's true. But also because I can't think of anything else besides, *Yes, please kiss me,* or, *Maybe being just friends is overrated.*

He's smiling so I smile back.

Easy as breathing.

"This is way harder than a test." He groans a little, rocking his head into my stomach.

"What is?"

"Not touching you," he whispers before gently extracting himself from my arms, swaying slowly into the shower, and fiddling clumsily with the knobs. "I need it cold before I do something you'll regret."

CHAPTER 37

Ro

Leaving him in the shower alone feels akin to leaving a mopey puppy alone.

But I need a breather, and so does he. We can't keep pushing the boundaries of our friendship like this. It's too valuable to me.

Instead, I pace back and forth across his organized mess of a room. Should I disappear before he's back to save us both?

The bathroom door opens with the shower still on in the background, steam billowing out behind him.

Freddy, with a towel slung around his waist sloppily, held together by a fist at his side, like he couldn't be bothered to really cover himself. Every step he takes flashes his thigh all the way up to his hip joint, water droplets tracing the butterfly tattoo across his pinkened skin.

I have the sudden urge to google "Can humans swallow their tongues?" to assure myself I'm not in need of a hospital.

As much as I adore Freddy, have tried to make every thought about him as "friend-zone" as possible, his beauty is hard to ignore. He's so handsome—the sharp cut of his jaw, his thick, pursed lips that I know taste like candy. His blond hair is darker now, still wet as it drips over his powerful shoulders and down the plane of his muscular abdomen.

"Ro?" he says. Like he's been trying to get my attention while I've been ogling him.

"Yeah?" My cheeks heat in mild embarrassment.

"You can shower." He steps aside, again flashing his thigh indecently. "I laid a towel out for you. And I'll grab you some clothes to wear—if you want."

Say no. Say, "Thank you, Matt, but I should call a car and go home tonight."

Instead, I nod and head right in, washing off the night under the steamy warm spray. I search the surprisingly large bin of different products his bathroom boasts, finding a few travel-sized face washes and moisturizers, and excellent hair care products, all in mismatched bins and drawers.

I shouldn't be so surprised at the selection. The boy is gorgeous, clearly well kept in terms of his appearance and hygiene.

Taking my time—not to avoid him, I swear to myself—I emerge with reddened skin, grabbing the clothes he's left at the threshold before closing the door all the way. There's a pair of short athletic shorts with a drawstring I'm able to tie up on my waistline, and a shirt that hangs just an inch past the shorts—which only adds to the illusion that I'm not wearing pants, thanks to the extreme length of my legs.

For some reason, I thought he might be fully clothed by the time I came back out. Instead, he's lying across his unmade bed in tight gray boxer briefs that leave basically nothing to the imagination. I dart my eyes to the ceiling, which somehow feels worse, so I shift and stare down at my feet.

"I, um—" I clear my throat, neck hot even though my curls are still piled high on my head.

"Can you . . ." he says before lifting himself on his elbows. His abs flex and relax with the motion, like some sexed-up underwear model. But his face is still very much "kicked puppy," brows furrowed and eyes sad. I hate it.

I walk a little closer, drawn in by his magnetism.

"Will you sleep here?" he asks, hand reaching out for mine. I take his, letting our fingers play along each other's. "Just, stay."

"Okay."

I flip off the light. Something plays on the TV, muted but colorful enough to cast a glow over us—the same two guys eating ridiculous food at a desk, a comfort show he often turns on. It's calm and relaxing, welcoming in a strange way.

Melting into the bed, I stay on the side he's left for me until warm arms wrap around my waist and tug me back to a hard, warm chest.

"Is this okay?"

His whisper dances across the skin beneath my ear and I shiver.

"Yes." The word is barely a breath.

"I just want to hold you. Just for tonight, please."

It takes far too long to fall asleep with the light puff of his breaths against my neck, distracting and lovely.

· · ·

It's Friday afternoon, and Sadie has given me free rein over her hair and makeup—besides her signature dark lipstick, which I would never change even if she let me.

"You haven't let me do your hair in a long time." I smile down at her in the mirror. "Actually, have you *ever*—"

"Shut up," she laughs, elbowing me gently in the hip. She bites down on her lip, inspecting the updo I've created for her. "It looks . . . incredible."

Her words are sincere, genuine in the way Sadie always is, no matter if it's praise or criticism. She's got a hard exterior, always has, but I can see the softer pieces of her shining through the more she's around Rhys Koteskiy.

He treats the tough-as-nails girl like she's made of glass, and I think there is something in Sadie that is slowly, finally relaxing under his care.

"Can I see the dress now?" she asks, the words a little disjointed as she keeps her mouth mostly open to coat her lips in the dark cherry color.

"Yes!"

Excitedly, I rush to the closet door of the spare room in the Hockey House—now furnished with two twin-sized roll-away beds that I *know* Rhys bought for Sadie's brothers so they can stay over with her and have somewhere other than their less-than-happy home to go to.

After taking out the black silk dress, simple and elegant in a way Sadie can pull off with ease, I turn and present it a little dramatically to my best friend.

Her pretty gray eyes go wide, skin flushing as she steps closer and runs her hand along the fabric.

"Oh my God," I blurt out. "Are you going to cry?"

"No!" She nearly shouts, batting at her eyes. "I— No, I didn't. I mean, I'm not!"

She very clearly *is* about to cry.

"Sadie," I whine, tears springing to my eyes. She bats me away as I try to hug her, shaking her head rapidly.

"No." She scoots back and I chase after her, still holding the dress. "You did this to me—I don't cry over this stuff."

Putting a hand over my heart, I stop and look at her like she's the last sweet little kitten up for adoption.

"I don't think it's my fault at all," I say, turning to hang the dress on the doorframe. "I think you're all soft and gooey cause you're in *loooove*." I say the last word in singsong and wiggle my eyebrows at her before ducking down in case she decides to throw one of her strappy heels at me.

"This is ridiculous," she grumbles. She pulls my fuzzy robe a little tighter around her shoulders, and it swallows her entire body. But still, she doesn't deny my claim.

She *is* in love with him.

"You should tell him."

Her lips turn down, brow furrowing lightly as she looks herself over in the mirror. Does she see the same thing I do when I look at her? The strongest, most self-assured girl I know. Someone to look up to, admirable in so many ways.

"Maybe," she whispers.

I remove the dress from the hanger and Sadie takes it from my hands, stepping into the bathroom, half closing the door to slip it on.

"Can you zip me?" she calls out seconds later.

I step into the pristine, empty bathroom, smiling brightly at how beautiful the dress looks on her, the slit perfect for her muscular thigh, the entire cut of the garment elongating her short stature.

"You know," Sadie says, a little glint in her eye as I find the zipper pull low on her back, pulling slowly so the fabric doesn't catch. "You could be coming with us. Bennett would be happy to take you. Rhys said he's never taken a date."

Bennett would be happy to take someone, but I'd bet we'll never know who that is if even Rhys doesn't know.

"Or Freddy?"

The question is pointed, and I want to prod her on how much she knows.

Specifically, if she knows that Freddy *did* ask me. After showing up at my classroom and waiting for me to get out, he asked me if I could *please, please* help him with finding a suit to wear, even offering to get me an extra-large dirty chai for going shopping with him.

The bribery was very unneeded, but I let him take care of me.

We spent the afternoon at a few shops in downtown Waterfell, eventually stopping at a vintage store I've frequented before—mostly because the blue suit in the window easily caught my eye. It didn't fit him when he tried it on, but I knew the alterations were easy enough for me to do for him.

And in the quiet of my dorm room late one night, after measuring his broad chest turned to labored breathing from us both and another almost-kiss, he backed away with a signature smile and settled himself on my bed, though he never looked comfortable, instead stiff and anxious.

"You know you could come with me—be my date."

It made my heart soar. For a long moment, I considered it. Imagined it.

But I remembered the date marked on the calendar hung on the fridge, circled in red with hearts. Sadie told me about it with true, blinding excitement when she asked me to watch Oliver and Liam.

"I can't. I'm sorry."

He shook his head with a pained grin that made my chest hurt and nodded. *"Right. Right, of course."*

I know Sadie would hire a sitter—which she *hates* to do when she doesn't know them—if I even hinted at wanting to go. But I want Sadie to have fun for once. Real fun that makes her feel full and not empty afterward.

Rhys is good for her. *Love* is good for her.

"Is this you playing matchmaker now?"

Sadie grins. "C'mon, tutor and athlete?" The question is playful, mocking how much I've teased her cliché of figure skater and hockey player making the perfect romance pair.

"Yeah, yeah," I say. The ache of Freddy's familiar words and knowing I'll face him downstairs in a pretty suit coat I helped him select is enough to have me fidgeting, desperate to get out. "Besides, you need someone to watch Oliver and Liam."

"The Koteskiys probably wouldn't mind if they came," Sadie says, but her words are tinged with anxiety, like she's not sure of the truth of that statement.

Do this for her.

"Honestly, I'm excited to have them for the night."

Sadie shakes her head. "No, just grab them from practice—they're having pizza night tonight, so it'll run late anyway. And then you can bring them to the dorm or wherever until the gala is over. But I figured they can stay here."

"You sure? If you and Rhys want to have time alone—"

"No, I don't wanna leave them for another night so soon."

Acquiescing, I nod and fix one of the fluttering strands of her curtain bangs that I know for a fact she cuts herself once a month. If I had the budget for extra, I'd send her to a proper salon. She has the perfect hair for something cool and creative—something more than my YouTube hair scholar information created tonight.

"Ready?"

To see Matt Fredderic in a suit that nearly made me choke on my dirty chai the first time? *No. No, I am not.*

Still, I nod and lend her my arm to help her slip on her strappy heels before she heads for the stairs.

CHAPTER 38

Freddy

I hate hospitals.

The gala was incredible, as it always is with anything Max and Anna Koteskiy throw their support behind. However, any good feeling and crowded-room high I was riding before evaporated the second Rhys found me standing by his parents, his expression stricken with clear panic, and a wide-eyed, terrified Sadie at his side.

We'd left, leaving Bennett—who was still missing—behind as we headed directly for the hospital. I couldn't ask what happened before we arrived at the massive building, the tension in the car too great for me to say a word, especially not to beg them to let me out on the side of the highway so I didn't have to go in with them.

My stomach is still roiling, and I've nearly excused myself to the bathroom to puke four times, but manage to hold it together for the kid currently seated in my lap, playing games on an iPad.

The smell of copper and antiseptic leaves me spinning out in a fog of memories I'm desperate to repress.

"Did you win your game, Matty?"

"My doctors said I might get to go to the next one."

"I'm sorry, Matty, but I don't think she'll—"

I shake my head a little too hard. My knee bounces before I can stop it, eliciting a sharp little "Hey!" from Liam, who lost his streak on whatever brightly colored game he was winning.

"Sorry, bud." I smile to hide the deep ache plaguing my every muscle, threatening to pull me under every minute longer I'm in this damn building.

My eyes track to the corner, where Rhys is still talking with a nearly inconsolable Oliver. He'd been borderline hysterical when we appeared without Sadie, screaming at the nurses not to touch him until Rhys settled his hands on the twelve-year-old's shoulders and whispered something in his ear. Oliver's entire body immediately slumped into my captain's arms, fight leaving him so suddenly, nothing left but fear.

Fear that only Rhys seems to be able to calm.

It feels like another shot directly to my exposed center.

A hazier memory surfaces, still shrouded in grief, of a devastated dark-haired man and a terrified eighteen-year-old both clad in uncomfortable black clothes. Too scared to hold each other the way Rhys is holding Sadie's brother now.

I shudder out uneven breaths, holding Liam a little tighter as he settles back against my chest.

The door clicks behind us, and before I can even turn, Liam is jumping from my lap, screaming for his sister. He elbows me as he goes, but the sight of him reunited with her is enough to distract me.

"Hey, bug." Sadie smiles. I realize I've never heard her voice like that, soothing and calm in a way that reminds me of Anna Koteskiy. That reminds me of my own mother. "Did they get you all checked out?"

"He's all right, just scratched up his elbow a bit—right, little man?" I say, ruffling Liam's hair.

I'm softer as I gaze at her now. Maybe it's the sick pool of memories I'm still drifting in, or the sight of her acting like a mother to her little brothers. Maybe it's the lingering regret of the judgments I've made of her in the past.

"Freddy said I'm the same age he was when he started playing hockey," Liam says. *Did I?* Probably when I was frantically trying to avoid any thoughts that involved the words *hospital* or *mother* or *father*. Hockey is my default setting.

"He says I'm gonna be even bigger than him one day."

Now *that* I definitely did not say. *The little menace.*

"I did not." I laugh, shoving him with my knee so he trips and starts up another round of giggles that seem more healing than anything else so far.

Oliver finally releases Rhys, looking at his sister from across the hospital boardroom. There's an entire unspoken conversation before Rhys presses a supportive hand to Oliver's back and walks them both across to her. He presses a kiss to her temple before greeting his mom—a discreet way of giving Oliver and Sadie a moment alone.

I look away from their little worried stare-off.

Rhys clasps my shoulder and pulls me off toward the door.

"Hey, do you mind checking on Ro? Maybe give her a call—"

The question works like an adrenaline shot and I'm nodding and reaching for my phone before he can even finish his sentence.

"Everything okay?"

"Yeah." He rubs the back of his neck and blows out a breath. "I just . . . I don't like the way I spoke to her in the moment. I'll apologize to her after I get Sadie and the boys settled, but . . ."

"What did you say?"

He hands his opened phone to me, forcing me to repocket mine to see it.

RO
They weren't there when I went to carpool—
I panicked and started calling you.
I went to the rink, but no one saw who
they got in the car with.

RHYS

Apparently their dad picked them up &
got in a wreck. Headed to the hospital now.
Everyone is okay.

RO

Leaving now. I will meet you there.

RHYS

It's fine, stay home. It'll only stress Sadie
out more than she already is. I'll keep you updated.

There is no response to that—and I know exactly why.

Keeping my voice calm and whisper quiet, I grit out, "You had to know how she would take that, Rhys. Goddamn it."

"I know," Rhys sighs, rubbing his eyes tiredly. They're red, watery, like he's been holding back tears. Like he's been the strong captain for the entire Brown family to lean on like a crutch—but he's barely sturdy enough for it.

But I know from experience that Rhys Koteskiy is nothing if not loyal and fiercely strong in his love. And it's only because of *that* knowledge that I know he's telling the truth—he didn't mean anything hurtful to Ro.

"I'll call her and take care of it," I say before poking him hard in the chest. "But apologize now. Rosalie's the most selfless person I know. She's probably crying alone in her apartment over that."

My stomach rolls.

"Rosalie?" he asks, eyebrows raised.

"Fuck off," I sigh. "I'm gonna go, but keep me updated. And take care of them."

"I will," he vows. "And, Freddy?"

"Yeah?"

"Sorry I told you to keep away from her. You're a good friend and Ro seems like she needs that."

A good friend. I smile but it hurts. "Yeah. Anytime."

CHAPTER 39

Freddy

The dorms are empty and quiet on a Friday night, but after several unanswered calls and texts to Rosalie, I decided to make a house call.

"I know you're in there, princess," I say again, banging on the door a little harder. I would feel bad if I thought she was already asleep, but I know Ro enough to *know* that she won't be able to sleep after that.

I know Ro—God, does it feel good for that to be true, to know her inside and out enough that I can be here, her support system when she's so often been mine.

"Please, Rosalie," I beg, pressing my mouth against the wood and projecting my voice.

Finally, the door opens. I'm leaning heavily enough on it that I stumble a little and reach out to steady myself by grasping Ro's upper arms.

To steady yourself? Or just to feel her skin.

Ro's so beautiful that seeing her always feels like I've been checked into the boards by some massive defenseman, breath knocked clean out of me.

Her hair is frizzy, bigger than I've seen it—like her curls took on the stress and anxiety of the evening as much as her body did. She's still wearing what she wore to work, I assume: jeans and a flowy sage-green top. The ribbon holding her hair up is sad and droopy now, the entire ponytail nearly undone.

Shaking hands with pearly nails reach up to wipe newly formed tears, her bottom lip trembling as she shakes her head. Her face is pale, hazel eyes red and watery.

"S-sorry."

I shut the door behind myself.

"Come here, Rosalie," I whisper, and she collapses into my arms. I press my back against the door and take her full weight, wrapping my arms around her and kissing her hair and along her forehead while I whisper, "It's okay. Sadie, Liam, Oliver—they're all okay. Everyone is safe and okay. You're okay, Ro."

"It's my fau—"

"It is *not* your fault," I say, pushing her away from me a little. "Hey, hey." I wait until her eyes are locked firmly on mine so she can see the ferocity in my stare. "None of this is your fault, okay? You didn't do anything."

"I tried to call—"

"I know, princess." I crush her back into my chest. "You're so perfect, so selfless. You do *everything* for everyone around you—and tonight was a freak accident. It could have happened to Sadie if she was picking them up, to Rhys, to Anna or Max—*any* of them. Would you want Sadie beating herself up over this?"

She shakes her head, forehead rubbing across my stiff button-down and suit jacket.

"Would you think Rhys was bad for Sadie if this happened to him?'"

She shakes her head again.

"Exactly. So let's get rid of any of the self-blame stuff, okay?"

"Okay."

I wait for her to release me, but she only hugs me tighter, which sends a thrill of being wanted, *needed* for pure comfort, zinging up my spine.

Until I feel her shuddering increase and realize . . . she's sobbing. Hard.

"Whoa." I gently try to pry her from my body but she doesn't budge. "Rosalie, please."

Finally pushing her back enough, I can see she's crying desperately now and my stomach drops.

"Hey, hey, hey." I smooth her hair back from her face over and over. "It's killing me to see you cry, princess. Please."

"I'm s-sorry," she splutters, words mangled and caught up in sobs.

"Don't apologize, love, just tell me what I can do to fix it. What's wrong?"

"I don't know. I think—" She hiccups a few breaths, trying to get enough air to speak, before whispering, "I miss my family," into the quiet, darkened room.

My body settles with the ache of a familiar pain. *Me too, princess.*

"Okay." I nod, pressing another kiss to her forehead and tightening my hug around her for one last squeeze. "Here's what we're gonna do. I want you to go shower, do whatever you need to do to relax and feel good again. Cry if you need to, take your time."

I can't stop fluttering little kisses across her skin, especially as it seems to soften her cries until they are fewer and further between.

"Okay."

"Can I use your computer while you're in there, princess?"

She nods before sliding from my arms and into her room with my hand in hers. She lets me settle onto the end of her bed with her opened laptop in my lap before she gathers more clothes and heads to the bathroom.

I wait until the water is on before biting my tongue to swallow the anxiety of what I'm about to do and hitting the call button on her screen.

They answer on the second ring.

. . .

She's washed her hair, which takes much longer with her curl routine, as she walked me through it mindlessly once when I asked. She waited after every step for me to get bored, but I could listen to her talk about the scientific process of paint drying without batting an eye. Everything she says is enthralling to me.

However, it means I've had nearly thirty minutes to chat and laugh with the kind, gentle woman on the screen.

Still, I go quiet as Ro emerges.

She's in the doorway of her bathroom. Her striped pink pajama pants flood her ankles just clearing the length of her legs, while a massively oversized shirt with a bespectacled teddy bear reading a book and bright bold letters saying Beary Yourself in a Book covers her down to midthigh.

Smiling bigger, I hold my finger up to the camera and prop the laptop in the corner of her half-made bed.

"Is that my mom?"

I take Ro's hand and lead her over.

"I ordered you some food to get delivered from The Chick," I say, knowing full well they *don't* deliver and that I used my scary senior privileges to get one of the team freshmen to make a trip for me. "Should be here soon. I'll leave it outside your bedroom door with a knock."

She looks a little shell-shocked, but not unhappy as she turns toward the screen where her mother is still smiling like she's won a free cruise.

I don't wait for the rest of her reaction before seeing myself out of the bedroom and into the living room.

. . .

"You're still here?"

My body shoots up, having almost fallen asleep on the couch. I raise myself up and look over at her.

Clearing my throat, I say, "Rhys called. Sadie is staying at her house with the boys. And . . . I didn't want you to be alone." *Not now . . . not ever, if I can help it.* "How was time with your mom?"

"Amazing," she says, walking over to sit opposite me on the sofa. "Thank you, Matt. I don't . . . I can't tell you what that meant to me."

"Good." I smile at her gently.

"And thank you for the food, too."

I laugh lightly. "The Chick really helps when in deep emotional turmoil. Can't say how many times I've eaten my feelings there."

She grins and shakes her head.

"You're still in your suit."

I only realize that I am, in fact, still fully dressed, suit coat and all, after she points it out.

"Only for you, princess," I flirt. "Figured you'd want to admire your choice in person."

There's a bright flush to her cheeks. "I knew you'd look good in the blue. And I can't really imagine you in a tux."

"No?"

She shakes her head, biting on her lip.

"You'd be right," I say, standing to slide my suit coat off and toss it over the back of the sofa. I take the opportunity to sit closer to her this time, my arm stretched out behind her. "I've never worn one before."

Ro grins again, her mouth on the straw as she takes another loud sip. She presses play on the TV, where the music has paused, Manchester Orchestra's "The Sunshine" serenading us.

"My junior prom date wore this godawful baby blue tux that didn't match my dress at all—a pink jacquard dress that I hemmed and changed the neckline on myself. I thrifted it."

"You know I'm gonna need to see those pictures," I say, and she smiles, eyes glinting with pride.

"Anyway, with his eighties powder-blue suit and my pink dress and heels, we looked ridiculous. Like lopsided Easter eggs."

A laugh bursts unbidden from my chest, head tilting back as my arm slips to her shoulders and pulls her in a little closer.

"I'm sure you were gorgeous, and he was just a bad accessory." I pull at a loose thread on the shoulder stitch of her shirt. "Did you redeem yourself the next year?"

Ro shakes her head. "No, um . . ." She trails off, hesitant, chewing mercilessly on her lip. "My dad had a stroke that May, my junior year. It was really touch and go for a while."

My heart thuds a little harder as I squeeze her tighter in my arms, a familiar, similar pain throbbing in my chest.

"After, I spent a lot of time taking care of him."

"I didn't know," I breathe. "That's . . . that's horrible, Ro."

"Yeah." She nods, head bobbing out of my hold on her. "But he's okay now. He can't really move that well anymore, and he has trouble speaking, gets stuck on words sometimes." She pauses. "It's why I started going by Ro, instead of Rosalie. It was easier for him to say."

"That's—"

There are no real words to say, all of them sticking in my throat. *You're the most amazing, wonderful person I've ever met, and sometimes I nearly make myself sick over what I'll do without you when this is over between us.*

In my dreams, I take care of you the way you take care of other people, and you're relaxed and calm. And before bed, you tell me how easy it is to love me. I'm starting to think I'd give up anything, even hockey, for that life with you.

Instead, I lean in and kiss her forehead, hard, taking a minute to feel her skin against my lips, still dewy and warm from her steamy shower. The crisp smells of tropical florals and coconut waft from her damp, springy curls into my nose.

"You're perfect, you know that?"

She laughs. "Yeah, yeah." She snuggles into my hold now, fully relaxed in a way that works like a calming drug to my system. Her giggles slowly die off before she asks, "What about your prom?"

I want to smirk and ask, "*Which one? The one where my history teacher showed me how to eat a girl out in a closet? Or the one where my girlfriend, for whom I'd already planned a romantic night and spent every dime to my name to make it special for her, asked if I wanted to try a threesome with her best friend in the hotel?*"

But something about the way she's looking at me, wide hazel eyes and a little soft smile, makes me want to be different. Makes me wish I was someone different. Her vulnerability pulls at mine, but I am drowning in humiliation.

So I lie.

"It was amazing. I look great in baby blue, princess."

Realizing I won't say more, Ro tucks her hair behind her ear and inches closer, so our thighs completely press together, knee to hip.

"Do you want to stay here tonight?" Her head tilts almost too close, voice dropping into a whisper.

"Yeah," I breathe, the answer coming easier than I expect. "Do you want me to?"

"Yeah."

Breaths come out slow but uneven as our mouths move closer and closer together. Kissing her now would be easier than *not*, and yet . . .

"Do you want me to kiss you?" I ask, lips brushing hers with the question.

She moans slightly in the back of her throat, but there's a hint of hesitation, and that's more than enough for me to pull away.

"Wait, I—"

"It's okay, Rosalie," I whisper, smoothing her hair back. "But just know—the second you ask me to kiss you again, I'm not holding back."

And though I have self-control, I'm not a saint, so I steal a kiss on her cheek, near the corner of her mouth.

"All I have to do is ask?" she asks, raising her hand to where I my lips had just been.

I nod. "All you have to do is ask."

CHAPTER 40

Ro

"*C'mon, princess, take what you need.*"

His voice is gruff, arms trapping me around the waist as I grind down. I'm panting, chest heaving as I grip his shoulders for leverage.

"*That's it, Rosalie.*"

The sound of my full name rolling from his lips has me jolting, rocking higher and higher, almost cresting that mysterious, elusive wave. My stomach hollows out, an edge of fear as I—

"*Rosalie—*"

My eyes whip open, sweat beading on my brow. That sounded like—

Oh my God.

Matt Fredderic.

Matt Fredderic in my tiny twin bed, pressed entirely against my back while I'm writhing and have my hand—I look down briefly—in my pajama pants.

The embarrassment shoots through my body so swiftly I feel like I might pass out from the intensity of the shame. That, or cry, eyes welling a little as I stay completely frozen, facing the wall of my room.

I'd taken that side at his insistence after asking him to stay with me for the night. I felt too raw to be alone, and Matt was worried I would fall out of the too-small bed attempting to fit both of our long-limbed bodies.

"Ro?" Matt asks again, chin resting lightly on the curve of my shoulder, breathing into my neck—which very much does *not* help my current predicament.

"I— I'm—"

Nothing. I have no words, just a lump in my throat, my skin hot with mortification. Shame rolls through my gut like lava.

"Rosalie," he breathes, his hand coming up to my waist, shifting my hips. The angle thrusts me against my hand, and I nearly cry out.

Instead, only a muffled whimper crawls from my tight-lipped mouth.

"I need—"

Matt's hand lands on top of mine, over my soft, thin pajama pants, working like an ice-water-level shock to my overheated system, or a gallon jug of gasoline and a lit match with how quickly my need and desperation notch up to an insurmountable level.

"Easy, princess," he says, voice stern, but with a morning scratchiness that has my toes curling. "Do you want me to help you?"

I want him to do *anything* to me.

"Yes, please," I breathe.

He chuckles, pressing a kiss to the skin below my ear. "So polite," he praises. "Such a good girl."

"Freddy—"

"No," he says roughly. "Call me Matt. Please."

Matt's hand flattens, firmly pressing my own hand to my sex. The pressure makes me gasp and thrust my hips forward a little desperately.

"Can you come like this?" he asks, not even a trace of teasing in his tone. Just a soft, genuine question. "I want to know what feels good for you, princess."

"It all feels good," I say, so shakily I'm worried it might've been gibberish. "Please."

"Move your fingers," he commands, though his voice stays even. "Do you want to feel me?"

"Please. *Please.*"

I'm not sure if I've nodded, or if my vision has gone hazy. But he directs my body to lie more on my back, one of his arms still beneath my neck.

Matt's fingers trail back up my stomach and under the waistband of my pants, feather-light touch slipping over my overly sensitive skin until the warmth of his hand meets mine.

It isn't what I thought he meant by *feel* him, but it's perfect.

My fingers swirl over my clit in slow but tight circles. His bicep brushes my nipples through my shirt, and that combined with the feel of his bare skin against mine, so close to where I need him, elicits an embarrassingly needy noise from me.

Embarrassment threatens, but before a single thought can derail my arousal, Matt is in my ear again.

"So beautiful, Ro. Just keep doing what feels good. Just like that, princess. Good girl."

His praise feels as good as his touch. The noises I'm making only grow as he angles his hand, fingertip pressing at my opening.

I nearly swallow my tongue, and a loud, keening noise—almost a sob—bursts from my lips. I pull my hand away from myself, biting my lip and furrowing my brow as he starts to inch his way into me.

He pauses, and my knuckles go white with their grip on the sheets beside me.

"Breathe, Ro. You can touch, baby," he says reassuringly, pressing a kiss into my hair.

His fingers feel thick, but I'm embarrassingly wet, clenching around him as he slowly stretches me.

"I need—" It's embarrassing. Tyler hated this, that I couldn't just *come* like other girls. That I didn't feel good enough with just him, hating when I tried to touch myself while we—

Matt stops touching me and I almost *do* sob this time. My stomach clenches, the heat of the lust coursing through my body mixing with the anxiety of asking for what I want.

But I don't need to.

His hand finds mine, guiding it back to the swollen wet flesh, moving my fingertips in a light, practiced circle.

"Don't stop," he says. "It's okay to want both at the same time. If that makes you feel good."

The relief is instantaneous, as is the flood of heat as he moves his finger back to push into me, soft and gentle.

"I want you to feel good, Ro," he breathes, pressing in and out— once, twice, before adding a second finger that has my other hand gripping his forearm. The need to keep him there and pull him away makes my stomach flip.

He curls his fingers and I jolt, shifting until the solid length of him is pressed into my hip. There's a heady rush of confidence in knowing he's just as affected by this, that he wants me just as much.

It's enough to have me relaxing a little in his grip as he works my body over. He's an award-winning musician, and I am his instrument, though the sounds he continues to pull from me are anything but musical. Still, I don't hold back, letting myself fall entirely into him.

The heat grows hotter and hotter in my core, tightening until I can't hold it back anymore.

"Rosalie," he moans into my ear, and I shatter with a breathy, "*Matt*," to match him, cresting the wave with abandon, knowing he'll hold me through it. Keep me safe.

It's quiet, only the huffed sounds of our breathing and the light press of his lips to my neck over and over. My body stays wired, but the energy shifts to panic and embarrassment. I pull abruptly from his arm and almost sprint to the bathroom, shutting the door and sinking against it.

A beat passes, and then, "Rosalie?"

God, will I ever tire of hearing my name from his lips?

"I need a second," I say, chin tipped to my shoulder. "Actually—um, I have . . . I have work. I need to get ready."

"Okay." I can easily imagine him nodding repeatedly outside the bathroom. "Okay—um, I can go. Unless you need a ride."

My heart is in my throat. "No, I'm, uh, I'm good."

Another, longer pause. "Okay. I'll see you later then, yeah?" I hate the sadness I can hear in his tone, carving lines in my skin like I'm rolling on broken glass.

"Yeah."

. . .

Dr. Tinley calls me to her office Monday morning, which leaves me unable to sleep Sunday night with the anxiety rolling through my system. Dreams about missing the meeting entirely, or even getting fired, plague me all night.

I knock rapidly and peek into her office, the warm ambience always soothing.

"Come in, Ro." She smiles over her coffee cup at me.

"Morning," I say, taking the seat at her desk and dropping my backpack to the floor. I cross and uncross my legs.

"So, you know I adore you, girlie." She laughs, tucking her hair back. "You're so smart and talented, and I'm so lucky to have a girl like you on our tutoring team and in my prep cohort."

"Thank you." I blush, relief settling my nerves.

"Of course." She takes another sip of coffee, leaning forward across the desk. "Now, here's the one thing I really need to chat with you about. Your cohort."

I swallow a little harder, wishing I had something to drink to clear my throat. Angry at myself for forgetting my water bottle.

"Tyler told me you broke up, which"—she raises her hands—"is none of my business. However, he also said you've been difficult? Making things harder on the team? Not coming to events anymore?"

I'm not difficult. I barely even see the team enough to be a "problem." I don't come to events because I'm not invited. Tyler is in charge of the entire thing—he is doing this all on purpose.

"Okay . . ." I trail off, unable to think of how to respond.

"Listen, Ro, I like you. I do. But I need team players on my team. Those willing to put their differences aside, to not be bitter about the past and be able to work with people they might not get along with."

My cheeks flame, her tone like she's chastising a child. I hate it, squirming in my seat, desperate to ask her if I can quit and leave.

"Hey—"

As if I've somehow fallen into the pits of hell and summoned the devil himself, Tyler appears in her doorway.

"Oh! Sorry, Dr. C., I didn't know you had a meeting this early. I'll come back."

"Actually, Tyler, we were discussing Ro's performance on the team."

"Really?" Tyler smirks, eying me in a way that makes my stomach drop. "Well, if you're looking for some more opportunities to work and get to know your team better, we're going to lunch today."

"That's great, Tyler!" Dr. Tinley smiles at him like he's announced a cure for cancer. "Perfect, right, Ro?"

No, not perfect. I have tutoring with Matt today and I promised I would meet him for lunch beforehand. Not only that, but after the other night, I really want to know where things stand between us.

"Sure," I say.

"And," Tyler says, "we're all meeting at my house on Thursday night to go over a couple of things before the applications are due. I think it would be really important for you to be there, Ro."

I think it's really important for me to be anywhere else but with Tyler, for my own mental health and healing. But losing my spot on the team or the respect of Dr. Tinley are both things I can't really afford right now. Not with decisions over the internship program looming in the distance.

"Sounds great," I say, despite the regret I immediately feel.

By the time I make it to the coffee shop inside the library, our usual meeting spot, Matt is unpacked and halfway through the homework from last week. His eyes drink me in as I slide in across from him, my cheeks heating to match his already flushing skin.

It's easier to see the embarrassment now that his summer tan has completely faded, his skin much paler than my deeper undertone. But we're both cherry tomato red and avoiding the elephant sitting heavily on the table between us.

We work quietly for a moment, only Matt's phone playing "As I'm Fading Into You" by Belvins adding limited relief to my anxiety. I tap my pencil against my mouth to the beat.

"Please don't be embarrassed about Saturday," he blurts out, his hands slapping the table, pen spinning out from his grip. "Seriously—we can just forget it ever happened."

It lands like a punch to the stomach.

"Is that . . ." I swallow a hard gulp, reaching for his pen and twirling it in my fingers. "Is that what you want?"

His brow dips, frustration and fear mixing plainly across his face, walls down, vulnerability intoxicating even now.

"Isn't that what you want? I mean . . . we're friends." He finally wrangles the words out. "But I—"

"Yes," I say, feeling more like I'm swallowing a knife than anything else. "Yeah, you're right. We're friends—we can just forget it ever happened." I hand him the pen. He hesitates, like I've offered poison rather than a writing utensil, before taking it.

We barely speak the rest of the session, and I find myself reaching to rub the aching spot in my chest every few minutes.

It aches more when I realize Matt is doing it, too.

CHAPTER 41

Freddy

The entire week has been hell, and Coach Harris is currently busting our asses *again* at Thursday evening practice, but I can't wipe the stupid smile off my face. Even when Garcy—Roman Garcia, a sophomore defenseman—checks me a little roughly into the boards.

Usually, that's Kane's game, but he's currently getting the dressing down of the century from Assistant Coach Johnson. It's bad enough that even Holden is wincing from where he lingers close to his defensive partner.

The two have grown closer—as close as I imagine Toren Kane will allow the kid. Still, Holden follows him around like a golden retriever trying to befriend a Doberman.

Either way, I'm riding a temporary high. My grades are improving, thanks to shedding the impossible math credit for the semester, and all my homework and tests are done and graded. I feel good about my test in biology, as does Ro. I haven't seen her since Monday, and the three days of short text conversations and her being relatively busy have made it a little harder to focus, mostly from the shift in my routine.

Or, because after coming in my pants like a teenager in her bed, and the most awkward tutoring session of my life, we haven't talked about our relationship.

Maybe, if I can wait until she's not tutoring me anymore, I'll ask

288

her on a date. All I really have left are finals before I pass and skip right out of probation.

Hey, now that you're not paid to spend your days with me, do you want to spend the day with me?

I shake my head a little at the thought. Ro likes me, *truly* likes me. I need to show her that I'm not a party boy or "the school slut" everyone believes I am. I can be serious and smart, like her.

"One more time, and we're done for the day," Coach Harris calls before nodding to the other two assistant coaches, as well as their two student interns, to finish out the practice. "I'll see you boys tomorrow. Freddy, a word?"

A couple of the guys *ooo* over the callout, but there are no nerves with Coach anymore. After watching him back up Ro in my adviser meeting, defend me, and believe in me enough to do so, I feel more than comfortable with him.

"Yes?" I ask, hard stopping on one leg by the bench and pulling off my cage.

"You've got a visitor, demanding to be let into my private practices."

"Who?" I ask, sweat that has nothing to do with the hard workout starting to bead at my temple.

"Your dad."

My stomach drops and I have a little wave of nausea as my fists tighten in my gloves.

Coach Harris watches my every move, but so does Bennett, currently parked on the bench while his tandem works the last exercise.

I don't talk about my dad, but it's not hard to make the connection—especially with how often my dad is begging for a media interview, anywhere he can get it. Just so he can call me his son, making a fucking mockery of the term, before tearing my technique and skill to shreds on a national stage.

Sometimes I can't tell if he wants me to succeed like he seems to push me for, or he's only setting up as many hurdles as he can, desperately wishing for me to fail.

"Okay," I say. "Do you want me to talk to him?"

"He's insistent. Nothing I can't handle, but I need you to tell me how you want to deal with this." Very subtly, Harris's eyes flick to Bennett and back to me.

Right, because out of the three NHL legacies on this team, Max and Rhys aren't the only golden father-son pair. Bennett and his dad have a privately strained relationship, easy to see if you're around them long enough. Bennett's dad wouldn't dare show up to a practice, while Max Koteskiy would have a red carpet rolled out for his appearance.

Coach doesn't know how to handle my dad, because in the three years I've been here, he's never shown up on campus.

He's waiting for my lead.

"I'll take care of it," I say, waiting until Coach Harris nods, giving me permission to cut out early.

"Locker room," he calls, crossing his arms. "You've got twenty minutes tops, Fredderic."

I can barely hear him over the rush of blood in my ears as I stomp down the tunnel into the locker room.

"Your little peewee coach needs some backbone if he sent you here to deal with me."

Having only heard his voice through a phone for three years now, the sound of it in person is crippling enough that my knees go weak, and I have to grab the wall for support.

We don't look alike—something that used to bother me as a kid. I wanted to be his twin once upon a time, before his poison infected everything around me, until the decay ate all the good in my life.

His skin is tan and damaged, like he's been drinking on a beach in Miami for the last three years—and maybe he has. His hair is a mix of gray and blond, brighter than mine in a way that immediately negates the serious persona he's trying to create with the cheap, ill-fitting suit. I'm taller, a fact I *know* bothers him even now, especially as I nearly tower over him with the extra inches my skates and my pads give me.

Flat brown eyes slowly take me in from across the room, so opposite the bright green of my own. Does he see *her* when he looks at me? Does it cause him pain? I hope it does.

And yet I don't want him to think of her. He doesn't even deserve the memory of her.

"What are you doing here?"

"Here to see my son skate. Check on his progress. I'm the one paying for this stupid school, right?" He raises his hands out to the sides and smiles—our one similarity. The fucking Fredderic grin and smile lines: *the lady killers; the Dallas playboy and his up-and-coming replacement.*

I *wanted* to be just like him once. It makes me nearly sick to think about it now, about how much time I wasted on him when I could have been by her side.

Stupid. Stupid. Stupid.

"Funny," I deadpan. "I'm on scholarship." *You couldn't pay for this preppy ass school if you wanted to, old man.*

I sit and start to undo my laces. I want him gone before a single skate leaves the ice.

One of the papers called him "Dallas's Biggest Regret" in giant bold letters after his second contract renewal. I remember because Archer laid the paper right next to my breakfast and winked at me before slipping to the corner of the kitchen to inconspicuously sip his coffee when my mom came in.

She laughed louder than I'd heard in a while before kissing the top of my head and ruffling my too-long hair, reading it aloud before I even had to ask her what it said.

I'm sure John Fredderic was the *biggest regret* of a lot of people, but none more than my mother and me.

"I'm bringing some coaches for other teams in to watch you practice. I want you to set up some of your fancier shit, speed it up, show off—"

"Coach runs closed practices."

He ignores me entirely. "And I spoke with your adviser and teachers about the math drop—"

"What?" I freeze then, disbelief running through me.

"That pretty Mrs. Tinley thinks it's a bad idea. That you're taking an easy out. Your adviser seemed to blame some girl—"

"You're not allowed to know my business with the school. That's the rule."

He smiles. "No, you signed that exception form during registration. I assume you thought Elsie would be around, that it was for her, but . . ." He shrugs, like he's discussing the weather and not delivering blow after blow.

"Why can you not leave me alone?" I'm breathless, like I've gone nine rounds in the ring instead of having a conversation with my father.

"Honestly, son—"

"Don't fucking call me that."

My voice is dangerous, a little too loud as it echoes around the empty locker room. I huff, slip off my skates, and yank off my pads, running a hand through my sweat-damp hair, trying to calm down.

His voice only rises to match mine. In the same way he has to be the *best* at everything, he has to be the loudest in the room.

"I'm your goddamn father, whether you like it or not, Matthew. Whatever poison that *bitch* spun in your head all those years is garbage."

Biting down on a scream, I barely manage to speak.

"Shockingly, John, she never said a fucking bad word about you.

Those were *your* games." I pull a gray T-shirt on, not bothering with a shower now. I want out of here as fast as possible. "Even Archer bit his tongue whenever *I* brought you up, more of a man than you've ever been."

John snorts. "Right. Innocent little Elsie, always playing the victim so some older scumbag would rescue her? Do you call Archer your daddy, too? Or was that an Elsie-specific term—"

I've got him pinned to the wall before I can blink, hands on his throat.

I want to stop—I *don't* want to be like him, but there is no stopping the terrifying fury coursing through me. I can't hear *anything* until someone is grabbing me, pulling me away, and my entire body folds in.

Is someone yelling? Is it me?

"Freddy?"

Holden's voice. *Holden.* Thank *fuck* it's not—

Kane is behind him, standing toward the exit with his arms crossed like some strange bodyguard, somehow keeping both my father in here and the rest of the team out.

"Get the fuck out of here before I kill you."

My father scrambles to his feet, darting a nervous glance at the scarred defenseman still in his gear and skates, bringing him to a roughly terrifying six eight—all hulking darkness with the stillness of a hunter with its prey in its sights.

"I begged her to get rid of you," John snaps, straightening his ugly plaid suit coat and heading for the exit. "And look at this—somehow you become an even bigger disappointment with every breath."

I wish his words rolled off me by now, but they don't.

They never do—it doesn't matter how much I smile or laugh at my own expense; my heart is exposed like a second skin, no armor. Every word hits like an arrow to its target until I'm bleeding out on the locker room floor.

I don't waste a second after he's gone before changing and storming out, ignoring my two teammates while praying they never bring
this up again.

• • •

I slam the door to my bedroom a little too hard, wanting to apologize one moment, then kicking it the next.

Fuck, I can't think like this. I can barely breathe.

Flashes of me in this same fucking boat at age six, twelve, fifteen—
over and over, with my mom to sit beside me and coax me back to
normal. But she's not here. I *have* to face it without her. Without
anyone, because I have no one—

You have Ro.

I'm dialing before I can think twice about it, the line ringing long
enough that I'm almost sure she won't pick up.

And yet, when she does, I almost wish she hadn't.

"Hello," she whispers, her voice airy and trembling.

"Ro?"

At the sound of my voice, I hear her curse under her breath. A
door shuts, and there's a few soft inhales and rustling before: "Freddy?"

"I need you to talk to me, princess." I shove the words through
my mouth even though it feels a bit like vomiting razor blades. *So
fucking pathetic.*

Running a hand through my hair and rubbing my eyes where
they've started to burn, I wait for something—anything. Ro can
make this better, I just need . . .

I don't fucking know what I need, can't fucking think through
the beating in my skull, but she's the only thing I *want* to need.

"Freddy, are you okay?" she asks, still whispering.

"Did I wake you up?" I look back at my phone to register just
how late it is. "Fuck, I don't even— I hate to ask, but can you talk to
me until I calm down? I can't fucking talk about it."

My words are harsh, but my tone is aching. Can she hear how desperate, how pleading I am through the speaker?

"Matt," she whispers, a gentle mumble of my name that makes my next breath come a little easier. "Hey, I need you to breathe, okay?"

Obeying her commands is easier than anything I've ever done in the last twenty years of desperately trying to do the right thing and failing repeatedly—but I can feel myself spiraling, the self-hatred growing, the need for her reassurance.

"Do you think I'm a bad person, Ro?"

My voice catches and I cough, desperate to cover exactly how much I'm breaking now. I spin away from the door and walk tight circles around the cluttered floor.

"No," she breathes. "Hey, hey. No, Matt. You're a good person. The best. You're—you're incredible—"

"Can I come over?" I ask, my voice shaking, because just hearing it isn't enough. And I don't care how pathetically needy it is.

She's so silent for so long, and my stomach sinks, the swimming sickness returning to my gut.

"Freddy," she says, and the change of name, the tone of her voice— *Fuck*, a knife to the stomach would've hurt less. "I can't—I—"

"God— Sorry." I bite my lip. "Of course you're busy. I'm sorry—please, ignore me."

"No, Matt, I can—"

"Everyone's really busy right now and I'm being selfish." I nod, agreeing with myself as the words come out. My shirt is sweat soaked and sticking to me, making my thoughts scatter until I can pull it off over my head.

I pull the phone back to my ear frantically, breathing heavy.

There's another sound, and then a deeper voice, muffled and far away.

Ro says, "I'll be right there," but it's not to me. It's to him.

I'm too frantic already not to blurt out, "Is that Tyler?"

She pauses. And then, "Freddy—"

"Fuck. I'm sorry. I . . . I shouldn't have called. I'll let you go."

I don't *want* to let her go. But she's with Tyler, the fucking super genius who doesn't sleep around and is older, smarter, less wild.

I think you'd be really easy to love.

I feel so goddamn stupid.

My entire body sinks down to the floor, head tipping back to rest against the door with a bitter laugh, my knee bouncing.

"Matt, stop."

"Don't," I rasp, eyes burning as I drop the phone into my lap. If she says something, I don't hear it over the thrumming of my heartbeat in my head and the trembling starting to take over.

"I begged her to get rid of you."

"Is it true you've slept with your teachers for grades?"

"You can barely read; you can barely add numbers together—what the fuck are you good for?"

"It was fun, Freddy, but I'm not . . . You're not a serious option."

"I'm sorry, Ro," I say, my breath still heaving as I pick the phone back up. I'm sure she knows I'm crying, can fucking tell by the sound of my voice alone. But she stays quiet as I continue. "I don't know why I called you. I'm fine. You're busy—everyone's busy right now with finals and no one has time for this kind of shit. Sorry, I should go."

She tries to say something, but I hang up before I can hear another word.

My texts to Bennett, Rhys, and Holden are all unanswered in the group chat. Even Toren Kane, who keeps removing himself from the group while Holden keeps adding him back, is silent.

I touch Archer's contact, the photo in the center of him with me on my signing day with Dallas.

But opening our texts is just a scroll through a year's worth of unanswered check-ins. My fingers hover over the keys.

But I can't.

When I was younger, my dad took me to Vegas for a game—and then a casino and strip club. It made eleven-year-old me queasy and uncomfortable, especially how he and his friends were with the girls, who looked so sad.

I was too scared to tell my mom, so I used a phone in the gas station next door and called Archer on the number he'd made me memorize.

Archer flew to Vegas that night to come and get me, still dressed in his pajamas. We ate at a twenty-four-hour diner, and after I apologized for making him come to my rescue, he looked across a full spread of breakfast food, burgers, and pies, and said, "Anything you need, Matty, I'm always a phone call away. Always."

It was easy then, to shed the shame I'd been carrying like a second skin, leaving it behind with the neon lights as Archer took me home.

Now, it's hard. The shame I carry is protection as much as it is a prison.

There's a desperation to use that get-out-of-jail-free card once more, but after six months of silence it's unfair to him. He shouldn't have to deal with this version of me.

I ball my shirt in my hands and throw it hard across my messy room before closing my eyes and letting myself sink further into the shadows of my self-hatred. It's like greeting an old friend.

CHAPTER 42

Freddy

I'm not in my bed. That's the first thought that swirls through my head when I wake up.

I rub my eyes furiously with one hand, the other reaching and fumbling across silky sheets until my phone is in my hand. I look at the screen:

11:30 a.m.
16 missed calls & 24 texts from Princess
10 missed calls from Captain PeanutButterCup
4 missed calls from Rein or Shine
30 texts in FIRST LINE FLIRTS

Fuck—

Someone's hand crawls across my chest, nails sporting a perfect French manicure sliding over the bare skin, down, down, down toward my hip bone before I grab the bracelet-clad wrist.

A sinking feeling hits my gut as I turn my head to see Carmen Tinley, wrapped in a sheet with mascara flecks on her cheeks, smile bright and seductive all at once.

I've been here before, several times, but this feels . . .

Wrong. It's always been fucking wrong—*this is fucked up.*

"I'm glad you're here, sweets," she whispers, and for a moment it

298

feels good—to know that for *someone* I did something right. That I pleased her. That I was enough for—

No. Stop.

"How did I get here?" I ask, raising myself up to lean against the headboard and rubbing my eyes. A deep ache has already settled between them.

She chuckles patronizingly, rising out of the bed and sliding on a robe matching her usual black silk set. "Someone got a little too crazy at the Howler last night."

The Howler.

God fucking damn it.

It shouldn't be that much of a shock that I sought comfort in the one place I vowed to never step foot in again. Specifically, the Howler, a dive bar nestled between Waterfell and Boston, somehow in both cities and neither at the same time. I think I was their youngest patron when I first showed up there freshman year, trailing behind my professor like a dog on a chain. I was probably still their youngest patron last night, considering the significantly older clientele of regulars.

Carmen and I utilized the spot for dates because she couldn't be seen with me in Waterfell. At the time, I thought it was because I was a student. I never imagined she might be embarrassed of me.

Or married.

But I was a game to her, probably the easiest she ever played.

Thinking about myself then, about what I did, the things I was so desperate for that I debased myself time and again, makes the nausea churn higher, so I shake my head and focus on what I can remember.

Which is nearly nothing.

"How did I get here?"

"They called me to pick you up."

That does not make me feel any better.

"Did we . . ."

"No, Freddy—we didn't sleep together. You didn't want to. Didn't even try to kiss me," she says condescendingly, stepping to where I've swung my legs over the side of the bed to stand. "You were embarrassingly drunk."

I scowl a little, peering up at where she broods over me. "I was drunk a lot." *Probably over half the times we slept together before.*

Drowning in grief that felt like a never-ending ocean that I couldn't get out of.

But . . . *You didn't want to,* her words echo. I said no to her—I didn't cheat . . .

Cheat on Ro? You're not dating her. Fucking stupid. God, my head is spinning.

"We were . . . together, then. We aren't now—it's different," she says, her tone the same one she's used with me forever, like she's correcting a wayward child.

And for a second, it's that same frustration and burning, the same weird feeling that used to flow through me as a freshman, grief ridden and angry, with the permission to take power from this woman with so much power over me—and be praised for it.

"*For what it's worth coming from me . . . I think you're amazing, Matt. You're a good man.*" Ro's voice plays like my favorite record on a loop in my head, building me up brick by brick again. "*I think you'd be really easy to love.*"

"How's it going with Ro?"

It all crashes back down.

I feel sick, so much so I press up and brush half-naked past Carmen to the bathroom, hating the three steps it takes to get there. Hating even more that I know where it is, the familiarity of this situation.

"Fine," I blurt out, leaning over the sink. I wish I didn't have to say *anything*, but I know that I have to say something. There's an insistent need to defend Ro, especially to Carmen. Especially in the aftermath of what I've done.

Selfish playboy asshole. This is why Rhys and Bennett wanted you to keep your distance.

Splashing cool water on my skin doesn't help, and I feel like my head is swimming—like I can't get enough air in, because I'm panicking, and I can't get one thought to stick long enough to decide what to do.

"Must be going well. Randall told me you begged him to call her and not me."

Randall, the bartender who probably called Carmen.

Carmen leans against the door, twisting and untwisting her smooth red hair. There was a time where this much nearness, the feeling that she *wanted* to talk to me beyond the sex, would've had me doing tricks for an extra treat.

Now, my shoulders tense, freezing like a cornered deer in the spotless marble bathroom.

"I was so sad to hear she and Tyler broke up; they were a real power couple."

My grip on the sink tightens.

I don't say a word—I probably wouldn't if I could. Even the thought of talking about Ro with Carmen makes my knees weak.

Damn it, did I drink enough to have some kind of alcohol poisoning?

"But it looks like things are working out for you two?"

My head whips toward her. "What?"

Carmen looks a little struck by my reaction and I close my eyes, trying a breathing exercise or a dozen. *Calm. The fuck. Down.*

"You're . . . Freddy, you're passing. That's incredible for you."

As it usually goes with Carmen, all her compliments are gently backhanded.

"I should go," I mumble, my limbs starting to feel numb.

"Freddy." She tsks. "So sensitive." *That fucking word.* It still chafes just as hard, like sandpaper on a bleeding wound that hasn't closed since that day on the front porch of the damn house I'm currently inside.

If she notices the color leaching from my face at her mocking tone, she doesn't say a word, continuing right on.

"I'm only asking as her friend. Tyler mentioned she's been difficult on their cohort . . . Has she seemed different to you?"

"What?" A flare of anger on Ro's behalf centers me again and I find myself grateful for it.

"Ro— She's been different lately. More assertive, but she's causing some waves with the boys on my team."

I want to roll my eyes—Carmen Tinley wouldn't take another girl's side if it was a life raft out at sea. She'd rather drown waiting for a group of young fishermen to be at her beck and call.

"She's a great tutor," I say. "Better than Tyler ever was."

She snaps and her eyes brighten. "Oh, that's right! He was your tutor sophomore year. You know that's when they started dating?"

I'm not surprised she knows. Carmen has always had a too-close relationship with her students, toeing the line of what's appropriate, but moderating it by being so well liked. I remember drunkenly trashing her in a review online, annoyed with her near-perfect score and the amount of anonymous accounts calling her *hot*.

"Don't care." I shake my head. "But he's not fond of me and has made that crystal clear."

I might as well have said he helped me pass astrophysics with the way she reacts, laughing and nodding.

"I—oh." Her head swivels toward the bed and she steps away, returning with my phone in her hand. "You're getting another phone call."

"I need to take it."

She smiles, and I feel nothing beyond the sinking ball of guilt and regret in my stomach.

"I'll make you some coffee before you go, sweets."

I flinch again at the haunting nickname but wait with a clenched jaw until she's gone before answering.

"Ro?"

"Goddamn it, Freddy." Bennett's gruff voice growls through the speaker. "Where the fuck are you?"

Shame threatens to overwhelm me. "I'm— I'm, I'm—"

"We had practice this morning and you, what? Slept in?" He lets out a long breath and I can almost see his thumb and forefinger start to massage his brow. "Are you at least with Ro?"

"What? No—wait, why?"

"He's not with her," he calls, away from the speaker. "Fuck."

"What's wrong with Ro? What's going on, Ben?" The panic claws my throat.

"We don't know," he mutters. "But she left voicemails for Rhys and Sadie last night in a panic saying she was worried about you and that she was getting a ride to you at the house, but she never showed, and no one has heard from her."

Dread curls in my stomach, and I feel a bit like I'm drowning. My hand trembles as I pull the phone away from my ear and click to her unopened texts—

"Freddy?" Carmen enters the room and pads over to hand me a coffee. "Everything okay?"

"Is that Ro?" Bennett asks.

"No," I grit into the speaker. I hear Bennett curse before he hangs up on me. But his disappointment stays with me long after.

Her text thread taunts me on the bright screen of my phone.

PRINCESS

Call me.

Please call me back. Text me. Let me know you're okay.

Freddy, please, answer the phone. I'm scared.

My stomach swoops at that one, but I shake my head and continue slowly. The texts are hard enough to read, but add my pounding heart and thunderous headache and they're nearly indecipherable.

PRINCESS

Just tell me where you are and I'll come to you.

Everything is gonna be okay, Matt. I promise.

Whatever it is, I'll fix it.

I click out of the messages, seeing mostly the same sentiments over and over. Like she was trying to soothe me while I was unreachable.

While I was drinking myself into a stupor and sleeping in Carmen Tinley's expensive bed.

If I got rid of any of it before, the self-hatred is back in droves as I grab my jeans and shirt off the floor before calling a too-expensive Uber to take me straight to campus.

CHAPTER 43

Ro

It doesn't matter that it's the middle of November; I'm sweating as I head back across campus toward the dorms, a longer trek than normal.

I spent the day studying in the vet school library, holed up in a private room since the building opened at 6 a.m.

Being a team player is bullshit—I practice the phrase over and over as if that will be my response to anything Dr. Tinley says to me next week. I don't want to play on their team anymore.

I showed up at Tyler's off-campus townhouse apartment last night with my backpack in tow, ready for hours of work with the others in our cohort. Instead, I'd been greeted by the sight of Tyler, alone, and a spaghetti dinner—complete with expensive wine—spread across his dining table.

Excusing myself to the bathroom, I'd nearly dialed Matt in my panic—only to stop when an incoming call with his goofy contact photo scrolled across my screen: the Hello Kitty tattoo selfie.

It made me smile before his panic melted my own anxiety.

"I don't know why I called you. I'm fine. You're busy—everyone's busy right now with finals and no one has time for this kind of shit. Sorry, I should go."

"Matt, please—just tell me where—"

The dial tone cuts me off. And then the knocking, which I'm sure had never stopped but I'd blocked it out.

Standing with a growl from my huddled position against the bathroom door, I rip open the door.

"What do you want from me, Tyler?"

It's clear my sudden change in demeanor has shocked him, mouth gaping like a fish.

I roll my eyes and stalk past him, grabbing my backpack and heading toward the door.

"Wait! Ro, listen—"

"No!" *I round on him.* "You need to listen. We are broken up. We are done, for good."

"Because you're sleeping with Fredderic?" *He laughs.* "Truly, RoRo. That's pathetic, even for you."

"Matt is a better person than you have a chance of ever being," *I snap.* "But, for the record, this"—*I gesture between us*—"has nothing to do with him. Freddy is my *friend*. That's something you never were to me. I should have done this a long time ago."

I take a settling breath, trying to press a calm I don't feel into every limb.

"This was inappropriate at the least, and an abuse of power at the most. I've let too much slide, and maybe that was naive of me, but I am reporting this to Tinley."

"Tinley won't take your side on this. I'm her cohort lead."

It's upsettingly true—something I've tried not to be annoyed or hurt with in the past. Trying to convince myself that she wasn't favoring the boys of our group over me—trying not to take it personally.

"Maybe Tinley won't," *I say.* "But I'm betting the dean will. Especially if I accompany that with proof that you've ignored a student's accommodations form."

His nostrils flare at the threat. "Fredderic tell you that?" *He laughs, and a chill works down my spine.* "He's a fucking liar and an idiot. Try it, Ro. I guarantee I've got more support in our entire department than you can wrangle together."

I want to argue more, but I can feel the threat, the way he's breaking pieces of me down to sink his claws back into me.

But I won't let that happen. He won't get the reaction out of me that he so desperately wants.

"Leave me alone. Leave Matt alone—just stop. Or I am going to get our department involved. I don't care anymore, Tyler."

Leaving his house had been the easiest thing I'd done concerning Tyler. I wanted to go to Freddy immediately, but he'd been unreachable.

And I was still so raw from the energy that standing up to Tyler took, still am, nearly twenty-four hours later, after spending the night studying and perfecting my research proposal—my original one, before Tyler tried to redirect me.

It'd been years since I pulled an all-nighter, but after the situation with Tyler and the inability to calm my mind of what-ifs concerning Matt, I decided being productive was my best outcome. My phone died somewhere in the middle of the day, and I hadn't had the energy to leave yet, so I just . . . disconnected.

I used the hours after finishing the proposal to journal, like I'd done when I was in high school. After my dad's stroke, our family therapist had suggested it, and it helped. But I stopped when I moved to Waterfell and got busy, stopped taking care of myself or putting myself first.

And then I read the books Freddy got for me—on the bookstore trip that felt like a core memory, melded into what makes me, *me*.

To be loved is to be seen.

An old adage, but also a quote from the shy wallflower character of my favorite romance, when she gains her strength and becomes the heroine of her own story.

Isn't that what Matt was doing? Seeing me?

I try not to think about it too much, because if there's anything tutoring Freddy has showed me, it's his extreme emotional intelligence.

That, tied with his desperation to please and keep everyone around him happy.

The sun set at four and the winds are getting brutal as I climb the steps to Millay and swipe my card, pulling the door hard against the breeze. Climbing the stairs instead of using the elevator that is definitely not up to code leaves a damp sweat on the back of my neck and an embarrassing heave of my breath before I get to—

"Freddy?"

Matt Fredderic is at my dorm room door, head tilted back with his eyes closed.

He's too big for this ridiculously ancient, small hallway—all six foot three of him stretched out lazily across the floor, making me wonder if anyone's accidentally kicked him while hopping over his long legs. His hoodie is scrunched up around his shoulders, almost like he's turned it into a makeshift pillow; his golden hair is messy, backpack held like a teddy bear in his lap.

"Matt?" I say.

He jerks, eyelashes fluttering. He's so beautiful he looks like a Disney prince in some gender-bent version of *Sleeping Beauty*.

"Ro," he breathes with a smile. "You're here."

You're here, in that gentle, happy tone that makes me feel wanted and needed.

"What are you doing here?" I want to laugh and hug him, enough that my fist tightens on the strap of my backpack.

"I went to the library first, to your office, everywhere. I started here, so I just . . ." He trails off with a light shrug. "Came back here after my class. I figured you'd have to show up sometime."

His class—meaning he's been sitting here since 2 p.m.?

"It's nine o'clock at night."

"Shit, is it?"

He struggles to stand up for a moment before I reach my hand out to help him. He doesn't use the leverage, but reaches for the skin contact anyway, not bothering to let go once he has my hand gripped in his.

"You sat here for seven hours waiting for me?"

"I'm really shocked they didn't call campus security." He furrows his brow, as if really considering it. "Actually, that's concerning. Maybe you shouldn't live here anymore. You can stay at the Hockey House."

His suggestion is so quick and mildly absurd I can't help but laugh. Until it dissolves into a hiccuped sob.

"Hey, Ro . . ."

He pulls me into a hug, arms over my shoulders so I shove my face into his neck.

"You scared me." I shake my head, nose rubbing against his hoodie and his throat. "I thought you . . . I was worried about you all night, dummy."

I pull away and shove his chest lightly.

"I know." He scratches the back of his neck, face still a little pale as he chews on his bottom lip. "Can I come in? I mean, unless you're busy. Which . . ." He smacks a hand to his forehead. "I can't believe I didn't think about that. I know you've been really busy and I'm sorry I take up so much of your time, but I *am* doing better."

He's barely pausing for a breath, even as I unlock the door and walk in, Matt trailing behind me.

Letting himself in while continuing to discuss whether he can *ask* me to come in.

"The math class substitution thing? It's great—I feel really good about it. And." He bites down on his pinkened lip. "I wanted to say thank you again."

"It's nothing," I say, dropping my backpack next to our shoes by the front door. "Seriously, it's what they should've been offering you from the beginning. Did you not test for your math credit?"

"I, um . . . no, actually. They let me put it off, for—um, because of my mom being sick. And then I think I got lost in the shuffle." He shrugs again, eyes stuck to the sticker tile of our kitchen flooring.

Matt pulls on the string of his hoodie, looping it around and around his finger, unwinding and winding it over and over. "Anyway." He huffs a breath and blushes as he looks around the dorm. "I don't remember where I was going with that."

"You were asking if I was too busy for you to come in and talk," I say before grabbing two juice boxes—all we currently have that's not from the tap—and handing him one.

"Right." He shakes his head, embarrassment coloring his cheeks further. "And I invited myself in anyway. I can leave—"

"Sit down, Matty," I say softly, passing him with a squeeze on his arm before settling into one of the mismatched wooden chairs.

"I don't have to, really," he smirks. "But I like when you boss me around."

The flirting would be fun, but it's not real. He slips it on like a mask, the same one he's used before—but it's chipped and damaged enough that I can see him through it. The insecurity. The shame.

"I want you here."

The words strike him, and the insincerity melts away to a shaky trust. "Yeah?"

"Matt," I say. "I called you, like, twelve times."

"Sixteen, actually," he blurts out, shaking his phone in his hand. "I'm sorry I didn't answer. I was—it was a bad night for me."

"We all have bad nights," I reply. "But you've helped me with mine. It hurt not to be able to help you with yours. You hurt my feelings, but you really scared me."

"I have a lot I want to say," he says. "But I don't know where to start."

The confession is genuine, as is the layer of anxiety dripping over him. So I stand up and reach for his hands with a soft smile.

"How good are you in the kitchen?"

He blanches. "Where's your fire extinguisher?"

• • •

"About yesterday. Do you want to talk about it?"

Turns out Matt Fredderic isn't as bad as he thought in the kitchen. Granted, he's mostly boiling pasta and using the pesto sauce I made from the fridge, while I've already cooked and diced the chicken.

We did most of the prep in silence, letting the movements and instructions keep him concentrated and calmer, while Phoebe Bridgers croons "Smoke Signals" over the Bluetooth speaker sitting on the counter dangerously close to the sink.

He pauses, shoulder hiking up while he stands stirring over the stove. I wait for him to laugh and make a quick Freddy-like excuse. But instead, he takes a deep breath.

"My, uh." He rubs the back of his neck, refusing to turn and look at me. "My dad showed up at practice."

His dad. A subject we've never truly broached. At first, I'd assumed that Archer was his father—because of the way he speaks about him so reverently—but I didn't understand why Matt called him by his first name.

"You and your dad don't get along?" I try the question, continuing to focus on the last chicken strip, cutting a little slower as I wait for him to respond.

He huffs a laugh that makes my chest hurt, an ache only worsened as he peers over his shoulder at me.

There's a deep hurt etched almost permanently into his eyes, the effect of a buildup of rejection.

"My dad would rather I didn't exist," he says frankly. It's like he's accepted it but still feels it like a fresh wound. "But I do."

I swallow the lump in my throat, demanding myself to be strong, for him. So he can share this piece of himself without having to comfort *me*.

"He . . . he played hockey?" I think he mentioned it once, or maybe I saw it in an article.

"Yeah. I think he wishes I never picked up a stick."

"Hates the sport now?"

He shakes his head, hanging it slightly as he crosses his arms and leans against the creaky countertop of my little dorm kitchenette.

"I think he doesn't want me to ever be better than he was."

I slide the cutting board to the side and meet his gaze.

"He pushes me to be better, to work harder, constantly there to remind me of every mistake I make along the way. But he doesn't want me to succeed—not if it means I'll be seen by anyone as the better *Fredderic*."

"Was this how he always was?"

"Not as bad, but . . ." He shrugs and nods. "Yeah."

Matt turns to the cabinet and grabs us bowls, telling me to sit at the table, but I decide to make us comfortable on the floor pillows in the living room, like usual.

It isn't until we are sitting in the glow of the golden lamplight on jewel-tone pillows with warm bowls of my favorite comfort meal that he opens up even further.

"My mom used to make this," he says, mouth still half full. He smiles a little cheekily and swallows.

"Yeah?"

"Yeah." He nods.

"How old were you when your mom got sick?"

It's the most direct I've ever been about this topic, trying to handle it with care. We've both danced around the other's hurt, both of us desperate only to make the other feel happy—even if that meant ignoring the bad.

But this is important. I want him to see me as a soft place to land.

His bowl is noisy as he sets it on the coffee table and runs a shaky hand through his hair.

"Um, I think sixteen? Originally. But that time she got better fast—she did chemo and it worked for a while. And then it came back around, but it was in her heart. An angiosarcoma, super rare and really aggressive. They gave her six months after the diagnosis."

My heart squeezes, but I stay still and silent, letting him speak without interruption.

"It was only four, though."

"Matt," I say, but stop because—what can I say? There's nothing I can say that would make this better, make it hurt less. How many times after my dad's stroke had someone said, "I'm so sorry," or God forbid, "Everything happens for a reason."

Four months.

A ten-year estimation would be hard to swallow—my dad's not-so-confident "he'll probably be like this for the rest of his life" was a living form of grief for my mother and me. But at least he is here, still breathing; he can still smile at me in his favorite leather recliner.

"Tell me about her."

CHAPTER 44

Freddy

Tell me about her.

When was the last time anyone asked me that?

A smile breaks out across my face—even thinking about the force that was my mom shoots a bolt of joy up my spine. I'm not sure where to start, so I blurt out, "She was really smart."

Ro rewards the quick confession with a smile. "Yeah?"

"Yeah." I nod. "She finished her master's early—sports medicine—and got offers, like, everywhere. But she had a friend from high school who was playing hockey already, so she took the offer with Dallas, because she didn't want to be alone—I think. Her parents were kinda cold and not that nice—I only met them once, when I was really young. I barely remember the visit, but Archer says they were never very kind to her."

"Was Archer her friend?"

"Yeah." I smile again, remembering the photo of them on our living room wall, a Polaroid tucked into the frame that held her diploma. A blurred photo of my mom and Archer at their high school graduation just as Archer lifted her in the air—joyous surprise on her face, a hand on her cap to keep it secured. She's looking at him. And Archer is grinning at the camera, cap half off his head with the commotion.

"She was really new to the team still, when she met my dad—" I

314

cut myself off at that, the mention of my dad starting to push away the good feeling that memories of my mom bring.

"You don't have to talk about him," Ro says, her voice sounding distant.

But . . . but I *want* to talk about him.

"He was—*is* a narcissist. He thought he was the best on the team, and I think it was more, at first, that my mom found him charming. He pursued her wildly—very publicly. Showed up to every practice or stretching session with her armed with flowers and extravagant gifts.

"Archer wasn't playing anymore; he'd gotten hurt bad the first year my mom worked there and he started coaching. She helped him through his injury, but then John Fredderic showed up and ensnared my mom."

Clearing my throat, I add, "My mom was the best person I've ever known. She was—"

I reach up to my eye, feeling an itch, and come away with my fingers wet.

Shit. Am I crying?

"Sorry." I laugh and shake my head, wiping my eyes earnestly. "I can't believe I'm crying. It's been, like, four years."

"Hey," Ro says before crawling over to my side of the floor and grabbing me in a hug—one I quickly return full force.

"I wish you could've met her. I told you that you remind me of her a lot—kind and gentle. Nice to everyone. Helpful and genuine. But my dad, he . . . he ruined it. All the time."

"Were they ever married?"

I shake my head. "No. She gave me his last name because they *were* going to get married—I think? It's kinda fuzzy."

Our pasta is cold now, half eaten and fully forgotten. And I feel like a used towel, wrung out and dried up.

She turns on our favorite internet show, letting it autoplay as I rest my head on her shoulder and she rests hers on mine. Her curls tickle my neck and cheek, the smell of her shampoo and perfume intoxicating and fresh.

I turn my head slowly until I can press my lips against her neck. Once, twice, and then I press my nose in to inhale her skin.

Flopping back away from her, I take her in—flushed cheeks, pupils wide, breath shallow.

I think the sight of her beneath me, being inside of her, would change me forever. She is so perfect, smart and gentle and kind. That same desperate need to please is like a living thing inside of me, begging me to push her back, put my head between her thighs until she feels good and happy—relaxed, sated.

I want that.

But there is something unsettling about sex now, especially with Ro. The need to please her in the way I know best warring with my need for her friendship. Her respect—and never have those things gone hand in hand for me.

So I grin and jump up from the floor.

"I should go."

"Do you want to stay tonight?"

I've slept next to her enough times to know my answer is a resounding yes, but I shouldn't. It doesn't matter—I'm nodding before I can talk myself into leaving.

She pops up beside me, stumbling a little in her excitement. It's thrilling and humbling all at once.

"I just need to shower."

Why does it feel like she asked me to get naked?

My throat goes dry. "Okay."

"You can come in, though." *The room? The shower? Her?*

"Sure." I nod stupidly, following her into the dim lamplit room. It's an instant hit of dopamine; the entire room is *her*. Same sage-green patchwork bedding and floral sheets. Same fairy lights and sewing machine in the middle of a project on her desk. Her perfect wall calendar meticulously filled out with—I stop to stare at it, hand drifting up to touch it. Ro's been to every home game we've played, and now I know why.

My finger grazes the black writing—all my games are written out on their respective dates.

"Oh," she says. She blushes, realizing what I'm staring at. "Yeah, I just . . . I don't wanna miss one, ya know? So I marked them all down."

I can't swallow, throat tight.

"I'll be right back," she says before swiftly turning on her heel and disappearing into the bathroom.

My thoughts are racing, warring with one another. Like a mental game of pulling petals off a flower: *she likes me, she likes me not . . .*

Ro marked my games on a calendar. She made me a tie, embroidered with stars and my number. She asked me about my mom. She asked me to stay the night.

Don't do this to yourself, I think, clenching my fists at my sides. *You've been wrong before.*

Carmen's voice echoes in my ears before I can stop it. "*It was fun, Freddy. Don't be ridiculous, you're—that's not what I need.*"

Ro is different. I have to believe that. Ro wouldn't play with my feelings like so many have before. She's *real.*

Barging into the bathroom doesn't seem right, but I can't stop myself. Steam billows around me as I cover my eyes and blurt out, "Do you like me?"

"Matty? What are you doing?"

"Do you like me? Do you have feelings for me?"

There's a creak of metal on metal and I uncover my eyes on instinct. Ro pokes her head out around the colorful shower curtain, curls piled high on her head, a few wet and stuck to the back of her long neck.

Hazel eyes inspect me until I'm aware of what I just did. What the hell was I thinking? I don't—

"Matt," she breathes, eyes softening. "Of course I like you. There's no part of you I wouldn't like."

Wanna bet? That same voice that sounds too much like my voice mixed with my father's.

White teeth nibble on her bottom lip as we lock gazes in the steamy, humid room.

"Will you kiss me?"

"What?" I nearly stumble, planting my feet a little wider so I don't make more of a fool of myself than I already have.

A touch of insecurity sinks into her features, her hand gripping the curtain a little harder like she might slam it closed and tell me to *get the hell out.* "You said I only had to ask you—"

I don't let her finish, straining toward her and planting my hand on the wall beside the shower, my other hand holding her neck as I kiss her. She tastes like candy and summer, warm, lips wet from the shower as I drink from her mouth.

My tongue pushes between her lips, the noise she makes sending shivers down my spine. She pushes back just as excitedly. Ro kisses like an overeager teenager, like she's just discovered French kissing. It ignites something in me, something that makes every touch feel like *my* first time.

Special.

I pull back, smiling with heaving breaths. She matches me, until we are both doe-eyed messes gazing at each other.

"Come in, Matty," she says before ducking her head back into the shower. My breath catches. She doesn't—

"You don't have to," she calls over the sound of the spray. "But I want you."

I want you.

It feels like I'm undressing for the first time, chucking my sweat-shirt and shirt into a pile in the corner before pulling my pants off too hastily, having to catch my balance using the wall.

For a moment I debate if I should take my underwear off, which is ridiculous. No one showers in underwear. *They do when they don't wanna pressure the girl in the shower.* But she's naked already—

Fuck. Rosalie Shariff is naked. And wet. In a shower, waiting for me to join her.

I don't think, just pull back the curtain and step into the tight space.

I'm greeted by the long, bare line of her spine, golden tan skin from head to toe, and I swallow my tongue as my gaze tracks down, down, down to her small, pert ass. She's tall, delicate, and so beautiful I can't stop flicking my eyes over her because I don't know where to look first.

She looks over her shoulder, down my body, before—

"Why are you wearing underwear?"

What?

Oh— Fuck. I am, though now the gray fabric of my boxer briefs is stuck to my skin, damp from the warm, wet air.

She turns, but brings her arms up over her chest, covering herself. "Shit."

I scramble, my hand swiping at the wet tile as I reach and shuck off my boxers, tangling them around my feet until I can kick them off, tossing them out onto the bathroom floor.

Ro inhales sharply as she takes me in.

I match her, both of us staring openly, admiring each other.

Her brain, her kindness—that's why I want her. But God, her body has me ready to drop to my knees and stay there, staring at her like a work of art, never getting my fill.

"Rosalie," I breathe, swallowing loudly. "You're so beautiful."

She blushes, letting her arms drop from around her chest, revealing small breasts tipped with small brown nipples.

My mouth waters. I want to press my lips to every inch of her, slowly taking my time down her tight body until I reach the soft brown curls between her legs. I know the feel of her, dream about it often, but I want to see her feel me, my fingers inside her, pulling pleasure from her.

"Can I touch you?"

Hearing her ask that question makes me moan, my own hand holding myself. I'm rock hard, practically straining toward her.

"Y-yes."

She reaches for me, slow and careful. Her delicate hand wreathed in little beaded friendship bracelets wraps around my length. Her fingers are long, but still barely meet.

I'm well aware of what I bring to the table when it comes to sex—pretty face, muscular body, objectively white-boy attractive. My cock is arguably perfect; a nice length, and thick. And, most important, I know how to use it. I'm good at sex, just like I'm good at hockey.

And yet, my dick is weeping like a virgin in her hesitant hold.

"I'm—I don't know if I'm going to do this right."

I almost laugh at the ridiculous idea of her doing anything wrong, but bite my tongue and step a little closer to her, touching along her bare shoulder with my fingers.

"Just stroke it; you can't do it wrong."

I can't remember the last time I got a hand job, but *fuck*, the feel of her hand on me is going to make me blow in five seconds like a fucking teenager.

"Like that?"

"Yeah, princess," I breathe, my hand coming up to cup her cheek. She's warm from the water and the blush of her arousal. "I wanna kiss you," I pant. "Please, please let me kiss you."

It's almost a whine, and maybe I should be embarrassed, but my want for her is so great I don't care.

She nods rapidly, eyes meeting mine—finally pulled away from her intense gaze on my dick. She sucks her bottom lip into her mouth and I collapse into her. I press her back into the cool tile, and the water splashes over my side as I angle into it.

She whines into my mouth, almost frantic, as I feel more than see her press her legs together.

"Rosalie," I coo, pressing her fully back. Her fist continues to grip me while I slide my knee between her legs. "Are you aching, princess?"

"Yes," she breathes. "Please, Matt—"

"Ride my thigh, baby. Make yourself feel good."

She does, humping against me with abandon. I feel feral, frantic in my movements to kiss her, nipping along her neck and trying desperately not to come.

Until—

"I think about you when I touch myself," she cries into my neck, biting down. "I—"

I come, hard, with a heavy, breathy moan. It zaps through me like lightning, no time to prepare for it or tell her. Come splashes against her bronze skin, washing away with the spray instantly.

She stops moving on my thigh immediately and I kiss her, harder now, as if I'm pressing *thank you* into her mouth. I wait for her to keep going, to rock against me, growing impatient as I grab her hips.

"You don't have to—" Ro says, shuddering as I push my thigh against her clit. "You finished. We can stop—"

I shake my head. "Not how it works. We don't stop till you come, Ro."

I pull her back with a light grip on her neck, looking into her eyes. They widen comically as I say, "Usually more than once, but the water's gonna get cold."

"But—"

"Does it feel good?"

She nods.

"Do you want to come?"

Her blush is furious, but she manages another nod. Her fingers tangle in the chain on my neck, pulling a little sharply. She could pull me around with it and I'd follow like a damn puppy.

I kiss her temple and hike her up again. "Then keep going, princess. Just like last time."

Ro whimpers, melting into a low, desperate moan. She rolls

her hips more quickly now, sharp nails sinking into my flesh as she climbs higher and higher before cresting.

"That's it, pretty girl," I mumble into her neck, kissing her while encouraging her. "Come on, Rosalie. Let go. Come for me, *please*, Ro, I need to feel you—"

Her shout bleeds quickly into a keening cry, nearly a sob of relief that has my cock rising again in record time. I grip her hips, slowly moving her as she slumps more and more into my body.

Placing her back on her feet, I wait until Ro regains her balance and smiles at me, sated and happy. I thought pleasing *anyone* released endorphins in my body, high on the feeling of being needed and wanted in the same measure. But with Ro, it's overdose level— and I'm raring to keep it going.

Grabbing her sponge, I lather an exorbitant amount of soap— soap that smells like flowers and coconuts and *her*—and scrub across her chest, stomach, gentle between her legs. I kneel to wash her legs in slow, sweeping strokes.

Looking up at her, I pause. Her eyes are on me, breath heavy and low—but it's not arousal I see. It's gratitude and awe, like she isn't sure if she's dreaming this.

I feel the same.

I think you'd be really easy to love.

Loving Rosalie Shariff would be the easiest thing I've ever done—I know, because I'm already doing it. I think I've loved her since the day she stood up for me in that conference room. As a friend first, something I've never had, but now it's more.

It's overwhelming, suddenly hard to swallow or even *look* at her. So I turn her around and wash her back reverently. I can't stop myself from pressing a kiss into her back, right at the top of her spine.

I think loving you would be the greatest thing in my life.

CHAPTER 45

Ro

I'm high on Matt Fredderic.

He leaves me in the shower with a quiet command to rinse off. I bundle into a big green towel and sit on the lip of the bathtub, feeling hazy and dazed. Like walking through clouds.

My clothes are folded neatly atop the sink counter, but it feels wrong to put them back on. Instead, I slide on an oversized shirt that looks a bit like a Lisa Frank art piece and pull my hair down. The curls are bouncy but frizzier from the extended steamy shower.

I *should* feel self-conscious, but it's impossible to feel anything even similar where Matt Fredderic is concerned.

Instead, it's only a floaty joy bubbling under my skin. He's like a shower and cool sheets after baking in the summer sun. A nap after the beach, all at once comforting and invigorating.

Healing.

There's a slight awkward silence when I come into the bedroom and stop across from Matt with a towel wrapped around his waist. We both hesitate, shy smiles and twitching hands.

He clears his throat. "Hey."

"Hey."

Matt leans over my desk, pushing aside the spread papers for the cardboard beneath, pointing to it as he angles his head over his shoulder to ask, "What's this?"

Every bit of syrupy warmth evaporates, ice in my veins.

"I don't—it's stupid."

He frowns but decides to trek on. I can't decide if I hate him or love him for it. "Why? It looks like a fun list."

It's a dare, waiting for me to play with his flirty comment. He waggles his eyebrows as he reads a few of them aloud.

I don't need the reminder—I remember them all.

> *Dance on top of a bar like* Coyote Ugly.
> *Third base in a car.*
> *Skinny-dip! (But don't get caught or go to jail!)*
> *Go on a crazy spring break trip. (But don't get arrested!)*
> *Get a tattoo.*
> *Lose my virginity to someone who loves me.*

There's more, but I stick on the last one. It aches to think about. To try and dissect the real way Tyler felt about me.

"It was something Sadie and I made freshman year. For me to check off all the things I'd never done but wanted to do."

He contemplates it for a second before grabbing the list and running over to my bed. It's hard to rip my gaze from him. He turns and winks at me over his shoulder, like he knows what I was looking at.

"Tattoos?" he asks. "I'm checking that one off. Do you have a Sharpie?" He opens my desk drawer without waiting a beat, grabbing a green one and a black one from my neat pile. "Which one should we do next?"

He's excited, and it frees a piece of me that's been locked away for years.

Tyler was excited, too, when he first saw it. Then the excitement wore off. I bury the hope beneath the memories of his laughter, warning myself away.

"None of them," I snap, grabbing the board away from him. "Seriously, it's something stupid from freshman year."

My own words sound so hateful I shut my eyes. But it's not toward him. The hatefulness and anger are all for myself, because there was a time when this was important to me. A beacon of hope after leaving home. But it faded away, along with my excitement. Now when I look at the list, the doodles and lipstick prints, I only feel the ache of the loss of time.

"Let's try this a different way," Matt says, but it's almost like he is talking to himself. "I would like to do these things on your list with you. I would love it, actually. But only if you want to. Do you want to try one with me?"

His voice is soft. I feel a little bit like crying.

"Now?"

He shrugs with a weak smile. "Yeah. Why not? If I'm the one you want to do these things with, then the only thing that'll stop us is you, because we're in this together. But you're in control of our direction, Ro."

His words are lovely, gentle. But something about it is wrong. I feel it like a pinch to my arm.

"What about you?"

"Me? What about me?"

He's still smiling—dopey-eyed and boyishly handsome.

"It's your body, too, Matt. You have just as much control as me."

The words feel heavy and awkward, and part of me wants to shy away. But there is another, larger part of me that's insistent *this is important*.

My words pull the carefree expression from his face, brow furrowing as he examines me. The fact that the idea is so foreign to him makes me feel a quick spark of anger in my stomach.

He raises his hands, like he's going to reach for me, but then he clenches his fists and rests them on the bed between us. A bitter laugh—then a smile, lips parted.

I wait quietly, watching as he tries to push back his usual move here—like he's actively unlearning the protective flirting that's so comfortable for him.

He glances back at the list like a lifeline before exclaiming, "I think we start with the whipped cream—do you have any?"

It would be so much easier to agree. To change the subject entirely.

"You know that, right?" I say. "That you have control, too? That you have a say?"

It's quiet for a long moment. Enough for us to both to sit in the discomfort of the conversation, yet be comforted by the mere presence of each other.

"I'm not—" He stops himself, clenching his jaw. "I know I sleep around. I know what people call me, but . . . it's not— I'm not *that* with you."

My stomach hurts, chest squeezing with empathy. "I know, Matt."

He nods. "I just . . . this is new for me." He laughs a little, scratching the back of his neck, ruffling his damp golden hair. "And I might not be good at it, so . . . I'm sorry if I mess it up."

He's kinder than Tyler ever was to me. More empathetic and understanding, more in tune with those around him than anyone I know. And he's apologizing because so many people have made him think he isn't good at this part—that he's not worth anything other than sex. Like he doesn't even deserve the opportunity to try.

"You won't," I say calmly.

He winces. "I might."

"By your logic," I say, stepping closer, "I will definitely mess it up."

"You?" He shakes his head vehemently. "Never."

I raise my eyebrows at him, extending my arms as if to say, *see*?

"Do you want to go out with me?" I blurt out.

He blanches, dropping the cardboard to the ground and scrambling for it, almost knocking his head into my bedframe on his way back up.

"What? Like—like on a date? Or . . ."

"Yeah," I nod, a little giddy with excitement. I've never asked someone on a date before. It's exhilarating, freeing where I thought I'd be anxious.

Matt takes a minute, eyes flicking across my face and down, reading my body language. An endearing smile, hesitant and bright all at once, spreads across his face and he nods rapidly.

"Yeah. That's—yes, Ro. I'll go on a date with you."

This isn't some magical healing conversation for Matt. Everything here feels delicate, like he's on the precipice of something. But it's a start—and a real date is exactly where we should start. To do this right.

Matt crawls across my bed and lies back against my headboard, beckoning me to him with a cheeky smile.

"Now come read me the list, princess. Some of the handwriting is horrible."

Sadie's handwriting looks like a physician's scribbles, where mine is intentional and loopy, decorative.

"Okay," I say, falling into him again.

CHAPTER 46

Freddy

It's the last week of school before Thanksgiving break. Most everyone is packed up or has gone home—half our professors canceled their last classes for the week, which means I've been riding a high.

Mostly, because of a pretty tutor propositioning me for a date.

We've met up only once this week, for our usual tutoring session—which was mostly filled with me trying to distract her. Fingers tracing the smooth skin of her thighs, whispering *I like your skirt, princess*, while I tried to get her to break the silent floor's rules.

Other than that, she's been busy. Between helping Sadie with her brothers and finishing her application for the internship she's applying for, I haven't wanted to distract her.

We lost our Harvard game over the weekend, which I am trying *not* to see as a reason we need Toren Kane—who, it turns out, is banned from playing in Harvard's arena. I found the concerning footage of his last game there before we left—only after scrolling through far too many fan edits of the six-five defenseman.

A weekend without Toren worked like a vacation, but we're back to our regular chirping now as he spins past me, clipping my shoulder.

"Heads up, superstar," Toren snarls.

I look over at him, ready to chirp back, when I realize the taunt is a real warning—a group of suits are standing at the railing of the seats, with Coach Harris and the assistant coaches lingering. All their arms are crossed, like some strange group domination standoff.

I skate over, followed by Rhys and Bennett at my back—Holden sprinting over from the other side. Even Toren lingers a little closer—nearly my entire line together.

"I've told you three times, Mr. Fredderic, it's a closed practice."

My dad sneers but hides it quickly. "Just a few minutes of seeing Matthew play. I brought some scouts from—"

Coach Harris cuts him off. "Did he tell you folks that Matt Fredderic is a free agent? Because he's signed with Dallas and doesn't have any plans to change that. Right, Freddy?"

"Right."

My dad rolls his eyes. "I don't think you're the expert here. And, as Matthew's future agent—"

"You're not my agent."

John Fredderic's attention slides to me, his face turning red in barely concealed frustration. "Your mom's not here." His voice barely drops. "A goddamn bitch—"

My blood boils.

"Don't fucking talk about my mom," I snarl, stomach cramping. Heart aching.

It's impossible to remove the memory of my mom from hockey. They're intertwined, more than with my NHL player father.

Mom loved hockey—always had. When I was young, we'd gone to all the games together. But something had shifted. I remember her turning sadder, her expression less hopeful and happy with each game. Until the last one we attended.

My dad has another girl here, dressed in his jersey and sitting in our spot. She's young, beautiful, but not like how my mom is beautiful.

Mom stands on the stairs only a few rows up from our reserved seats, frozen in her pretty black overalls and Dallas beanie with the fluffy bit on top that I'd asked to play with the whole drive in. I'm wear-ing my Dallas jersey with Dad's number on it, staring at the ice with a bright smile as I try to catch his attention.

But he's blowing kisses to the woman in our seats. His eyes flicker lightly over my mom with a slight hesitation before giving me a quick wave and turning back to warmups.

He said hi. But something about it feels wrong.

The feeling worsens as Mom pulls me back up the stairs too fast, tripping up them. We're in the empty back hallway toward the exit when someone shouts for her.

"Elsie!"

I look over my shoulder at the man in the suit, squinting until I realize it's Coach Ace.

He's as tall as my dad, broader but dressed in a dark suit with a Dallas green tie. Dark hair, dark eyes, and dark caramel skin that makes my mom's fair coloring look even lighter.

I tug on my mom's arm a little, trying to make sure she can hear him yelling for her. She slows, but doesn't stop, wiping her longs-leeve shirt under her eyes in a way that makes my stomach hurt as I look up at her.

"You okay, Mommy?"

"Yeah, baby," she sniffs, trying to give me a smile, but it doesn't look right. She's so pretty, even with red eyes and flushed cheeks. She says I have her eyes, but hers are so much better, like spring grass under sparkling sunlight.

"Elsie, wait," Coach Ace says, stopping right in front of us, smiling quickly at me as he pats my head. "Hey, champ."

"Coach." I smile. He's always nice to me, always plays with me when I come to practice and Dad's too busy. He tells me to call him Archer, or Ace, but sometimes I like calling him Coach—it makes me feel like I'm part of his team.

My mom is looking at Coach Ace like she's going to cry, and some-

thing about her expression makes him heave a deep breath and wrap his arms around her in a tight hug.

"Archer."

"I'm sorry, Els." He holds her like I've seen moms and dads hold each other, his hands gentle. He kisses her forehead, petting her hair the way my mom does when my brain feels too loud.

I've never seen Dad touch Mom like that.

But I have seen Coach Ace hold Mom before, I remember. When Dad crashed the car and pulled me out of my car seat, I remember crying for her, but my dad was walking us away, leaving her there as he sat me down on the grass. And someone was screaming, running from behind us toward her.

Then Coach Archer was there, wrenching my mom's door open and pulling her out, holding her in his arms.

I remember it most because he was crying hard, harder than I was, and he was shouting at my dad.

"Call 911!" he was screaming as he laid her on the grass like a sleeping princess, pressing on her chest hard. She'd been okay, but sometimes I still had nightmares about it. And now, with Archer holding my mom while she cries, I have that same hurting feeling that makes me use both my hands to press hard on my chest. Like I can make it stop.

Make it stop.

I shake my head, feeling the tears forming. *Make it stop. Make it stop.*

"Fuck you" is all I can say, my voice torn and broken.

"You wouldn't know what was good for you if it slapped you in the face, son," he growls.

"Get out of my fucking rink."

Everyone freezes at the slightly raised, threatening tone from Coach Harris.

"Now," he shouts, and I *feel* my team's response.

The men in suits behind my father are already leaving, and I can't stop myself from smiling sardonically and waving my gloved fingers to them as they scurry up the stairs and out.

My dad, however, doesn't move.

"William—"

"Harris to you, asshole," he snaps. "You're banned. No games, no practices, nothing that involves you stepping foot in this arena. Do you understand me?"

"Are you fucking kidding me?"

"Not at all. Hell, I'd ban you from campus if possible. And if I find you sniffing around the Dallas GM or anywhere *near* Freddy's contract, I'll find you and deal with you myself. Get the fuck out of here."

"Do you know who I am?" The cliché slips from my father's mouth a little shakily.

"A washed-up has-been who never touched a Stanley Cup? Yeah, I know who you are. How many years have you been punishing Freddy for being better than you?"

My stomach drops.

I wait for the embarrassment to completely overtake me, my skates slipping and sliding on the ice beneath me before someone— Rhys, I realize—grabs me across the middle of my back. He gives me a quick nod, a check-in to ask if I'm good, all while keeping his arm around me.

I nod back, huffing a little breath. Thankfully my cage covers some of the redness of my cheeks; thankful even *more* for the pillar of strength Rhys personifies.

"That's what I thought." Coach Harris nods when my dad doesn't answer him. "Now get the hell out of my arena."

This time, John Fredderic does something I've never seen him do before: listen and follow directions.

Bennett and Toren, the giants of the Wolves, stand like sentries on either side of our core group, the rest of the team that was practicing before all watching from the sides of the rink. I would bet my entire scholarship and contract deal with Dallas that it's because of Coach Harris's shouting—the man never raises his voice.

The entire rink is silent enough that the sound of the door closing at the top of the stairs seems to reverberate.

"Practice is over. See you all tomorrow for the last one before Thanksgiving. Just because we don't have a game this weekend doesn't mean we're resting." He claps his hands twice and everyone sets into motion, scattering toward the tunnels in small, quiet clusters.

"And, Freddy?" he calls before I can even unstick my skate from the ice enough to turn.

"Yeah?"

"Keep the head up, kid."

His voice is so gentle it reminds me of Archer, and I close my eyes, if only to bask in the warmth of it for one more moment.

Rhys and Bennett stay with me on the ice as everyone else exits, both quietly offering support. But it's Rhys who finally says, "Your dad's an asshole, Freddy."

I snort and nod at him. "Yeah. I can't say the same, Rhysie."

Bennett raises his hand and pulls off his mask, shaking out his curls with a smile. "Don't look at me. Adam Reiner would never."

There's a slight chuckle among the three of us before I slap them both on the back to start toward the tunnel.

"C'mon, slackers. I've got places to be and people to see," I say, my signature Freddy smirk back in place.

The truth is nothing my father said today can fully stop the soaring feeling within. Coach Harris's defense of me only ignited me further.

I've got a date with Rosalie Shariff. I'm beaming inside, even if it's slightly dimmed with a pinch of anxiety. I'm determined to be good enough.

CHAPTER 47

Freddy

My hands are sweaty—way too sweaty to lay on her thigh, though I want to, *very* badly. To touch the exposed length of her leg in her denim skort, trace it all the way to the top of her tall, heeled boots.

I also tried to clean up nicely, changing about five times before settling on black jeans, a white T-shirt, and a dark cream wool shirt jacket. The combo makes my skin seem more golden than it is now that I've been without the heat of the sun for a few months, my summer tan fading off.

I'd nearly swallowed my tongue when Ro came out of Millay, the setting sun dancing off her glowing face and beaming smile.

We both stood there for a few minutes, staring brightly at one another, matching blushes and fidgeting hands.

Finally I swooped in for a quick, tight hug before ushering her into the passenger seat of my car.

Music plays softly from the speaker, her choice, of course. Nat and Alex Wolff sing "Glue" while she directs me every so often as we head closer to Boston.

"You know, I think this is the first time someone has planned a date for me," I say, turning off the highway onto our exit. Actually, it's one of the only dates I've ever been on, but I don't divulge that.

"Is it selfish that I'm glad I'm your first?"

A laugh bursts out before I can help it and Ro blanches.

"No—I, I mean . . ."

"I know what you meant," I say, leaning over at the red light to kiss her on the cheek, leaving my palm just below her knee as I straighten.

There. Easy as can be.

"Here?" I ask, looking a little bewildered toward the nondescript building with black painted windows and antique lamps outside where a lone bouncer sits. "You bringing me all the way out here to kill me in the freezing cold?"

She nods, and I slow to park in the extended lot near the back for an easier exit if the half-empty lot fills up a bit more.

"It's not even snowing yet—"

My eyes scan her. "I thought you were a California girl."

"Maybe I'm not a baby when it comes to the cold," she says before opening her door and hopping out into the frigid night.

Chuckling under my breath, I follow her lead and wrap my arm around her against the whipping wind. "*Jesus*, it's cold. Sorry to ruin your fun, princess, but I think I'll be frozen before you have a chance to murder me *Saw* style in this creepy building."

She punches my shoulder lightly with a glint in her eyes that makes me want to do a backflip or become a full-time court jester and keep her giggling all night.

"You've been out of Texas for four years. You think you'd have toughened up by now." She smiles, all proud of herself, and I swallow any retort in favor of just looking at her.

She's so beautiful, smiling as she flashes her ID to the bouncer and waiting inside the doorway for me to follow.

It's warm, a little hazy with smoke, and it looks like not much has changed since it opened in the 1960s—as stated on the painted signs above the bar. It's mostly high-top tables and a few red vinyl sofas. The lights are dim, blue and green shimmering accents flaring across the black-and-white-checked floor.

There's a singer with a guitar up on the small stage in the corner, singing a gorgeous acoustic cover of some popular radio hit. Even the dance floor is crowded, couples slowly spinning to the music.

Ro had warned me it was a "small bites" place, which meant it would cost me my entire spring grocery budget to feed myself. Looking over the short menu as we step up to the bar, I'm glad I ate before.

I order us both a drink, opting for their whiskey-themed special and grabbing Ro a fruity seltzer. We toast and smile at each other, and it's seamless—tinged with the awkwardness of overexcitement. I can *feel* the thrill thrumming between us.

"Do you want to dance?" I ask.

She nods immediately, grinning like a loon as I down my drink and wait for her to finish hers before taking her hand, leading her to the crowd of bodies sluggishly swaying.

Ro's head is on my chest, soft curls across my arm, as she's left it almost all down in a swirling cascade of dark brown. The woman on stage croons, smoky and beautiful as she sings "We Don't Have to Take Our Clothes Off" with the soothing piano and strings echoing behind her.

I want to press the words into Ro's skin, to make sure she can hear what I'm thinking without the terror of speaking it out.

Your touch feels different. Your words feel different. Everything with you feels different, better. I press a kiss to her hair, then to her forehead, and watch as her plush lips slip into a smile and her eyes bat up at me.

The words almost tumble out then and there. It's our first date, but forget the rest. I'm done, I've decided.

Be mine. Let me call you my girlfriend, not just my friend. I'll be so fucking good to you.

I close my eyes and contentedly breathe in the familiar scent of her clean floral and coconut perfume. Everything here with her seems perfect, like the pictures already in frames at the store of happy families—frozen, beautiful moments. I want a million of them with her.

But when I open my eyes, I see a ghost.

Carmen.

Carmen Tinley is here, in my bubble of bliss, like a haunting reminder of everything I don't want even *close* to Ro. I try blinking, hoping somehow it was a trick of the light, that she'll just disappear.

But there she is—at the bar, drinking a glass of wine the same color as her painted lips and vibrant hair, looking every bit the sad, lonely woman she was the first night we were together. And just like the last time, she's staring at me.

I tuck Ro tighter to me, almost accidentally, and she lets out a breathy sigh of contentment.

"I like this," she whispers, and her vulnerability makes me feel a little dizzy and sick. Enough that I pull away from Ro and run my hands through my hair.

"Matt?"

Even in her confusion, her tone is nothing but soft, gentle encouragement.

"Let me, um—" I shake my head. "I'm going to grab us some more drinks. And close out." Because as much as I need some goddamn alcohol in my system, my need to get out of here is far greater.

"Okay." She smiles. "I'm gonna run to the bathroom."

I watch her all the way to the hallway, while the back of my neck pricks with that same feeling of being observed. Once Ro is safely away, I turn and walk right up to the little bar and order a shot of whiskey for myself and a fruity hard seltzer for Ro.

I'm far enough away that we shouldn't be able to touch, yet when Carmen turns in her barstool, she presses her shoulder directly into mine where I'm leaning on the bar top.

"Funny seeing you here," Carmen says, smiling. White teeth

gleam beneath red lips, eyes darkened with glittering shadow that I once reveled in.

"Keeping tabs on me?" is my curt response.

She takes a long swig of her wine and shakes her head. "Total coincidence, I swear," she says, crossing her heart like a promise.

"I'm here with Ro," I spit out, jaw tight, my entire body wound like a spring toy, barely holding everything down.

"I saw."

She leans close enough that some of her bright red hair trickles over my jacket. It makes my shoulder jerk, as if she's touched bare skin.

"How's that going, then? She gives you the answers and you give her an orgasm?"

The accusation makes the alcohol in my system sour to poison, and I don't really want to do the shot the bartender places in front of me. Instead, I'd like to run to the bathroom, knock on the door until Ro lets me in, and kiss her. Tell her exactly how I feel.

Carmen's allegation toward me is one thing; I can handle it. I'm used to it. It's the slight against Ro that makes me furious.

I finally move, tossing back the shot and shaking my head at the woman I once looked at like she was everything I'd ever wanted. Whose attention I basked in nearly constantly, whose approval I craved.

Letting the flames of whiskey lick down my throat, I shove off the bar top.

"It's not like that and you know it."

"Right," she says, and shakes her head.

I start to leave, but Carmen stands, her heels clacking as she steps to me and wraps a hand around my bicep to stop me.

"I'm not trying to be cruel, Freddy," Carmen whispers, and I pause for a moment, my back to her. The sympathetic pity in her voice makes my head swim with memories. "I worry about you.

You get these fantasies in your head, and I don't want you to get hurt."

"She's not going to hurt me," I say, but the conviction in my voice is gone.

Carmen is smart. So is Rosalie, both bound to do big things and wanting someone steady. Someone brilliant and well bred by their side. I was a fun-time distraction to Carmen—is that what this will become with Ro? Will she grow to resent what I can't be for her?

You're the joyride, man. Tyler's voice taunts me.

"*I begged her to get rid of you.*" My dad, a mockery of my own voice.

"*It was fun, Freddy. Don't be ridiculous, you're—that's not what I need.*"

I shake my head to clear the old Carmen, speaking softly to a younger, crying Freddy on the front porch while her husband watches.

"Ro is brilliant, and she has a beautiful life ahead of her. Don't make a mockery of her. And don't expect her to want . . ."

She trails off and my eyes flash.

"Don't expect her to want more from me, yeah?" I laugh, feeling sick. "Trust me, I won't make that mistake again."

I say it like a promise, to her and myself.

Shaking her off, I slap down a few bills and step away, spotting Ro moving toward me with a bright smile that slowly disappears as she looks closer at me.

"Hey," Ro whispers. "Are you okay?"

"I wanna go," I snap, tone desperate and restless. "Can we go?"

She nods apprehensively but doesn't ask before taking my hand. I'm shoving our way out as fast as I can because I can't. Fucking. Breathe. Even the walk in the cold to the car does nothing to soothe me or cool my overheated skin. I'm sure my grip on her hand is too tight but my muscles won't cooperate.

"Was that Dr. Tinley?" she asks as I spot my car.

"No." I lie so fast I surprise myself.

She pauses a second before, "Who was it?"

"No one," I huff, eyes wild as I turn back to her and unlock the car, whipping open the back door. "Get in here, princess. It's freezing and I wanna warm you up."

This I can do. This is who I am—the one thing I'm good at.

CHAPTER 48

Ro

Something is wrong.

My ears haven't adjusted to the quiet, and the last song from the club—an acoustic, airy version of flora cash's "You're Somebody Else"—is still repeating in my head enough I almost started humming through our trek to the back of the lot.

Until I saw the wild, ragged look in Matt's eyes when he spun me and lifted me into the car.

"Hey—"

His hands are clammy and shaking as he grasps my waist. I lean back, falling contentedly against the leather backseat. I want to take a minute to appreciate how delicate I feel beneath him, but I can't. Because Matt looks devastated beneath the huffing breaths and slipping mask.

"Freddy," I say, even as his mouth presses to mine again, his hand playing along the waistband of my skort, sliding under and making my belly drop pleasantly despite the war in my head.

"Does that feel good, baby?" he asks, his face buried in the crook of my neck. I want to relax beneath him, let his touch carry me away but—this is wrong. Everything about this is wrong.

It feels . . . fake.

Stop him. He's not okay. Stop him.

"Freddy—"

He cuts me off with a moan. "Yes, baby. Say my name."

He trails his fingers down my now-exposed stomach, where he's pulled the fabric of my shirt up high. My abs clench, his shaking hands fumbling with the fastenings on my high-waisted skort. But his face is pale, eyes red.

"Matt," I snap, my stomach hurting from the gymnastics of feeling him but not really feeling *him*. The mix of desire and worry and every confusing emotion between them is nauseating.

He pauses at hearing his name, darting his eyes to my face, pupils swallowing up all the green. The flickering streetlamp in the half-empty parking lot is the only real light. The orange glow cast upon his skin makes him seem almost ethereal.

Ethereal but broken, like a fallen angel.

There's a moment then when he hesitates, his eyes slip, his mask falling as he locks his gaze with mine.

But as quickly as his vulnerability is there, it's gone.

"Let me make you feel good," Matt says, hands tightening on my hips as he licks his lips and the vulnerability that was *just* there slips away behind the Freddy mask. "I'm good at that, at least, right?" His voice is ragged, like he's run a marathon. "So fucking good at it. Let me show you."

Something happened tonight that made him go back to this. And . . . I hate it. I want to scream and cry, because I want Matt more than anything, but not like this, never like this.

"Matt, no," I breathe, heart breaking for him, for the boy beneath the mask who is terrified of getting hurt. "Stop."

That's all it takes. His body jolts back, nearly toppling over as he pulls away. Fear and embarrassment race across his face, flushed from the wind or exertion or the raging emotional turmoil—I'm not sure.

He looks almost horrified, hands up in surrender before another heavy gasp escapes from his mouth, like he's on the verge of hyper-ventilating.

"I'm— Oh my *God*. Rosalie. I'm so sorry. I don't—"

"Hey," I whisper, pushing awkwardly off my back as I slide out of the car to walk toward him. He trips again as he tries to put even more distance between us. "Matt—"

"I need—" He looks around desperately, and for a second I think he might run despite being half an hour from campus. "I need to go home. Can we go home?"

Pressure builds behind my eyes and ears, and I blink away the tears. I don't want to startle or upset him further. I want him to be okay. He looks like he accidentally killed someone, not like he got a little too intense while making out. *Something more is wrong.*

"Yes. Do you want me to drive?"

"No." He shakes his head, then dips his chin to his chest and wipes his eyes. "But I don't think I can," he whispers, voice small and broken, like a scared child.

I don't say a word, only walking to stand beside him. I'm careful as I slide my hand into his front pocket for the keys, while I distract him with a soft kiss to his hot cheek.

"Okay, Matt. Just sit up front for a second and I can get us home."

He settles into the passenger seat while I climb into the driver's side and start his car.

"You've been drinking—"

"I had a seltzer. That's all. I didn't drink the one you got me before we left."

Something I've said there makes him flinch, but he nods and tilts his head against the cool glass of the window, his entire body shifting away from me.

It's a slow ride. Music plays in the background, like some sad soundtrack to the foundational breaking of Matt Fredderic. I have to clench the steering wheel to resist the urge to rub the aching pain in my heart.

I've barely parked in front of the Hockey House before Matt is opening the door and spilling out of the car. I follow as quickly as I safely can.

"Wait, Matt—"

"I'm sorry, Ro. I just . . . I need to be alone, okay?"

The front door opens, Bennett stepping out with his keys in his hand. He passes by Matt, saying something to him. He brushes the goalie off, shaking his head and whispering back.

"You said you wouldn't push me out," I call toward him, a little thread of panic pulling in my chest.

"Trust me, this is one thing you really don't want to know." Matt lets out a bitter laugh. "You'd hate me."

He enters the house and slams the door.

Bennett walks to me, seeming exhausted and sad.

"I'll take you home," he says quietly.

I wipe my eyes, their burning outweighing my need to keep from smearing my mascara.

"No, you don't have to, I can call an Uber—"

"I was already heading out. Besides . . ." He shrugs a little. "I'm, like, a five-star car service at this point."

If he meant it as a joke, there isn't even a hint of humor behind it. If anything, he sounds frustrated.

"Sorry, really, I don't need—"

"No, no. I'm sorry. It was a bad night for me, too."

"Yeah?"

"Yeah."

We climb into the car and his music kicks on, soft in the cabin— soothing in the way I've always found his presence.

He clears his throat before quietly offering, "Sometimes the people we love most hurt us the easiest, even if they don't mean to."

I pause, struck a little by the statement.

"And do you forgive them?"

"Yeah. At least . . . for her. I'll always forgive her." He grips the steering wheel harder. "Don't think I could hold a grudge against her if I tried."

The confession strikes me a little. It's the most I've heard him talk, really.

"Why?"

"Why what?"

"Why keep trying when it hurts?" I nearly choke on the words, but Bennett only grants me a sad smile, rubbing his mouth a little as he turns down South College.

"Because they've been disappointed by too many people," he says. "And I won't be one of them." He pauses and heaves a heavy sigh. "And . . . she deserves it."

Matt does, too.

Everyone who has touched Matt Fredderic has only fed that monster in his head, the one that says he isn't good enough beyond what he can do for them.

I'll be patient this time, because he's hurting. Deeply—and he's been there when I hurt, repeatedly. Matt needs someone who stays, who is willing to prove that he is worth it all. That he deserves good things in his life.

CHAPTER 49

Freddy

This is wrong.

I'm eighteen. A freshman, and too hungover to see straight.

My body slams into someone smaller, nearly knocking us both over into the brick outside the corner of the building—is this the one I'm supposed to be in?

"Whoa there," a voice is saying, helping me lean against the wall. "You don't look so good. Are you all right?"

Do I look all right? *I want to snap, but that only makes the pain in my head worse, so I smile and nod, eyes still closed. "I'm fine. Promise."*

Just keep smiling. *Isn't that what the fish from the Disney movie said?*

Either way, I do.

The shower goes cold before I realize how long I've been standing in the spray. I shake my head, desperate to clear the demons clinging to me for dear life. But it doesn't work, not really.

Standing at my dresser for too long, I start to forget what I'm there for.

"What's your name?" the feminine voice asks. I manage to open my eyes, the haze making everything a little blurry. But I can see her, sleek vibrant red ponytail, concern etched across pale skin. She's kind of beautiful, in a startling way.

"Freddy," I say. It wasn't my name a week ago—but everyone's call-

ing me that, and hearing Matty *out of anyone else's mouth might send
me off the deep end . . . again.*

A loud, banging knock against my door—three in quick succession.

"Freddy?" Bennett's voice calls. "You okay?"

"Yeah," I gasp.

When he doesn't respond right away, I'm worried how much my
tone has given away exactly how *not* okay I am.

*"Okay, Freddy," she sighs. "I think you're . . . sick." She means drunk,
but she's too polite to say it. "Maybe you should go home."*

*I nod, but don't move, hoping she'll eventually give up and walk
away.*

"Let me give you a ride."

"Practice in fifteen. Be in the car—I'm driving you."

"I'm good."

"I can drive myself—"

"You're not. Are you in the dorms?"

"Yeah, I can walk." *If I can figure out where the dorms are, and
possibly where* I *am.*

*"That's the other side of campus. Let me just drive you—my car's
right behind the building in the lot."*

"I'm driving you." Bennett's words leave no room for arguing, so
I don't bother responding.

*"I can't miss class." I choke back an angry sob, feeling stupid and
scared. But every single breath hurts deeper. "I need—"*

"It's Saturday," she says. *Somehow that's more embarrassing than
showing up drunk to class, getting my days mixed up. It's happened
before, but I had a system. And I had my mom—*

*I swallow through pure fire, rubbing my eyes hard enough to physi-
cally push back the tears. But it doesn't help, and they spill out anyway.*

"Oh," she breathes. "Do you— I don't—"

She sounds as awkward as I feel, which only makes everything worse, shame amplified by a thousand. I shake my head. "Sorry, I— Just give me a minute."

She does, stepping away and eyeing me a little strangely, like she's not sure what to do with a crying six-three mess. I swallow back everything that I can, until I feel shakily in control again, a firm grip on my own reins.

I smile at her, and that seems to relax her—as it does with everyone—as I follow her to her car.

"What's your name?" *I ask, halfway out of the parking lot, feeling regretful for not asking earlier.*

"Carmen," *she says.* "Nice to meet you, Freddy."

I barely dress for practice before I decide to lie back down.

Just for a few minutes.

The bed is all silken smoothness against my bare back as I stretch my arms out over my head, relaxing a little after a strenuous round. Carmen smirks, satisfied and picturesque as she carries two glasses of dark liquor back into the room, skin shining in the moonlight from her balcony and grand windows.

I run my finger along the hem of her black satin slip, grinning up at her as the room finally stops spinning.

"Feel better?" *Carmen asks, handing my glass over. I nod and gulp the shot down quickly.* "You did beautifully tonight, Freddy. So talented."

The praise makes me blush—makes my stomach flop at the strange mix of commendation and snark.

"I have a good teacher," *I say, watching her eyes flare a little.*

We ran into each other again, once, before school started—and the realization that the woman I'd kissed impulsively in her car in front of the dorms was my new professor should've deterred me. I'd been embarrassed by the entire thing at first, until she asked me to come home with her.

So I did.

And it made me feel good.

I'm late.

Like, nearly twenty minutes late. Which I haven't done since freshman year. I'm off my game entirely.

I miss a loop on my laces distractedly, cursing beneath my breath.

When she wanted to keep things going, it was almost too easy to say yes. I'd been sexually active since arguably too early, and this unfortunately wouldn't be the first time it was with a teacher.

But this was different. It was strange, how brutal she wanted me to be with her, and I aimed to please her. I wanted her praise, which I only really received when I fucked her hard and fast, furious. As if . . .

As if I hated her.

I didn't like it. But I did like the way she soothed me afterward. Let me cuddle her or stay the night. Agreed to dinners or away trips with me in lieu of aftercare. She fought me on it often, but I was growing desperate for it.

My goalie won't look at me as I skate onto the ice, head ducked, embarrassed. Coach Harris doesn't say anything, only sends me a vastly disapproving look. Which makes me think *someone* told him something they shouldn't have.

It only feeds the anger and self-hatred churning through me.

"Seriously?" The yelling is what wakes me up, cheek sliding off silk sheets, brow furrowed at the deep male voice yelling in the distance. "You couldn't have waited a few more weeks?"

"Henry, please, just go. We can talk about it tomorrow."

That voice is Carmen, I know it. The same thread of snark embedded into every word until you don't know her real meaning.

"No. It's my home. Let me through."

I'm at practice—not there, I almost have to remind myself.

That has me jumping up, pulling on my sweats and almost tripping over my feet, trying manically to get to the commotion in the foyer—no, at the front door.

Carmen is at the door, hip to the frame, blocking someone from getting in.

"Can you just come back tomorrow? You weren't supposed to be back until—"

"Let me in, Carmen."

I can't focus. My skating is choppy, shots sloppy and wide. Toren accused me of playing keep-away once, but this time I really am.

Instead, I try to poke the bear—aka Toren Kane.

Protectiveness rises in me like a tidal wave, ignoring the niggle of wrongness that pinches at my mind.

Carmen eyes me over her shoulder before slipping out and shutting the door behind her.

It makes me pause for a moment. She's tried to shut me out over and over, but I want her to see how much I care.

I open the door, heart pounding, ready to defend Carmen—show her how much I care.

"What's going on?" I ask, eyeing the tall older man in a full suit standing across from Carmen. I come to stand by her side, arms crossing over my bare chest as I flick my eyes between them.

She looks . . . embarrassed.

"Everything okay?"

Toren doesn't go for it the first few times, even as I wait for his quick clip to my shoulder and shove into the boards once he's playing defense against me. He's brutal, but he's more controlled with the team. Purposefully so.

"Oh my God," the guy laughs. "You've got to be kidding, Car."

"Henry," Carmen sighs, rolling her eyes. "Don't—"

"He's a fucking kid, Car. Please tell me he's not a fucking student."

She doesn't say anything, her cheeks practically glowing bright red now.

Carmen's hesitation works like a confirmation, and he shakes his head, eyeing me with a strange, sympathetic expression.

I don't want that Kane—I want the asshole who almost ruined Rhys's career, who nearly killed him.

"*Leave him alone. It's . . . it's nothing.*" *She steps forward, looking back at me regretfully.* "*Freddy, can you go? We're—*"

"What?" I ask. *It's not the right question, but I feel lost and confused.* "I thought . . . I thought we were like—I love you," *I blurt. It isn't what I should've said. Carmen curses and Henry laughs before stepping past us toward the door.*

"*Sorry, kid,*" *he says, patting me sharply on the back.* "*I doubt she mentioned me, but I'm her husband, Henry.*"

I flinch, rearing back like he might try to fight me. But he shakes his head. "*She does this a lot. It's fine.*"

"Playing nice now, huh?" I chirp, pushing him as he circles me. "I saw the video of your freak-out. The one that got you banned from Harvard—"

Wrong, wrong, wrong. *Everything about this wrong and backward, and I cannot figure out what I'm supposed to do.*

"*Carmen—*"

"*Freddy,*" *she says, her head slumping into her hands. She's embarrassed, has been the whole time . . . but I'm only now realizing it's me she's embarrassed of.* "*I think you need to go home.*"

Toren's eyes flash, golden flames, as he stops short. "You got something to say?"

"*I thought we were . . . I thought we were together.*" *The words sound as stupid as they feel, and I rub my face, tears wet against my cheeks.*

"Why? Do you?" I get closer, our bodies so near it looks like we're whispering game plans, not skirting the edges of a brawl. "Who was it? The guy? Or the redhead—"

"*It was fun, Freddy,*" *Carmen says, voice sharp.* "*Don't be ridiculous, you're—that's not what I need.*"

She turns on her heel and heads back into her grand house, calling for her husband. I keep my head ducked, humiliation blazing on my face while I stand on the wide front porch in some rich neighborhood like a lost, sad puppy.

Without hesitation, Toren slams me back against the boards and grabs me by the collar.

"Get off it, superstar. You're on dangerous *fucking* ground. That's off-limits."

He lets me go, starting to skate away—and I'm not sure if it's because he doesn't want to fight or because I went too far, though I'm leaning toward the latter.

Either way, I'm too desperate for something to get the gnawing under my skin *out*.

I shove him a little harder as he passes me again, grabbing his collar to be clear in my intentions.

"Hit me," I snap. Toren's eyes go a little wide, and a strange smile bleeds across his face.

"Hey," Rhys calls, ending the play, rushing toward us. He's been more irritated with Toren since the Harvard game weekend but won't tell any of us why. "Back off it."

He's snapping at Kane, not me, the instigator.

"Fuck off, Koteskiy," Kane says lazily over his shoulder.

"You wanna fight someone, you can fight with me," Rhys says, which makes me feel slightly embarrassed knowing *I'm* the one who wants to fight.

Does it piss Kane off that everyone assumes he's the one trying to fight? Does he feel the same way I do when people call me a *playboy*, *the school slut*?

"Yeah?" Kane laughs, mildly distracted by our captain while he keeps ahold of me. "I don't know, Rhys, seems like you're all bark and your girlfriend's all bite."

Rhys jumps toward us—I've almost *never* seen him fight, but the mention of Sadie has him furious, tossing his gloves down.

"Stop," Bennett snaps, sliding into the fray. He rips off his cage. "Back off—all of you." He yanks Rhys back, pulling him away. "Go cool off. You too, Kane."

"Nah." Toren sneers, finally releasing my jersey and tossing his gloves off. "Our pretty superstar needs this. Right?"

"Let's go," I snarl.

"Hurting, huh?" Toren huffs with a Cheshire cat grin.

"Just fucking hit me, asshole."

"Sure," Kane smirks, grabbing my collar and jerking me forward. "But it won't make you feel any better. Trust me."

"Yeah, yeah."

"I'm serious," Toren says, jerking me again. "I've been doing this for years."

"And?"

"And what? Still feels like I got shot in the fucking stomach and I'm bleeding out." He lands a hit square to my abdomen, but I tense, seeing it coming. "It never stops, and it never hurts less."

And then, Kane lets it go.

I'm an instigator—a great chirper—but I'm not a fighter. I've gotten into a few scrapes, but I'm too good of a player to really fight, to risk a suspension or the penalty for it. But this time I want it—to distract from the pain.

But it doesn't work.

"You get these fantasies in your head, and I don't want you to get hurt."

I hit him again, clipping his jaw.

"I begged her to get rid of you."

Another one, but it feels slow already, sluggish. I'm panting, sweat pouring down my face.

"Of course I like you. There's no part of you I wouldn't like."

Flashes of her last night, beautiful and hurting, barrel through my mind. In the backseat of my car, laid out beneath me, streetlights shining over the tanned length of her legs. Her face crumbling, eyes wide like she doesn't recognize me . . .

"*Matt, no. Stop.*"

"*You said you wouldn't push me out.*"

I'm distracted, so much so that Toren hits me hard enough to knock me down, jumping on me quickly like he'll follow through.

But he stops.

"Whatever you did," Kane snaps, all the enjoyment from the fight rapidly fading. "Fix it."

He leaves me lying there, the dark threat of his words hovering over me.

CHAPTER 50

Ro

I know it's Freddy before he even knocks.

Opening the door slowly, like I'm afraid to truly rip the Band-Aid off, only hurts worse. Revealing him inch by inch—head ducked, eyes to the floor. He looks so small standing in my doorway, a cut on his lip and eyebrow, red around his eye—which I was expecting, considering the text Bennett sent me ten minutes ago.

I was expecting him—but not like this. He's sweaty, hair damp, and not from a shower. It looks like he shucked his skates and hockey pants, threw on sweats, and sprinted across campus to the dorms.

"Hey," I say, gentle and quiet. He doesn't look up.

The dorm is empty the day before Thanksgiving break officially begins, and Sadie is gone with her brothers for the holidays—staying at the Koteskiys', which fills me with an overflowing bittersweet feeling. Endlessly happy for Sadie, Oliver, and Liam having a *family* to call home. But a little bit lonely in our empty dorm apartment.

Now I'm thankful for it as I step back to let the dreary figure of Matt Fredderic into the room.

"Come in," I say, like a light command. He follows me, shuffling, but stops just inside the threshold, holding his bag up on his shoulder with a white-knuckled fist.

"I—" He stops short, voice thick as he clears his throat. "I'm sorry."

355

He still won't look at me.

"Are you okay, Matty?"

A nod, slow and trembling.

He needs someone to care for him, to look after him. So I take his tightened fist in my hand and slowly uncurl it, pulling the bag off his shoulder. I prop it by the door to my room.

"Come with me."

I keep my voice whisper-quiet, pulling him through my room and into the bathroom. Turning the water on hot, I grab a fluffy towel from beneath my bathroom sink and lay it out on the counter.

"Shower. Take your time, and I'll get some stuff to clean up the cut on your face. Okay?"

He nods, finally lifting his eyes to meet mine. "Okay."

• • •

Matt looks worse somehow when he comes out of the bathroom, hair dripping and only dressed in the boxer briefs I left him. He rifles through his backpack where it lies on the floor next to the door, grabbing soft gray sweatpants.

He's exhausted.

Mazzy Star plays quietly on the speaker on a looping playlist, "Quiet the Winter Harbor" softly serenading us.

"Come here," I say, calling him to me. I've changed and am sitting against the wall on my bed. The lights are off, only the twinkling of the fairy lights glowing as Matt kneels heavily on the bed, unsure.

"You want me to—"

"Lie down." Another command, soft but clear.

He lies next to me, head in my lap.

I take the antiseptic wipe, ripping it open and pulling it across the cuts on his face. He doesn't wince, but I do, something like a sympathy pain shuddering through me.

A Hello Kitty bandage, which made me laugh when I found it in our little first aid tin, feels wrong right now, but he lets me put it on the broken skin of his eyebrow without complaint.

Only staring up at me, wide-eyed and in wonder.

"I wasn't there when it happened," he croaks, turning onto his side. "And, after . . . I wasn't— I was not okay."

I want to stop him, to ask questions already, because I'm so desperate to understand this beautiful, sensitive man. But I don't, instead raising my hand to gently scratch his bare back.

"I wasn't there when my mom died. When I got there, she was gone. And Archer was . . . We both couldn't handle being in that house. I came back a week later.

"It wasn't good, I didn't want to feel any of it anymore. So I started drinking a lot. And then she was there—"

He closes his eyes and shakes his head, body tightening for a moment.

"Who?" I say.

"Carmen," he replies, shame coloring his cheeks. "I was . . . I had a relationship with Dr. Tinley."

My stomach drops—somehow it isn't at *all* what I was expecting, and yet it's not surprise I feel. It's sickness, because my imagination is running wild. I want to ask a thousand questions, but I hold them back.

I just hold space for him to talk.

"She was my biology professor freshman year, and I was . . . I was fucked up, Ro. It was so stupid. I don't even know why—"

He cuts himself off with a hard swallow.

"It's stupid," he repeats. "But we just—I never stopped. I was so depressed, and I was drinking all the time. It wasn't smart, and it's embarrassing now—"

"It's not embarrassing," I whisper, unable to stop the words from spilling out. "You were grieving."

He nods slightly. "I think that she knew that. And I think it was easier for her, to have me like that. To keep me—but she was married." His voice turns almost frantic. "She was married, and I didn't know. I swear I didn't know, Ro."

"I believe you, Matt."

The confession settles him, his head relaxing back into my lap, hair damp and soft against my bare thigh where my T-shirt has ridden up.

"It was embarrassing. Her husband was standing there, and they were fighting while I just stood there, like a fucking child. It's disgusting and I hate . . . I hated myself after. I was drunk and sloppy and sleeping with my professor, destined to become exactly what everyone said I would be. The school slut."

The hateful words are strangled, caught in his throat as he forces them out.

"But I thought it was real. I thought I was in love with her," he laughs, but there's no humor in it. "And I thought she *loved* me."

The admission is broken, heart wrenching, and makes my chest ache. Has he *ever* told anyone about this?

"She told me she was *sorry*—that she didn't mean for me to 'get the wrong impression.'" A chuff this time. "But she was so surprised that I thought . . ."

He pauses almost too long, eyes filled with unshed tears. Reliving this time in his life is draining him, his body growing heavier and heavier.

"That I thought I meant something to her—that it was anything but sex. That I was a 'serious option.' And I was good at sex, I'm good with my body, but I thought she liked me for *more*. And then, when I realized everyone was only gonna see me as this? I embraced it. And . . . everyone liked me more for it. So I just became *Freddy*—the good-time guy, hockey star. A partying playboy legend."

Matt shudders once, which devolves into shaking. "My mom would be so disappointed in me."

"No, Matt, don't say that."

His whole body is trembling now, tears finally spilling across his cheeks. He rolls onto his back, hands rising to cover and rub his eyes, trying to hide, but floundering without his usual flirty, humor-filled mask.

I turn him, slowly and deliberately, until he's facing my abdomen, my fingers scratching his scalp and stroking his hair gently.

"I'm s-s-sorry. I don't k-know w-why I'm shaking," he chatters quietly, tears still spilling silently. "I'm n-not cold-d."

"It's okay, Matt." I tuck his head into my stomach, bending over him to kiss his temple. "It's okay."

I wait until his sobs have subsided, then pull him off my lap and put a pillow beneath his head, covering him with a blanket. He's so tired, eyes blinking rapidly, but he won't close them; he's too focused on trying to keep watching me. I turn off the music and reach for the lights on the side of the bed before his hand flops out to stop me.

"Leave them on," he whispers. "I want to be able to see you."

"Okay," I say, heart still in my throat while I crawl into the too-small bed beside him.

We don't cuddle this time, instead holding hands, foreheads pressed together.

"Get some sleep," I say, pressing a soft kiss to his nose.

I know I won't sleep. I'll spend the night watching over him, because I can't do anything else. It's a want as much as it is a need, to care for him, to protect him. My mind is flying a million miles a minute with the information he's dumped into my lap.

For a moment, I think he's asleep and I start to pull away. To grab my laptop and set all my plans into motion. But he snuggles deeper, closer to my body as he grips my hand a little harder.

"I miss my mom."

I keep my crying silent as I grieve for the woman I'll never know, and the boy she loved more than life. The boy I *know* she'd be proud of, even if he doesn't know it.

I'll take care of him, I vow to her silently. *I promise.*

CHAPTER 51

Freddy

I feel a bit like I've been hit by a semi or have a raging hangover from alcohol I definitely didn't drink.

Sporting a headache courtesy of Toren Kane's left hook, I finally blink my eyes open to see Ro, propped up uncomfortably, still asleep with her head resting against the wall. My head is smooshed into her thigh, arms hugging her leg to my chest like a body pillow.

Memories from last night flood my system, but instead of regret or anxiety, I feel . . . relief. Like the giant boulder forever resting on my chest and shoulders has finally been chipped away. Not gone, but lighter.

I slowly untangle myself from her, happy that she doesn't wake up, so I can gently angle her down to lie on the bed, tucking a blanket around her. She shifts, body relaxing into the pillows with a serene smile.

There is so much that's beautiful about her, her vibrance and infectious joy. But Ro like this—cozy, sleepy, and undone—turns my heart into mush.

I tuck her hair back and kiss her cheek.

Actively trying *not* to think too much about last night doesn't stop the anxiety from rolling through. Not knowing how she feels about my entire confession and subsequent breakdown is fraying the edges of my nerves.

I should do something for her.

The kitchen in Ro and Sadie's apartment is too empty, in my opinion, but there's a can of biscuits in the back of the fridge that are easy enough to make and a half-full carton of eggs.

That's enough—except—

I grab my sweatshirt—giving it a quick sniff test—and Ro's dorm keys, slipping on my shoes by the door before taking off to the stairs and out into the cold, empty campus.

There's a coffee shop two buildings over—which is thankfully still open for the break—where I grab an iced dirty chai latte for her and a hot black coffee for me. There's only one guy working, and he's slow enough that I'm fidgeting around like a lunatic while waiting for him to finish it, mostly because I forgot my phone and have no idea how long this is taking.

When I get back to Ro's dorm, she's awake, looking a little struck at the sight of me.

"You're here."

"You're awake."

We speak over each other, both laughing as we finish.

"Sorry." She shakes her head. "I didn't—is that coffee?"

"Um, no." I shuffle my feet, regretting it for a moment. "It's an iced dirty chai. I thought . . . I can go back and get hot coffee. Or you can have mine."

She steps forward and grabs the cold drink out of my freezing hand. "It's my favorite."

I nod. "I know."

We both stand quietly, but the silence is too much. I try not to ask her what she's thinking, trying to give her the space to be vulnerable, until I'm too spinny not to start talking.

"I'm sorry," I blurt. "I'm sorry about last night and—and I know I shouldn't . . . I don't know if I should even still be here or if you want me to leave. But before you say anything, I—I promise I didn't know she was married."

"Married?" Ro snaps. "What are you talking about?"

"I don't want you to think I'm a bad person—or, like, more of a bad person than I—"

"Stop," she barks. "Matt, I . . ."

She starts, opens and closes her mouth again and again, but can't get the words out.

"I'm withdrawing from her program," she blurts, brow furrowed.

It's not at all what I expected her to say.

"What?"

"Tinley's program," she grits out, disgust evident in her tone. "I'm withdrawing from it."

I've never heard that voice from Ro—ever. Never seen the heated, angry look in her eyes, either. She's hardened and resolute, but barely able to spit out Carmen's name without a shiver of fury.

"What she did to you? That's unforgivable, Matt. She took advantage of you, used you, manipulated you—"

"She didn't pressure me— I was willing. I wanted to—"

"Just because you were willing and wanted to doesn't mean that she wasn't in a position of power over you, that she didn't use it against you—use it to manipulate you. And I know she did it, even without you telling me, because she does it all the time!"

She's nearly shouting by the end of her tirade, metaphorical steam shooting out of her ears.

She's . . . mad. She's mad at Carmen—not me. She's mad at Carmen for me. My head spins.

"You don't want to work with her now?" I swallow against the lump in my throat. "I was . . . I was worried that you'd be mad at me."

"Why would I be mad at *you*?" She sounds genuinely confused.

"Because I messed up your internship—your whole plan for grad school, everything. And, Ro, I promise, if you want to work with her, I would never be mad at you for that—"

"Be mad?" Disbelief sinks into her beautiful features. "Matt, no one who cares about you would ever want to be around that woman again. I would never— *God*, I don't even know how I'm going to manage being in the same room as her until the end of the semester. Of course I'm withdrawing my application to her program."

Admiration swirls with affection, my breath catching at the fierce determination on her face. It's the same look she had in my adviser meeting, facing off with tenured professors twice her age and experience, not batting an eye in the face of their frustration or doubt of her.

I love her.

I do—and it's more than that; I admire her, every piece that makes her my Rosalie.

"Okay," I say, nodding stupidly.

"I've already started my application to Khabra's program. And she's actually going to be a much better fit. I'd picked her first anyway, before Tyler messed with my plans."

"Ro—"

"And you won't need a new tutor next semester. You're passing, you're fine. And if you need help, you'll ask me. So we don't even need to worry about that being a factor in January, and I can just tutor privately."

She uses *we* so casually my chest tightens, making it hard to speak.

"Ro?"

"The guys in my program are just"—she shakes her head with an eye roll—"just terrible. A horrid work environment that I was already worried about. Besides, I feel much more confident that Dr. Khabra's entire curriculum is better suited to what I want. And—"

I cut her off. "You're doing this for me?" She stops, blinking wide hazel eyes across at me.

"And, for, like, all the reasons I've said. But . . . yes," she says softly.

A grin bursts free, my heart turning to a pile of goo in my chest because it's the most selfless, protective, incredible thing anyone's ever done for me.

"You're doing this for me." I repeat the statement, to her or to myself I'm not sure.

The three steps it takes to get to her feel too long. Having her in my arms has always been healing, like something soft pressing away the lingering cuts that I've never managed to patch.

"I'm going to kiss you now."

"Please," she whimpers, barely getting the word out before my lips are on hers. I try to be gentle, but the freedom to really be with her makes me frantic, needing to touch every part of her.

We trip backward into the wall, giggling a little into the kiss. And I breathe a sigh of relief. There's no pressure to perform, to be what Ro wants me to be, because what she wants is *me*.

With or without the sex. With or without the hockey. She thinks I'm smart and kind and a good person. And, as hard as it is to admit, she's the first one to really see me like that.

If I'm honest with myself, this is the first time I feel comfortable and excited to give myself over entirely.

Ro pulls back, pushing firmly on my chest for a second as I break the kiss. This time, it's her eyes searching mine, lips freshly kissed, cheeks pink. She's so distracting, and yet my focus is best when it's on *her*.

"You're not going home for Thanksgiving?" she asks.

I shake my head, and she smiles shyly.

"Are you?" I ask, rubbing my hands up and down her bare arms beneath the big sleeves of her oversized T-shirt.

She shakes her head and I grin, scooping her up into my arms.

"Great, then we can spend the entire break together." I nip at her neck and gently toss her back into her disheveled bed, basking in the warmth of her laughter as I follow.

CHAPTER 52

Freddy

We spend our first day of the break watching a ridiculous number of YouTube videos, napping, and eating in bed—which is only after I let *Chef Ro* boss me around in the kitchen and snap at me for my continuous attempts at distracting her.

At night I try to tangle us into the bedsheets and slip my hands down her body, but Ro's having none of it.

Instead, she makes me lie facedown on the bed for a massage that has noises ripping from my mouth that I'm not proud of. But judging by the flush on Ro's cheeks when I do inevitably peek up at her, I'm not mad about the noises, either. The effect on Ro is always worth it.

After she finishes and my body feels like goo, we cuddle and put on a movie that neither of us watches, quietly sharing breath and too afraid to close our eyes or move closer.

"I want to do you now," I finally say, pulling her shirt away from her body, and Ro's eyes go wide.

Chuckling, I shake my head and roll her onto her stomach, leaning down to her ear to mutter, "Such a dirty mind." Her hands grip the bedsheets, gooseflesh rippling across her neck, shoulders, and arms.

My hands reach for the lavender-scented lotion that she used on me, warming it in my hands before I press into her skin.

A groan pulls from her, low and unbidden, and my dick is immediately hard as a rock. It would've been hard either way—touching Ro is a kink of mine—but *hearing* her? Another level of bliss.

"You don't have to—" Her sentence cuts off into another moan.

"I want to. And you deserve this, too," I whisper, selfishly pressing a few kisses to her spine. I reach for the lace back of her bra, the tiny clasp taunting me, before angling beneath it to rub in the lotion when she stops me.

"You can take it off."

Ro's suggestion is as quiet as a breeze, but I hear it like a megaphone in my ear.

Without hesitating, I deftly snap the clasp open and massage her skin reverently, growing braver as I tease the low hem of her soft, thin sleep shorts.

Her relieved moans from the easing tension of her muscles slowly turn to . . . something else.

I pull away when I realize how quick and heavy her breaths are, the white-knuckle grip she has on the sheets of her bed. Ro is panting, grinding lightly into her mattress, hips undulating.

It's so fucking hot I have to swallow back a deep groan, gripping my dick hard through the material of my sweats.

"I'm sorry," Ro suddenly says, flipping over onto her back, hiding her face and shaking her head. "I'm— I don't know what's wrong with me—"

"Ro." I hover over her body. "Stop it, okay? Don't apologize. There is nothing wrong with you."

"I'm—that's not—"

I brazenly grab her hand off the sheets and pull it to cup my cock, rock hard and straining against my sweats.

Her eyes go wide, pupils blown as she stares up at me with no more protests. Hesitantly, she pulls her hands back from my body and tucks them behind her, sitting half up on her elbows.

"I want to do something," I say, sitting back on my knees. "I want you to touch yourself."

"W-with you watching me?"

There's anxiety all over her face, but there is also interest and curiosity. She's still turned on, but she's nervous. Nerves I can deal with.

"Will you do it, too?" she asks. "Please?"

"You want me to touch myself for you? Give you a little show while you play with your pretty little pussy?"

A gasp bursts from her, and her legs snap together, squeezing. Her lust-soaked embarrassment is as intoxicating as always. She's so brazen and wanting, even beneath the anxiety that I know for a fact Tyler put there.

I'm certain there will be a day Ro will take charge of her own pleasure. When she'll be completely unafraid to ask for what she wants. But until then, I am happy to lead her. To show her that I *want* her to want things, to ask for anything. For her to feel good.

"Take your shorts off, Rosalie. And lie back."

She does, slow and careful, as she keeps her eyes on me.

"Good girl." She whimpers and I sit back, stripping off my sweats and taking myself in hand. "Open your legs for me, princess."

Again, without hesitation she does, her glistening tan upper thighs showing how fully turned on she is.

"You're so goddamn beautiful, Ro," I breathe. "And so wet for me."

Her hand reaches for the place I know she's *aching*, but I snap forward across the tiny bed and grab her wrist, relishing her needy pout.

I kiss her, quick and chaste, before leaning toward her ear and nibbling there.

"Matt—"

"Shh, baby, I know. I promise I'm gonna let you touch, but you're gonna do it when I say. Okay?"

She whimpers as I pull away, but nods profusely.

"That's my good girl." I stay kneeling between her legs but back far enough away that I can watch her entire body move with the wriggling of lust and need.

"I want you to lick your fingers first, then play with your nipples, okay, Ro?"

"Okay," she breathes, following my instructions. Her chest is heaving, skin glowing rosy gold.

I keep a firm grip on the base of my cock, reaching to squeeze my tip a little harshly to stop the continuous onslaught of tingling at the base of my spine.

"Now, slowly, I want you to trail your hand down to your thighs." My voice is gruff, I'm so turned on, but I lean into it. "You can touch anywhere but your pussy."

She does as I say, hands trembling as they glide along the flushed length of her body, rolling her nipple in the fingers of one hand. The other one grips her thigh for a second, as if she's trying to restrain herself from touching.

I wait patiently as she teases herself for—

Her hips pump up into the empty air, toes curling.

"Matt," she cries, nearly a whine. "Please—"

"Touch yourself, Rosalie," I whisper.

There is no hesitation, her hand diving between her legs and pressing firmly against her clit before pulling back and circling with two fingers around and around.

I start to stroke myself, and she immediately stops all her movement, eyes locked where my hand roughly rubs my cock. Growling out a firm, "That's it. Show me how you make yourself come when you're alone." I watch her snap back to the moment, though her eyes never leave the motion between us.

Ro bites down on her lip, like she's trying to stop her own noises of arousal.

Angling over her body again, I pull her bottom lip away with my teeth.

"I want to hear everything. All those noises—I wanna know my girl is having a good time."

A moan rolls through her at my words alone, and seeing her eyes flash up close like this is too intoxicating. So I adjust to rest up on one elbow, jacking myself off with my other hand, while I watch her face as she rubs faster and harder between her legs. The hitches in her breath tell me how close she really is.

"Is this how you come when I'm not here for you, princess?"

"Mm-hmm," she squeaks. "I—I think about you, a lot."

Fuck. She's said it before, in the shower, but now, while I'm hanging on to threads of self-control not to come before she does, it's enough to have me nearly snapping my jaw in half with the force of clenching it.

"Yeah?"

"I imagine you. H-how you'd be during sex. How good you are at it . . ." she breathes. "Sometimes I think about you teaching *me*, like I'm your student and you're my tutor."

Goddamn it. I can't hold on, my orgasm is building, rushing through me almost too fast.

"Rosalie—"

"I'm coming," she whimpers, legs snapping up around me where I'm still kneeling between her thighs. "Matt."

The sound of my name as she comes, with the fantasy she painted to get herself there, are enough to have me coming so hard I see stars, arm trembling to keep me upright as I paint myself across her stomach.

We both stay still, panting for a long moment, before I turn to kiss her cheek, the corner of her mouth, her forehead, reverently.

"Stay there," I say softly. "I'm gonna clean you up."

"Okay," she mutters, lax and sleepy, arms stretching out above her head as I walk backward to the bathroom, tripping hard into the wall. It gains a laugh from Ro on the bed, which is enough for me to be thanking the immediate shoulder pain.

I return with a warm, wet washcloth to clean her skin, then roll her away to scoot in after her. Drawing her to my chest, I play with her hair and press lingering kisses to her curls as she grows softer and heavier in my arms.

"Sleep, princess."

CHAPTER 53

Ro

I have a date—with Matt Fredderic.

Not our first date, but I am determined this one will be our *best* one.

After having toast and jam for breakfast, Matt left me to get ready for *our first real date*, advising me only to dress warm and cozy.

But it's a *date*, one I am giddy with excitement for, which means I try on about fifteen different outfit ideas until it looks like my wardrobe exploded onto the floor. When the tears of frustration start up, I open my laptop and dial my best friend.

"Hey," Sadie says slowly, looking half asleep. Her hair is a knotted mess of a braid, one eye still closed, a gray shirt almost hanging off her shoulder with how stretched the neckline is.

"Did I wake you up?"

She huffs a breath. To some it might sound sarcastic, but that's a Sadie Brown laugh.

"Considering it's nearly 11 a.m., yes, but I should've been up hours ago." She mutters under her breath something about *overprotective hotshots*.

"How's the ankle?" I ask, settling on the end of my bed with my computer in my lap.

Sadie sprained her ankle the weekend of the guys' Harvard away game. She hadn't really told me directly what happened, but it had to do with overtraining the muscle. Accompanied by the sudden firing of her figure skating coach, and I'm getting a better picture—especially with her boyfriend, and his entire family, being *very* protective of Sadie and her brothers.

"Fine."

She rolls her eyes, just as a faraway male voice shouts, "Not fine," over her.

I laugh and shake my head. "Is that Rhys?"

"No," she says before he pops up over her shoulder in the frame, slumping back on the bed.

"Yes." He grins into the camera, pulling his shirt down like he put it on to be polite for me. "Good to see you, Ro."

"Hey, Rhys."

His brow furrows slightly as he wraps his arm around Sadie's middle and pulls her to slump against his chest.

"Are you at the dorms?"

"Nothing like Millay for the holidays," Sadie and I say together in singsong. We've spent almost every holiday together at Millay— apart from my week trip home at Christmas. In the past, I've gone all out making ridiculous decorations or themed parties for the boys.

We giggle at our inside joke, but Rhys clearly does not find it funny.

"We have room here," Rhys says. "If you wanted to get out of the dorms. You can always come hang out with us."

Sadie softens, gray eyes filled with wonder as she gazes at her boyfriend out of the corner of her eye. "Yeah, Ro. It would be fun. Liam and Ollie would love it."

I shake my head with a smile. "Thanks, guys, I really appreciate it. But I'm actually going on a date tonight." I tuck my hair behind my ears and bite down on my lip. "With Freddy."

Sadie laughs and nods. "I knew it. You owe me, like, thirty bucks, hotshot."

Rhys blushes furiously and shakes his head. "I swear, Ro, I did not bet on you and Freddy—"

"Right—you bet against it. You owe me."

Rhys smirks down at her, eyes dancing. "You wanna do this now, Gray—"

There's a flurry of knocks at the door before both Sadie and Rhys look over their shoulders, both of their expressions softening as someone opens it.

"Hey, bud," Rhys says.

"Can someone please play with me?" It's Liam, his little voice tugging at my heart. "Oliver is with his new girlfriend and won't play—"

"I'll come," Rhys says, kissing Sadie twice, once on the cheek and one on the corner of her mouth, before making a *yuck* face at Liam and sliding off the bed.

"Girls are so gross," I hear him say just off camera, inciting Liam's infectious giggles. Sadie sticks her tongue out at them both as I hear a door close.

"New girlfriend?" I ask through a giggle myself.

Sadie shakes her head. "Liam won't stop with that. It drives Oliver up a wall—it's a new friend of his that happens to be a girl. He's barely mentioned her, but God forbid Liam misses an opportunity to annoy his brother."

"Aww." I grin. "I miss the little nuggets."

"We miss you, too. Now, important stuff." Sadie walks into a bathroom, setting the phone against the mirror and turning on the faucet to wash her face as we talk. "What are we wearing to said date?"

My eyes go wide. "You don't have questions? About—"

"About you dating Matt Fredderic? Hmmm, let me think." She rubs her chin dramatically, pursing her lips before deadpanning, "Is he nice to you?"

"Yes."

"And you like him?"

"A lot, yeah."

"And you're happy? Having fun?"

I blush, nodding silently. A rare smile pulls at Sadie's permanently stained lips, and she nods. "Then no, I have zero questions. And I'm super happy for you."

"Me, too," I say. "But for you. You seem relaxed, finally."

"Forced relaxation," she grumbles. "Rhys won't let me do anything with my ankle wrapped. He'd probably have a conniption if he realized I even walked myself in here."

"Don't tell me he's been carrying you to the bathroom every morning."

Sadie blushes, her pale skin flaring red. "No comment."

I burst into laughter and shake my head, standing and angling the laptop toward my closet and the mess spilling from it onto the floor.

"Okay, show me your options."

• • •

I'm pacing my apartment, nervous excitement thrumming in my veins until I'm a live wire twitching and popping electricity with every movement.

Which is a little ridiculous, considering it's still twenty minutes before he's supposed to be here.

Knock, knock, knock.

A rapid series of thumps on my dorm door has me popping into my bedroom to double-check my outfit—comfortable dark denim, a soft white long-sleeve, along with my thick green-and-purple flannel currently hanging by the door.

And a ribbon in my hair. I feel girly and feminine and, most important, I feel like *me*.

Smiling once more at my own reflection, happy with my makeup and aesthetic, I run to answer the door.

Matt Fredderic looks flustered, like despite the continuous knocking he wasn't ready for me to open the door. Dressed in black tech pants and a dark green sweater, his hair freshly washed, Matt looks handsome as always. But for once, he's not what has my breath stuck, heart in my throat.

It's the giant bouquet of out-of-season flowers wrapped in parchment, with black Sharpie writing across the paper, which I can't read because his arm is blocking it—almost protectively.

"Oh my God."

"Hey," he stutters. "You look so beautiful."

I blush under his attention, *feeling* beautiful beneath his gaze. "Thank you."

"I'm sorry, I know I'm early—"

Shaking my head, I try to cut him off. "Matt—"

"—and it's fine if you want me to wait out here, you can take your time, but I . . ." He pauses, shaking his head and smiling, looking as dazed and dopey as I feel. "I was too excited to wait any longer, so I came over. And I got these for you, but I— There's something on there. I had the girl at the store write it for me because no way you'd be able to read my handwriting, and my hands were shaking, honestly—"

"I've been reading your handwriting since the beginning of the semester, Matty." I laugh, taking the flowers from his outstretched hand.

He blushes and scratches the back of his head. "Right. Of course."

He sounds distracted, and it takes me a minute, as I step into the kitchen and pull the flowers back from where I had the petals shoved under my nose, before I see it.

Will you be my girlfriend?
—Matty

Signed Matty—not Freddy. He's mine, in that way. To everyone else he might be Freddy, smiling and joking at his own expense. To me, he is Matty, or Matt—walls down, the *real* him.

"Matt, this is . . ." I trail off because I don't have the words for it, for the overwhelming infectious joy coursing through me.

"You don't have to say anything right now," he says slowly. "But this is how I feel. I want to date you, officially. And I don't want you to feel confused about where I stand with you. And . . ." His voice softens, quieter in the space as he looks down. Like he's embarrassed. "And I don't want to be confused about how you feel. I don't want to play games."

My heart squeezes.

He's embarrassed to ask for anything more, because no one has ever given that to him.

I set the flowers down on the counter, turning and stumbling back toward him, grabbing his hands in mine.

"Matt," I breathe, emotions bubbling in my throat, overflowing. "This is the most romantic, wonderful thing anyone has ever done for me. And that's not even the first time I've said that to you." We both laugh, but it fades quickly in the nervous energy filling the air almost suffocatingly.

"I just want to be clear about how I feel."

"I want to be with you. I would *love* to be your girlfriend. And I want to be clear about that, too." I sense the weight of my own words as I say them. "I know how you feel. I've been confused about how people feel before. Tyler made me feel ashamed of the fact that I wasn't wanted when I thought that I was. He played games all the time. And I never want to feel that again; I don't want *you* to feel that way again."

"So then, we promise not to ever make each other feel that way." He hesitates for a moment, searching for the words. "To be . . . careful with each other?"

Matt says it all as if it's as simple as breathing.

And maybe it is.

"Yeah. Careful with each other." I smile and squeeze his hands in mine, raising one to my mouth to kiss it. Just because I can. "I think you are one of the best people I've ever known. And I think it would be almost too easy to fall in love with you."

Something I've said makes his entire face light up as he pulls me in for a tight hug.

"Yeah?"

He trembles in my grip, but his smile is infectious, pressed to the skin of my neck.

"Yeah," I breathe. "Now, I want to go on a date with my boyfriend."

He kisses me, and just like the very first time he kissed me, freshman year, my knees go weak.

CHAPTER 54

Freddy

"Ice skating?"

"Yep." I grin up at Ro from where I'm kneeling with her foot shoved into a crappy rental skate. I almost full-body cringe *again* just looking at the unsharpened blade. "It was one of your *never have I ever* things that we didn't do on our hooky day."

"Kinda busy for a holiday," Ro blurts out, eyes darting around at all the families skating around the community rink. Her cheeks flush. "I'm a little nervous. Maybe we could come back when I've practiced more in an empty rink."

"Nope." I pop the *P* extra hard. "Look, it was either this or 'dance on top of a bar' from your bucket list. And all the bars open on Thanksgiving are gonna be sad and weird. I'd rather not put you on a bar top while divorced dad music plays on a loop and people are drowning their sorrows in beer."

She giggles and my entire body lightens.

I grasp her hands, watching her weak little ankles wobble as she stands in front of me, still shorter than me but taller than every other girl here.

"I'm so tall and uncoordinated," she moans, reading my thoughts easily. Her head tries to dip in embarrassment. "I'm gonna look like a baby giraffe."

"Aww," I coo, stepping backward onto the ice with her hands in mine as she treads slowly onto the already cut-up ice. "A very, *very* cute giraffe, though."

Ro stumbles two steps onto the ice, legs immediately sliding like she might slip into a split and rip her jeans. She cries out lightly before I'm looping my arms around her waist to get a better grip on her body.

Blowing a breath to push her messy curls out of her face, Ro angles a fierce look over her shoulder at me. I manage to maintain my *very innocent* demeanor.

"I thought you were some superstar hockey player."

A laugh rips from me. "I thought getting on the ice would be easier than that." I adjust my grip, hands digging a little harder into her waist. "I'm gonna let go of you—"

"Wait, no—"

Her tone is desperate, pulling easily at my heartstrings.

"Relax, princess." I try to soothe her. "I'm going to get in front of you. You just need to stand up and I'm gonna pull you, okay?"

"Please don't let me fall," she says, real nerves making her words come out a little panicked. My stomach hollows, but I nod, schooling my features into a calm, neutral expression. *Be solid, like Bennett. Let her rely on you.*

"I won't," I vow before releasing her carefully and moving in front of her. I grab her hands again, skates spreading a little wider. "Ready?"

"No," she blurts, shaking her head rapidly. "But we should probably move away from the entrance."

"Probably." The truth is, I'd just stand here with her for as long as she needed. But my girl is fierce and determined in a way not many really know or appreciate.

I skate backward easily, pulling Ro toward the curve of the ice. Ro overcorrects and almost tips backward immediately. A few kids pass by us, struggling alongside their parents but going three times our speed easily. Ro eyes them precariously.

"I think I need one of those."

Flicking my head over my shoulder, I bark out a laugh seeing the toddler holding on to a walker, making good progress across the ice toward his mom, who stands at the red line in figure skates.

"A walker?" I shake my head, hair flopping lazily into my eyes before I flip it back again. "Nah, you've got me. You're fine. You're getting better already."

My words are confident and strong—but the truth is that she's *not*. We're barely moving, the slowest people on the ice. And every time one of the little hockey shits skirts a little too close to Ro, she tenses and almost falls again. I'm tempted to check one of them into the boards, but they're probably twelve and I'd easily get us kicked out.

A smile tugs the corner of my mouth. It might be worth it.

She makes a little more progress, but she keeps overcorrecting because she's too scared.

"I think I should let go."

"Please don't."

Her voice is desperately pleading. It hurts to hear. I grip her hands a little tighter. "I won't. I promise, I won't let go of you until you say I can." Hesitating only slightly, I finally say, "But I think you need to fall. Safely."

"Fall? That's exactly what I *don't* want to do."

"I know. But I think it'll make you more confident. You fall once and see how it feels, and then you're less scared to fall again. You might skate a little better."

Her eyes are expressive pools of hazel, and as they fill with even more fear, I start to regret ever bringing her here.

"Can I try a different day?"

"Of course," I say, happy to hold her and pull her around and around. We skate a little ways farther before Ro's face hardens into a mask of determination.

"Okay, let me go. I'm gonna try it."

My grin is uncontainable. I release her hands, hovering around Ro's body as she wobbles like one of those inflatable tube men in front of a car dealership. Still, she manages to stay upright, pushing off only on her right foot, keeping the left one planted as she moves.

"I'm doing it!" Ro shouts, overly excited. Her head flips over her shoulder, like she's making sure I'm watching her—before she loses her balance and crashes onto her butt on the ice.

And my goddamn stomach falls out of my ass—I speed over to her, stopping and kneeling at her side to check her over.

"Are you okay?"

She nods, eyes a little moony as she stares up at me. A deeper breath stutters out of me as I grab her hands and help her up.

"I did not like that," I grumble under my breath, messing a hand through my hair.

"You told me to fall!" she says on an incredulous laugh.

I shake my head. "Because I'm an idiot. When will you learn to stop listening to me? I think it scared me more than you."

She turns in my arms, petting my hair as we lean into the boards nearby. "I feel better, though. You were right. I'm not as scared anymore."

My eyes flutter as I lean into her palm. "Yeah. Me either."

The words feel heavier. Like we aren't talking about skating anymore.

"All right, you ready?"

"To skate more?" Ro smiles—this time more genuine—and nods. "Yeah. I think I can do it holding your hand this time."

I bite my lip, trying to resist leaning in to kiss her cheek, then realizing how *stupid* that entire thought is. I lean forward and press my lips to her blushing cheek. "I wanna pull you around a little faster. Do you trust me?"

"Yeah." She smiles like that question has made her happier than even the kiss.

I start slow, checking over my shoulder every now and then. It's closer to dinnertime, so the rink is starting to clear a bit and there's less traffic to maneuver around.

The speakers, which have been playing deep cuts of Christmas music—mostly indie covers—kick on Summer Camp's "I Don't Wanna Wait Til Christmas" as we pick up speed.

"You sure Sadie's not working here still?" I ask with a teasing grin. Her roommate's music taste has infiltrated my life, and not just through Ro, but through my obsessed hockey team captain. Her music is in our house, in our locker room, everywhere.

A small laugh bubbles out of Ro as she teeters and holds her balance while I take the curve quickly, backward crossovers helping me pick up more speed. They also seem to mesmerize my girlfriend, who watches my skates like I'm performing a magic trick.

"The music?" she asks. I nod and she only shrugs, bobbing her head to the music. "It wouldn't surprise me if she's engineered the entire rink to only play her music over the speaker system."

"I'm not complaining. She has pretty good taste."

"She does." Ro's face shifts slightly before she confesses, "I, um, told them. About us."

My face falls before I can control my reaction, slowing to a stop against the boards. Ro rushes to apologize, which only makes my stomach turn over again.

"I'm sorry. I should've asked you first. I thought—"

"No," I rush to say. "I'm glad you told them. This isn't a secret. I want everyone to know we're dating."

No games. Just you and me, princess, being real.

A flush darkens Ro's cheeks. "Yeah?"

"Yeah." I grin for a moment. Before my mind is assaulted with every single time Bennett and Rhys—hell, even Sadie—have warned me away from her. My face falls, insecurity scrambling my words so it takes a bit longer to speak. "But, um . . . did they say anything? Were they mad? Or—I don't know. What did they say?"

"They were happy for us."

"Really?"

Now it's Ro's turn to furrow her brow, tone soft. "Why do you seem surprised by that?"

"It's not that. It's just . . . I think I'm a little anxious."

"About?"

This is way too hard to say. I wish we were back home. The harsh fluorescents of the rink, the music—it all feels like the backdrop is too overwhelming to strip myself down for her. To be as vulnerable as I'm about to be.

"I know I have a certain 'reputation,' and that's my fault," I say, heart fully lodged in my throat. Even my voice sounds strained. Uncomfortable. My hands reach up to cover my face because I'm a little afraid I might fucking *cry*. "I don't want it to be on you, that you have to explain why we're together or for people to make fun of you for it—"

"Matt," Ro says, stopping me and pulling on my hands. I let her reveal my face, biting my lip. "I really don't give a fuck about your reputation. It's stupid and completely baseless. All I care about is who you are with me. And with everyone around you. You're a good person. The most emotionally intelligent person I think I've ever known."

Every word she says settles in my soul, building something new around the soft, damaged parts of my heart that have felt unlovable for too long. Around the version of me at ten, fifteen, eighteen, *now*, who watched his dad choose not to love him, who watched women take advantage of his desperation to be loved . . . who broke himself time and again.

I hear the words she doesn't say, too: *I will not abandon you. Your heart is safe with me.*

No games.

"So I hate that you're surprised that our friends are happy we are dating. Rhys and Sadie are thrilled; the rest of your teammates and friends will be, too." Rosalie smiles up at me where we've stopped short of the exit. "I only have, like, two people to tell, but if it would show you how little I care what people think, I'll wear a shirt with your face on it that says I'm Matt Fredderic's Girlfriend."

A chuckle breaks through my lips. "I think you'd probably look really good in that."

"Mm-hmm," she sighs, relaxing into my arms as I hug her. I don't want to let go of her. "I bet you do."

"I think my jersey would be better, though."

"Deal," she says. "Next home game, I'll be in your jersey."

My eyes sparkle with humor and delight. "Wanna go around again?"

"Sure," she says, hands locking back onto mine. "But I wanna see you go faster, Twenty-Seven."

The challenge thrills me and I take off, dragging Ro swiftly behind me until she's a giggling, giddy mess.

CHAPTER 55

Ro

After a Best Pizza in Massachusetts dinner, we opt for the empty Hockey House tonight. Matt stops by the dorms for me to grab everything I need to stay with him.

He ushers me to the shower, setting out a towel for me. The entire thing feels familiar and yet the tension feels turned up to a thousand.

Matt Fredderic is the hottest man I've ever seen—he was when I was a freshman, freshly eighteen and could count on one hand the number of boys I'd been that close to. Now, he's breathtaking, stretched out across his messy bed, though the floor is clear.

"Did you clean in here?" I ask after my shower.

He huffs and scratches the back of his neck self-consciously. "Yeah. I wasn't assuming we'd come here, but I . . . I wanted it to look nicer for you."

"Do you have a shirt I could wear?"

My face heats up as soon as I ask. I wait for him to call me on it—he just spent fifteen minutes in an idling car waiting for me to stuff my things into a bag, and now I'm asking him for clothes that I definitely have.

"Yeah." He nods like a bobblehead, stalling for a second before jumping into action.

Rifling through one of his drawers, he grabs an old volunteer shirt from some Christmas event. It's soft and well worn, and most important, it smells like him.

After thanking him, I turn to face away from him and drop my towel brazenly, slipping the shirt up and over my head before pulling my messy bun down, letting my curls cascade down my back over the green material.

Everything feels lighter now, instead of the weight of some unknown responsibility that being Tyler's girlfriend always came with. There are no games, no constant second-guessing or fear that I'm going to misstep or do something wrong. I don't feel anxiety over the future, just a thrilling excitement for what's next.

Matt is by the bed now, eyes blinking like an owl, unable to tear his gaze from the length of my legs. It makes my stride that much more confident before I'm crawling onto the end of the bed and relaxing into the sheets with a soft, calculated groan.

Matt audibly swallows, watching me intently.

"Ro?"

"Matt?"

"I, um . . . You're really pretty."

I smirk happily up at him. "Are you gonna just stand there or come cuddle me?"

"I'd like to do more than cuddle you," he blurts, flicking the lights off and his bedside lamp on before coming to the foot of the bed to face me where I'm sitting.

"How do your feet feel?" he asks, his voice calm and sweet. But I can't focus on anything except him kneeling in front of me, knowing I'm wearing nothing but his shirt. Knowing *he* knows I'm wearing nothing but his shirt.

"Swollen," I say. Matt is all athlete, where I'm tall with the athletic abilities of a toddler learning to walk. Bambi on ice, Sadie would call it. So the nonexistent muscles in my core and legs are aching, and my feet have a heartbeat.

He lifts my foot and massages the sole, a moan crawling from my throat.

"Does that feel good?"

My imagination is going to get me arrested for public indecency at this rate. There's not an ounce of heat in his voice, but I might as well have heard him say, "*Do you want me to get naked for you, princess?*"

"Uh-huh."

Matt looks at me like he knows exactly how low my thoughts have gone, which only makes the heated blush on my cheeks feel so warm I'm convinced I've been lit on fire.

He works on each foot slowly, pulling obscene noises from my mouth as his hands rub leisurely up my calves to the underside of my knees. I shiver. His touch grows softer, more teasing than anything.

As he works his hands up, up, up my thighs, my entire body feels shaky, hands trembling as I struggle to hold myself up. He's standing now, to lean over me.

"We should have sex."

The sentence spills out of me, syllables rushing together until they're one long word.

"Should we?" Matt asks teasingly, not letting up where his thumb works the inside of my thigh. I nod like a cartoon character in my eagerness, head bobbing outlandishly.

"Yes, but . . ."

The fire goes out, my body feeling cooler as Tyler's voice lurks at the edges of my mind.

Sensing the change immediately, Matt hovers over me and tucks my hair back from my face.

"What's wrong?" When I don't answer, he asks again, pulling back to really look at me. "Ro, where did you go? What's wrong?"

My throat is thick, voice scratchy and quiet as I warn him, "I might not be good at this. I don't think . . . I haven't been, in the past.

And I know you're experienced. So I don't want to be a disappointment."

"A disappointment?" he says, disbelieving. I nod, covering my face with my hands. He pulls them away instantly. "Rosalie—I'm—I don't even . . . damn it," he growls, shaking his head with a clenched jaw. All his relaxation and carefree enjoyment are gone, wiped clean. "I actually thought I couldn't hate anyone more than my father, but I think Tyler takes the cake."

I start to open my mouth, but I don't even know what I'm planning to say.

"I'm sorry, Ro, that Tyler is a piece of shit and made you feel like that. I'm sorry he did this—that he chipped away at you until he broke your confidence. You are so perfect, so real and raw and enthusiastic. So responsive." He shudders. "If anyone was *bad* at anything, it was him. Do you understand?"

I nod.

"Say you understand, princess."

"I understand."

"Good," he sighs.

"Now give me your mouth, Rosalie. I need you."

Everything shifts, the room growing hotter, my blood thicker with need.

My breath catches in the silence as his warmth invades my space. He hovers over me, both of us quiet. Music plays softly in the background, "Kissing in Swimming Pools" by Holly Humberstone— which tells me he found my playlist, not Sadie's.

He kisses me slowly, purposefully, less frantic than he has before.

"It's been a long time," I whisper, biting my lip.

"Yeah? How long, princess?"

My gulping swallow must be visible from outer space. "Since February."

Matt lets out a sound of approval as he kisses up my jawline, nose inhaling my skin. "And are you needy because of that? Or are you so needy because of me?"

"You," I cry. It's almost embarrassing how desperately I want him, mouth watering at just the sight of his body over mine. "Because of you."

"That's my girl."

His praise washes over me, working like a drug, loosening every muscle in my body. Matt Fredderic is intoxicating.

He's always been so tactile, even as a friend, but having his full attention is almost overwhelming. I could drown in him.

Skirting his hand down my body, he pulls up my shirt and ducks his head to lick and suck my nipples. I arch into his mouth with a silent cry, every single inch of my skin unbearably sensitive.

Too soon, he pulls away, standing over me at the end of the bed, eyes scorching a path down my overheated body. He trails his hand over my skin as he steps toward his nightstand, grabbing a condom.

"I was going to take my time with you," he says, sauntering over to climb back onto the bed, hovering over me as he revs me up again. "Bury my face between your thighs until you soaked the sheets before I took you."

Moans escape from me as his fingers play gently, teasingly, across my swollen sex.

"Please."

"But," he says. "You're so soaked, so ready for me already, I don't want to wait."

"Don't wait," I pant. "Please, Matt, I need you."

He sits back on his knees between my thighs, shucking off his sweatpants, hard, thick cock bobbing up toward his abdomen. Even just watching him roll on a condom feels like some private Magic Mike–style performance, bold and sensual.

Slowly, so slowly I'm worried I'll combust before I get him inside of me, Matt lays his big body over mine, sinking into me gently. I gasp out a breath at the first push, grabbing for him.

"You feel so good, princess," he whispers into my ear, and a pathetic, needy whimper spills out of me. I'm holding him around the neck, squeezing him like a cobra, my heart thundering against my rib cage. The pendant on his chain dips between us, sticking to the skin between my breasts.

He kisses my jawline again, down my neck and to my chest, sneakily sliding from my grip on him. I plant my hands on the sheets, gripping them tightly between my fingers to anchor myself, my body so light I'm worried I might float away. It's so overwhelming.

"You gonna let me in, sweet girl?" he says. The smile on his face is gentle, but his face is lined with tension, like it's physically taxing to hold himself like this.

"M-Matt," I gasp, taking a shaky breath. Then, another one, as praise starts to pour from his mouth.

"I know, princess. I know. That's it." A kiss. Two more, covering my face gently. "Breathe and relax. Let me in."

I do, breathing slowly as I take him in, inch by inch, feeling a little ridiculous at my lightheadedness, body feeling almost floaty.

"God," he says, shuddering, pressing his hips to mine. I'm so full I feel like I might burst open and turn completely to starlight. "You look so beautiful, full of me like this."

"You're so big," I say, slurring my words a little, lust-drunk on him. I shift my hips, realizing it feels even better to move. I raise my hands and dig into his biceps, begging him to move.

He kisses me again, lips and tongues tangling, before he's moving—slow at first, deep, hard thrusts that turn faster, slightly more frantic.

And he never stops talking to me, praising me over and over.

"Good girl."

"You take me so well, princess."

"Don't—I want to hear how good I'm making you feel."

"I want to keep you like this forever—with me inside of you."

"You're so perfect, Rosalie. Come for me."

I do, riding the wave easier now. His fingers work over my clit—not too hard or too soft. He's mastered my body already, learning everything from my reactions.

"I w-want you to come," I gasp. "I want to know what it feels like when you come inside me."

"Fuck," he growls, thrusts already frantic, now uneven and harder as he climbs with me this time. "Oh, *fuck*, Ro—you're squeezing me again. You gonna come with me, princess?"

I nod wildly.

"Good girl." He drags the words out slowly and I cry out, coming hard. He follows me, shuddering as he explodes inside me.

Matt melts over me, body heavy on mine. I want to stay like this, the weight of him on my skin so warm and comforting.

Tears prick at my eyes, because sex has never been like this for me—and I've always wanted to feel this way. I want to tell him that. I want to thank him for making me feel so cherished and wanted and *free*. Tell him that I'm falling in love with him.

But the words catch in my throat.

"You okay, Ro?" he asks, smiling down at me, pushing my sweat-damp hair back around my ears. "Did I . . . did it feel good?"

"That was amazing, Matt," I say, grinning so hard it feels like my cheeks are splitting open. I play with the chain hanging around his neck. "I . . . how long until we can do it again?"

I'm embarrassed to have asked almost immediately, but the shameful feeling washes away with Matt's huffed laughter against my neck as he ducks his head.

"Be gentle with me, you nymphomaniac," he says, teasing.

I dissolve into laughter, curling in his arms as we whisper quietly to each other far into the night.

CHAPTER 56

Ro

We spend the rest of Thanksgiving break wrapped in each other. It goes by too fast.

But at the end of it all, I find myself giddy to start back despite the anxiety of what comes next—because Matt Fredderic is my boyfriend, and he has my back.

It's like an extra burst of confidence, one I rely on heavily as I wake early Sunday morning and set up in the empty kitchen downstairs at the Hockey House to type out my email.

I started the draft the night that Matt told me about his relationship with Dr. Carmen Tinley. Hatred fueled the majority of it, so it was unprofessional and rude. Rereading it now, I don't disagree with a word I typed. But it won't work to CC the dean on an email like that.

The front door slams noisily and I blanch, worrying my lip as I wait to see who's home first.

Bennett Reiner saunters in, stopping in the doorway of the kitchen, staring at me for a moment.

"Hi," I squeak, tucking my hair back. "I just needed to do some work in the quiet—but I don't want to get in your way."

He shakes his head. "You're fine, Ro." The words are kind, but completely flat, his furrowed brow never letting up as he turns his baseball cap backward with a heavy sigh and starts grabbing ingredients from the shelves and fridge methodically.

Large shoulders heave with a deep breath, head ducking between them before he tosses a towel over his shoulder and turns back to me.

"Are you hungry?"

"Me?" Every thought scatters—direct eye contact with Bennett is heavy. "I, um, yeah. But you don't have to—"

"Cooking helps me think," he admits, turning toward the stove. "It makes me calm, too."

The admission is gentle, soft, despite the gruffness of the words that sound like they've cut him as he says them.

"Sewing does that for me. Making stuff—like, I don't want to be a fashion designer or seamstress or anything. I just like it."

Bennett nods and grants me what I think is his version of a smile over his shoulder. "Yeah, same. I don't want to be a chef. I just like to cook for people."

The rest of the morning passes in silence—besides the various sounds of Bennett cooking and the *click-clack* of my keyboard as I write and rewrite my email. Eventually, Matt stumbles down the stairs and plants a kiss on my cheek, sitting next to me at the bar top. Bennett sets a plate of malted vanilla waffles with fresh fruit, a traditional French omelet with a garnish, and a plate of fresh maple-glazed bacon—which I think he *made* that way—in front of me, and my mouth drops open.

"I don't like that." Matt frowns, his finger pushing my chin back up to close my mouth.

"What?"

"You looking at my goalie like he's performed some kind of miracle," he says dramatically.

"Learn to cook, then," Bennett says quietly, a hint of a smile on his face as he hands Matt a plate with a stuffed omelet, veggies and chicken overflowing.

"Orrr," Matt says slowly, eyeing me with a mischievous smirk. "I can take you back upstairs and—"

"It's like a family reunion in here," another deep voice chimes in, perfectly on cue. "And smells like Bennett's home."

Sadie is on Rhys's back like a very reluctant, very angry koala bear. Her ankle is wrapped tightly still, but I know it's a sprain and she's good to walk. She might even be nearly cleared to skate.

My roommate waves at me before beating her fist against the hockey captain's chest. He bats her arm away like a buzzing fly.

"Sadie," Matt says with a salute. "You look . . . taller."

"Ha-ha," she deadpans. "I'm rolling over here."

"Rolling! That's a great idea—we should get you a wheelchair to run around Waterfell in. I'll even volunteer to push you around."

"I can walk," she grumbles. "Put me down, hotshot."

Rhys turns his head to catch her lips with a little smirk before ordering his left winger out of the chair, dropping Sadie in next to me.

"Ridiculous," she grumbles, snatching a piece of fruit from my untouched plate. "Do you see this?"

Rhys snaps his finger at her, face serious as he orders, "You need up, you tell me."

"Wanna bet?"

She looks like a feral kitten facing off with a calm, stern labrador.

"Walk and see what happens, *kotonyok*." He accents the Russian heavily, and I melt a little. Even Sadie's eyes go a little hazy before she can help it.

"Hey," Matt snaps, pulling out of the hug he'd just granted his friend. "Not cool—either of you. No foreign language shit, that's cheating." He points toward Bennett. "And you? No cooking in front of my girlfriend—that's . . . that's even worse, I think."

I nod with a beaming smile, biting into the waffles with a groan.

"See?" Matt says with an annoyed huff.

Sadie is giggling next to me, snatching my food and nodding along with me.

"Definitely the food, that's the most romantic."

Rhys and Matt stare over at us, arms crossed. Bennett blushes and excuses himself from the room.

"We've got practice tonight," Rhys says to Matt. "Wanna catch a ride with me? The girls can hang out here."

The words alone make me giddy—my best friend and me having a girls' night, while our *boyfriends* go to hockey practice. It feels like a movie, but better because it's Sadie and it's Matt. They're better than anything I could've made up in my head.

It feels like the warmth of being home. For the first time since I left California, I don't feel homesick.

• • •

The COSAM offices are quiet Monday morning, which gives me some time to go over my speech a few times. Fortunately, I don't have to speak directly to Dr. Tinley in order to withdraw.

Unfortunately, I have to speak to Tyler Donaldson, head GTA of the program.

Clearing my throat, I finally work up the courage to walk over to him.

"Can I speak with you a minute, Tyler?"

He's surrounded by his friends, his posse, which is basically everyone we work with. I tried for years not to feel isolated and alone. Because I was dating Tyler, I thought maybe I could count these guys as my friends, but they aren't. They never were.

That's okay. I have real friends—people who care about me. Sadie, Matt, Rhys, Bennett.

Real people who support me. Who like me exactly as I am.

"Now?" Tyler grumbles, turning to say something condescending—no doubt about me. I ignore it, staying focused on my task.

"It'll only take a minute."

He sighs heavily, crossing his arms and rolling his eyes as he turns to me. "Whatever it is, go ahead."

"Okay." I move my eyes over his group. A few of them look awkwardly away from me, not really wanting to be part of this. Mark smirks, mimicking Tyler's stance entirely. "I'm withdrawing my application to Tinley's internship track. I just wanted to let you know, formally."

Tyler frowns. Mark's smile only grows.

"Why?" my ex-boyfriend blurts, catching himself off guard. I watch him slowly regain his composure; I'm sure it wasn't what he expected me to say. "I mean, clearly you weren't going to make it into the program anyway, but you were so determined to try. So, please, RoRo, enlighten us. Why the change of heart?"

"First," I snap, watching my attitude shock him back a step. "Don't call me that. We aren't dating. And I've always hated that name. Second, it's actually none of your business why I'm withdrawing."

Fury paints his cheeks and the tips of his ears bright pink.

"You know what, Ro? I tried to be nice to you, to *gently* lead you down the right path. You've never been at our level. You were never a serious contender to Tinley or me, so good for you for figuring that out soon enough not to be embarrassed by the rejection."

I swallow, my throat tight. Shame bubbles in my stomach like acid.

It isn't that I believe him. But it doesn't make the pain of hearing someone who once told me he loved me say as much as he can to hurt me.

"I earned my spot on the team just as much as any of you."

Good. A surge of pride at my quick defense of myself rolls through me.

"And you really think you were here on merit?" He laughs, and I deflate. I'm desperately trying to hold back the tears. But if I cry in front of them, then I'm proving them all right.

"Tyler—"

He steps into my space and tugs lightly on the silk bow tied to one of my braids, and suddenly I'm ten and my teacher is telling me not to antagonize the boys, even though they're the ones making fun of me.

"You dress like a kid and act like one. I don't know why I ever thought I could take you seriously as a girlfriend." He peeks behind him at our entire team and laughs again.

I want to scream. Or cry. Maybe throw up.

"That's enough," I spit out, choked by the anger that's making my eyes water. "Stop it."

My obvious reaction to him, the engagement with his barbs, only spurs him on.

"No." Tyler shakes his head. "You should be thanking me for even taking a chance on you. It was never enough for you."

"You're trying to hurt me, and you *know* you're not smarter than me." I cross my arms, trying to stifle the overwhelming urge to run and hide. To appease him enough so that I can just leave. "So you're trying to attack, what? My clothing? My previous mistake in dating *you*? Grow up and move on, Tyler."

It's like I didn't even speak, his voice only growing in volume to continue over my protests.

"You acted like a slut when we were together, so I don't think it surprises anyone that you jumped into bed with the school's whore."

I can only hear the fury and anger and pain roaring in my ears until it all pushes out of me.

"Considering I wrote your entire research paper that got you into this program in the first place *for* you, I think it's *you* who should be thanking *me*."

Someone is trying to get our attention, calling out to both of us, but we're locked in this face-off. Years of pent-up frustration against one narcissistic circular argument.

"Thanking you?" Tyler sneers, dropping his voice. "You pathetic bitch—the only reason you work here is because I vouched for you. I *asked* for Dr. Carmen to put you in, to consider you for the internship." He steps closer, all menacing fury. It's like a switch has flipped and he's revealed the monster buried beneath the mask of privilege and fake confidence.

"No one ever thought you'd actually make it into the program. Grow up, Ro."

Tyler pulls the ribbon from my hair on his way past me, clipping my shoulder with his harshly enough that someone shouts.

Matt—Matt is here.

In my corner, just like he promised.

"Get the fuck away from her," my boyfriend growls, stalking through the room.

I don't know how long he's been here, but the second his hand makes contact with mine, relief floods my system like a shockwave. Sinking back until I'm almost in his arms, I let a few tears escape. Because it doesn't matter that I shouldn't listen to Tyler. Even knowing I don't believe a word he said about me to be true, the pain is still there. Still real.

Matt Fredderic's entrance has only reignited Tyler's frenzy.

"Did you tell your new little boyfriend about how obsessed with him you were?" he asks, spinning back toward us. It faintly registers that Dr. Tinley is here, too, practically hiding behind her office door, watching us all.

"How you lied about meeting him freshman year? Telling me he was your first kiss?" He barks out a laugh and winks at me. "I mean, I knew you were pathetic, Ro, but—"

"What?"

Matt's brow furrows and he glances at me, only for a millisecond before he's back to glaring at Tyler.

"Oh—she's never told you?" Tyler claps, almost gleeful. "I'd think that would've been your first words to him—reminding him that he was your first kiss, freshman year, right? So romantic."

"Ro?"

"I—I—"

Nothing comes out. Humiliation and anxiety war for dominance in a match that has me searching for the nearest trash can in case I *do* decide to throw up.

"God, for such a smart girl, you really act pathetically stupid sometimes." Tyler rolls his eyes. "RoRo here has had a crush on you since freshman year. She's told everyone that you were her first kiss—that you shared some magical night together."

He shakes his head at Matt, as if he's chatting up one of his buddies and not a guy he's relentlessly mocked, a student he insufficiently tutored and someone he's claimed to hate for years.

"I thought at first it was to make me jealous. Then she wanted to go to your games all the time. And finally, she *begged* us to let her tutor you—right after we broke up." Tyler huffs a laugh and tucks his hands into his pockets. "Hate to break it to you, Freddy, but she's, like, a stalker. I mean—we only started dating *after* I started tutoring you."

The room goes quiet, ice cold against my skin that still feels like it's on fire.

That's . . . that's not true.

I mean—yes, parts of it are, but . . . But, I begged *not* to be Matt's tutor. And I never had any clue that Tyler was tutoring Freddy at all.

Terrified to look at Matt, to see the belief or disgust on his face, I close my eyes tightly.

"Matt, I swear I—"

He holds his hand up, stopping the word vomit on my tongue. My cheeks flame hotter, shame eating me from the inside out.

"Listen to me, Donaldson—you're an asshole. If anyone is pathetic here, it's you. I know you think I'm too *stupid* to remember exactly how we met, but I haven't taken *that* many pucks to the head yet.

"Ro is the best person in this department—she's smart, a genius, really, and you're so threatened by her you can't *stand* that you don't have some weird control over her. But you can't stop her from being better than you anymore."

"She's not—"

"I'm not done, Donaldson." Matt calmly cuts him off. "My dad is just like you. A narcissistic, abusive asshole. And he turned out just as washed-up and miserable as I'm sure you will be. Now back off. You love telling everyone else they're stupid, but you're a full-blown idiot."

He laughs, eyes dancing as he flicks his gaze to me. "You're telling me my girlfriend and I kissed freshman year? That she's been crushing on me since then—*while* she was dating you?" The smile that takes over Matt's face is beaming, his arms stretching out around my shoulders lazily. "That's the best thing I've heard all year."

Tyler is furious, and my emotions are so jumbled I feel a little nauseous, leaning into Matt's body for support.

"Now, princess." Matt turns to me and kisses my cheek. "Do you need anything else? Anything you wanna say before we leave?"

I shake my head, eyes wide and wonder filled as I gaze up at him.

"Great."

He walks to my desk, leaving everyone else frozen in shock as he grabs my bag and anything off my desk, setting it all inside and zipping up the sage-green backpack with a ribbon still hanging off it. Sliding it onto his back without a second thought, he grabs my hand and starts to lead me out.

We strut past Tyler first, and my boyfriend leans in to whisper, "Thanks for the info. You can't imagine how good it feels to know that all five times you slept with *my* girlfriend, she was thinking about *me*." He grabs Tyler's shoulder and jostles him slightly. "Good talk, man. And hey, if you ever talk to her again, I'll kick your ass. For real this time."

He ends it with a big beaming smile, grabbing my hand again as we walk out of the main area, passing by the Dr. Tinley's office door on the way.

Carmen Tinley is still standing half in, half out, looking a little shellshocked at the entire outburst.

"I'm done, Dr. Tinley," I say, barely restraining my tone. "I quit—tutoring, TA'ing, any of it. I want to be dropped from consideration for your cohort in the spring."

She clears her throat. "May I ask why?"

Her gaze flicks to Matt and I stand a little taller, wishing I could cover him entirely.

"I think you know why."

We exit the door in silence, waiting until we've cleared the entire COSAM building and are walking across the greenery of central campus before Matt whips around and clasps me in a hug.

"I'm so proud of you!"

Our words are identical, overlapping so perfectly that we dissolve into happy laughter.

It feels like a fresh start—a real one, this time.

I can be whoever I want to be.

CHAPTER 57

Freddy

I finish my last final with a beaming smile on my face.

I'm sure I look like an overexcited idiot as I exit the classroom where my extra-time private block testing took place. But I can't bring myself to care, because I know I passed. I can feel it in my gut.

It's like shooting the game-winning goal.

Because not only did I pass, but I have someone rooting for me. And I know I'm going to graduate—something my dad swore I'd never do. Something my mom wanted.

God, I hope I'm making you proud, Mom.

I burst through my bedroom door back at the Hockey House where Rosalie Shariff sits cross-legged on my bed with a textbook by her curled-up feet, her laptop balanced precariously on her knee.

She spots me and nearly drops her computer in her haste to stand up and greet me.

"Hey!"

I'm grinning like the Joker now; I can feel it—but she knows why.

"You passed!" Ro squeals, launching herself into my arms. "Oh, I'm so proud of you, Matty."

She presses the praise into my neck, and I spin her around.

"I'm proud of me, too," I say with a chuckle, setting her back on her feet and fluffing her hair playfully. "How was your meeting?"

Ro met with Dr. Khabra, the other professor with an internship track built toward her grad school plan. Something to do with neurological testing and creativity. I'm trying to learn more about it, to understand Ro's work and interests more, but she's so brilliant most of what she says goes right over my head.

That, and I'm usually distracted by the urgent need to kiss her or lay her back and pull more of those little noises from her. Which is exactly how I'd like to celebrate now.

"Great," she giggles, dropping back onto the bed. I fall on top of her gently, pushing her shoulders into my mattress. My mouth presses to her neck, hands sinking into her waist. Her hands meet my shoulders, pushing me up off her slightly. "Actually, there is something I want to talk to you about, though."

"What?" My stomach drops a little. "We need to talk" is never a good thing to hear, but I bite down the frantic thoughts. "Everything okay?"

"Yeah—I just." She clears her throat. "I'm going home for Christmas."

"Oh." I nod. "Yeah, that's great."

It is great, asshole. Be a little more excited for her—she misses her parents as much as you do. Encourage her to see them.

"It's a long flight," she says, but it feels like she's dancing around the topic. "Do you want to come with me?"

"To California?"

"Mm-hmm." She glances up at me shyly. "I know it's probably way too soon to meet the parents, but I would really love for you to meet them in person—you've kind of already met my mom."

"Yeah, and she's awesome."

"Right." She smiles. "So . . . will you think about it?"

"I don't need to think about it, Ro. I'm in." I barely manage to wait a beat before I ask, "Can I kiss you now?"

She bites down on her lip and nods. I unleash myself, grabbing her in my arms and picking her up off the bed, eliciting a quick squeal.

"I have work tonight—"

"We have time."

Ro smiles before biting her lip and asking me to set her back on her feet. "I have a request. For you to . . . teach me something." She clears her throat and says, "Sexually, I mean."

My entire body lights up, eyes dancing across her fidgeting form. "Yeah?"

"Yeah. I don't . . . I want to know how. To do it."

"To do what, princess?"

"To . . ." She hesitates again, and I can see the retreat begin, like the slight fear of whatever she wants is enough to make her shrink.

"Rosalie." My voice is louder, a mix of low, soft tones with a sharper snap. "To do what? Say it."

She shivers. "To suck your cock."

"Such a good girl," I say, tightening my hand into a fist reflexively at the dirty words from her lips. Leaning in to kiss her cheek, I move her hair to the side and press my mouth to her ear. "I think, since I earned the grade, I can teach you something now."

A moan pours from her lips and she nods almost frantically.

"*Yesyesyes.*" Her words come out slurred into one. "Mr. Um . . ."

"Matthew, please, Ms. Shariff." Her eyes twinkle. "First lesson— she comes first."

I press her back onto the bed, kneeling so I can pull her cozy sweats off her body along with her underwear. Her skin is warm and soft beneath my hands, pliable as I pull her legs apart.

Licking a solid stripe down her pussy, I tuck my tongue slightly into her opening before circling up and around her clit. My fingers press into her with precision as I stay focused and steady with my mouth until she comes, beautiful and unreserved.

"Perfect," I breathe, pressing a kiss to her thigh and then her slightly exposed stomach. "Beautiful. A-plus, Rosalie."

She laughs, tossing an arm over her eyes and shaking her head.

"That isn't—that wasn't what I wanted."

"No?" I ask, furrowing my brow in mock surprise.

"Please?"

Every part of my act melts beneath her plea. I unbutton my jeans, shucking them off entirely, before starting to pull my boxers down—but I'm cut off by her hands pushing mine out of the way, her bracelets scratching my skin lightly as she finishes undressing me and drops to the floor.

"Like this?" she asks, eyes wide as she looks up at me from her kneeling position. I stumble back at the sight of her, knees weak, smacking back against the bed.

"Just like that, princess." I try to keep my voice low and sensual, but I'm shaking. I can barely stop the tremors in my hands as she reaches tentatively for my dick, tongue darting out to lick her lips— and then my skin.

My hands reach for her—hair, shoulders, anything I can hold myself up with, the sensation of her hot, wet mouth over just my tip enough to have my entire body tensing.

Get it the fuck together, I chide myself, closing my eyes because the sight, sound, and feel of her has me ready to blow.

She pulls off again, eyes peeking up. "Show me, please."

I gently help her, guiding her mouth back onto me and to a pace that I would usually enjoy a slow build from—with Rosalie, it's like I'm walking a razor's edge for control.

"Perfect," I breathe. "God, Rosalie, I'm not gonna last."

Her eyes crinkle, like that thought pleases her, and she picks up the pace and sucks *harder*—

"Fuck," I moan. "I'm gonna come, princess."

She sucks more firmly, hips gyrating like she's humping against the air, searching for friction. I come, *hard*, managing to keep my hands soft in her hair as she swallows me with a happy, energetic smile.

After I catch my breath, I mutter, "You turned on again, Rosalie?"

She nods eagerly, cheeks blushing. I lean to scoop her from the floor and deposit her onto the bed, ready to sate my insatiable girlfriend again.

• • •

Once she's relaxed from my overeager mouth and tongue, I carry her to the shower and slip away to grab us snacks from the kitchen—not bothering to dress because I know we're alone. We eat in bed, giggling and laughing, playing with our food more than we're eating it.

I've waited long enough, and it's been torture even waiting the few days until her finals and my extended time blocks were completely finished. But I don't think I could wait longer to ask if I tried.

"So." I clear my throat, passing her a blue sports drink that she downs greedily. Her clear exhaustion sends a burst of satisfaction through my body. "I want to talk about what Tyler said."

Her entire body freezes, then blushes, like she hasn't just been screaming and crying out for me to "Please, please make me come" while I praised her and talked her through the entire thing. My heart swells again, like it wants to leap from my chest and sink into hers.

"Oh," she stutters, tucking back her hair self-consciously, avoiding my gaze. "Right—um, thank you, by the way. For standing up for me."

I shake my head, reaching a finger to pull her chin up. "I always have your back, Rosalie."

There's another prolonged silence, but as usual, with her it feels comfortable. Like we're both holding space for each other.

"He was . . . it wasn't all a lie. I mean, we did meet, freshman year. At a party. And you were my first kiss."

My smile is killing me, so wide my cheeks hurt. "I was your first kiss?" She might as well have told me I won the lottery, or the Stanley Cup. She nods shyly.

"Yeah?" I duck my head to meet her gaze, to show off my grin. It seems to soothe her and her words pour faster.

"Yeah—I had my first drink of alcohol, courtesy of you. And then you kissed me."

"Was it a good kiss?" I can't keep from asking.

"Yeah," she breathes, biting her lip into a smile. My heartbeat speeds up, reacting to a memory I don't have. It also makes me wish for a time machine to slap myself over the head for clearly doing something stupid and fumbling this girl.

This girl who cares for me, defends me, likes me—not for my body or skill, but for me. For who I am. With Rosalie Shariff, I am unequivocally myself, maybe for the first time.

"We spent the night hanging out together. Playing beer pong and laughing and—" She shakes her head with a bittersweet smile. "And it was incredible."

"But . . ." I let the word hang, feeling the charge of the air around us. Something happened. *Think.* Only I can't—I have no memory of it at all, zero.

"But then you just kinda . . . disappeared."

"What?"

"You told me you'd be right back, and you left me there."

Think, think, think. My heart pounds, stomach churning as I soar through my awful, spotty memories from freshman year. *Think, think, think.*

Only every memory I can reach includes things I wish I could forget—and I'd never want to forget her. I know myself—even at eighteen and grief-ridden, I would've been crawling toward her light and kindness.

"And." She shakes her head, burying her face in her palms. "And I know you don't remember. It's okay—I just—"

"Do you remember when this was? Freshman year?"

She nods. "It was the weekend before the start of fall semester."

My heart drops into my stomach, skin turning cold. I pull a blanket up around my waist, eyes downturned. It feels wrong to be naked right now, when I know the exact weekend she's speaking of.

Freshman year, my first big party with the team after spending the summer at practices and flying back to Texas to be with my mother. It was an under-the-table condition upon signing with Waterfell—a condition, actually, that bought my eternal respect for Coach Harris and made me utterly loyal to this team. And he kept my secret.

I'd planned to play for them, but had excused absences whenever I was needed at home. It turned out I wouldn't need even one.

She was gone before the semester started.

I search for that memory now—a hazy party scene, not even a clear face of one team member who was with me. And then, a phone call—shrill and unforgettable.

Painful, even now.

Archer, whispering a broken "Matty" and then, "I'm so sorry." A stumbled walk to the dorms, which were nearly too far—and Bennett fucking Reiner, with his dad, taking care of everything. Flying in a goddamn private plane and shaking, legs bouncing, the entire time.

The rest blurs and my eyes water, hands reaching up to rub them.

"Matt?" she asks, her voice trembling. "Can I hug you?"

"Please," I rasp.

She doesn't know why I'm crying but she doesn't ask—she doesn't even try. Ro holds me, her long arms winding around my broad shoulders and pulling me closer.

"I'm sorry, Matty," she says, but her voice overlays with Archer's in my head.

After my tears subside, I manage to wrangle the story from my brain and out of my mouth. It takes awhile and I stutter over a lot of it, but Ro sits patiently, listens, all while keeping my hand in hers.

Patience. Kindness. Love. It pours from her like water.

"I need to stop unloading on you like this." I laugh, releasing her hand from mine and wiping my eyes until I've pulled it together. "It's ridiculous." *It feels like I'm leaching your strength and love and warmth*, I don't say. *And I don't want to be that to you.*

"No," she says lightly. "I want to be there for you. You've been there for me more times than I can count. And besides, I like this part of a relationship. I think it's healthy, and I haven't had that before."

"Me neither."

In the quiet of my room, we stare at each other, until adoring smiles burst beneath our sparkling lovestruck gazes. It is still and perfect.

She stands, slowly and almost begrudgingly, to get ready for her shift. I grab her and pull her back to me.

"I can't believe you're leaving me," I mutter, pouting my bottom lip and moping up at her. She laughs and shoves me off gently, grabbing her clothes and dressing carefully.

"I'm going to work—not the military." She bites her lip and walks into the open bathroom, messing with her hair. I scoop a few butterfly clips off my nightstand and follow her, coming up behind her. It's comical—me, completely naked; her, fully dressed. I comb a few strands back like I've watched her do a thousand times before, securing a clip into one side and then repeating the process with the other.

"Perfect," I whisper, leaning down to kiss her, arms around her waist. She blushes up at me and my cock starts to harden all over again—which only works like a vicious cycle, making her cheeks hotter. "Give me a second and I'll drive you."

"Okay," she says dreamily. I perch her on the counter so she can watch me change in the way I watched her. We descend the stairs hand in hand and out to the driveway, where I parked a little haphazardly on the sidewalk.

"I have a request," she says once we're inside the car, music playing softly.

"What's that?"

"I think you should call Archer."

My throat closes up almost immediately, sweat beading at my brow. "I . . . I don't think he would want to talk to me now. I ignored him for forever—"

She shakes her head, looking at me softly, affection and warmth heavy in her gaze. "I don't think that's true, Matt. I think he loves you and he probably wishes you would call him."

I hate that she's working today as I pull up in front of Brew Haven to drop her off for her shift. I want to ask her to stay, to talk to me until the echoes of shame are drowned out by her nearness.

She kisses me twice on the mouth, then once more on the cheek before she hops out, shivering from the icy wind immediately whipping against her.

"You don't have to do anything you don't want to do," she says. "Just think about it. I think it would be really good for you. Both of you."

CHAPTER 58

Freddy

The phone ringing sounds as intensely loud as an opposing team's goal horn at an away game, but I'm filled with more nerves than a hockey game has ever given me.

Archer answers on the first ring.

"Hey," he drawls, a door slamming in the background. "It if isn't my favorite kid. How are you?"

An instant calm washes over me, water bathing a too-dry beach.

If it isn't my favorite kid.

But his words blend, old voices and new. The memory blares through me like electric shock.

Me at nine years old. A private rink practice with an NHL coach.

Saturdays after early skate are my favorites—especially when Coach Ace comes to pick me up, because it means I get extra practice time with him. But today is harder, because my dad is supposed to spend the rest of the weekend with me.

The rest, because he didn't show up Friday like he was supposed to, again.

"I don't think my dad likes me very much."

The words spill out of me accidentally, shame and embarrassment coloring my cheeks. I didn't mean to say that, but things always spill out when I talk to Coach Archer.

Archer frowns, and I feel like I shouldn't have said it. But . . . maybe he should know. I'm not good at being a son.

When the other guys on my team asked me about my dad playing hockey with me, I almost told them about Archer. Sometimes in my head I pretend that Archer is my dad, especially before I go to sleep at night, imagining the picture in the kitchen with my mom and Archer and me, as if my dad didn't exist.

Still, I blanch a little.

"Don't tell my mom I said that," I add, skating to the next puck he's pushed out for me. "I don't want her to think she's doing a bad job."

"Okay," Archer says. "Just between us."

He waits to speak again until I make my next shot, perfect up top, just barely under the bar.

"Great shot, Matty." He pats my helmet before skating to face me and ducking his head so he can meet my eyes through the cage. Grabbing my shoulders, he says, "And for the record, I think you're the best of all the kids."

My eyes widen. "In the whole class?"

He shakes his head. "In the world. You're my favorite kid in the whole world."

I can't help the smile on my face through the rest of our practice and dinner that night. One that Archer mimics, sitting beside my mom.

"Hey," I say, swallowing down the immediate swell of emotions. "I'm okay—I just finished finals, actually."

"Yeah? How is that going?"

"Good." I nod like he can see me, then feel a little ridiculous and smack myself in the head. "I—it was hard, for a bit. But I got a great tutor and I passed. Like, more than just eligibility. I'm a B student now."

"God, that's great to hear, kid. I'm so proud of you."

It warms my chest, healing something that's been broken in me for far longer than I can remember.

"Yeah," I sigh, feeling a twinge of nerves pinch at me. *What else do I say? What does he want to talk about?*

I must feel like a stranger to him now. So I pick the only topic I can, the one thing people *like* discussing with me.

"Hockey is great—we're having a killer season. Rhys is back, which, I don't know if you watch or keep up with us—"

"I always keep up with you, Matty."

Rubbing at the slight pulse in my chest, I continue. "Well, then you know Rhys got hurt last Frozen Four. And now, actually, the guy that hit him? That Kane kid that was all over the news a few years back? He's on our team—a defenseman on my line. By the way, I am first line now. I actually made my way there sophomore year."

I'm rambling—I can hear it, but I can't make myself stop. Even still, Archer never interrupts me.

Finally managing to trail off, I swallow loudly. "So . . . yeah. That's about it."

That's about it? Have I ever had a conversation with a human before?

"That's great, kid. The hockey has always been grand for you, but . . . What about *you*, Matty? How are you?"

"Good. I, um, passed my classes." *I definitely already said that.* I clear my throat and try again. "I had this really great tutor—but she's not my tutor anymore."

"Oh?"

"Not because of anything bad, she . . . She's my girlfriend now, actually. She's—her name is Ro. Or, well, it's Rosalie, but she goes by Ro. But she's super smart. Kind of a genius, like Mom."

My head sinks into my hand and I go silent, as if I just dropped a bomb on the conversation. A strange urge to hang up hits me, but I managed to hold on.

"Yeah?" he asks, his voice sounding as relieved as I feel.

Archer is the *only* person who knew my mom, who shares memories of her with me. Blocking him out of my life felt like the right thing when I was spiraling deeper into my grief, desperate not to pull the one person I cared about into the shitshow that was my brain.

But losing that connection, the place where I *could* talk about her when it eventually felt right, was more brutal than I anticipated.

The way Archer grieved my mom was how I imagined one would grieve the loss of their soulmate.

I remember being so confused and frustrated in the aftermath. The way my dad reappeared, suddenly concerned with my hockey career, or when I was going back to school—trying to pull me out entirely when he *knew* how much it meant to me and to her for me to graduate. My father never cared about her or me.

When Mom got sick, Archer quit his job and moved in with us. Spoon-fed her when she was too tired. And I'd been so blinded by my own grief and anger that I didn't see it was because he was so in love with her. Devoted, and then distraught afterward.

I remember the night I found him doubled over in a panic attack because he couldn't breathe through his sobs.

Had it been acceptable, I think he might've followed her. But he didn't. And I'm realizing he didn't because of me.

To take care of me. It shouldn't matter that my dad's never been a father to me because Archer is here. And he would've been my dad, if I'd let him.

"I miss you," I blurt out, feeling relief just to say it. "Maybe we can . . . get lunch sometime? If you're ever near Waterfell. Or even Boston."

"Name the date and time, kid," he says wistfully. His voice is just as deep and settling as it was when I was a kid. "I'll be there."

. . .

"Are you sure you're gonna be okay?"

"Yep," I say. "I'm not sick, Rosalie. Just nervous."

"I didn't know you were afraid to fly."

I'm not. I'm terrified *of meeting your parents—officially, as your boyfriend.* But I can't tell her that, so I stay quiet.

Her slender hand rests across mine, stopping the incessant drumming of my fingers on the armrest. Ro intertwines our fingers and dog-ears the page she's reading in one of her sexy romance books before checking the flight path on the screen that I've been diligently watching the entire time.

"Want to listen to a book with me?"

I perk up at that. "One of your sexy ones?"

"Whatever you want." She tosses her phone onto my lap. "You pick."

I decide on the one with the best cover, in my opinion, and Ro is already giggling as I start the first chapter.

By the fifth chapter, I'm flushing bright red.

I nearly jump three feet into the air when the flight attendant asks what I want to drink. Ro can barely stop giggling to order a ginger ale.

"Keep it up, Miss Poker Face While Listening to Sex Scenes on a Plane."

"That's a really long nickname," she laughs.

"Just know, whatever the spiciest thing in this book is, that's what I'm doing to you in your childhood bed when we get there."

Her laughter dissipates almost immediately, skin flushing hot as she bites down on her bottom lip. The urge to kiss her is strong, but the urge to tease her is even stronger, so I manage to keep my distance.

As we land, I discreetly try to wipe a few tears from my eyes, but Ro catches it easily.

"It's an angsty one, I know," she says, rubbing my back as I shove our headphones back into the bag. "The first time I read it, I cried buckets."

"I didn't know it was going to get so emotional. The cover is two hot people ripping each other's clothes off."

She laughs and nods. "They're *romance* novels, not erotica. But I'm really happy you liked it."

"I loved it, actually," I say. "Make sure you pick a good one for our flight back."

．．．

The Shariffs live in a modest, dark brown wood bungalow-style home near Solvang, which I'm realizing is a major tourist destination—especially for Christmas.

Our Uber drove us straight through the town, and I was in awe of the eclectic style and unique designs of the entire downtown strip. It must've shown all over my face how enthralled I was, since Ro leaned over and whispered, "I promise, we'll come back and see it at night."

Now, as we grab our bags from the trunk and send the rideshare off, the nerves catch up to me.

On the porch stands Ro's mother, olive skin and dark curly hair cropped to her shoulders, dressed like a modern-day hippie. Beside her, in a wooden rocking chair, sits a man who I can only assume is her dad.

He's a weathered man, a full head of gray hair and a darker beard. His body looks like he's tall when he stands, and he might've been muscular at one point, but now he's thin and frail. He smiles at Ro more slowly than her mother does, but seems no less enthusiastic to see his daughter.

I hang back, letting her greet them alone first.

"Mom," she sighs, slumping into her tall, slender mother's arms. They hug for a long, long moment, and her dad eyes me briefly.

Smiling like a loon, I keep my distance, sweating in the California sun.

"Hey, Dad." She smiles, fluffing his hair lightly and bending down to hug him in his chair. Slowly, he wraps his arms around her in return, holding her tightly to him.

"Ro," he croaks. "Who—?"

"I brought my boyfriend, actually." Ro gestures for me to join her. "Mom, Dad—this is F—"

"Matt," I say, cutting her off. "Nice to meet you both."

Usually, it's Freddy. I prefer that *only* Ro calls me Matt or Matty—with the exception of Archer. But I *know* how much easier Matt will be for her father to say. I want him to feel comfortable around me. I want him to *like* me.

And I haven't had much luck with that in the father department.

"So nice to see you not on a screen, Matt," Mrs. Shariff says, squeezing her husband's shoulders. "Let's go inside and eat. I'm sure you're both starving."

I grab our bags and dump them inside the foyer, out of the way, but quickly return where Ro and her mother are helping her dad out of his chair.

"I can walk," he says, speech sluggish.

"Go ahead," I say to my girlfriend and her mom. "I'll help you in, Mr. Shariff."

"Don't need help," Mr. Shariff grumbles while grabbing my arm and using my body like a crutch.

I was right, he's tall, and grumpy—though that seems to be a trait he's reserved for me.

"Where do you wanna go? Kitchen table or the couch?"

He doesn't speak at first, just eyes me skeptically.

"Or I can dump you right back outside and let you start over."

His hand grips me tighter and I think he's angry at first, before I realize he's . . . laughing. He's laughing so hard he's about to fall over, so I wrap my arm around his waist to steady him.

"Kitchen," he says, smiling now as we walk slowly into the house together. I settle him in his seat of choice. Ro flutters around him and her mother like she can't quite decide what to do.

"Ro said you play hockey?" her mother calls as she continues stirring a large pot on the stove.

"Didn't say whether you're any good," her dad huffs, a glint in his eyes. Ro explained to me that sometimes he speaks easily, the words flowing. Other times he struggles to get a one-word response out.

"Yes, ma'am, I play hockey for our school. But I'm actually signed to play for Dallas after graduation, in the NHL."

"Oh, that's amazing," Mrs. Shariff says, reaching for something behind Ro, who stops her and grabs the stack of bowls for her. "Your parents must be so proud."

The ache that is permanently etched into my chest throbs a little. Ro walks around the table to stand at my back and squeeze my shoulders.

"Yeah. My mom passed a few years ago, but she was very proud of me."

It comes easier now—a wave of grief—but there is something beautiful about allowing myself to speak so openly about her. About the loss of her.

Ro shifts the conversation away from me, for which I'm grateful. The reprieve is enough to settle me into their dinner routine, stomach growling as they set a bowl of curry in front of me and a smaller cup of rice.

We eat and laugh and talk across the dinner table, and then move to the back patio where we eat and laugh and talk some more. Ro's mother tells stories of her in her youth. Her dad holds her hand, scratching her palm and fingers as she lays her head on his shoulder.

Watching Ro with her parents is eye-opening.

They baby her and she grumbles about it, but she softens under their attention. And she's so fucking beautiful. I want to keep her here, comfortable, away from the shit at school and Tyler and my fucking past. I want her to be able to be like this. *Always*.

CHAPTER 59

Ro

"You really didn't have to do all of this."

"*Yavrum*," my mom says. She squeezes my biceps and peers around my shoulders to inspect the dough I'm molding. "I wanted to. I think manti is good for dinner, right? How much do you think we should make?"

My mother's eyes dart around the massive piles of lamb-filled dumplings on which she's just sprinkled more flour. Her hands are still powdered as she sets them on her hips.

"I think this is more than enough, actually."

"Matt is a growing boy—"

"He's not a giant," I laugh, shaking my head as I finish off the last of the dumplings. My mom gives me a look that screams *He definitely is a giant*. "You've made plenty of food, okay? Let's get these into the water before it boils over."

I start on the sauce, pulling the ingredients out of the fridge as my mom sings low. The nostalgia of it all—her voice, the smell of her food—soothes me. My muscles relax even further—more than they have in years.

She watches me work, but not in a way that makes it feel like she's looking for errors—it's like she's taking in the sight of me, committing this once-familiar sight to memory.

"What?" I smile at her, blowing a curl out of my eyes. We look the most alike—my father's fairer complexion and blue eyes didn't stand a chance against her brown skin, hazel eyes, and mass of black curls. My own strands might be a little lighter, a brunette hue more like my dad's, but I am my mother's daughter.

You have my heart. I heard the sentiment from both my overly loving parents. Where my father has a gruff exterior, my mother is as soft as they come. Fragile, yes, but strong in her fragility and vulnerability. In a way I've always aspired to be.

I just got a little lost along the way.

"Mom." I find my voice, shaky as I concentrate on stirring the red sauce in front of me. "I'm really, really happy that you're getting to meet Matt. He—he helped me a lot this semester, and . . . it's just special to have him here with you and Dad."

My boyfriend is currently watching the prep games for World Juniors—which one player from Waterfell is playing in—and from what I overheard, he's spending most of the time explaining hockey to my dad, answering all his questions.

Matt is patient, and to see him be so comfortable with my dad, never annoyed with the slowness of his speech or responses, makes my heart thunder even harder with that one truth.

I am in love with Matt Fredderic.

"We didn't meet your other boyfriend."

I refocus my attention, moving the pot from the heat as I stir. I look at my mother's intense, love-filled gaze. It says *I'm here* and *Nothing you could ever say will change the love I have for you.* There is shame in admitting this, a double-edged sword—I am embarrassed that it happened at all, but I am even more embarrassed knowing I never told her.

"It's hard to put into words," I say. My mother is patient, reaching to take the sauce from my hands and setting it to the side, walking us farther into the kitchen, away from the open walkway to the living room. "Tyler was . . . very mean to me."

I talk. She listens, never cuts me off, just nodding even as her eyes well up with tears.

At the end, we both cry.

"I didn't want to tell you because—I just wanted things to be easy. For you. For Dad—and I know—"

"Rosalie Defne Shariff," she whisper-shouts, reaching to grab my shoulders and shake me a little. "You are *everything* to your father and me. You have been the greatest blessing of our lifetime. I would not trade a second, only wishing you felt like you could tell me this sooner." She pauses and looks around for a moment, clearing her throat before adding, "And maybe, wanting you to bring this Tyler boy here so I can slap him myself."

"Mom," I laugh.

"You think I'm kidding."

We hug, laughs subsiding into more tears. She builds me up with every whispered, "*You're so strong, yavrum. I'm so proud of you.*" It warms my heart, healing even more of my soft, sad pieces.

"I'm making simit in the morning," she says, pulling away resolutely.

"Mom," I say, but don't *really* want to tell her no. It's my favorite—especially with jam—but she only makes it on special occasions. The bread dish is time-consuming, so it's a treat for her to cook.

"I'm making it," she snaps back, elbowing me as she takes the pot of cooked manti off the stove and starts to plate them. "You deserve it, *yavrum.*"

· · ·

I wait to take Matt downtown until the day after Christmas, our last day before flying home.

Solvang is packed, but so beautiful that you forget about the crowds underneath the twinkling lights.

We've spent the last four days with my parents—exchanging gifts quietly. My parents say they don't celebrate Christmas, but we always give one gift to each other and watch my mom's favorite holiday movie, *A Charlie Brown Christmas*. It's a favorite tradition of mine, one I was thrilled to include Matt in. With the four of us, it somehow felt even more like home.

We grab Danish treats from one of the multiple bakeries downtown, ordering anything and everything seasonal. Matt dons a Santa hat, tucking red and green reindeer antlers with bells on them into my loose, long curls.

Playing tourists in a town I've been to a thousand times is entirely different. Because it's with him, it feels like the first time—bursting with excitement and endless laughing fits. We take pictures at every stop, until I run out of storage on my phone and we switch to his.

By nightfall, we down the last of the hot chocolate we've been sipping, trading it for hot mulled wine from a darkened tiki bar on the corner.

Matt pays for the jukebox—which is really a requestable streaming service—to play the song from our ice skating adventure over the crackling speakers.

"Time to check off another one, Rosalie," he says, smacking my backside gently as he hoists me to stand and climb up on top of the bar—

—but only for a moment, before we're getting kicked out, my long legs tossed over his shoulder as he carries me out, both of us laughing as we sing "I Don't Wanna Wait Til Christmas," fumbling most of the words.

Matt gifted me a crafting service subscription, which lets me try all kind of artsy things I've always wanted to. My gift to him was this mini getaway before our flight home. Just us tonight.

He puts me down before stumbling forward with a laugh, turning back to me with his arms stretched out as he keeps singing. My voice trails off, just watching him. Completely sick in love with him.

Matt eyes me, too, realizing I've frozen on the sidewalk under the glittering lights, making me feel like we're in some romantic snow globe. He's smiling, lines carving his cheeks, dancing side to side.

"What?"

I laugh, a bright, bubbling feeling shooting through me like stars in a night sky.

"I love you," I say.

He freezes, a tender smile tentatively spreading—nervous, worried I'll take the words back.

"Yeah?" he asks, disbelieving and wanting in a way that pulls at my chest.

"Yeah," I say to reassure him, voice strong. "And I'm not scared, because it's *you*. I was terrified that it would be hard to trust someone again, to be this vulnerable, but . . ." I bite my lip before the words spill like tipped-over wine. "I think falling in love with you is the easiest thing I've ever done."

It's his turn to laugh, but his eyes shine, glimmering with tears. A thread of worry worms through my stomach.

"What?"

He shakes his head, stepping toward me. "Nothing. You just . . . you said something really similar once."

My brows furrow. "I did?"

"Yeah." Matt reaches out and takes my waist in his hands. "At the party, back in August?"

"Oh God," I moan, trying to cover my face with my hands. He nudges them away with his nose. "The one where I sang karaoke in your car like a drunk crazy person."

He grins broadly. "The one where you called me your celebrity crush—"

"I didn't—"

"And jumped off the shed into the pool to 'feel something.'"

"I—" The words don't make it out this time. I shake my head as my cheeks heat. "God, that's so horribly embarrassing—"

"No." He cuts me off with a quick press of his lips to mine. Then another, much slower and softer. Keeping our foreheads pressed together, he continues. "I jumped with you, and when we were in the water together, you told me that you thought I'd be really easy to love."

My eyes pull from their locked spot between his pecs, meeting the spring green of his intense gaze. "I did?"

"Yeah," he breathes. "I thought about that a lot. Like, every day. It's the first time anyone has said anything about me being easily loveable." He tries to joke, but I can see how deeply this affected him and I want to hug my drunken self for being honest.

"Oh," is all I manage to say, intoxicated by him in this moment.

We kiss, gentle, almost tentative, and it still leaves us both breathless.

"And, if it wasn't clear, I love you, too," he says. "I think I've loved you for a long time."

• • •

When we get to the hotel room, he presses me into the mattress, and I preen under his ministrations. We undress each other in slow, languid movements.

Every time we're together now, intimate, it's comfortable. Matt so completely commands all of my attention he banishes the threat of self-destructive, painful thoughts of before.

He kneels on the hardwood floor, pulling my knees over his broad shoulders as he kisses my thighs, teasing me and avoiding the place that aches for him until I plead breathlessly. I can barely get the words from my lips before his tongue is firm and insistent over my clit.

My orgasms are so heady I barely notice how loud or intense

I become vocally, but it pleases Matt—pulling throaty moans and, "*That's it, princess. Let me hear you,*" from his mouth over and over as I turn to liquid in his hands.

He moves over me languidly, mouth shining with my release as he grins and lowers to his forearms. The comforting press of cool metal to my overheated skin ignites me further, hands reaching, twining in his hair.

Beneath the intensity this time, there's an inherent softness. It's always been there, in the corner of the room as we explored each other's bodies. But now, with the weight of shared *I love you*s, it seeps into every movement. Every touch.

Matt is so much more than his body, more than sex. But he has always shown love physically—and I can feel it with every press of his skin to mine. Every lingering kiss. The catch in his breath as he slides into me. Our mouths nearly touch, but we don't kiss, sharing breath—the scent of warm mulled wine heavy in the air as we pant and he pulls another orgasm from me.

His pace is slow, the feel of him dripping like syrup over my skin. I want to feel this way forever, keep him clutched between my thighs, holding still as I chase my own release, riding every wave.

"You feel so good," I moan, watching as the praise ignites him. "God, Matt—please, baby. *Moremoremore*," I slur, head tossing back.

Matt's hips pick up the pace, the slow intimacy melting into a light frantic energy as he gets closer.

"Come for me." I say it this time.

He comes, moaning my name. I press kisses into his neck and jaw. He returns them, his lips meeting the sweat-damp skin of my hairline before he meets my eyes.

We gaze wonderstruck at each other, silently asking one another *are you real*?

"I love you, Rosalie," he breathes, grinning broadly, smile lines cutting his cheeks sharply. "God, it feels so good to say that."

"I love you, Matty," I whisper, tucking my fingers into the gold chain and looping it around. He curls down to me, nose to nose, both of us smiling still, even as we kiss, teeth nearly clacking. Joy bubbles under my skin like champagne.

This, with him, forever. It's the best thing I've ever felt. And it's love. And it's real.

CHAPTER 60

Freddy

We spent New Year's Eve kissing under Rosalie's floral pastel sheets and the twinkling lights hung round her bedroom, saying *I love you* until it wore out on our tongues.

It never does.

Our first hockey practice back is always earlier than the start of the semester, so I needed to be in Waterfell. Now we're a week into the new semester, preparing for the first game of the new year. Ro and Sadie are both downstairs in the Hockey House—decked in their now-signature jackets, our numbers painted on their cheeks—as Rhys, Bennett, and I descend the stairs with our bags in tow.

"What's this, Gray?" my captain says, a smirk evident in his tone.

When Ro and Sadie indulged in a girls' night last week, Rhys spent the evening with me, sans Bennett. We grabbed burgers from our favorite local spot and he told me everything—his struggles after the hit last spring, his PTSD and night terrors, going to therapy. All of it.

And then, after several tight hugs, he told me a bit more about his angry figure skater girlfriend and her brothers.

"I should apologize to Sadie," I told him, hand to my forehead at the high-top.

Rhys shook his head. "No. I can almost guarantee that response won't be ideal. And she feels just as bad for judging you with Ro."

He smiles at me, reaching out a hand to squeeze my arm. "You're both protective people. And I love that about you, Freddy. You and Bennett—I wouldn't have made it through the last six months without either of you. I need you, just as much as I need Sadie."

Every crack that had formed between us started to mend from there. It didn't hurt that our girlfriends were best friends.

"Personal cheerleaders?" Rhys asks, crossing his arms.

"You wish, hotshot," Sadie snaps at the same time Ro grins and yells, "Yeah!"

I laugh openly and jump the last two stairs to grab my girlfriend's lanky body up in my arms. I spin her, delighting in her squeal, before kissing her forehead as we watch the other couple in the room.

Rhys mutters to Sadie in Russian, low and sultry—and though I *know* Sadie doesn't understand the words, she flushes red beneath his attention.

"I'm so proud of you," Ro says, pulling my attention. "You're gonna kill it, Matty."

• • •

Before we left, Ro tied one of the ribbons from her hair onto my bag. *For good luck*, she told me. I'm practically preening, shuffling my bag nearly into the center of the dressing room for the guys to see it. To ask me about it.

It's from my girlfriend, I almost scream when Holden finally asks. I'm made of smiles. Every one of them finally *real*.

As I leave the tunnel and step onto the ice for warmups, I spot them.

Rosalie, in her usual spot, but not alone—an entire crew decked in Waterfell colors surrounds her. But not just Sadie and the boys— Ro's parents are here. Her dad is bundled up and seated, smiling. Her mom holds up a sign with Ro that says *I Love 27!* with hearts and stars doodled all over it.

And on Ro's left, right at the glass, is Archer.

My stomach somersaults, memories swirling. Archer at my games; Archer and my mom at my games, together, shouting at the refs and cheering me on.

I shake my head, realizing I'm standing just off the ice, blocking everyone's path, when Rhys gently pushes me aside.

"You good?" he asks.

"Yeah." I smile. "Just surprised."

"I like the fan club over there." My captain slaps my helmet and shakes me. "No one deserves it more, Freddy. Let's go win a hockey game."

• • •

I'm playing the game of my life—barely into the second period. Sweat soaks my uniform, hair wet as I readjust my cage and hop the boards for another face-off.

Rhys wins it easily—he's nearly perfect on face-off wins, shooting it to me quickly. I pass it back to my captain, but one of the opposing players scoops it away. I hard stop on my skates, shaking my head and trying not to get too caught up in the anger.

I can't help but flick my eyes toward Archer, seeing his concentrated gaze on me—always on me. *You got this, kid,* he shouts when I get close enough to hear. It pumps in my blood like a shot of pure adrenaline.

You've got this.

One of the guys on the other team makes a bad pass and it bounces off his defenseman's boot, swinging right toward me. I check my placement—there's *no one* around me, most in the middle of a change.

So I take it—racing toward the net on a breakaway. I can hear the screaming ratcheting up to immeasurable levels, only spurring me forward.

My shot is a goddamn beauty, soaring in glove side, high.

Cheers erupt from all around as my entire line excitedly slams into me, but I'm looking at them—Archer, arms around my girl-friend in a hug as they jump up and down and scream for me.

They're here for me. *My family.*

Is this how it feels for Rhys when his parents show up? For Ben-nett with Adam Reiner in the stands? I can't imagine they're riding this kind of high every game. And *God* is it a high—having the sup-port of people I love, people who love me, cheering me on at the game I love. At the sport I'm fucking incredible at.

It's the best game I've had. And I owe it all to the girl I love.

• • •

We win.

I score my first hat trick of the season, racking up points. My third goal is on the side where Archer sits and I slam face first into the glass, like I can hug him through it.

It's a highlight reel night.

The boys award me the trophy—a frayed rope of nets cut and tied together. A sacred tradition for the Wolves. I can barely speak, because I'm too excited to see my . . . my family.

I give a quick speech, showering and changing out faster than I ever have before. My whole body is tense and twitching, thrum-ming with energy as I dismiss myself and head through the exit where friends and family—and fans—wait for us to leave the arena.

It's early enough that there are only a few lingering nearby, but I bypass them, eyes flicking around until I spot him.

Archer, hands tucked into the pockets of his jeans, standing down a little hallway, away from the commotion of the crowds ex-iting.

Part of me wants to run to him—hug him, if only to expel some of the bundled nervous energy I'm carrying. Instead, I hurry toward him and stop, getting his attention immediately.

"Hey, kid."

His voice is exactly as I remember, soothing and soft, deep. I've never heard him raise it in anger—as a coach or as a man. He looks the same, too: black hair, a beard of wisps of silver and gray, deep olive skin, and a nose that looks like it's been broken one too many times. Brown eyes that are kind and empathetic, that look over me now with a watery gaze.

"You were incredible out there, Matty."

"Thanks," I manage to push out, eyes glistening. "For coming."

Archer smiles and shakes his head. "Thank your girl. She and her parents got me out here. But, I'm glad that . . ." He clears his throat, like he's feeling the clog of emotion stuck there the same way I do. "I'm glad that you wanted me here."

There's a pause then, where we both stare at each other, unsure. Apprehensive.

But then his head tilts toward my collar. "Do you remember when she got that chain?"

I remembered everything about that day. She'd gone through each myth that was depicted on all the pendants in the store, telling me each story, patient with all my questions.

"*But this one is my favorite,*" she'd said, fingers ghosting over the Psyche and Cupid carving as she told me their story, her hand on my arm, Archer's hand on her shoulder.

"Yeah." I nod. "On the beach trip, after Granddad's funeral. I was like five or—"

"You were six."

His words are confident, sure. I don't think my dad would know my age *now*, let alone back then, when he had even more of himself and his life to focus on. But Archer . . . he's always been there.

"Were you . . . You were there, but I thought it was because my dad sent you. That he couldn't come and didn't want my mom to be alone."

Archer shakes his head.

"No. I came because your mom had just lost her dad and didn't need to be alone—no matter how much she thought that. And because I loved her." Tears well in his eyes, and he tries hopelessly to wipe them away before they truly fall. "I still do. I always will.

"And I'm sorry I wasn't there for you after her death. I s-should've tried harder. I know John's mentality, and I knew it wasn't good— that he wasn't good to you. But . . . he's your dad. And I was—"

"You were important to me, too," I say, but it doesn't feel like enough. "You were important to Mom. She—she loved you, I think. I didn't understand it before, but I'm starting to."

He smiles, blinding and brilliant even with the redness of his eyes and tear-stained cheeks.

"Elsie was the best thing in my life. I loved her when we were kids—she was my best friend, my personal cheerleader for our small-town hockey team. And then I fell in love with her when she spent an entire summer dedicated to helping me recover enough to play. When she cried with me after the second injury, drank with me all night when I found out I'd never play again . . . I *always* knew . . . I knew I was hers. And for me, that was enough. Just to be there for her, even if she'd never be just mine."

God, why does my heart feel like it's exploding?

He lifts the chain out of his own collar, the pendant shiny, clearly well taken care of—and an identical match to the one around my own neck.

"It was the only thing I had of her for a long time." He huffs out a near sobbing breath. "Besides you."

"Me?"

"Matty." He steps forward, putting a hand to my neck. "I love you like you're my own son. And I will always, *always* be here for you. If you want me."

A broken sound bursts from my lips as he presses his forehead to mine before tucking me into his embrace.

"Cut yourself some slack," I mumble into his embrace. "I wasn't doing that great, either. I did some stupid shit freshman year."

He pulls away. "Yeah, well, at least you kept it together at her service."

My brow wrinkles. "What do you mean? You were like a freaking statue while I cried my eyes out."

Archer nearly chokes on a laugh. "Matty, I nearly tried to murder your father when he showed up to the funeral. We got into a fight in the hallway until a few guys pulled us apart."

A shock of laughter bursts from me, and we stare at each other.

I don't look like Archer, but right now it *feels* like I do—watery eyes and happy-sad smiles to match.

I hug him again and he lets me. That's better than any goal.

CHAPTER 61

February

Ro

"Jump Rope Gazers" by The Beths plays from the Bluetooth speaker.

A light humming sounds, enough that my eyes snap up to where Matt is sprawled lazily, as if he just woke up from a nap and is not mid-study session. His skin glows under the lamps and string lights glittering around my room. He looks larger than life on my twin-size bed.

He's so beautiful it hurts.

"Are you singing?"

He smirks. "You play this one a lot."

"It makes me think of you." Matt pays attention. He knows the lyrics, what I'm really saying.

"Yeah?" He smiles. "Me, too."

I laugh lightly, eyes tracking him as he stands and walks toward me. He looms over me as he settles his palms on my desk, effectively caging me in his arms.

"You're supposed to be studying," I chide him, but my voice shakes.

I'm not his tutor this semester, and his course load is fairly easy, but we prefer studying together. Prefer being together as much as we can.

436

Matt hums deeply, his face pressing to mine so I can feel his skin, before his nose skims the exposed skin of my shoulder, up my neck to my ear.

"I was. But you're distracting me."

"Oh?"

It might as well be a moan, and my cheeks heat from the embarrassment of how well he knows my body. He's barely touched me, and I'm already keyed up.

"Yes. You chew on your pencils."

"And that's distracting?"

"It is when I can't stop staring at your mouth." His hands are creeping under my sweater onto the bare skin of my stomach. Playing with the waistband on my sweatpants, before reaching over to pull open the closed panels on my vintage desk vanity mirror.

"Oh," I breathe.

"Do you how much you tortured me last semester? How often I had to go home before my practices, barely making it to the rink, because I needed to jack off after watching your mouth as you chewed on that fucking pencil during our tutoring sessions?"

Another whimper escapes from my throat as I desperately bite down on my lip to smother my sounds. He tsks, retracting his hands from where they'd started to graze over my lace panties, and using his warm thumb to pull my lip from my teeth.

"We've talked about this, Rosalie," he says, stretching out the syllables of my name in that smoky way that makes it sound like he's moaning it. "I want to hear when my girl is having a good time. Now, don't interrupt my story."

"I—o-okay—"

He smirks into the mirror, locking eyes with me and pressing a quick kiss to my cheek.

"Good girl," he whispers, and exhales a long breath, blowing across my exposed neck and shoulders.

My eyes threaten to close as his hands make their way slowly down the front of my body, grazing over my pebbled nipples beneath my sweater.

"Unfortunately," he whispers in my ear, fingers playing at the hem of my pants. "I have practice."

Matt jolts away from me, leaving a firm, wet kiss on my cheek and laughing at my pouty expression.

"You should rest some," he says. "But don't nap too long, princess. We've got a big date tonight." He tilts my chin, meeting my gaze. "Hey. I love you."

I melt into a puddle. "I love you more."

He grabs his backpack—his hockey gear is in the car where it won't stink up the entire room—and gives me enough kisses goodbye that I'm pulling him back to bed with me.

• • •

Our local Thai restaurant is full, but not overly crowded for a weeknight.

And I'm sitting at a large wooden table with my boyfriend, my best friend, and her boyfriend. On my very first double date.

A smile has taken up permanent residence across my face, full and glimmering because my joy feels so massive and uncontainable I might burst with it all. It's like a movie.

Sadie looks a bit ridiculous next to us at the same chair height, tiny compared to our lengthier upper bodies. She swipes her drink and nurses it, dark red lips leaving an imprint on the straw. Meanwhile, her boyfriend relaxes back, just watching her like she might disappear. Completely taken with her every huff or movement.

"Weren't you supposed to graduate early and be gone already?" Matt asks Sadie, setting his arm over my chair.

"Weren't you supposed to keep your dick out of my best friend?"

Rhys shakes his head, but quietly observes the snippy argument between them, only reaching forward to kiss Sadie's temple or take a sip of his ice water.

I would be worried, but I've realized this is what Matt and Sadie's friendship will be—sharp barbs and snippy comments.

Matt with a smirk, Sadie with a scowl.

"Touché." He nods, leaning forward to take a sip of his fruity margarita. "But can you blame me? Look at her."

I blush as Matt pinches my cheek and points to me like a piece of artwork on a museum wall. Sadie's stern frown slips into a gentle smile. Secretly romantic underneath her tough exterior, she's happy to see us together.

And I'm happy we're all together.

It's almost surreal, if I think back to last year in comparison. My roommate barely hanging on by a thread, hurting and angry, now happy and loved and taken care of by someone who loves her. My misery at a job where every person I worked with openly hated me or treated me differently. Now, I'm learning from the top-performing professor in our department with a direct line to two of my top grad schools, studying the topic I wanted all along. My desperation to be good enough for a boy who didn't love me, who didn't deserve it, now replaced with the gentle surety that I am wholly and completely adored by Matty.

I am so thankful—for all of it.

Matt now calls my parents more than I do. He has lunch with Archer once a month, sometimes more, if his schedule isn't insane. We do a date night every other week—but we're both understanding when plans change.

Being with him is *easy*. Loving him is even easier.

"Sadie and I are gonna try to go into Boston next weekend, since we're off on Saturday. Do you two wanna come?" Rhys asks, settling a hand over the back of Sadie's neck.

Matt sighs a little and shakes his head. "I told Archer I could spend the day with him." He turns to me, pulling my chair closer to him so our knees knock. "You should go, though."

"Oh." I shake my head. "No—I don't have to, really."

"C'mon, princess. You can spend the day with your best friend. I trust Rhys and Bennett to take care of you. It'll be safe."

Trust. Concern—but only for my safety and comfort. Sometimes it feels surreal, but I have to remind myself that this is normal. This is a good relationship, how it's supposed to be.

"And"—Matt leans in, pressing a quick kiss to my cheek—"I'll come up right after. We can spend Saturday night and Sunday together, okay?"

"Don't cut your time with Archer short."

"Never. It'll be perfect."

It already is.

EPILOGUE

Five years later . . .

Freddy

"You're gonna be late."

"I'm not gonna be late, Mrs. Shariff. I promise."

"You are," she moans, tinny through the speaker. "I can *feel* it."

I quietly chuckle a little as I grab a program from the man at the door who eyes the phone at my ear like it's some type of vermin I grabbed off the street.

"I've gotta go. I'm here."

"Matt—"

"See! I told you I wouldn't be late."

She sighs heavily, her voice trembling slightly. "I feel like a horrible mother for not being there—"

"Hush with that," I say. "You need to be there for Daniel. Besides, I'll be sure to film the whole thing, okay?"

Daniel Shariff's condition took a turn for the worse in the year after graduation, a second stroke leaving him nearly completely bed-ridden. I was in talks with a contractor on building them a one-story house closer to Dallas, but Daniel all but chewed my head off at the suggestion.

So we're still negotiating.

Still, I know Ro's mother and father both feel awful about missing

441

out on her graduation today. Fortunately, it's being livestreamed, and I spent most of last night's flight home using the Wi-Fi to make sure they could find and load the page to watch.

"Okay, *oğlum*." *My son.* She's called me that since long before we married. "Call me after."

I agree quickly before hanging up and switching my phone to Do Not Disturb. I spot Archer near the front, knowing he probably showed up as early as they'd let him to grab good seats. He waves to me using the soft, little baby hand currently grasped his wrist.

Shuffling into the center of the row, I smile warmly at the sight of Archer holding baby Elsie—the sweetest, most darling girl I've ever seen. The cutest baby in the entire world. If Ro would let me enter her in competitions, I'd have a trophy to prove it.

"How's my girl?" I ask, taking her from him to rub my nose on her plump cheek, absorbing the new-baby smell.

"Excited to see her daddy." Archer grins, petting her hair. He turns to the giant diaper bag he always totes around and pulls out a little beanie for her pretty curls. "But it's freezing in here, so put this on her."

Talk about a mama bear—that's been Archer since the hospital.

Overcoming my fear of hospitals happens in seconds—which I think is normal when your wife goes into labor at midnight and waits until 2 a.m. to wake you up, because she's worried about you getting enough sleep.

Terror really makes the body react.

Not a single bad memory can plague me when I'm too concerned over Rosalie's cries of pain and the death grip she has on my hand.

Archer makes it there first. He paces around outside her room until I finally invite him in. It doesn't matter that he's been an important part of our lives for four years now. There's still a slight hesitance to him every now and then, that same self-doubt that I've seen reflected in myself time and again.

We both wanted the same thing but feared the same outcome—acceptance and rejection.

"She's beautiful," he says, leaning over the bassinet by the bed. Ro smiles sleepily from the bed and looks at me.

We planned this, and Ro has made it clear that I'm the one who's going to tell him.

"Her name is Elsie. Elsie Rose Shariff."

Ro rolls her eyes at the middle name, but I'm beaming. Named my favorite girl after the two most important women in my life.

And she's a Shariff. Like her mother. Like me, because I'd taken Ro's last name after we married. My mom wasn't a Fredderic. The only father figure I truly knew, Archer, wasn't a Fredderic. I shed the last name with the haunted memories of my past. My Waterfell friends still call me Freddy, but to everyone else I'm Matt, Matty, or the Sheriff—my new team nickname.

Not to mention, wearing Ro's last name on my back every game had become something of a bonus for me. It feels even better than seeing her in my jersey.

Tears wet Archer's cheeks almost immediately, and I follow suit. Until we're both staring across at each other, flicking our eyes to the sleeping baby girl and back, over and over, crying. There's so much love in the room I feel like I might burst.

"Can I . . ." He clears his throat, voice thick. "Can I hold her?"

I nod and he sanitizes his hands before I lift my most precious possession into his arms. He holds her close, mesmerized as he looks down at her.

"Hi, Elsie," he whispers. "I'm your uncle Archer."

Ro clears her throat, and her eyebrows jump a little as she not-so-subtly gestures to him.

"Actually, about that," I say, nerves rattling my voice. I lean a little more toward Ro for strength. "I want baby Elsie to know about her namesake, about Mom. And I want her to know how much you loved *each other." I clear my throat now, feeling almost sick at the mix of nerves and excitement. "You've always been a father to me, and I want her to know you as my dad—as her grandfather."*

He chokes out a sob with a swift nod. "I'm . . . God, kid. I'm honored." His eyes immediately dart back to the baby in his arms, and he coos even softer now. "I'm your Grandpa Ace. And I love you very much."

"Am I your second favorite now?" I laugh, massaging Ro's shoulder.
Archer looks up at me with a blinding smile.
"No, Matty. You'll always be my favorite kid."

He's nearly moved into our house now, a live-in nanny during the last months while Ro finished school and I traveled. Fortunately, baby Elsie came to us after my season ended—not making it past the first round of play-offs.

I commiserated with the guys, but I was thrilled to have that extra time with my wife and our new baby.

That, and I'd found a new hobby—home videos.

Ro cried nearly every night of her fourth year, deep into the research for her dissertation and constantly feeling like she was missing something every time she stepped out the door for school.

So I started videoing everything Elsie and I did—Archer, too—in hopes that Ro never felt like she missed a second. I really put my off-season time to good use.

They read off the names rather quickly before Archer leans over with a quick, "She's next." He takes Elsie from me so I can film just off stage where I can see Ro, green high heels the only pop of color—other than the numerous cords decking her black robe.

"Dr. Rosalie Shariff!"

"That's my wife!" I shout, hand cupped to project my voice. Archer bounces Elsie up so she can see her mom. She coos and giggles, clapping her little hands together. I film one handed and shoot a thumbs-up to Ro as her professor settles the hood on her shoulders.

It jostles the funky cap nearly off her head, but Ro puts a hand on the cap to hold it and returns my thumbs-up with one of her own.

Her smile is dazzling.

My cheeks feel wet, tears tracking across as I watch her. She waves to us again, and I look at Archer, realizing he's crying, too.

I've never been so proud in my entire life.

I love you, I mouth. We're close enough for her to see it and she blows me a kiss and mouths the words back.

These girls—this family we've made. This is what I was made for—for loving them, protecting them all.

I know my mom is gone. But she is here, in me. In my softness with Ro. In Archer's love of me. In Elsie's vibrant green eyes. I can feel her everywhere, even when I'm not looking for her.

One year later . . .

Ro

I'm having one of my bad days. With my new job, these days are few and far between, but today has been exhausting. I've gotten sick too many times today, until the professor I currently work with finally sent me home.

Tears burn my eyes as I sit in the car inside the garage, so I open my phone and flip through the videos in my Life with Elsie folder of all Matt and Elsie's videos together.

"*Hey, Mama.*" Matt's happy tone crackles from my phone speaker. The video doesn't show him, only baby Elsie in her highchair. "*We're trying something new today.*"

Elsie slaps her hands on the pink plastic tray and giggles, eyes shining as she watches her dad. She's been smitten with him since her birth, eyes sparkling whenever he enters a room and calls for her.

Like mother, like daughter.

Matt opens a container, propping the phone up so I can see them both in the wide-frame shot. He takes a tiny baby spoon and dips it into the beige-colored mush.

"*Okay, I'll go first, Els,*" he says to our daughter, ruffling her head of dirty blond curls as he plops the baby food into his mouth. His face wrinkles up. "*Oh my God, this shit is disgusting!*"

Elsie giggle-screams like she can understand what he's said. He blushes and shakes his head, a smile splitting his face even as he struggles to get the baby food down.

"*I feel bad even giving it to you,*" he mutters, but zooms the spoon toward her like an airplane—complete with loud, animated noises. Elsie easily eats it, her grin never wavering.

I click out, feeling lighter, as I always do when I watch one of the videos he sends me. They were mostly for when I was away for too long during school, but I've begun returning the favor when he's away for games or practices. Even Archer sends videos into our group chat.

Stepping into our house, I hear Mouse before I see him—our boxer, who is clumsy and overeager as he rushes my legs with a yelp. Right after him, I hear an excited, "Mommy!"

Elsie comes stumbling in, Archer hot on her tail. She's fast—tall for an almost-two-year-old. I scoop her up and greet Archer quickly as she babbles to me, half-real words, half-garbled.

"Is Matt home yet?"

Archer nods with a smile. "Yeah, I was watching her while he made dinner."

My eyebrows shoot up. "He made dinner?" At this, Archer blushes and shrugs before kissing my cheek and then Elsie's.

"I'll see you guys later."

"Bye, Grandpa Ace!" Elsie shouts, waving as he leaves. He doesn't have to go far—when we built the house, we had a father-in-law suite built across from the garage. So we all have privacy, but he's always here.

My dad finally agreed to Matt's offer to build them a one-story home that would make it easier for them to continue to live independently, but in Dallas, where they could be closer to me. And closer to the medical research facility I work for.

I don't anticipate some major breakthrough that can heal my dad. I'm thankful he's here. That he's happy. And that they both get to see us as much as possible.

Pictures line the walls—team dinners we've hosted for two years now as Matt earned the C he now wears proudly on his jersey; photos of us at our wedding; us at Rhys and Sadie's wedding—the family network we've built together for seven years now.

Music plays in the kitchen, Matt dancing to Noah Kahan's "Forever" as he cooks chicken for what looks like taco night.

"Hey there, Matty," I shout over the music. He spins with a massive grin, smile lines deep. His hair is shorter, shorn on the sides and perfectly styled on top. He's bigger now, muscles from his intense discipline carved into his body, which he keeps at the peak of sport performance perfection. His eyes wear the wrinkles of constant smiles, his skin tan from swimming in the pool with our daughter, his arms thick and warm as they wrap around us both.

"Princess," he says to me, leaning in to kiss my lips before kissing the top of Elsie's head. "And my little mermaid."

We both giggle at our respective nicknames.

"Elsie," I say, dropping her to her wobbly feet. "Can you go get Mouse's toys?"

Once our daughter toddles off, where we can still see her, I turn to Matt with watery eyes.

He drops the spatula, grabbing my biceps and pulling me a little closer. "Rosalie?"

I look up into his emerald eyes, his concern and protective nature bleeding through. This man—who I kissed at eighteen, who I fell in love with because of his gentle heart, who I've grown beside for the last seven years of our life . . . who I love more every day.

"I know we had a plan—" My voice breaks. "But . . . I'm pregnant again."

We'd planned to wait, to enjoy our time with Elsie and not add to our insanely hectic, though very happy, lives.

Matt's head tips back and he curses at the ceiling before grabbing me in a tight hug.

"*God*, Ro. I thought something was *wrong*." He kisses every single spot of my face he can reach, laughing. Pure joy in his tone. "We're gonna have a baby?"

"We're gonna have another baby," I laugh, tears streaming onto my face to match the ones on his cheeks. "Are you happy?"

"More than you know." He looks over at our daughter, who babbles to our dog and plays with him. "I never thought being this happy was real. That it was possible. I love you."

"I love you."

Loving him is the easiest thing I've ever done.

"And I love this life we've built together."

We're never alone. We always have each other.

In our house, there is so much love, it overflows.

ACKNOWLEDGMENTS

This book is, at its core, about grief and love—isn't it kinda beautiful how gently hand in hand these two things go?

So, first this book is for my fellow Dead Dad/Dead Parent Club members. It's the club no one wants to be a member of, but you'll never be alone in that grief. And for every one of you readers who has shared your own experiences with grief and this loss.

To my mom, this one's for you, too. I am forever proud of your strength. You are my hero. Thank you for sharing your own difficult experiences with narcissism; with the formation of this book, somehow we've grown even closer. I'm endlessly grateful for that.

To my dad, as always. There is so much of you in everything I write, and I think there always will be.

This book is also for you, Isabella, my little sister and my forever partner in grief. Thank you. Let's keep holding each other close. Dad would be so proud.

To Austin—because I truly wouldn't be able to do anything without your everlasting, patient love and support. I love you. Thank you for taking such gentle care of my heart and pulling me from each dip of depression that threatens.

To Bal, I truly believe I would not be able to do this big scary publishing journey without you by my side. Thank you for holding my hand through this entire thing. You make me a better writer. I love your books, I love you.

Caitlin. There are not enough words in the English language (or any of the other languages you might know) to express how much you mean to me. I am forever grateful that you found my book and me. You are the best partner, guard, gal pal, magician, etc. (I could go on for pages) I could ask for. Here's to a long partnership side by side.

Melanie, the editing QUEEN. Truly this book would be a mess of ideas tossed together without your valuable input. Thank you for the quick meetings, random texts, and also fun chats at our BB table. So thankful this book has allowed us to grow closer. (PS—our dragons miss each other.)

Dayna and Holly—the dream team! So happy I get to call you mine (hehe). Dayna, your cleverness and care for each plan has made each release magical. Holly, thank you for keeping me sane and prepared (two things I struggle with daily). You are the most joyous presence to be around—I'm smiling just typing this.

To Jo, who listens to every random idea I ever have and encourages the good ones (and very gently tells me to trash the bad ones), thank you for reading way-too-long text messages and listening to endless voice notes. I'm so thankful we found each other on a silly little app. Our friendship means the absolute world to me.

To Monica, for your careful guidance and advice. Thank you for helping me showcase Freddy's learning differences and ADHD, as well as the effects of narcissistic abuse in the correct way. And thank you for always hyping me up.

To Grace, my sweet kiwi. Thank you for drawing these characters to life. I'm so happy that I get to see your artwork on the cover of my book every time I look at it. I adore you, truly.

To you, the reader. None of this would exist without your unending support. I can never express what you've done for me, for this book, for my life. I love you all, dearly.

And last, to myself. I'm making a habit of thanking myself. This book was harder than *Unsteady* to write—I've struggled over this one more than usual. It turned out that might've been because of how close to home these character's struggles really hit. So, to the me from months ago who cried over the fear of writing this, we did it, babe.

ABOUT THE AUTHOR

PEYTON CORINNE is the author of *Unsteady*. A writer of romances with imperfect characters, angst, and lots of heart, she grew up on swoony vampire books and endless fan fiction and has wanted to be an author since she was very young. When she's not writing, she's probably at home making *another* cup of coffee, rewatching *Twilight*, or frantically reading through her own never-ending TBR. Visit PeytonCorinne.com and follow @peytoncorinneauthor on Instagram and @peytoncorinne on TikTok for more.